Politically Corrected

"The only thing necessary for the triumph of evil

is for good men to do nothing."

—Edmund Burke

Politically Corrected

Kurt M. DiClementi

The Good Shepherd Press

Foreword

—~~—

"Politically Corrected is a novel whose characters are capable of offending us and making us laugh at our . myopic political divisiveness at the same time. DiClementi's characters unabashedly take issue with our current political narratives and use them to their advantage while they are pursued by the FBI, ATF, DEA, and NSA. The alphabet agencies become their own worst enemies as they pursue nine highly trained Special Forces veterans, one of whom is a genius at breaching national and international weapons systems. This novel is like Rambo on steroids. This is a rare, must read work that unfolds more like prophecy than fiction."

H. Gene Lawrence

H. Gene Lawrence
AO1 US Navy Veteran &
Retired Pierce County, WA Deputy Sheriff

Contents

—⁓—

Chapter 1
In the Still of the Night

None of us would come to know Salvino Scorzoletti the way the rest of the world did. His story began even before that fateful night that would be the critical mass bringing us all together. In the still of the night, on July 31, the ill-fated intentions of nine heavily armed men would not go as planned. These guys were looking for more than a fight. They were looking for a considerable sum of money that they planned to divide after their scheme played out. It would end in the death of Scorzoletti, a murderer, a thief, and a traitor who escaped justice, or so they thought.

They were dead wrong in their plans. This was due to their sorely misguided source of information. It was the least credible source of information one could have wanted because Philster was ONI's fall guy, but nonetheless, they took his fast talk as the gospel truth. Steve Philster, aka Lupe, or "the mouth," as the other cons called him due to his affliction with lupus, was a fast-talking ONI black ops specialist looking for his freedom. Operation Lotus Blossom was his brain-child, and it had the approval of the brass in the shadowy world of black ops because it generated revenue that could support black ops without having to seek funding that required Senate or Congressional oversight.

Philster had the highest security clearance and reported to only one person: the deputy commander of ONI, Richard Pierpont. The commander of ONI was kept in the dark on the nature of Lotus Blossom for reasons of plausible deniability and because Lotus Blossom was the total antithesis of ONI's core values, especially honor and integrity. So, a cover story was created for the commander, and he was made to believe that ONI operatives were seizing funds from drug lords in Southeast Asia who were in league with corrupt officials in Cambodia and Vietnam. So, while Pierpont knew the cover story, Philster, an outside mercenary, and a few others were the only ones who knew the truth about Operation Lotus Blossom, or so they thought. The other operatives within ONI were simply bagmen who were fed the same cover story as the commander. After the fall of Pol Pot's Khmer Rouge, Cambodia was culturally, financially, and morally decimated. Had the SEALS not been a part of fighting the Khmer Rouge, Lotus Blossom would never have come to fruition. Unfortunately, corruption, torture, and genocide were fertile grounds for the dark machinations of Operation Lotus Blossom that would continue to operate with impunity for over a decade.

Scorzoletti, a SEAL Team Master Chief with extensive contacts throughout Southeast Asia, and particularly in Cambodia, would learn of Operation Lotus Blossom through the mercenary both he and Philster knew who used the code name Wrecking Crew. He was part of Operation Lotus Blossom and he was tight-lipped about his role because the money was good. He bought in to Philster's platitudes about serving a greater good that Operation Lotus Blossom was making possible. As time passed, and he began to see vast sums of money being diverted to personal accounts that were purely for personal gain, he became disillusioned. That notwithstanding, he felt repulsed when he saw what was being done to innocent children by those with wealth and privilege who could victimize these innocent souls with impunity to gratify their perverse desires.

Operation Lotus Blossom wasn't just an operation that used prostitutes who freely chose to sell their bodies to survive. All military personnel was familiar with this and most of them accepted it as a legitimate vice like smoking. They saw no wrong in indulging in it occasionally. Operation Lotus Blossom, however, was the advent of human trafficking in what became the dark world of the child sex slaves, and it was far from anything that could even remotely be considered as a legitimate vice or a necessary evil. It was the darkest form of evil depravity imaginable. Its victims were typically between the ages of four to eighteen years of age. On occasion the packages, as they were called, were even infants. Infants were typically used in Satanic sacrifices that required innocent blood. A sexual orgy would precede the sacrifice wherein female infants would be vaginally raped and male infants would be sodomized.

These rituals gave birth to the films in the porn industry known as "snuff" flicks, which typically involved teenage girls who could follow simple directions and act like innocent girls who were being abducted and raped, or naughty girls who wanted to offer sex to their partner in return for drugs that they would consume while filming. Sometimes the victims were boys because some films catered to those who had a taste for homosexual sadism and murder. In either case, the victims never knew that the film they were appearing in would be their last. Unless the film plot was an abduction rape scenario, the films started out with innocuous kissing and foreplay even though the adult's identity was concealed by black leather sadist masks. As the filming progressed and the participants became increasingly intoxicated on either marijuana, methamphetamine, or cocaine, the level of violence would gradually begin to escalate, but the victims had been told that this was all a part of the script up until they were murdered. Death came to the victims in such grisly manners that one could only conclude that these scripts were conceived nowhere other than the depths of hell, yet these films were considered delicacies by the most depraved sexual connoisseurs. They were never circulated in the public. There was a select clientele within private circles of the wealthy elite and among certain prominent politicians who could afford their price tag. The films were far outside the reach of the average sexual predators, sadomasochists, or serial killers one might imagine were the typical consumer. Instead, their consumers were highly respected in society. senators, congressmen, and an assorted array of lifelong Washington bureaucrats.

These acts were unfathomable to Wrecking Crew until he peered into the set of a snuff flick that reached its culmination. He witnessed a boy who was perhaps twelve years old guillotined face up as two hulking masked men relieved themselves on his face and into his mouth and the gleaming blade descended upon his tender neck. Wrecking Crew was filled with disgust when one of the men turned around to see him and smiled, tilting his head back and exhaling before saying, "Man, that felt good!"

It had been ten years that Wrecking Crew had turned a blind eye to things of a less heinous nature, but this gruesome act summoned his wrath and a desire to live up to his code name and unleashed a fury like a tornado ripping through a picturesque village without warning. Wrecking Crew was as lethal as any man could be, but he knew that Operation Lotus Blossom was too big for him to handle alone. So, he connected the dots that Scorzoletti had been seeing from afar in different villages but had been unable to put together into a comprehensible big picture. Wrecking Crew also knew that making his misgivings known to Philster or anybody else in Naval Intelligence would be a death sentence to him. Nobody in ONI or any other intelligence network that was profiting from Lotus Blossom would think twice about eliminating him. He was an outside contractor who stood closest to the altar in this den of evil. He was the only one besides Philster who possessed enough information to shut the operation down and destroy the reputation and careers of some enormously powerful men if he channeled information correctly. But no breach of information would be correct.

Wrecking Crew knew that Operation Lotus Blossom would raise the ire of Scorzoletti, and if given the necessary information, he would decimate the infrastructure of the operation. That's exactly what Scorzoletti did through a two-pronged attack after Wrecking Crew killed the perpetrators who murdered the young boy, before he himself disappeared into the shadows and became a ghost. The first part of Scorzoletti's attack employed psychological warfare that targeted key individuals by letting them know they were compromised. An anonymous package was sent to the commander of ONI with graphic photos, videos, and names of those involved. The only information he

4

omitted was that of the black ops accounts holding billions in revenue. The deputy commander of ONI did what was logical in his situation. He set Philster up to take the fall for the entire operation and he protected his own position by letting one senator and one congressman know that he was aware of certain perverse proclivities of theirs that would mean the end of their careers and the lifestyles they had grown accustomed to if his position and stature in ONI were jeopardized. Philster and those who were part of Operation Lotus Blossom were portrayed as a corrupt, rogue element within ONI who would receive federal prison sentences. Details of their operation remained classified on grounds of national security.

In the meantime, Scorzoletti set up shell accounts and transferred all the ill-gotten funds to them. He then slowly funneled that money to organizations helping victims of human trafficking and prostitution, and those families he was able to reunite with their children through the help of a pastor named Stan Brunsler, who worked with organizations designed to help victims and their families. Finally, he set about doing what he did best. He began to eliminate corrupt politicians and police who supported Operation Lotus Blossom as it operated amongst the indigenous people of Cambodia, where it was based. He killed in a signature manner that left no doubt these assassinations were retribution for the innocent children whose lives provided the bulwark of their evil empire. He delivered justice that was swift and uncompromising. His was a judiciousness that could not be bribed or plea bargained with. He was the voice of those whose voices were forever silenced. While nobody could say for sure who was the arm of retribution for the victims of Operation Lotus Blossom, Philster recognized some of the trademark signatures of Scorzoletti's kills, and one thing he was utterly obsessed with was what happened to all the money acquired through Operation Lotus Blossom.

Like every con who has nothing but time to think, Philster felt if he offered up information about all that money to the right person on the outside, he could cut a deal and buy his way out of Leavenworth. As fate would have it, Special Agent in Charge Gary Bickens of the

ATF's Washington field office, who had attended college with the deputy commander of ONI, was coming to Philster. Philster never admitted to having any knowledge of the operation's funds, but the deputy commander of ONI believed that Philster had a silent confidant who could be made to relinquish that money to him. The deputy commander, who knew of the assassinations in Cambodia, also knew that only one person was in that area who could kill with such precision, using methods that eliminated participants in the operation who were indigenous personnel. It was also a person whose most successful black ops were planned by Philster. That man was none other than Salvino Scorzoletti, and while it would be too risky for the deputy commander of ONI to visit Philster, it wouldn't seem suspicious in the least for Special Agent in Charge Gary Bickens to visit him and gather information on Scorzoletti. Philster's knowledge of Salvino Scorzoletti seemed encyclopedic, but it was padded with ninety-eight percent bullshit and two percent truth.

That didn't matter to Special Agent in Charge Gary Bickens, who was in collusion with the deputy commander of ONI to secure a retirement nest egg for himself and the deputy commander. The prospect of an unfathomable cash windfall for both of them, as well as a public relations coup for the ATF, would more than justify sifting through a mound of shit to find that diamond in the rough. The ATF had suffered several humiliating public relations defeats in the national press and news media, and Gary Bickens was out to restore the image of the ATF. Moreover, he and his members were going to get some payback. They were going to profit from their latest siege in the still of the night. It would take place under cover of the night and within the darkness of the human heart, the place where all evil has its origin.

So, it was at night that Gary Bickens would visit Philster, whose illness often caused lethargy during the day and almost constant insomnia with co-morbid mania at night, hence his nickname: "the mouth." His real name was Steven Philster, but nobody in the joint called him that. The other prisoners had beat him so often that all his teeth had been broken to the point of needing extraction. As such, he wore false teeth and was housed in his own cell. Even there he learned to keep his incessant chatter to a low whisper as he paced back and forth. Before this happened though, enough of his talk about his hidden caches of automatic weapons circulated through the prison to actual snitches who sent word to the ATF, hoping to cut deals for themselves, but Bickens went straight to the source. The man who had direct contact with Salvino Scorzoletti. He wanted facts, not jailhouse hearsay, but Philster would weave a carefully crafted quilt of misinformation and disinformation to cover the life of a man who was his former comrade in arms, even though he suspected that Scorzoletti was the one who shut down the operation. In the end, Philster respected him and didn't hold him to blame for his imprisonment. Instead, he saw Pierpont as the one who rolled over on him, and he suspected there was some connection to Pierpont when Bickens came to visit him. However, he said nothing of his hunch.

Bickens led Philster to a private interrogation room with a small package that resembled a diplomatic pouch, but there was no diplomatic material in it. All it contained was a document that would increase Philster's time served to the twenty years he was sentenced to due to good behavior, health issues, and cooperation with federal authorities. Aside from that, it contained Philster's favorite contraband: a carton of Winston cigarettes, a ninety-day supply of Xanax, and a six-pack of cold Coca-Cola. It would be enough to last Philster until his release. All this was allowed to pass through the prison unchecked on the grounds of national security.

Once inside the interrogation room, Philster quickly went through the ritual of applying his denture adhesive, inserting his false teeth, applying some Chapstick to his lips, and placing some moisturizing eye drops into his eyes and some vitamin E oil to his face. For reasons unbeknownst to anybody but himself, Philster was very vain about his appearance, but it started to wear Bicken's patience a bit thin.

"All right, Philster, I didn't come here to make love to you, even though you have the nickname of a Spanish senorita. You can get plenty of that when you hit the showers here. I came here for information."

7

Bickens removed the plastic-sleeved documents from the pouch along with the contraband, slowly placing each item on the table with a slight bit of force for emphasis.

"Yeah, yeah, of course, I knew you didn't come here because you think I'm a stand-up guy, even though I am. You know I was set up. ONI needed a fall guy for the neck-deep quicksand pit of shit they were sinking into, and I was their middleman. I was the liaison between them and the flesh purveyors, so I was the perfect patsy. I laundered those mothers untold billions from the sex trade to finance their black ops and other shit that Congress wouldn't approve, or they didn't want congressional oversight on… It was all highly classified shit. We called it Operation Lotus Blossom. Then of course there was the very unknown foray into Mindanao, where we slaughtered the Abu-Sayyaf Muslim extremists who were kidnapping and killing Americans and other foreigners. We also trained the Filipinos to develop their own SEAL Teams. The cash from Lotus Blossom did a lot of good! And let's not forget how we got Noriega out of Panama! Where the fuck do you think that money came from? The only thing that turned that mission into a disaster was Congress's involvement! Those motherfucking bureaucrats can fuck up a two-car parade!"

Bickens opened the carton of Winstons, peeled open a pack, slid them over to Philster with a lighter and a Coke as he jabbered on, and placed both his arms on the table with the vial of Xanax clasped between them.

"Holy moly, is that what I think it is, Bickens?"

Bickens nodded with a smile as Philster leaned over the table and stretched out his hands.

"Well, I didn't come here to listen to your conspiracy theories about the military industrial complex, Philster."

"Well, you sure as shit brought the right stuff. All these guys in here get off on this shit. They go for five bucks a hit! Can you believe that shit! You see, if you grind these babies into powder and swallow two or three with a Coke, it's like shooting heroin. The citric acid in the Coke combined with your stomach acid melts these pulverized babies instantly. Then the CO_2 in the Coke shoots this shit straight into your intestines, where it's propelled to your brain like a bottle rocket. Oh man…instant karma! No need for matches or a rig, no telltale tracks… Perfect nirvana! Give me a few of those."

"Not just yet, Philster," Bickens said, nodding his head negatively. "For now, you can satisfy your chain-smoking desires with the Winstons and quench your parched lips with Coke."

"Yeah, yeah, of course, that's why I put my teeth in. It burns my gums when I take a heavy drag off a butt. All that other shit was just for the lupus. I get dry lips from talking to myself too much. These guys in here don't want to hear any intelligent conversation, so I can only talk to myself, and even that gets them pissed off. I wasn't trying to float your boat or anything. I don't swing that way, Bickens. The young guys in here will do that because they can't get a bitch, but I can wait. I'm no butt-banger, and as far as I'm concerned, my ass was made for only one purpose.

"You know, Bickens, I don't even yank my hog. Some guys in here do it two or three times a day because there's nothing else to do, but not me. I read. I'm not talking about smut rags like *Hustler*, *Penthouse*, or *Asian Beauties*. Well, actually I do read *Playboy* now that there's no nudity because they actually provide a forum for decent writers, but…"

Bickens let out a somewhat frustrated sigh.

"But that's not what I came to hear about, Philster, so why don't you take a few of these damn Xanax so we can slow your motor mouth down to a speed that will yield some relevant information. Otherwise, your ass can sit in here talking to yourself for another twenty years."

Philster grinned sarcastically and nodded his head. "Fuckin' A, twenty years off as time served for information…

"Well, I beg your pardon, Mr. Bickens, but you didn't tell me what information you wanted. For instance, I can tell you about how the military industrial complex created lupus and even AIDS…it didn't come from some goddamn green monkeys in Africa. AIDS began in this country after a series of hepatitis shots were issued in New York, Chicago, and California among the heroin addict and homosexual populations. That shit is documented. That's a mother-lovin' fact! They were considered worthless guinea pigs for a virus the military was developing that would have a refractory effect on the immune response system. The military wanted biological weapons that appeared viral in nature and could wipe out huge swaths of populations considered a threat or otherwise undesirable... Green monkeys, what a crock of shit!"

Bickens opened the bottle and poured two bars of Xanax into the palm of his hand and leaned across the table with the tablets cupped in the palm of his hand.

"Open the damn Coke, and then open your mouth!" Bickens demanded with obvious annoyance as he handed the yellow bars to Philster.

Philster complied at once, and Bickens popped the whole tablets in Philster's mouth as a priest might administer the eucharist.

"Now drink, damn it! I don't want to spend the next twenty years in this room with you."

Bickens listened to Philster's incessant rambling for about another five minutes after he swallowed the Xanax, and then a calm smile stretched across his face, and in a composed manner he inquired of Bickens:

"So, what exactly do you want to know?"

"I want to know everything you know about a man named Salvino Scorzoletti," Bickens said, looking Philster directly in the eyes.

"Jesus H. Christ...for the love of God, why didn't you just say that when you came here?" Philster said with a tone of growing annoyance. "I thought you were after some leftist moolies who had a briefcase nuke! You know the democrats are using these fucking radicals these days... Fucking divide and conquer is their strategy... AntiCap, CLM... All those fucking billionaires like Morros that are financing those caravans to storm our southern border! Have you ever seen those luxury caravan buses CLM has? Where the fuck you think they get all that money? You think that's all a coincidence?

"And what about that fucking tech billionaire and his wife...

10

Belinda and Mel Bates? Those fuckers want to microchip everybody, and if you don't submit, you can't fucking work! I mean, can you believe that shit? That rich fucking twit isn't even an elected official, but he's making global-reaching demands!"

Bickens exhaled somewhat exasperatedly.

"Is there a possibility I could get a word in edgewise between all your woes of the world! I did have a specific agenda in mind."

"All right, all right, you're not the first one who said I'm a bit verbose at times, but before I tell you anything, what are you going to do for me?"

Bickens took the documents out of the vinyl sleeve, slid them across the table to Philster, and quickly summed it up.

"It's no doubt a fact that you have some health concerns; you've also been a model prisoner, despite the terrible physical suffering you've endured, and you are needed to assist the United States government in a matter of national security. Therefore, your sentence will be commuted and you will be a free man in thirty days. You just need to quickly read through the two-page document I've passed to you, sign it, and provide me with everything you know on Salvino Scorzoletti. Moreover, you'll be working with us on the outside. We'll provide you with a cover job."

Philster smiled, shook his head affirmatively, and signed the document. "I like the sound of that."

"Don't you even want to read it?" Bickens asked.

"Why? Any time you guys start talking about national security, it essentially means you mothers have the right to screw somebody seven ways to Sunday without just cause. So, who gives a shit whatever it says as long as I get out of this stink hole in thirty days?"

"All right, let's get on with it."

"I can't believe a backward hillbilly is going to buy me my freedom! I don't know how in the hell a guy like him becomes a matter of national security when I've written to congressmen and senators about shit I know, and I don't even get a response. The only thing my information earned me is a repeated shanking one day that almost killed me. That, and two beatings that took me to within an inch of my life."

Bickens shook his head and focused his gaze straight into Philster's eyes.

"Well, maybe they just think you're a conspiracy theory nutbar... who knows...who cares. You have my attention and I represent the government. I also hold your freedom in my hands, so let's hear what you know about this guy you call a backward hillbilly. You can start by telling me why you refer to him as a backward hillbilly when his name is as Italian as a Giordano's pizza and he held the rank of a Master Chief SEAL?"

To the annoyance of Bickens, Philster took his time extinguishing his first cigarette by grinding it into the ashtray as if it wouldn't go out before casually lighting another cigarette and resuming his conversation.

"Oh yeah, that...well, his family immigrated to Georgia's deep south when he was just a baby. So, even though they spoke dago in their household, Scorzoletti took on that Southern drawl when he started speaking English. I guess you could call him a Daglish southerner," Philster said with a sense of amusement. Bickens, however, was not amused.

"All right, how about if we fast forward to the part where you came to know him."

"Yeah, yeah, I was getting to that. Maybe you should take a couple of those Xanax yourself and chill out a bit. Anyway, like I told you earlier, I was a liaison between ONI and the bad boys in Cambodia after the fall of the Khmer Rouge. I'd purchase boys and girls at pennies on the dollar and we'd turn around and go selling ten- and twelve-year-old virgins into the sex trade for huge returns."

"What kind of investments and returns are we talking about?"

"I'd buy in volume at ten to fifteen dollars a body."

"How did you secure the kids? Did you have Khmer kidnapping them for you?"

"Kidnapping them...what, are you nuts! Do you fucking ATF guys have to take a stupid exam and get less than fifty percent on it before you can qualify for a position?"

"I don't think I like what I'm hearing, Philster," Bickens said, pushing his chair away from the table. "Maybe I'll just call it a night and forget about my offer."

Philster licked his lips and applied some more Chapstick to them.

"All right, all right, I didn't mean to insult you. All I was trying to say was that after the fall of Khmer Rouge, Cambodia was so piss-pot poor that parents would line up to sell their children, especially when they had five or six of them. Seventy-five dollars back then was worth over 304,000 Cambodia riel. The purveyors would take a fifty percent cut, and the rest would go to the family. It was like winning the Powerball lottery for those families back then! Depending on how many kids they sold, they could live well for three or four years! We didn't need to kidnap or resort to violence. The products came to us. We could probably still do it today because that country is still impoverished beyond belief. The same situation existed in Laos."

"What did you get out of it?"

"My take was ten percent of the resale value."

"What was the resale value?"

"It depended on the market, but the low end was five hundred thousand on up to a high end of two million dollars! The US usually ranged on average between 500K and 750K, but the Saudis and other Middle Easterners would often pay up to two million or more for a virgin...boy or girl. It just depended what they were into."

Bickens placed his hands over his mouth and slowly slid his fingers across his cheek while shaking his head as he retracted his hand from his face.

"So where does Scorzoletti come into the picture? SEALS weren't a part of the Cambodia conflict in the seventies or the eighties."

"They sure as fuck were! It was just classified...they simply didn't exist as far as Uncle Sam was concerned. If the truth be told, they were the ones who drove those cock-sucking Khmer Rouge out of the highlands and into the hands of the North Vietnamese army, who slaughtered them and toppled the regime. The SEALs made that happen."

"So Scorzoletti was a SEAL in the seventies?"

"No, he was infantry…no, no, a Marine sharpshooter at that time, and he had a thing for machine guns. Like this guy was so precise with a machine gun that when he knew the windage and elevation and all that crap of a certain area, he could write your name on a target five hundred yards out."

"Really, you know this for a fact. You saw him do this?" Bickens countered with disbelief in his tone of voice.

"I wouldn't have believed it myself if I hadn't seen it with my own eyes. Groups of military personnel from all branches of the service were brought to see him give demonstrations…and get this," Philster said with growing excitement, "he wrote one guy's name in cursive with a fifty-caliber machine gun. Like, the recoil had no effect on his precision, man! It was like his body automatically adjusted his aim to compensate for the recoil or something…it was incredible shit, a real sight to see!"

"And what else?" Bickens probed.

"This mother was deadlier than a heart attack with a sniper rifle. In one demonstration, they had one of those snake charmers sitting profile to the side of three cobras taken about a quarter of a mile away in open terrain. We had to use binoculars to see this. One at a time in rapid succession, we saw Scorzoletti shoot the heads of each cobra clean off. It was incredible because those mothers were swaying, so he had to compensate for their movement precisely so he didn't shoot the charmer, who was only twelve inches in front of the cobras. That notwithstanding, he was shooting at a target that was as thin as a quarter inch."

Philster paused for a moment, took a puff off his cigarette, a swig off his Coke, and then continued.

"I heard from one of the guys in his outfit that he learned to start shooting at the tender age of six from some old Vietnam vet that took a liking to him because he reminded him of his brother who

14

got whacked in Nam or some shit like that. The guy was like a second father to Scorzoletti because his own father was always working. Scorzoletti really loved this guy; he taught him how to shoot, take apart and clean guns, and then reassemble them as well as build trip wires for Claymores and other lethal shit."

"What did Scorzoletti's family think about this?"

"Oh, they never really knew anything about the guy until Scorzoletti was about ten or eleven when he started learning to trap and hunt with this guy, and at that point they didn't care because Scorzoletti was coming home and putting food on the table...pheasant, duck, venison...and that helped a lot because they were poor. Scorzoletti just told his mom and dad it was some old farmer about a mile off from where they lived. They had six kids, and their dad was a laborer. So, Scorzoletti's dad told young Salvino to teach his brothers to hunt, and he did."

"Was it the vet that taught his siblings?"

"No, according to Scorzoletti, the vet asked Scorzoletti to take a vow of secrecy about their friendship."

"Why?"

"My guess is that he was afraid of guys like you. He didn't want anybody knowing that he had Thompson submachine guns, fully automatic AK-47s, and other firearms that are illegal for civilians to possess without paying a buttload in taxes to your agency."

"So, this vet was the one that taught Scorzoletti to fire machine guns as well?"

"Yeah, the first fully automatic weapon he fired was at the age of nine. It was a Thompson submachine gun. Scorzoletti fell in love with it instantly because the low caliber of the ammunition allowed him to see and feel the destructive power of the machine gun while being able to control it at the same time. He started in with the AK-47 when he was eleven years old. He said he liked its power and durability, but he didn't feel it was as precise as an AR15 or an M16. The Thompson, however, would always remain his favorite."

"Were these things the guys in his outfit told you."

"No, Scorzoletti himself told me."

"Did you become friends with him?"

"I wouldn't say friends because he was as dumb as a stump. I mean this guy must have had an IQ of about sixty-two. He wasn't much of a conversationalist unless the conversation was about guns. He even told me he was a bit of a recluse or loner as much as anyone can be when they're in the military. Snipers, however, typically spend a lot of time alone, so what he said made sense. Anyway, I always did most of the talking."

"I can believe that," Bickens said with a wry grin. "So, go on."

"He said he never really made any friends in grade school because he always failed every class he took except PE. The only other exception was his love for football. He especially loved practice because then he got his aggression out on the guys who teased him and called him a variety of names like dummy, wop, dago-ding-a-ling, and other shit like that. The offensive linemen feared him because he was built like a brick shithouse. The vet made him start working out with weights at the age of eight, and when his hormones kicked in, he was muscularly well built. Scorzoletti took his school to the championship in their division, so the coach convinced the principal to give him a diploma and pass him on to high school."

"What about high school?" Bickens asked. "Did he get along better there academically and socially?"

"He got along with the jocks because he continued to excel in football and other athletics like wrestling and gymnastics, but he was even worse academically in high school. In fact, he got dropped from both the gymnastics and the wrestling teams due to poor academic performance, but the football coach managed to curry favor with the principal again as they were both fishing and drinking buddies. There was just one catch…the principal didn't want Scorzoletti to have a diploma with their school's name on it, so he'd have to take a GED course in the summer after graduation. He did miserably with that, but the principal did some old-fashioned southern politicking and arranged for Scorzoletti to get his GED."

"What happened after that?"

Since Philster was taking a swig off his Coke when the question was asked, he laughed and started choking and coughing. When he regained his composure, he looked at Bickens and smiled.

"What happened after that?" Philster repeated in a slightly mocking tone. "What…don't you guys have computers or databases that provide you with information or a profile of someone you're investigating?"

"We do," Bickens countered, "but that doesn't necessarily mean a person is going to surface on our radar, especially if they haven't been associated with or convicted of any criminal behavior. So, what happened next and how does that lead to you and him knowing each other."

Philster smiled and shook his head.

"Well, isn't it obvious? He joined the Marines. It's one place on the earth where a guy like him would fit. You don't need to be intelligent; you just need to follow orders and learn how to shoot and kill anything you're told to. Scorzoletti could do that better than most kids can play video games or hack computers. Hell, he had been learning that from a vet before he started junior high!"

"I must say that your information sounds entertaining. You're a delightful storyteller, Philster."

"What do you mean?" Philster asked with a quizzical look on his face.

"There's no military record of anyone named Salvino Scorzoletti being in the Marines," Bickens answered bluntly.

"Well, maybe he shortened his name or changed it. I mean, I never called him Salvino. I called him Sal or Scorzo."

"Been there, done that," Bickens countered, clasping his hands behind his head and stretching as he inhaled. "Your friend Scorzoletti may be as dumb as a stump, but I'm not. Are you sure you're not confusing the man I'm talking about with someone else?"

Philster took another mouthful of Coke and shook his head negatively.

"I'm sure! A person doesn't forget someone with a name like Salvino Scorzoletti who possesses such lethal skills. Besides, I kept in touch with him until he was discharged. I even have letters from the guy dated after his discharge."

"Letters…as in love letters?" Bickens said with a laugh. "Who in the hell writes letters these days? It's all SMS, text, or email. Now why would a guy as dumb as you say he is write letters in a forum where there's no grammar or spell check?"

"He never liked the fact that whatever you do online leaves an electronic fingerprint. He had these trust issues…who knows, maybe he picked it up from the Vietnam vet that taught him how to hunt and how to shoot."

"But earlier and just now you said he communicated with you and kept in touch with you after his discharge. He must have trusted you."

"He might have liked me because I listened to him and respected him, but liking someone and trusting someone were two different things to Scorzoletti. Can't you check in holding among my personal possessions that were seized when I was taken into custody?"

"You have no personal possessions, Philster. They all seem to be missing, and what few things do exist are sealed as highly classified and out of my reach."

Again, Bickens slid his chair back away from the table.

"You know, it's a shame you won't be getting out of here next month, because I do believe that you're a wealthy man who's tucked away mountains of money in offshore accounts. It's a shame you're not going to be able to enjoy it for a long time. In fact, I'm going to run a very thorough check with the help of the IRS and a few other agencies to see what kind of electronic fingerprints are associated with you during the days you were profiteering off the bodies of Cambodian children."

"I'm a patriot, Mr. Bickens! I did what I did because I thought I was serving a greater good. Besides, those kids probably lived better lives wherever they were sent than they would have if they'd been left in Cambodia…their families were better off too!"

Bickens leaned over the table and stared into Philster's eyes with contempt.

"Oh sure, every ten-year-old boy and girl lives a better life when they're repeatedly sodomized and raped. Is there anything else in that vivid patriotic imagination you'd like to share before you live out the remainder of your twenty years in this stink hole?"

"Yeah," Philster said with resignation.

"Well," Bickens replied, shrugging his shoulders, "I'm all ears."

"Two years after Scorzoletti's discharge, I received letters from him postmarked in and around Cambodia, but there was never any return address on the outside. At about that same time, our purveyors started having their heads blasted right off their shoulders without a flash or without a sound anywhere near."

"You can always tell where a shot comes from if you examine the entry and exit wounds and follow their trajectory," Bickens retorted as if his interest in Philster was suddenly restored.

"No, you don't understand…there were no entry or exit wounds. The rounds that hit them had to be exploding tip rounds on large-caliber bullets fired from an extremely high-velocity rifle. Sometimes even the neck and shoulders were blown off the bodies. Months before I was busted, we couldn't find a purveyor that would deal with us or even talk with us. They said they were being eliminated by the *tevta morn* because they dealt with us."

"You'll have to forgive me, Philster; I took Spanish in college, not Cambodian. What or who exactly is the tevta morn?"

"Roughly translated it means angel of death."

"So, you think I'll find Scorzoletti if I do a Boolean search on tevta morn?" Bickens replied with a chuckle.

"No, I'm asking you to honor your offer to me because I provided you with information. You've got to connect the dots. I can't do that while I'm in here."

"You haven't provided me with anything more than a bunch of unsubstantiated bullshit. I could probably get more by attending one of his class reunions than I did from you."

"What about his family? I'm sure they can back up what I say."

"Unfortunately, none of them have seen or heard from him since

19

he left home. Moreover, they don't have any fanciful stories for me to connect the dots with. So, I'm afraid I'm going to have to say good night to you. Enjoy your contraband, and get used to Coca-Cola and Xanax for the next twenty years."

This time Bickens pushed his chair away from the table, rose, and pounded on the door to be let out.

"Check with the fifth infantry company commander. He'll substantiate what I'm saying. Poke around town where Scorzoletti grew up...talk to his teachers, his principals, and people who knew him... find that vet, and you'll probably find Scorzoletti. Have you considered that maybe he went black, and that's why there's no records of him? Coordinate your efforts with Interpol if our people won't help you! Scorzoletti could have went rogue and blackmailed clients to the tune of millions. He must be worth millions because another thing we heard about the tevta morn hits is that all the money vanished from the purveyors. Even the money in our accounts was wire transferred to different banks presumably under different corporation names that were basically shell companies."

Philster looked at the vial of Xanax sitting on the table but left it there to pursue Bickens at the door.

"Well, are we good?"

"Oh, I'm always good." Bickens chuckled. "I uphold the law."

"Yeah, yeah, sure...but do we still have a deal?" Philster asked desperately.

"Yeah, I'll work on your release. I'm sure I'll find something of value in what you told me, especially after you're out and you can provide me with a little more information about these wire transfers of money. Mr. Scorzoletti must have left some electronic tracks. All we have to do is follow the money trail."

There was something within the impassioned sound of Philster's voice that made Bickens believe there was some truth in what he disclosed. However large or small, he wouldn't be satisfied if he discredited Philster's story because he was a con. Perhaps Philster had an axe to grind with Scorzoletti and would like to see him behind bars, especially if there was a sliver of truth that Philster's loss was Scorzoletti's gain.

Bickens looked at the vial of Xanax that he left on the table and nodded to Philster to take it. He knew Philster wouldn't be checked for contraband due to his visitor being a federal agent. While Philster would take another Xanax and drift off into a pleasant slumber, Bickens would return to his office and continue to ponder the things that Philster had to say on the evening of June fifth. After an hour of examining and re-examining the story that Philster told him, Bickens was questioning himself about the how and why of the purveyors being killed. It wasn't the style of rival gangs nor a house divided within the military that wanted to shut down a lucrative means of financing ops off the backs of foreign nationals. Who would have the intel to know about what was happening, eradicate the purveyors, and anonymously blow the whistle on Philster and his unit to shut it down? And the money...where did all that money go, and why?

Bickens mapped out a plan of action to locate Salvino Scorzoletti, a man who had fallen off the public radar after his service in the SEAL Teams ended. Bickens and the eight men under his command would connect the dots and charge Scorzoletti with firearms violations as well as murder and possibly treason for interfering in military intelligence operations. Finally, they would steal his ill-gotten profits and make the decision to eliminate him.

Chapter 2
Don't Speak

—⁓—

Bickens interviewed everyone from former classmates and teachers to school administrators, neighbors, store owners, and anyone else who might have had any association with Salvino Scorzoletti. Much to his chagrin Bickens' expedition into Georgia led him to believe there were only two words needed to define Salvino Scorzoletti: don't speak. Far from being the academic loser that Philster described, Bickens came to learn that Scorzoletti wasn't picked on for being so dumb, but rather for being exceptionally brilliant in a school district where the average male student was considered smart if he had straight Cs. To the contrary, Scorzoletti had straight A's on all his report cards from elementary school through high school, and while it was true that he had to attend summer school to receive his diploma, it was not a GED nor was it due to academic ineptitude. He simply became ill from a tick bite and missed a substantial amount of school.

The doctors seemed to be at odds with each other about whether he had contracted Lyme disease or not, but when he shared what was happening with the Vietnam vet, things changed. The vet made him a salad from herbs he gathered in the woods that made him sweat and urinate frequently all day and night. The next morning, he was symptom free. He attended summer school and received his diploma with a handshake from the principal. He was described by all his teachers and school administrators as being essentially nonverbal and somewhat aloof from his classmates, but when called on to give an answer, he always had the correct one. It left Bickens wondering if the Vietnam vet had served as a mentor to Scorzoletti as well as a role model.

Unfortunately, the Vietnam veteran would remain more of a mystery to Bickens than Scorzoletti. There was nobody who could recall anyone fitting such a description. There was nothing to suggest that such a person existed except for a very comfortable abandoned log cabin on the outskirts of town. Whoever lived there had cleansed it of all traces of any former resident. About a quarter of a mile away from the cabin, there was an area that appeared to be a shooting range, but there wasn't a single spent cartridge or a slug to be found anywhere around. It may have been a misguided hunch, but it was one of those dots in Philster's story that could be connected to other information that simply had to be turned 180 degrees in the opposite direction to arrive at the truth.

Finding no help from other agencies like the CIA or the FBI, Bickens took Philster's advice and connected with a man named Devereaux from Interpol three days after his visit with Philster. He had set everything in place for Philster to be released on July first, 2019, so he wanted to make sure his plan would be based on solid intelligence before Philster's release.

Not wanting to travel to Lyon, France, Bickens simply called, identified himself, and asked for the agent who oversaw investigations in Cambodia. Bickens knew that most of the police forces in Southeast Asian countries were integrated with the military. This meant that Devereaux would have military connections as well.

"Good afternoon, Agent Devereaux, this is Special Agent in Charge Gary Bickens with the United States Bureau of Alcohol, Tobacco, and Firearms. I need information on someone that fell under your investigative jurisdiction in Cambodia during the years ranging from approximately 2004 until the present."

"Before I can discuss anything with you, Agent Bickens," Devereaux began in his heavy French accent, "I must confirm your identity. Can I have your badge number please."

"Yes of course…that would be 30666," Bickens said warmly.

After a pause of about ten seconds wherein Bickens could hear the clicking of a computer keyboard, Devereaux resumed his questioning.

"Agent Bickens, can you please tell me the office you work from and your role there?"

"I'm the special agent in charge of the Washington Field Division. My office is located at 1401 H Street Northwest, Suite 900, Washington DC."

"Thank you for confirming this information, Agent Bickens. Now how can I assist you?"

"I need information on a man by the name of Salvino Scorzoletti, who may have been involved in a series of murders of Cambodian nationals and American military personnel, and I need that cross-referenced with the words 'tevta morn.'"

"I remember that name well," Devereaux began as he rapidly clicked away at the keyboard of his computer.

"You do?" Bickens replied with enthusiasm.

"Yes, he was considered a subject of interest as he was one of only three men in the region at that time who could have killed in the manner that came to be associated with the tevta morn."

"Was he enlisted with the US Marines or any other branch of the armed services at that time?"

"Unfortunately, Agent Bickens, due to the level of your security clearance, I can only confirm that he was enlisted as a Marine and honorably discharged after four years. Immediately thereafter, service records for him as a US Marine were abrogated."

"Abrogated?"

"Yes, it was made to appear as though he had never had any association with any branch of the armed services in your country, yet he re-enlisted in another branch."

"Well, what happened to him afterwards, and where is he now? Why couldn't your people bring him in?"

"I'm sorry, but what I have told you has been more than generous given the security level required to discuss this individual."

"Could you at least give me a clue as to his whereabouts. You can be as vague as you need to be. Is he still in Southeast Asia…Europe? I mean, throw me bone, and I'll run with it after that. Nobody needs to know we spoke."

"I can tell you only this much more…the last we saw of him was at Chiang Mai International Airport in Thailand. We have surveillance camera pictures of him boarding a flight bound for the US in 2014. I am sorry, but this is all I am at liberty to discuss…and this stays between you and me, Agent Bickens."

"Why, yes, of course."

"Very well…good day to you, Agent Bickens."

The receiver clicked before Bickens could hang up. It was less information than he had hoped for, but it did confirm what Philster said, especially his hypothesis about the possibility of Scorzoletti being the tevta morn.

It was also Bickens' hope that Scorzoletti was within his reach. Bickens wasted no time contacting the IRS to determine if Scorzoletti was in the US as the tax filing season ended a couple of months ago. They could provide him with a location where new leads and information could be gleaned.

Bickens was disappointed to find that Scorzoletti used a post office box in New Augusta, Mississippi, on his return, so he couldn't get an exact fix on Scorzoletti's home at that point, but his check with USPS confirmed that the box was still listed to Salvino Scorzoletti, and a home address was on file with them as of June 3, 2019. Next, Bickens selected a satellite imagery map he could zoom in and get an exact picture of the residence.

Bickens immediately picked a team of eight of his most experienced agents and briefed them on their target. These were agents who had given the better part of their life in service to the ATF and were villainized as jack-booted thugs by the right-wing voters. None of them had any aversion to profiting off the coattails of a murderer and a traitor as Scorzoletti was portrayed.

"Gentlemen, tomorrow night we are going to pay a visit to the residence of Salvino Scorzoletti in a remote area on the outskirts of New Augusta, Mississippi, where there will be no spectators to take videos of our operation with iPhones or any other type of social media recording devices. I have obtained a FISA warrant to enter Mr.

Scorzoletti's home for the possession of automatic weapons, suspected murder of foreign nationals, interfering with classified operations, and possibly divulging classified information. In addition, he has secured vast sums of money that are undisclosed on his tax returns. He lists only his employment as a light vehicle mechanic for the National Guard out of Camp Shelby, which is about ten minutes west of his residence."

"Excuse me for interrupting, sir, but what evidence do we actually have that he's a foreign operative, and what type of resistance are we likely to meet in serving this warrant. Do we actually know the suspect has arms in his residence? Are there more individuals in the dwelling other than him?"

"Excellent questions, Agent Dixon. I was actually just getting to that information." Bickens reached behind himself to pick up some bottled water and take a drink before proceeding. "Our suspect is a former marine sharpshooter and a SEAL master chief with a love for machine guns. That's why we will be going in with night and thermal vision equipped with fully automatic AR-16 machine guns after first breaching the premises with stun grenades on every side of the house where there are windows. Upon our approach there will be two men to every side of the building. Upon entry, the two men on the south perimeter will join the two men on the west side, where the four will then enter the rear of the residence while the two men on the north side join the men on the east side front entrance as the two teams enter both the front and rear entrances to the residence. The rear team will be first in with the front team breaching that entrance moments later to evoke an element of surprise and confusion.

"You see, gentlemen, the FISA warrant allows us broad reaching powers in the absence of any substantiated proof. It's all based on conjecture and the premise of a threat. That's the beauty of it all.

"As for possible resistance and other residents in the dwelling, I can say with confidence that Mr. Scorzoletti is the lone resident of this small, two-bedroom, one-bath dwelling."

"How can you be sure, sir?" another agent questioned.

"Well, Agent Johnson, he declared himself single on his latest tax return a couple of months ago, so I don't see how he could've gotten married and impregnated his wife, who would thereafter give birth to a child in slightly under two months."

The room filled with laughter and some jocular banter before Bickens proceeded.

"If I may continue, gentlemen…according to other sources in my investigation, all of them, except one, seem to concur on the fact that Mr. Scorzoletti is very bright but extremely introverted, so he's not likely to give any resistance whatsoever in the face of overwhelming force and firepower. He's smart enough to know that he won't stand a chance in a siege against an unknown number of heavily armed men, especially when we convince him that our primary objective is to recover the assets that he sapped from illegitimate covert operations when the shooting stops. He's in his mid-forties; I'm sure he'd prefer to go on living than to die in a clearly no-win situation. Our angle is going to be that if he cooperates and provides us with information he has on hidden accounts, as well as cash he may have hidden in his residence, we don't need to speak about that in court. We can also look the other way about the war crimes for the killing of Khmer nationals, as well as treason for divulging classified operations."

"Pardon me, sir, but if we throw out all of those things, what is our case going to be?"

"Another excellent question, Agent Daniels! Mr. Scorzoletti will absolutely have a Thompson submachine gun on his premises, but, more than likely, he'll probably have a plethora of other machine guns and their corresponding ammunition, and not one of these weapons is registered with the ATF last I checked. We all know the charge for the possession of one unregistered machine gun is ten years in prison and a 250,000-dollar fine. Trust me though, gentlemen, this one is never even going to have to go to trial. Mr. Scorzoletti is going to be terminated after we get what we want, and we're all going to enlarge our offshore accounts. That's the essence of this mission. That's why it's called Operation Don't Speak. Mr. Scorzoletti's social profile is perfectly aligned with that of a lone right-wing zealot who may resist our attempt to peacefully serve a warrant to bring him in on weapons violations. I think we all remember the incident in Diamond Ridge, Idaho. We'll fire off a few hundred rounds into the surrounding trees from his weapons to support our allegations that he was killed in an unprovoked firefight."

"Will local authorities be alerted or involved in any way, sir?"

"Well, Agent Marks, I suppose they can be informed after the fact, but there is a reason why this mission is called Operation Don't Speak. Now, if there are no further questions," Bickens announced as he glanced around the room at the eight men, "we need to gear up and get airborne because we have a hot date in Mississippi tomorrow evening. One last thing…hand signals only…maintain radio silence during the operation. Don't speak."

Chapter 3
Darkness Falls

As darkness fell in Mississippi on the eve of July 3rd, 2019, Scorzoletti had no reason to believe it would be unlike any other night. He read a story to his five-year-old daughter and tucked her in her bed. He watched a baseball game in the living room while his wife was knitting Independence Day scarves to donate to the Vietnam veterans. She knew her husband was a marine, but she didn't know that he was a Navy SEAL team leader, and she never knew about his cherished old friend and mentor who was a Vietnam veteran. The first time she asked her husband why he wanted her to knit scarves for vets from a war he never fought in, he simply replied, "Because they fought, died, and were taken as prisoners in a war that everybody was against, and when they returned home, they were not welcomed but they were despised and even hated. That war was about one thing, and one thing only…who got rich, and who got dead." That was a good enough reason for her, so every year she knitted a scarf that she would embroider with the words "You're not forgotten," or something to that effect.

At 10:00 p.m. he joined his wife for some pillow talk and at 10:30 the lights went out. The two of them drifted off into a relaxing sleep to the backdrop of crickets clicking and frogs croaking, unaware that danger was fast approaching. It was 11:00 when the nefarious eight, led by Special Agent Gary Bickens, would come to a slow stop and exit two black Cadillac Escalades parked a quarter mile from Scorzoletti's home and silently walk to form a perimeter around it.

At the same time Philster was enjoying his freedom and celebrating by drinking all evening at the Tilted Kilt in Chicago. He was getting friendly with the waitresses, who were doting on him because he was generously tucking twenty-dollar bills into their skimpy skirts and talking about his entertaining clandestine activities like they were episodes out of a James Bond movie. The waitresses were not only enjoying the generosity of Philster; they were genuinely intrigued by him until one of the waitresses wanted Philster to validate his experiences in some way.

"Here, here, look at this," Philster said, pulling out an anodized Navy distinguished service medal with the signature white, five-pointed star above it.

"Oh my God, that's so cool. That would look so awesome on my blouse. Could I get this from you," the waitress asked.

"No, no, no," Philster said, chuckling and motioning with his hand for her to give it back. "Civilians can't wear anodized medals. They're government issued only to those who have distinguished themselves in a military combat situation."

"Let me see it, Kelli," another waitress pleaded as Philster reached in his pocket and retrieved an anodized Navy cross. Instead, Kelli pinned it on her blouse and took a quick selfie with her cell phone.

"Here, pin this on your rack," Philster said to a waitress named Rayanne. He then handed his cell phone to another waitress. "Here, you take a picture of me with Kelli and Rayanne sitting on my lap. One on each thigh. My arm isn't long enough," he said, beginning to laugh. The waitress took two pictures of Philster and her coworkers sitting on his lap.

Suddenly Philster stopped laughing and his mind flashed back to Bickens and Scorzoletti. He knew Bickens' intent and he knew why Scorzoletti did what he did in Cambodia. He dug into his wallet and pulled out a number that he hoped was still Scorzoletti's. For security reasons, he didn't keep any classified contacts on his cell.

"Hey, give me back my phone. I have to make a call."

"Do you have to call your wife and tell her what a naughty boy you're being?" asked Kelli.

"No, this is personal, classified business."

"So, do you want us to go away?"

"Go away…no, you can keep your little buns parked on my thigh until I shut this place down."

Philster carefully dialed the number and when it began to ring, he put his finger up to his mouth. "Ssssshh, this is very important."

Scorzoletti put his phone on vibrate as he always did at night. By the fourth ring Philster began to think the number was no longer Scorzoletti's, but Scorzoletti was awoken by the second vibration. He never received calls at this hour of the night, so he was instantly summoned to consciousness by instinct. He was just straining to focus on the number and trying to discern if it belonged to anyone he knew past or present. He recognized the 312 prefix as a Chicago area code, but he didn't know anybody in Chicago. Then, by the fifth vibration, Scorzoletti noticed the crickets weren't clicking; the frogs weren't croaking. It was dead silent, and this was unusual. His instincts told him someone or a group of people were approaching his home. When Philster was just about to hang up on the sixth ring Scorzoletti picked up.

"Who is this?"

"Scorzo, is that you?"

"Who is this?" Scorzoletti demanded in a raspy whisper.

"It's the Philster…Steven Philster. Don't tell me you forgot me?"

"I remember you, but why are you calling me now, after all these years, and in the middle of the night?"

"Because you need to watch your six, comrade."

"What's the deal?"

"Pierpont and the ATF believe you bankrolled all the cash from Operation Lotus Blossom. There were only three marines in the entire armed forces that could have made the kill shots on our purveyors. The other two were nowhere near that area, so that leaves you. They're probably on your ass as we speak."

Philster had forgotten all about the girls as he spoke. Time stood still and he could only hear the man he admired. Suddenly the phone went dead. He hoped it meant that his tip-off prompted an immediate call to action from Scorzoletti. Scorzoletti silently slid to the floor of the bed and quickly crawled around to his wife's side and began to shake her gently.

"Julie, Julie, wake up, baby," he whispered sternly. "Get out of the bed and get down on the floor and get under the bed. Don't move. I'm going to bring Angela to you."

Julie knew that something was terribly wrong by the tone of her husband's voice and the bizarre nature of his request, but she knew well enough to obey him. Scorzoletti quickly went downstairs to a special vault he had built and retrieved a Thompson submachine gun and affixed a 100-round drum magazine to it. He took an extra one with him. As he raced toward the stairs, he heard first one then a second stun grenade go off in Angela's room, which was wrongly presumed to be the room where Scorzoletti would be. The first one landed directly on her abdomen and the second one landed near the left side of her head. She died instantly. The other grenades followed almost simultaneously in other rooms, and Scorzoletti knew he had only seconds before his home would be breached by a standard rear and front entry.

He quickly raced up the stairs knowing he could not check on his daughter. The best he could do was position himself behind the kitchen counter near the back door. The rear team entered twenty seconds before the front team, which had to wait for Bickens to run around the house from the south end to the north end to signal that team to join the east team by breaching the front door. Those few seconds were all the window of opportunity that Scorzo needed. He let the four men enter and then opened fire. Aiming at their thighs, he hit all four in rapid succession and pulled two of them to the rear door and laid them on top of each other like human sandbags as they groaned in agony. He positioned his gun and did the exact same thing to the second group, who had wrongly assumed it was the rear team firing on Scorzoletti. Bickens proceeded to enter through the window of Angela's room as Scorzoletti quickly collected most of the men's arms and placed them on the bed in his room.

Bickens lowered the barrel of his rifle and placed his hand on the lifeless girl's throat to see if he could feel a pulse, but there was none. Scorzoletti silently entered the room as Bickens was overcome with grief by the murder of an innocent child.

"Drop the weapon or die…it's your choice," Scorzoletti muttered with anger, sensing his daughter was dead.

Bickens obeyed and slowly laid the weapon on the floor as his left hand slid off the lifeless child. He then proceeded to raise his hands in the air.

"Kick the rifle away from your side," Scorzoletti ordered. "Do you have any other weapons on you?"

"A nine-millimeter Glock tucked in my back," Bickens replied.

Noticing the watch on Bickens' left wrist, Scorzoletti knew that he was right-handed.

"Take your right hand, place it in your pants, and grab your balls."

Bickens paused momentarily and grimaced before Scorzoletti gave him a more menacing directive.

"Mister, you reach into your pants and grab your balls, or I swear to Jesus I'm going to write my name on your chest, and believe you me, I can do it!"

Bickens grudgingly complied in humiliation that one man took down him and his entire team of ATF agents in a matter of seconds.

"Now go sit down next to my daughter, who you and your men just murdered, and turn your head to the wall behind you. Take your left hand and slowly take your weapon and place it under my daughter."

Bickens slowly did as he was ordered.

"Now stand up, clasp your hands behind your neck, and go on over and face the window."

"You know, Scorzoletti, you can still get out of this. Nobody knows about this operation. It was a 'do not file' op."

"So can you," Scorzoletti said, raising his weapon in the air and slamming it into Bickens' back as hard as possible. He heard a sharp snap just before the front of Bickens' face slammed into the raised window. "You'll get out of this and into a wheelchair for the rest of your life! And every time your smelly diapers have to be changed, because you won't be able to feel your bladder empty or your bowels moving, you can remember my innocent daughter, who you murdered on the third of July!"

Before Scorzoletti even finished talking, Bickens' legs buckled beneath him and he fell to the floor. He couldn't feel anything from his waist down. He knew he was paralyzed. His mind drifted back and forth between his own future and the sounds of his men groaning and groveling about on the floor in the other rooms. Scorzoletti took the gun from beneath his daughter and the rifle that Bickens had laid down and brought them into his bedroom with the cache of other weapons. He gazed about, looking at the other men in the living room, and checked them for other weapons, but in doing so he noticed that they seemed to be in no condition to do harm to anyone. Some seemed to be going into shock from blood loss, but Scorzoletti wasn't leaving anything to chance. After collecting all the additional weapons from the agonizing specter of dying men, Scorzoletti returned to his room.

"Sweetie, you can come out now. The threat has been neutralized."

"Where's Angela?" Julie asked as she began to cry.

"It's not good, baby."

Julie looked at all the weapons piled on her bed in disbelief.

"What on earth is going on? Why would an entire army descend upon our home? Did you do something wrong, Sal?"

"No, these men came here with the belief that I had a lot of money, and they were wrong."

As Scorzoletti's voice trailed off, Julie began to sob.

"I want to see my baby."

"Honey, it's not good. She's gone," Scorzoletti said in soft and low tone.

Julie's hands were drawn up to her mouth as if by the suction of a vacuum, and she gasped before her eyes widened with the fire of retribution blazing.

"I want to see her, and I want to know which one of these bastards killed her."

Scorzoletti took his wife and led her into the room where Angela lay lifeless and Bickens lay on his back with tears streaming down his face, knowing that his condition and his life had been irrevocably changed for the worse. As Julie buried her face in Angela's chest and sobbed, Scorzoletti walked over to Bickens and looked down at him.

"What are the tears for, Bickens? You realize how pathetic your life is now? Do you realize what a coward you are, or is the realization setting in that you waged war on the family of a man who's going to make you wish you had never been born?"

Bickens simply closed his eyes tightly and shook his head in disagreement, and Scorzoletti spit on his face. He walked over to his wife.

"Baby, I need you to turn on the computer, log in to your YouTube account, and bring me my phone," Scorzoletti said softly with a flattened affect that suggested his mind had shifted into a different mode. Julie looked at him and winced in confusion, but Scorzoletti just stared at her like he was looking through her as he said numbly, "Please, baby, just do what I ask."

Upon complying with his request, she re-entered the room with his phone and Scorzoletti began recording and narrating the scene in his home, starting with his lifeless daughter, Angela.

"What you see before you is not a dramatization. It is the lifeless body of a five-year-old girl who never got to see her sixth birthday on July fourth…a day that celebrates our country's victories…Tomorrow it will memorialize one of America's worst tragedies." Scorzoletti came in real close to show the third degree burns on her chest and abdomen around her massive wounds and the blood oozing from her nose, eyes, and ears and then he panned in on Bickens and continued his monologue. "And this is the face of the man who ordered eight other men to shoot stun grenades through her bedroom window and on to her bed. His name is Special Agent in Charge Gary Bickens of the United States Bureau of Alcohol, Tobacco, and Firearms…better known as the ATF. He and eight of his men could have been anywhere in the

35

United States pursuing dangerous criminals that commit heinous acts like this on law-abiding citizens, but they weren't. Instead, they chose to deprive a helpless, sleeping little girl of life, liberty, and the pursuit of happiness on the day our country will celebrate the fourth of July. Instead, they drove out of their Washington, DC district to pursue what they thought would be a large cache of money and murder their would-be perpetrator." Scorzoletti walked through the house, turning on the lights and panning in on each of the suffering agents. "These men carried out a covert operation called 'don't speak' against little Angela and her family. Their mission was accomplished with the death of little Angela. She will never speak!" Scorzoletti said with emphasis and a moment of silence as he walked toward the living room and panned in on the suffering men there before continuing. "There's just one thing that went wrong with their mission: They didn't know that Angela's father was trained by the same government to neutralize terrorists and enemies of the state…both foreign and domestic. In this case, you're looking at domestic terrorists posing as agents of justice.

"What would you call nine men who deprived a little girl of life, liberty, and the pursuit of happiness before her sixth birthday?" Upon asking this rhetorical question, he came back to Special Agent in Charge Bickens, who merely said, "Help us." Scorzoletti zoomed in on Agent Bickens' jacket where the bold letters ATF were printed and said: "These men went beyond the law, and they are beyond help." Then he stopped the recording. He then rifled through Bickens' pockets until he could retrieve keys to his vehicle. He walked over to his wife Julie, who was staring at their daughter and crying in disbelief at what had happened, as well as the drama that was unfolding in the aftermath.

"Baby, let's go over into the other room; I need to talk with you."

Scorzoletti walked his heartbroken wife into their bedroom. He sat down on their bed and pulled his wife onto his lap before he began to speak.

"Julie, I'm going to have to do the hardest thing there is for me to do…I'm going to have to leave you for a while."

She attempted to speak, but Scorzoletti put his finger on her lips.

"Baby, this isn't something that I want to do. This is something I must do to protect you. I'm about to publicly humiliate our government by uploading this video to YouTube and an alternative, conservative news site. They'll try to kill me and anyone who is with me, including you, my precious wife. They'll brand you as an accomplice to my activities and thereby justify eliminating you as well. We've already lost our daughter; I can't lose you too. As much as I hate to leave you behind, it's the only way I can guarantee your safety. You're a foreign national, and killing you would create an international shit storm."

Scorzoletti embraced his wife and kissed her before easing her off his lap and going to their computer to upload the video he had just made. After uploading it to YouTube, he uploaded it to three other conservative sites and gave it the title "Don't Speak: The ATF's Nefarious Nine" before unplugging the auxiliary cable from the computer port.

"Salvino, what did you do that these men came here and did all this to us?"

"I saved a bunch of young girls and boys from being sold into sexual slavery."

Julie shook her head and winced in disbelief.

"This is all so crazy," she replied. "Why would our government send these men into our home because you saved a bunch of young children from a terrible thing like that?"

"Because our government was directly sponsoring and profiting from this terrible thing?"

Again, she shook her head.

"It all sounds so crazy."

"I know, baby, I know, but it's the truth. ONI, the CIA, and several other foreign intelligence agencies were all involved. We've been married for seven years and I never lied to you once. Why would I start now under these circumstances?"

"You never lied to me, but you didn't tell me about this, and now I wonder what other things happened in your past that I don't know about. And why would our government approve of such a thing?"

"It's hard to explain, honey…our government isn't one unified body, especially where the intelligence field is concerned. It's very compartmentalized, and very often one part doesn't know anything about what another part is doing, or why, and most of the stuff they do in other countries as well as our own country is illegal. The ends always justify the means to them."

"It just doesn't sound rational," Julie replied, coughing, and then sniffling.

"It isn't, baby, and I'll bet you that the ATF and no other law enforcement agency knows anything about these men being here."

"I still can't understand why they would come after someone who saved young girls and boys. Is it really about your guns or something else you do, or that you did in the past?"

"No, that's just the pretext they used for obtaining a warrant to enter our home, but it all boils down to greed."

"Greed," Julie exclaimed in confusion. "You lost me."

"When I shut down military operations involved in sex trafficking, I also tapped into the accounts that were being used to hide their profits and diverted the funds. Bickens and his men obviously thought I was hiding the money for myself. He and his men wanted it for their own personal profit. It's that simple."

Scorzoletti finished uploading the video as he talked with his wife.

"Honey, I've got to get one of their vehicles and load up my guns and ammunition now. There's no time for me to discuss things."

"What if these guys set a trap for you while you're gone?"

"Honey, I'm more worried about these scumbags bleeding out than setting a trap for me. They're really in no condition to pose a threat to anybody, but if they die the scenario gets a lot worse for us. I'll only be gone for about five minutes. These guys probably followed textbook protocol and parked their vehicles no more than a quarter mile down the road. That's just a minute's run for me."

Scorzoletti hugged his wife briefly and bolted to the door. Within minutes he was back again. He quickly loaded the entire contents of his vault into the back of the Escalade within about fifteen minutes.

"Salvino, why do you have weapons that look like rockets in your vault? And what about those other things…those small boxes?"

"Those rocket-looking things are LAWS rockets, and the small boxes are Claymore mines. The soft bars are C-4 explosives."

"Honey, I know you never cared much for talking about your time in the military, but what exactly did you do that you would need to keep these kinds of weapons around the house?"

"I did all kinds of things…like the things that brought these men here looking for money. I also made enemies around the world."

"What's going to happen to me," Julie asked with tears streaming down her face and her voice choking up.

"Trust me, baby, these people are going to treat you like a big azure diamond because you're the only living link to me, and, moreover, as a green card holder, you're still a Chinese national who they wouldn't dare to hurt if you're alone. However, if you go with me, they'll shoot you like a rabid dog in broad daylight on the city streets and get away with it. They'll spin the story that you were an accomplice, or even my foreign handler."

"What about you," she asked helplessly.

"Well," he began tentatively, nodding up and toward the stairs, "you see what I did to those guys."

"Then you can protect me, Sal?" she asked, with her eyes looking for reassurance.

"Baby, your safety isn't the only reason you have to stay behind. You're also the only living witness that knows exactly what happened here. If you come with me, they'll try to change the story of what happened. You have to stay here and call this in to extricate yourself from appearing as a conspirator, but you can't say a thing about the operation or anything in my past that I disclosed to you. All I need is a forty-minute lead."

"Won't that be a red flag to them?"

"No, not under the circumstances…You were in shock…grenades had exploded, a gunfight ensued, and suddenly you were all alone… your daughter is dead; your husband is gone…and it all happened so fast it was unreal. Then you contemplated committing suicide for quite a while before even thinking to call 911."

She looked at her husband with stoic resignation because she believed in what he said. In the seven years they had been married, Salvino had never been apart from his wife…no skiing trips or solo vacations with the guys, and no weekend retreats that separated Julie and Angela from the presence of his tender love and affection. Those days were gone now.

"Julie, I can't say exactly when or how, but we will be united. I promise you, baby…"

Before Scorzoletti could continue, Julie put her finger on her husband's mouth and then planted a kiss upon his lips.

"I know; I believe you, Sal…just hurry…don't speak."

Chapter 4

Sunrise, Sunset

At 4 a.m., Philster was drinking champagne and talking to himself while surfing the net when his phone rang.

"Philster here...talk to me or I'll talk to myself," he answered before laughing momentarily at his own comment. With silence on the other end, he took a more serious tone. "Hey, who the shit is this?"

"Philster, it's me. I'm coming to Chicago; where are you?"

"Jesus H. Christ, do you know the video you posted on YouTube is going viral. You not only beat the record set by Adele and that retarded video of hers, but you have more views than her, Taylor Swift, Nicki Minaj, Miley Cyrus, Justin Bieber, and Rihanna combined...close to a hundred million views! That's about a third of the literate part of the country, and the other two-thirds are still sleeping! You're a freaking rock star!"

"How did you know I posted a video on YouTube?"

"Jesus H. Christ, Scorzo, what the shit do you think I do all night long? I mean, what the shit does anyone that stays up all night do? You know, I check out social media...Facebook, YouTube, Instagram, and a bunch of other shit. By the way, you don't have to be an Einstein to put a voice to a video. After all, I knew you were going to get hit by the ATF. I just didn't know exactly when, so when you answered your phone, I figured maybe they were just watching you, and weren't going to strike for a day or two...or maybe later."

"So why did you sell me out? I never mentioned your name when I leaked Operation Lotus Blossom."

"Sell you out! What the shit are you talking about? They were already on to you. All I did was give them a few worthless bona fides so they'd believe me, and then I served them a crock of shit. I made you out to be some dumbass retard that they could take down easy-peasy-Japanesey! That's why they only came down there with nine guys and small arms instead of with tanks and BZ gas and armored personnel carriers and that sort of shit!" Philster exclaimed with exasperation.

"They killed my daughter, Philster. Why didn't you call sooner?" Salvino retorted coldly.

"Sooner…sooner…fricken A…I just got out of the joint yesterday when I called you last night! Do you think I had the privilege of making personal calls inside a federal penitentiary whenever I wanted? I'm sorry about your daughter, Sal, but I had no idea you were even married. I mean, let's face it…you were never a very social guy, so I couldn't picture you as the marrying type…the mercenary type yes, but the marrying type…no. So, what now…you're going to come to Chicago and whack me?"

"No, I need to lie low, and the last place anybody would think to look for me is with you. So, I need your help. Especially if my post has gotten as many views as you say it has."

"Hey, I shit you not, Sal! Your post has gone over the edge viral. The posts on YouTube are just the tip of the iceberg. I've already seen your post reposted on Facebook with friends I have in Thailand. There's also a search engine called Baidu I know of in China that has picked it up. Then there's those three conservative sites you posted to that are running it every few minutes. It was midday over in China when you posted this, but what I don't understand is how they got wind of it. YouTube and Facebook aren't even allowed over there, but about a quarter of a billion people over there have seen your post. For the life of me, I can't figure out how that shit happened, but you are a freaking global, viral phenomenon."

"I posted it to China and a few conservative news outlets that post stuff on the USA for China as well as controversial stuff here to YouTube," Salvino said coolly.

"Why, I mean…how does China figure into this?"

"It was an insurance policy." Salvino replied.

"An insurance policy for what, and how? Did you do some ass kissing with the Chinese that I don't know about when you were a SEAL?"

"It's an insurance policy for my wife. I had to leave her behind. Once they know she's a Chinese national, she has a de facto form of diplomatic immunity. If the ATF does anything to her, it becomes an international incident. That's why I included her in the video."

"Was she hurt at all?"

"No, but as you can imagine, she was traumatized and in a state of shock when I left. I had no choice, though; it was the best possible thing to do. So, with that said, I have no intention of taking you out. You were one of the few people in the military that I liked."

"No shit...really?" Philster replied with surprise.

"Yeah, really...and your conspiracy theories were a lot more palatable when I found out what kind of stuff you were into once I became a SEAL. They just made common sense because the strength of a conspiracy, no matter how logically defined and refuted, is that the average masses won't believe in it."

"Yeah," Philster agreed, "they'll gladly wolf down the shit sandwich the media hands them before they'll even take a nibble on the truth."

"Yeah, it's the God's honest truth, Philster, but we haven't got time to talk about that. I need to know where you are, but you can't tell me directly because the ATF will use the NSA to intercept our conversation. Remember how we conveyed information when I was a SEAL?"

"Do I remember? I wrote the fuckin' book on that shit...of course I remember!"

"All right, give me a phrase, Philster...something that will allow me to lock in on you while they waste days trying to decipher what we're talking about."

"Shit, shit, shit," Philster muttered as he frantically paced around the room, "shit, okay, I got it! Shit! Am I good or am I good!"

"Give it to me now, dammit, or they'll triangulate your position before I get there!"

"A musical question was asked while Pisces, Aquarius, and Capricorn were overlooking Chicago from an elegant abode!"

"Gotcha! Be there at 0800."

"Hey, they got me under an assumed name."

"Don't need to know that. Meet me on the outside of the building where the sun rises but casts no light, yet the diamonds still sparkle… understand."

"Roger that, Sal. If I were you, I'd swing by little Italy first and pick yourself up a Belfry Fedora hat to obscure that mug of yours. You're bigger than the Courtland towers! I mean you really stand out."

"See you at 0800," Sal said abruptly before hanging up.

"Watch your twelve, three, six, and nine, Geronimo… They're going to be coming at you from all sides," Philster said even though he knew Sal had hung up.

Scorzoletti monitored police radio transmissions as he cruised at a steady speed of eighty-five miles per hour, but he was also keenly aware that a traffic stop would result in a lethal firefight with whomever was unfortunate enough to engage him. Scorzoletti was vigilant in his belief that he acted in self-defense against a debased federal gestapo, but he also knew that all the members of law enforcement now perceived him as an armed and extremely dangerous felon on the run. The use of lethal force against him would be deemed necessary.

As day broke on the city of Chicago, Philster was preparing to meet Scorzoletti. He conversed with himself as though he was talking to Scorzoletti, trying to rationalize his past transgressions. Suddenly, he realized it was nearly eight. First, he turned over the nightstand and quietly broke the lamp. He then cracked the mirror on the bedroom dresser as well as the flat-screen monitor before he placed it face down on the floor. Then he quickly dressed, threw on a cap and some sunglasses, and left his room at the Palmer House and went down to wait for Scorzoletti on the east side of the Palmer House Hotel facing Jeweler's Row. Much to his surprise, Scorzoletti was already curbside awaiting as Philster walked up. Scorzoletti honked the horn quickly and called out to Philster.

"For Christ's sake it's good to see you, Sal. Man, you look as young as you did the last time I saw you," Philster opined enthusiastically.

"I wish it were under better circumstances," Scorzoletti answered.

"Yeah, yeah, that's some hard shit losing your daughter and leaving your wife behind and all that, but you got to believe me when I say that they were already on to you, Sal. I didn't sell you out...your daughter's blood is not on my hands," Philster said in a somewhat pleading tone. "It's that Bickens...he's bad shit...him and his crew are as dirty as they come...that whole raid on your place was all about money."

"Look, I'm not here to take you out," Scorzoletti said flatly. "If I wanted to do that, I would have never told you I was coming. I would have hunted for you, and I would have found you, and then I would have put you down."

Philster shook his head nervously and chuckled.

"Nah, I'm not so sure about that, my friend. The ATF figured you would be coming after me, so they gave me an assumed identity. I'm now Ahmed Al-Sayed because I have dark hair and dark eyes. Can you believe that shit! I mean, do I even remotely resemble one of those fucking Muslim rag heads? They even wanted me to grow one of those bushy beards and wear one of those stupid fucking Muslin skull caps!"

Scorzoletti laughed.

"Oh yeah, that's real funny. I do Uncle Sam's dirty work for half of my life and then for the rest of my life I'm branded with the name of a motherfucking sand nigger Muslim...real funny, Scorzoletti! Remind me to laugh if I forget to."

"Judging by the place they put you in, you're getting the royal treatment. Did they throw in the standard amenities?"

"Oh yeah, shit, they gave me a Citibank Visa and a Chase MasterCard...both with a ten-thousand-dollar limit."

"Tell me something, Philster, what's the badest neighborhood in Chicago?"

"Well, if you're going for per capita murder rate, it would be Englewood, but Austin can't be far behind it, why?"

"Because those are the two neighborhoods we're going to throw your credit cards out the window at."

"So, you're going to whack me and plant my body in a shitty neighborhood to make it look like I was in the wrong place at the wrong time, huh? Blame it on the gangbangers?"

Scorzoletti smiled and shook his head.

"Come on, get over that, Philster. I need you to put a crew together for me, so I have no intention of wasting you."

"What happens after I put the crew together… Then you waste me?" Philster asked tentatively.

"Look, you and I were both ONI at one time. We both got screwed by the same puppet master. I don't agree with what you were doing, but I went rogue myself and started killing friendlies because their moral compass was so fucked up, I felt compelled to do something about it. So, you would have every bit as much reason to take me out."

"Are you fucking kidding me," Philster said, beginning to laugh as he pointed to his gut. "I couldn't kick a piece of dog shit down an alley! I'm so out of shape from eating prison lard and laying on my ass all day. The only way I could kill anybody is if I pulled down my pants and pulled up my shirt. All a person would have to do is look at my distended belly and my shrunken half-inch penis. They'd die laughing. That's the only way I could kill anybody."

"You can still fire a weapon, can't you?"

"Yeah, sure, but I don't own a weapon and I doubt I could even get one."

"Yes, you do," Scorzoletti replied.

"What the shit are you talking about? Do you know something I don't?"

Scorzoletti nodded toward the back of the car. Philster craned his neck over the seat to see a large cache of weapons and ammunition.

"Holy moly! What the shit are you planning on doing with all of that?"

"I'm planning on proclaiming liberty and justice for all. When I was over in Cambodia undoing the work of a certain faction of our government, I was merely nipping at the tail of the behemoth. Now I'm going to prepare to strike at the heart of the behemoth."

"What are you going to do, blow up the White House or something?"

"No, I have no beef with the president... In fact, he's the first president that's a businessman, DC outsider, which is exactly what this country needs. We've had too many career Washington bureaucrats in the White House. Besides, I am absolutely convinced he had no knowledge of the operation that killed my daughter. Lotus Blossom started and ended long before his tenure."

"Well, what then... why all the firepower? You going after Bickens' crew?"

"No, I could've taken them all out the night they decided to wage war on my family. Killing Bickens would have been an act of mercy. I wanted him to live the rest of his life as a helpless cripple. The other half of his crew that died were simply collateral damage."

"Okay, then who the shit is this behemoth if not the ATF or the federal government?"

"The behemoth is the one who controls the federal government from sunrise to sunset. The people who control the wealth in this world dictate what countries can or can't do, and, as a direct result, the quality of life for people who live in those countries. Cambodia should have taught you that, Philster. Saloth Sar, better known as Pol Pot, was from a well-to-do family, and he was educated in France. That's where he established his communist affiliations. He was no fucking working-class peasant seeking equality for the poor. Moreover, he grew rich from arms and money he was receiving from both the US and China all throughout the 1980s. We sent the SEALS in during 1989 because we reneged on our deal to pay off the North Vietnamese for their decade-long occupation of Cambodia."

Philster began nervously looking from side to side of the windshield as well as the passenger window as Sal drove and talked. "Yeah, yeah, that's right around the time when Lotus Blossom bloomed. Hey, Sal, I don't mean to cut you off because I definitely think you've got a point, but we've already passed Sixty-third and Ashland and it's starting to look pretty fucking scary. It's looking like the yard in the big house, only it's all Black instead of eighty percent Black."

"Just a minute." Scorzoletti pulled up to a corner where a group of young men were gathered. He quickly scrawled on a Post-it note the words "From Uncle Sam." "Give me your Citibank card."

Philster quickly complied, extracting it from his wallet and handing it over to Scorzoletti with his hands shaking slightly.

"Now crack your window just enough to toss that card out the window and we'll get out of here," Scorzoletti said.

No sooner had the card been tossed than Scorzoletti stepped on the gas and made a U-turn on Ashland Avenue and headed northbound to the Eisenhower Expressway.

"Now it's on to Austin," he said with a tone of satisfaction and determination.

"Oh, shit, Sal! Why couldn't we have dropped both the cards there?"

"Because we want to add an element of confusion. We want our adversaries looking in two separate places where we'll never be found."

"Well, that screws up everything I tried to make them assume by trashing my room at the Palmer House to make it look like you came after me so I could really disappear."

"That will still work. They'll just think I forcibly extracted you from the Palmer House, took you down to the badlands, and left you to the mercy of the gangbangers. Their obvious conclusion will be that you were looted and disposed of."

"Yeah, that would be very neat and convenient if you had just dumped both the cards off there, but when charges start showing up from places on the west side as well as the south side, it will blow the shit out of that theory now, won't it?"

"No, not necessarily. They'll just have to waste a lot more time widening the perimeter of their investigation trying to establish what happened to you. As for me, they'll most likely assume I'm heading west to get out of Illinois."

"So that's the plan...we head west out of state, which you anticipate they're going to assume? What the shit kind of plan is that, Sal?"

"No, that's not the plan. The first plan is that you tap into some money you have hidden in some shell corporation and get another vehicle. After that, you need to produce someone for us who is a genius when it comes to computers and who we can lie low with for a while."

Philster nodded as if processing Scorzoletti's instructions while licking his lips and applying some Chapstick before responding.

"Shit, that's like asking a server at a McDonald's counter for a beer-battered, deep-fried Big Mac...but you're in luck! I happen to know this nerdy ex-naval officer who was dishonorably discharged for getting caught smoking dope on duty. I couldn't believe this guy... an IQ of about 180 but so shittin' stupid. His CO was standing right behind him watching him, but he thought nobody would know because he was using a supposedly 'smokeless' pipe. After a few seconds observing him, the CO calls him to attention, so he slips the pipe into his shirt pocket still lit, turns around, and stands at attention. When the CO accuses him of smoking dope and orders him to hand over the paraphernalia, he denies it and tries to play dumb, saying that he doesn't smell anything like marijuana. The next thing you know, he says he has to take a piss really bad and starts leaning forward because the pipe is burning him. So, he races to the upper deck with his CO on his tail and he heaves the pipe overboard. What a dumb-ass!"

"He was a terrible liar, but he did think fast!" Scorzoletti replied.

"He was a dumb-ass."

"Well, if you feel that badly about him, why would you suggest him as our man?"

"Because when it comes to computers, this guy makes Mel Bates of Microspan look like he's mentally challenged. He just doesn't have any common sense. He only made officer because he had a degree from MIT before enlisting, but he always told everybody his ultimate goal was to be an 'ethical' hacker. Have you ever heard of such a stupid thing? There's no such thing as an ethical hacker. All of them do shit that causes other people a pain in the ass in some way or another."

"He's just the type of guy I'm looking for," Scorzoletti said flatly.

"Really?" Philster replied with dismay. "Why?"

"Because he's not opposed to using malevolent means to right a wrong. Where does he live?"

"He lives up north in this rich-ass suburb called Kenilworth...really nice house on the lake front. He made a shitload of money creating a super popular game that all the kids got addicted to called Popper, and once he got them hooked, he started creating additional levels of it. Anyway, he's a dumb-ass when it comes to anything other than computers and hacking into sophisticated systems, so I'm sure he'll take us in."

When Scorzoletti and the Philster were in the Austin neighborhood, it was well after noon. Scorzoletti told Philster to take anything he wanted out of his wallet, but to leave the credit card, new social security card, and state ID in the wallet and toss the whole thing out the window along with his cell phone as they approached a group of guys near a curb. They then quickly sped off and found a car in an alley about two miles away. They got out and put new plates on the SUV, and then drove to the branch of a bank where Philster had warehoused some of his ill-gotten gains during Operation Lotus Blossom. He had a check made out in the amount of $29,500 to Wilson Nissan, where they purchased an SUV with tinted windows that could hold all their cargo and then headed to Kenilworth after abandoning Bickens' vehicle with the old plates on the west side of Chicago.

At the same time this was happening, a media frenzy that began at eight a.m. continued to display the YouTube video of the decimated ATF team, but muted Scorzoletti's voice-over. His picture was displayed along with a newly supplied cache of arms the Mississippi ATF had brought in to justify the ATF's reason for the deadly encounter, even though Scorzoletti left no arms behind. Unfortunately, and unbeknownst to the American media, the Chinese media ran the video non-stop with the English voice-over and Chinese subtitles. It was no different in England and America's other allies. The conservative media outlets did the same.

Scorzoletti was being portrayed by the American media as an

emotionally unstable loner with past connections to Neo-Nazi extremists and an ongoing affiliation with the Montana militia. Books of Hitler and extremist right-wing groups were placed in his bedroom and repeatedly shown to present a convincing portrait of the government allegations against Scorzoletti. His wife was initially depicted as a devout Chinese Communist who approved of her husband's attack on an unwitting ATF team. Viewers worldwide, especially in China, were horrified by Angela's murder at the hands of the ATF. There was no mention about Bickens and his team being from the Washington, DC field office. Nothing was mentioned about treasonous activities, classified information, or Scorzoletti's military background. The Chinese media portrayed the ATF assault as a brutal attack on a decorated military hero simply because his wife and daughter were both Chinese nationals. The conservative outlets, who were first on the scene, said that all neo-Nazi and militia books were planted by federal authorities. They were followed by officials from the Chinese government.

The official American story line was that the ATF went to the Scorzoletti home to serve a warrant on weapons violations, and suspected Scorzoletti had plans for armed sedition against the United States of America with right-wing extremists to counter the growing threat caused by leftist groups like CLM and AntiCap. It was further alleged that Scorzoletti was an adherent to KKK values, even though his wife was Chinese. The ATF spokesman out of Mississippi said that the ATF had credible sources to substantiate their claims, but names could not be divulged due to the ongoing manhunt for Salvino Scorzoletti. An international war of words ensued between the American and Chinese media outlets. Meanwhile, the KKK vehemently denied any affiliation with Salvino Scorzoletti, claiming it was an attempt to further villainize them. They even noted that the KKK literature found was from the 1960s during the civil rights conflicts, a rather odd coincidence to say the least.

While Julie was disparaged and portrayed as a passive participant in her husband's alleged attack on the ATF, Bickens had briefed the Mississippi SAC not to mistreat her or label her as an accessory to the shootings. He maintained that Julie seemed remorseful and likely to cooperate with them, and, as such, she was to be treated kindly. Bickens was keenly aware of the reason why Scorzoletti left his wife behind and didn't want to incur the ire of Washington bureaucrats who would have to answer to China about any alleged abuses to one of their citizens by the USA as well as the murder of an innocent Chinese child.

Scorzoletti was the reason that what the ATF assumed would be a simple domestic case turned into an international incident. Scorzoletti had already notified the Chinese consulate and the Chinese ambassador in Washington of the ATF's murder of a Chinese national, since Angela was born in China and immigrated to the US with her mother, and, in addition, the abusive treatment being unleashed on Angela's mother. Unlike the video images displayed in the media coverage, the Chinese officials could see the video evidence on YouTube and hear the narration of events that led to Angela's death. They quickly copied the video and sent it to China in a diplomatic pouch. They saw the incident as an unprecedented violation of human rights against two Chinese nationals. Moreover, they reasoned, a girl of such a tender age could have no responsibility for anything alleged against her father. Therefore, they saw her death as a senseless and barbaric disregard for an innocent child who was a Chinese national. Though they maintained silence on the issue within the US, they immediately reported it to Beijing, supplying them with lethal ammunition to silence the US claims of human rights violations perpetrated by the Chinese government on their own citizens.

Chapter 5
Virtual Disaster

Scorzoletti stood to the side of the front door as Philster rang the doorbell of the imposing home where Jerry Alvarez lived. It had been years since he had seen or heard from Steve Philster, but Philster came off like their relationship had never ended as soon as Jerry opened the door.

"Alvarez, how the hell are you?" he began, but continued without waiting for a response. "Man, you haven't changed a bit! You still have that dopey look of confusion written all over your face."

"It's just that I didn't expect to see you show up at my front door the day before never," Alvarez replied.

"What the shit are you talking about? Don't you remember when we docked in the Philippines and were partying all night with those three whores from Manila? You said I absolutely had to stop in and party with you when we got back stateside! Did you forget that?"

"Well, no," Alvarez began hesitantly.

"Well, hey, here I am…in the flesh, ready for some action at this fabulous place you have."

"Oh man!" Alvarez said with astonishment. "Is this who I think it is?"

"Indeed, it is, so how's about letting us get the fuck off your front porch before everyone in your neighborhood comes to the same realization that you just did!"

"Yeah, sure, get your asses in here," Alvarez replied as he pulled Philster in by his arm and motioned for Scorzoletti to follow. "Fuckin' A, Philster, you know how it is when you're in the service…you say a lot of shit to the other guys, but I didn't think you would just show up at my front door out of the blue with America's most wanted."

"So, what the shit are you saying…that was all a load of crap you were talking when we were having fun every night in Manila?" Philster spouted off in an accusatory tone of voice. "You know it was my ass who kept your ass out of the brig and made sure you weren't court-martialed for smoking dope on duty, and this is how you treat me when I take you up on your invitation?"

"No, man, it's not like that, Philster…"

"It's not like what? You mean I'm okay to hang out with when I keep you supplied with a barrage of supplicant Filipinas to go muff diving in, but I'm not good enough to hang out with now that you're living in highfalutin Kenilworth."

"Philster, you don't understand…things are different now."

"Oh, I understand all right, you virtual nerd… You live in a nice neighborhood, you've got money, and now you're too good to hang out or even be seen with the Philster…is that about it?" Alvarez attempted to speak, but the Philster continued. "Yeah, yeah, things are different now because your ass isn't in a sling and you have a small fortune tucked away living in this ivory tower of yours. Just remember that none of this shit would be possible if I didn't intervene on your behalf and keep you from getting court-martialed, ya dumb-ass."

Just as Alvarez was going to answer Philster, Scorzoletti put his hands together in a sign indicating that he wanted a time-out. For the first time since Alvarez set his eyes upon Scorzoletti, Salvino began to speak in a genial Southern manner.

"Mr. Alvarez, could we go into the living room and sit down for a spell. I'd like to get your opinion on a few things that I believe are within your area of expertise."

Alvarez led them to the opulent living room and beckoned them to make themselves comfortable. As soon as they were seated, Scorzoletti looked at Philster and put his finger up to his mouth signaling that he wanted him to remain quiet.

"Mr. Alvarez, do you believe that all people who obey the laws of their country at the federal, state, county, and municipal levels are entitled to have law enforcement at each of those levels protect their right to life, liberty, and the pursuit of happiness?"

"Yeah, of course I do. That's a no-brainer."

"I guess it's safe to assume that you haven't logged on to any form of social media today?"

"No, but I have had the TV on in the background while I was working on a new game, and all I saw were pictures of you and a team of ATF agents you massacred when they came to serve you a warrant on weapons charges."

Scorzoletti nodded his head in agreement and smiled amiably.

"Of course you did…because that's what they wanted you to see and hear. What you didn't see was my five-year-old daughter who they murdered. Do you know any five-year-old girl who violated weapons charges and is considered so dangerous that nine heavily armed men have to toss stun grenades directly on her body before entering her home?"

"No, I can't say that I do," Alvarez replied in a stunned tone.

"Do you know any American expatriates in China who abide by the laws of China and have the Chinese military storming their house in the middle of the night using lethal force, and thereafter hold the Americans hostage?"

"Not to my knowledge, but I heard from the Philster that you stayed over there for a few years."

"That's correct…that's where I met my wife and that's where she had our daughter because there wasn't anything I could do back home. You see, I went into the Marines when I was eighteen, and after serving four years in the corps, I immediately enlisted in the Navy and joined the teams, where I remained until I was forty, or should I say… until I developed a conscience." Scorzoletti ended with a brief chuckle as he shook his head in regret.

"I remember you from that demonstration where you shot the heads of three cobras off at about a quarter mile or some insane distance like that."

"Yup, that was me, but with all my skills and medals, ONI cut me loose from active duty and abrogated my entire military service history, so I had a twenty-two-year black hole in my work history that I couldn't explain to any employer back in the States. I had no choice but to live as an expat teaching kids English in China and believe it or not, I was treated nicer by the people and the government of China than I was by my own country. I wish I could say the same for my wife right now, but I can only imagine what she's going through."

"Man, that really blows," Alvarez said, looking down at the carpet, shaking his head in disbelief.

"I'll say," Scorzoletti responded. "If it hadn't been for a colonel who had taken a liking to me in the Marines and recommended me as a civilian mechanic at Camp Shelby, I'd most likely still be in China... maybe better off too. Anyway, that's neither here nor there now. What I'm interested in is whether you want to do something with your life that's meaningful?"

"I'm already doing something with my life that's meaningful," Alvarez replied with a puzzled look on his face.

"Right now, you're doing something you're passionate about," Scorzoletti said as he began shaking his head in disagreement. "Sad but true, it's not meaningful."

"It's meaningful to me; I make a lot of money doing it, I live in a beautiful community, and I have the freedom to do the things I want to do."

"Unfortunately," Scorzoletti countered, "you're not seeing the big picture. The reality is you produce a product that has no beneficial outcomes for the end user. It eats up his or her time, alienates them from their family and friends, and desensitizes them to violence while inculcating a low threshold for patience and goal-oriented behavior... the payoff in those games is the instant gratification of attaining a high score and going to the next level of the game, but what does that translate to in real life. Is being a good gamer something that's of value to an employer?"

"I guess not," Alvarez replied

"Will it help them develop social skills that will benefit them in their life?"

"No," Alvarez replied flatly.

"Well then, in the final analysis, you're simply steering a whole generation of kids into a narcissistic world where their threshold for tolerance is slim to none, their ability to demonstrate empathy and compassion is absent, and their capacity for engaging in senseless violence is enormous. Does that really sound like a meaningful legacy to leave behind when you're dead and gone?"

"You sure as shit can't drag this wonderful place and the town of Kenilworth into the grave with you," Philster finally piped in.

"He's right," Scorzoletti concurred, "and because you have no wife or kids, guess who's going to inherit all you worked for."

"I guess the government," Alvarez offered in response.

"Yeah, yours truly, Uncle Sam. Now does that seem fair that the government gets to inherit everything that resulted from the fruits of your labor when they didn't contribute one iota to your efforts?"

"No, it surely doesn't, but what are you proposing I do that will provide a lifestyle I've become accustomed to while providing a meaningful existence?"

"Use your talents as a hacker to undermine the efforts of a government that's trampling on the life and liberty of its people and making it impossible for them to pursue happiness, much less find it."

"Yeah, but if I do that, I won't be obeying the laws according to your explanation and therefore I won't deserve life, liberty, and the ability to pursue happiness."

"Do you think those ATF agents who declared war on my family were obeying the law? They had absolutely no proof that I even possessed weapons. Their sole reason for laying siege to my home was predicated on a conversation Mr. Bickens had with Pierpont at ONI while they were out drinking at a DC bar. Pierpont was the one who put the idea in his head that I wired millions of dollars earmarked for clandestine ops into private accounts for my own use. The truth is, I wire transferred that money to accounts to help a pastor named Stan

Brunsler, who helped victims of sex slavery recover. I also transferred portions to Hapha House in Cambodia so they had funding for safe houses and other resources they needed for victims of trafficking they recovered. Huge amounts were transferred to Israeli Defense Forces shell accounts as well as to organizations assisting aging holocaust survivors, and other worthy causes here in the United States, such as the Appalachian food project. I never kept a penny of that money, but Bickens and his men had other ideas, and they were fully intent on acquiring that money and keeping it for themselves. Think about it… why wasn't the ATF in Mississippi in on this, and why weren't the local law enforcement at the state and county level involved?"

"Yeah, that makes no sense at all given what they said about you being involved with the militia of Montana. I'd think the Mississippi ATF as well as the FBI would be all over your ass, especially with all those books and pamphlets you had in your house."

"That stuff was all planted for the media. I never had a single piece of hate literature in my home, and as for me being a KKK sympathizer…I don't think I'd win any favor with those guys being married to a Chinese national and having a Chinese-American daughter. In fact, they themselves denied any affiliation with me."

"I guess it does sound like a crock when you start putting the pieces together, but let me ask you this… Are you looking for revenge in your quest to promote life, liberty, and the pursuit of happiness for people?"

"No, if I wanted revenge, I wouldn't have let one of those guys live that night. I'd also be going after key individuals in ONI that were perpetrators and co-conspirators of the operation. I'd shut down the bastards that brought my military service to an end. I simply want you to use your skills as a hacker to give us access to information and weapons systems we'll need."

"How will this add meaning to my life?"

"As time goes by, you'll see wrongs being righted and justice being served, and in being a part of it, you'll know in your heart that you're a part of something greater than yourself. It was once said that the only thing necessary for evil to prosper is for good men to do nothing. I believe you're a good man, Alvarez, and I'm going to give you a chance to do something about evil that exists in our country, and which we actively export to other countries."

"I'm good with that," Alvarez said, nodding in affirmation.

Philster got up and started pacing around the couches they were sitting on.

"Oh, for Christ's sake, I feel like I was sitting at a Yalta summit or something listening to you two. All right, all right, can I say something now? Jesus H. Christ, I think this is the longest time I've gone without at least contributing something to a discussion."

"What's on your mind, Philster?" Scorzoletti asked.

"Well, I think the first thing we should do is fire up YouTube and show Alvarez the real version of what happened at your house, so he can see for himself what a ruthless bunch of bastards you're talking about...so he can see your daughter and your wife...you know they say a picture paints a million words or some shit like that...come on, come on, let's let him see for himself. The Tube tells no lies, unlike our fucking media that only broadcasts the party line on every channel every day!"

"But the Tube censors, so we'll have to see it from my USB."

Alvarez led Scorzoletti and Philster to his lavishly decorated basement, and then to another part that was like a hidden alcove where he had all his electronic equipment. He logged on to one of the computers hooked up to a thirty-six-inch monitor and pulled up the "Nefarious Nine" YouTube video. As Alvarez watched the carnage and listened to Scorzoletti's voice-over, he kept shaking his head and letting out breaths of sighs, especially when he looked at Angela and her distraught mother. At the end of the video, he looked at Scorzoletti in a silent, sullen manner that attested to his talent in neutralizing overwhelming forces relying solely on his own expertise.

"Whatever you need me to do, I'll do it," Alvarez said somewhat emotionally and with a firm sense of commitment in the tone of his voice. "What's first?"

"First we put together a team of guys that can help us. You will get me all the information on how we connect with them without surfacing on any government radar. Then we get them here and map out our game plan."

"No, no, no," Philster interrupted. "First we need medicinal aids that are going to give us clarity as well of peace of mind when the shit starts to fly."

"What are you talking about?" Alvarez asked.

Philster turned and looked at Scorzoletti first.

"Now, Sal, I know you have a legitimate beef with the feds. I would too if they killed my little girl and took my wife hostage. But think for a moment…who's the second biggest group of rip-off artists the American people are subjugated to after the United States government? They're the number one whore politicians are in bed with when they ain't banging teenage boys or girls."

Scorzoletti and Alvarez looked at each other, and then looked at Philster. Scorzoletti shrugged his shoulders and Alvarez shook his head, dumbfounded.

"I give up, Philster…who?" Scorzoletti asked.

"The shittin' pharmaceutical industry. They sleep with the FDA and the DEA and rip the American public off seven ways to Sunday. Shit! The average price of a thirty-day supply of Dexedrine, which they've renamed Vyvanse, is about $287. Do the fucking math, Sal! That's almost ten dollars a pill! The price of Seconal, an effective sleeping pill, is over nine hundred dollars at most large, retail pharmacy chains. That's higher than black market street prices, and those motherfuckers have the government's blessing because of mandatory insurance, which half the time won't even pay out on those kinds of prescriptions!"

"Excuse me, Philster…what in the fuck has this got to do with anything we're talking about right now?" Sal asked nonchalantly.

"Well, as I see it, we're going to need pain relievers if someone on our team gets wounded…we'll also need stimulants to sharpen our reaction time and focus if we end up in a firefight, and we'll need something to help us chill out after the adrenaline has been pumping."

"Essentially, you're saying we knock off a drugstore for drugs, correct?"

"Well, yeah, essentially," Philster replied somewhat sheepishly.

Scorzoletti looked at Alvarez tentatively and said:

"Well, the Philster does have a point, and since this is your neck of the woods...do you know any small, independent pharmacies we could hit that aren't on major intersections where there's not a lot of foot traffic? I don't want to be hitting any 24/7 Walgreens or CVS pharmacies where we have to worry about possible casualties amongst innocent civilians or store personnel. I want one of those old-fashioned independent stores that closes at eight or nine that we can enter during off-hours, and where there's no street video surveillance."

"Yeah, there's a place up in Winnetka, called Sonny's. It's about a mile northwest of us. They open at nine and close at seven p.m. After 21:00 that area is a ghost town."

"Okay, you use your virtual genius to get into their system and examine their inventory for the stuff Philster requests. The most important thing is to get some schematics that show the layout for their controlled substances. This is going to be Philster's show. He's going in solo, so we don't want him to be in there all night searching for stuff."

Philster laughed momentarily.

"What's so funny?" Scorzoletti asked him.

"Shit, back in the Navy we used to call this guy Virtual Disaster because he could get into any other country's automated weapons system and jam it or even aim the weapons back on their own country, but he was always getting wasted on weed and playing video games on duty."

"Virtual Disaster...huh?" Scorzoletti said in a quiet and reflective manner. "I like that name. It fits because now he's going to create virtual disasters. Only this time they're going to serve a purpose and right some wrongs that have gone on for far too long."

Scorzoletti took a deep breath.

"Okay, Alvarez, you get to work on everything we need to know about Sonny's, including breaching their alarm system. Philster, you and I need to come up with some people we can add to our team."

"Yeah, sure, I know a few people who have been screwed over by Uncle Sam who would be glad to sign on with us."

"We need six more."

"Six more! Shit, that's a nine-man team, Sal! What are you planning on doing, storming the White House and pulling off a coup d'état?"

"No, I told you before...I have no problems with our current commander-in-chief. He's the first president in a long time that makes any sense. He doesn't need to play politics because he was already wealthy and powerful before he took office. He's simply a businessman trying to run the country like a business, and that's why the democratic-controlled press, the Congress, and the Senate are all against him. They want to continue running the country like a bunch of ruling elite royalty that have the people and powerful companies serving them. No, nine is a symbolic number. Nine men laid siege to my home, killed my only child, and separated me from the love of my life, so the 'nefarious nine' have given birth to their 'nemesis nine.' We are going to be the posse comitatus for the people of the United States of America."

"Hey, look, Sal, that's an admirable thought, but why don't we just blow up the Washington ATF building and call it a day."

"Because we couldn't get close enough to the building to pull that off, and if I'm going to die for a cause, it's not going to be just for revenge. I'm going to die serving and defending the people I swore to protect."

"No, no, no, Sal, you're not getting it...I mean, you don't even know what Virtual Disaster here is capable of doing. This guy is so shitting good he could launch a cruise missile from one of our own ships right at the Washington ATF headquarters and they'd never know what the shit happened because those things fly below the radar."

"Yeah, but the ship's crew would know a weapon was fired and they would know the coordinates of the target."

"No, no, wrong!" Philster said, starting to pace back and forth from end to end of the couch using his index finger for emphasis.

"That's where the genius of this dumb-ass shines brightest! He developed a launch program that will totally redirect the tracking of the weapon's trajectory to a nonexistent path, so the crew will assume it was an accidental firing heading toward the ocean where no harm will be done. Their obvious course of action will be to have a couple of fighter jets launched to head to that target zone to have a visual accounting for the loss of a missile. You know, those fucking things aren't like M-80s. They're fucking expensive! Shit, back in 2011 one of those fuckers cost 1.4 million dollars.

"Anyway, since that would take some time after the missile is launched for them to get some birds in the air, they'd never catch up with the thing, even if they could find it! The only thing they can report to the crew is that it hit the ocean where the coordinates were programmed," Philster exclaimed with excitement as he stopped momentarily to rub some Chapstick on his lips before continuing. "Prior to that, we plant some radical Islamic propaganda and the photos of some known terrorist near the scene the day before, and our stupid media picks up the story and reports it. Perhaps then they'll stop harassing the president about his nonexistent travel bans on Muslims. Think about that, Sal! You'd actually be helping our president because Islamic Jihad and all those other radical ragheads over in the Middle East would be out in the streets cheering and celebrating, and they'd even want to take credit for it because they hate America so much… and guess who'd be panning in on all those crowds and giving them free publicity for their insane causes?"

"Our media of course."

"Fucking bull's-eye, Sal! Our media would be stirring up public outrage against those whack jobs instead of portraying them as poor, persecuted minorities who simply want to coexist with other Americans in this country. Coexist my fucking ass…their Koran says that we're all infidels, and we're to be slaughtered! The problem with most people is that they don't even know what that fucking revolutionary manifesto piece of shit says. I bet ninety percent of the Muslims never even read that piece of shit from cover to cover! I'm so sick of those fucking ragheads. Everywhere they go they want to change things in their host country so that the laws operate according to Sharia law. It just fucking kills me, Sal! Look at that bitch Osira Ilhar in Congress. She came over here because the leaders where she grew up, in a fucking refugee camp, of all places, are a bunch of crazy yahoos that are killing everybody, but then they want to turn our country into Tehran, Bagdad, Africa, or wherever else it is that they come from.

"You know I was just reading how this one Muslim bitch enrolled in the Star Point military academy and she refused to take off her hajib or habib or whatever the fuck they call those scarves they wrap around their head, and the school said she had to observe the academy dress code, so she couldn't wear it. So, what do you think the bitch does? She turns around and tries to sue the fucking school for religious discrimination. The goddamn bitch is probably a sleeper agent for one of the Islamic terrorist groups and she's not only attending a school that teaches our battle strategies, but she's trying to sue the school as well. And the sad thing about it is that she'll probably get some liberal-ass lawyer from the ACLU or the Southern Poverty Law Center to take her case and give her lots of publicity so all the rest of them ragheads will be saying they're persecuted in the US. Oh, fuck me!

"And of course, everyone else must adhere to the bank dress code, but not those Muslim bitches! They're allowed to go into banks in a wardrobe that conceals them from head to toes. The only thing you can see is a slim patch of their face where their eyes are, and sometimes those fucking cunts even wear sunglasses so you can't even see their eyes. I mean, how the fuck do you like that? They're allowed to go into a bank better concealed than any bank robber, but the bank can't do shit about it! Isn't that just the shit! I get so pissed off by that shit! I mean, if those fucking ragheads want to have everything the way it is in their country, then they should just go the fuck back to where they came from, but that would be too fucking easy, Sal. These assholes would much rather stay here where they won't get their eyes gouged out for looking at pornography, and of course the bitches would rather be in a country where they can't be married off at eight years old and be sodomized by their sixty-eight-year-old husband. In the meantime, they find all sorts of loopholes in the tax code so they can get out of paying taxes and then they find ways to get welfare benefits like disability benefits for their kids and food stamps and all the while they're driving taxis and making about two hundred and fifty dollars a day. That's why they own a string of Dunkin' Donut shops and a few Subway shops five years after they arrive here. Nice fucking system we have here for them! Man, I don't even want to talk about it anymore because I get so pissed off!"

"Look, Philster, it may be as you say, but all I know is that no group of radical Islamic fundamentalists stormed my house, killed my daughter, and took my wife as a hostage. A corrupt faction within our own corrupt government did that. That's my focal point. I can't change the entire world, nor do I intend to do so. I do, however, want to shake up the thieves and the power brokers that have taken control of our country. So, let's focus on our team."

"Okay, okay, give me a minute. Let me calm down so I can think. You got me all riled up thinking about that fucking piece of shit Koran. I mean, what you ought to do is recruit about five of those Muslim bitches to hit a bank because not only can they conceal themselves with approval of the US-fucking-government, but they also know how to fire an AK-47 and they'd just love to shoot any American infidel who made a move on them. I can't believe you got me started on this topic!"

Scorzoletti just shook his head, knowing the way Philster would go off on tangents and then accuse someone else of starting the conversation.

"Hey, Jorge would be great!"

"Don't know him," Scorzoletti replied

"Sure, you do…George Gonzalez…remember, we partied together in the Philippines. We just called him Gonzo for short, remember? His mother is the only one who called him Jorge. He was really close with his mother. That's why he went into the Navy and joined the teams. His family was living over in Humboldt Park and he

was a gangbanger…a real fuckin' cowboy, not afraid to take on anyone. The only way out of gang life was the military, so he enlisted for
his mother. He was a stand-up guy. I remember this one time he fucking singlehandedly took out a group of six Abu Sayyaf guerillas that
had kidnapped some western vacationers. I remember he was with
a couple of Marines we were supporting, and they wanted to call in
some backup. Gonzo just looks at them and says, 'No fucking way, you
pussies. These guys will move before backup can form a perimeter.'
Then he marches right into the middle of their camp and says: 'You
guys know any place there's a big hole that can fit a lot of shit in?'

"Then he's told to put his hands up. Well, what the fuck do you
think he does? He shoots the motherfucker right between the eyes and
starts blasting away at all the other bastards who had their guns on the
ground. During the commotion, the last one grabs a woman and puts
a knife to her throat, threatening to kill her.

"'Go on, motherfucker, slice the bitch. I don't give a shit! I don't
know her,' he said to the fucker. 'Then it will be just you and me, and
you think that knife is going to save your life.'

"Well, all of a sudden Gonzo throws his gun down and steps right
up to the guy, who pushes the girl aside. Gonzo grabs his knife hand,
twists it around the rebel's back until you could hear his shoulder dis-
locate and the knife drop. The he starts stabbing the shit out of the guy
while saying, 'So you like to play with knives, huh motherfucker? Well,
Gonzo's gonna teach you how to use one! Too fuckin' bad for you it's
the last lesson of your life you're gonna learn!'

"It was like the gangbanger in him came back to life, but as soon
as the killing was done, the first thing he did was apologize to the
woman for what he said and asked her if she was okay. He asked everyone when the last time they ate or drank any clean water, and then he
broke out his rations and his water for them. When he was sure they
could move quickly, he informed them that they had to put as much
distance between that site and their group as possible. He was a perfect gentleman after he got a taste of the old Humboldt Park warfare."

"Yeah, I know who you're talking about. I do remember him. All right, he's in," Scorzoletti replied after patiently listening to the story. "Who's next?"

"Maxwell Peterson...he was a friend of Alvarez, and he was a medic, so he'd be very useful."

"Be that as it may, how do you know he'll want to join up with us?"

"Jesus H Christ, Sal...the guy is an MD and he was good friends with Alvarez. They used to smoke dope together, and he was the guy who invented the nickname Virtual Disaster for Alvarez. What more do you need?"

"Something a little more substantive than paling around with Alvarez while they were in the service. A lot of things may have changed in his life since then. If he's currently a doctor, I can't see him wanting to take himself out of a cushy lifestyle and join ranks with a crew of outlaws."

Philster rubbed some more Chapstick on his lips after licking them and then started pacing around.

"Substantive, you want substantive. All right, I'll give you substantive. How about the IRS seized his family's home, cars, and bank assets because his father made a seven-thousand-dollar cash deposit from his legitimate business? The bank was forced to notify the IRS without informing Peterson's dad because he allegedly violated the IRS 'structuring' laws. So, his family lost everything and had to borrow legal fees from relatives to prove Mr. Peterson's innocence. Even though he eventually prevailed, his home and cars were already auctioned off and his financial assets were lost in the maze of the government coffers. Max had a shitty childhood because of the IRS, and he was old enough to know that they were the reason for his family's demise, so I'd say he has a bit of an axe to grind with the feds. So, how's that for fucking substantive? An American citizen with constitutional rights that assume innocence until guilt is proven, but along comes the IRS and deems his father guilty until proven innocent. Then when all is said and done, the IRS offers no admission of their own guilt or any wrongdoing on their part, and, moreover, they don't even offer any restitution or even a fucking apology for ruining this guy's business, his life, or the life of his family! They just fucking walk! Now that's some fuckin' substantive shit!" Philster said, wiping sweat from his forehead. "The only reason why Max became a doctor was because NYU had a special tuition-free program for MDs because of a severe shortage of doctors."

"Maybe you better sit down a spell and calm down before I ask you about anybody else," Scorzoletti said, with a slight smile.

"No, no, I'm fine. Let's strike while the iron is hot as they say. I got two more people. Miles Sano was really tight with Maxwell. Whatever Maxwell was into he would follow. They grew up together. Sano is really into martial arts and weapons. He started studying Aikido when he was just five years old! Even unarmed the guy is a fucking weapon himself. If he knows Maxwell is with us, he'll follow. In some ways, he's a bit like Gonzo…not in a gangland sense, but he's a bit of a juice junkie. He likes action and excitement."

"Well, believe it or not, I actually led a few team missions with him under my command. He's everything you say he is and more… very precision- and plan-oriented. He executes orders like a machine, but, if necessary, he'll improvise to keep his team out of harm's way. I definitely want him with our crew."

"Jake Sturgis would be another good man. He was a Marine sniper. He served in Iraq and Afghanistan, and has been continually jerked around by the VA on his health coverage and medications."

"Medications?" Scorzoletti interrupted. "We don't want anybody with health problems that could compromise us."

"No, no, it's not like that. He just suffered from PTSD after he got out, and the VA was trying to deny him coverage because he got in some scuffles with the police at a Second Amendment gun rally. After that the VA tried cutting him off by claiming that they weren't responsible for veterans' actions and subsequent after-care if the incidents were due to criminal activity."

"Do you know what he does these days? When was the last time you saw him?"

"It was a couple of years back. It was in Vegas. He was working as one of the casino security personnel on the gambling floor."

"Maybe he's content with that," Scorzoletti countered.

"Nah, he just settled in Vegas because he enjoys the legal prostitution on the outskirts of town, and his boss is a really easy-going guy. Before that he said he just drifted from job to job, more often than not, getting fired for one reason or another."

"Perhaps that's not a good thing for us. We need people who are willing to fit in with a team and take orders from me."

"He can definitely get along with our team and take orders from you. He never had any issues during military life."

"Then why did he leave the Corps?"

"He whacked three Iraqi civilians he saw raping a young girl. It wasn't part of the mission, so he was charged with murder and dishonorably discharged, and served a couple of years stateside."

"How about after he got out?"

"He just had problems dealing with civilian life. You know how people can be on jobs…you got the lazy guy who can show up late every day, take long lunches, and slip out early because he would kiss the boss' ass. Shit like that drove Jake crazy, and he wasn't shy about letting his opinions be known. That just doesn't cut it in most places. You have to play company politics, and that shit always rubbed Jake the wrong way. So, he'd either move on or end up getting fired for giving the boss a piece of his mind."

"Well, given what you've told me, it seems like he could get behind my cause, if he can play by my rules."

"I know he could because the one thing that's missing in his life is a sense of mission. I could feel it the last time I saw him, and if there's one thing Jake hates…it's powerful motherfuckers getting away with shit simply because they have connections, influence, and money."

"Okay, let's look him up and recruit him. Who's next?"

Philster stopped his pacing for a moment and put his hands up to his chest with his palms facing Scorzoletti as if to signal that he wanted Scorzoletti to hear him out.

"Now, I know you're going to have some reservations, but there's this guy named Mohammed Hussain who I think would be a great asset.

I mean, ordinarily I can't stand anyone with the name Mohammed...just the sound of it pisses me off, not to mention the fact that all these dumb-ass Muslims think their sons are gonna be some fucking prophet or great man because they give him the name of their high priest of pedophilia...Mohammed! But this guy is solid and he can get any weapons we need or want!"

Scorzoletti tilted his head sideways and squinted as he looked at Philster.

"I don't think I know anybody who hates Muslims more than you do, Philster, and now you want to bring one into our crew?"

"This guy isn't a Muslim. Believe it or not he hates Islam, hates the Koran and Sharia law, but he does know a few folks in the Jihadist network who would be happy to take the credit for any federal agents we grease and any of the collateral damage that arises. Not only that, but he could probably get some of those jihadist turds to help us out in a tight situation. You know those shitheads aren't like the federales, my friend. If faced with the prospect of dying in a firefight or going home at the end of their shift, the feds will run their chickenshit asses off, but not the ragheads. They'd rather die for the cause of killing a few agents of the 'great Satan' than getting back home..." Philster ranted as he began to pace and furiously puff on a cigarette he had lit. "...and I'll tell you why...you want to know why? Because they're thinking about the forty fucking black-eyed virgins they're gonna be banging once they get killed and end up with Allah!"

Scorzoletti shook his head as Philster exhaled a huge billow of smoke.

"All right," Scorzoletti said, nodding in agreement. "It makes sense, so connect with him but don't bring him into our group. He stays on the outside as ancillary support. He might not object to dying in a firefight, but he'll sing like a choir boy if he gets caught and they waterboard him at Guantanamo. We need one more person," Scorzoletti said flatly.

"Jamal Nixon," Philster shot out without a thought. "Not only can he drive a car like a stunt-man, but he can shoot with precision while he's driving. He can also fly Apaches and F-18s. Not bad for a former

Englewood gangbanger."

"I've never worked with him," Scorzoletti conceded, "but his reputation precedes him. The only thing that worries me is that I heard he has a rap sheet, and I don't want to be bringing any problems into our mix."

"Sal, we're not looking for choir boys! We're looking for people who can perform under pressure and get a job done when their back is against the wall."

"Okay, okay, point well taken. We bring him on, but you make it clear from the get-go that we won't tolerate any gangster thug life attitude. When we bring him in, you make it clear in no uncertain terms that he operates like he's military, and, if necessary, he dies like he's military! I couldn't give a shit less how well he drives a car, a chopper, or a plane. We each have our individual talents, but we work as a tight-knit team. We're the Nemesis nine, and our mission is to politically correct this country.

"We're not going to have Washington bureaucrats indoctrinating second graders with LGBTQ+ material before they even know what sex is. Senators and congressmen are going to stop raping kids from orphanages. And that criminal enterprise known as the Federal Reserve is going to stop stealing money from the people of the United States, and the CIA is going to honor its charter to stay out of domestic affairs and politics! And without a doubt, CLM and AntiCap have to be neutralized!"

"What you do you mean when you say neutralized…infiltrated…disbanded? What?"

"I mean terminated! They have nothing to do with freedom of speech or seeking equality for people of color. They are radical Marxists, cut from the same cloth of the ones we fought in Cambodia, Laos, the NPA in the Philippines, the FARC insurgents in Colombia, et cetera. They go by different names, but their agenda is always the same. We were never allowed to win when we fought in foreign countries, but I'll be goddamned if we're going to lose to these fuckers in America!"

"This sounds like a much bigger theater of operations than the loss of your daughter," Philster said, shaking his head dismissively.

"You're wrong!" Scorzoletti shot back. "You're just looking at the scrambled pieces of a puzzle in disarray. You're not seeing the pieces all put together to form a unified picture. I see the picture, and soon you will too."

Chapter 6
Fuel for the Fire

——♪♪♪——

Scorzoletti's viral YouTube post entitled "The Nefarious Nine" and the ATF's media counter-spin were certainly enough to sear the name of Salvino Scorzoletti into the consciousness of the American people, for it begged the moral question of what circumstances and by what individual or group of people can killing be seen as acceptable. Under previous presidential administrations, there's no question that the ATF would have won the media spin, but under the administration of Neville J. Courtland, the 45th President of the United States, who rightly condemned the American media as being purveyors of liberal propaganda and deceit that bordered on being treasonous, Scorzoletti's post garnered a huge amount of sympathy for him and an equal amount of vitriolic wrath directed at the ATF. Intuitively, Scorzoletti focused his video on his wife and daughter, people of color who had faced as much discrimination as Blacks and Hispanics. As fate would have it, every one of the ATF agents was white. So, both CLM and AntiCap descended on the area to harass ATF agents, riot, loot, and burn businesses in the more populous areas outside of New Augusta. But now, others joined the cause of CLM and AntiCap, although their cause was lacking in the Marxist battle cries of CLM and AntiCap.

A confluence of events created an environment that was ripe for ordinary white middle-class Americans to rally in favor of a perceived underdog that was attacked by agents of the federal government. The attack on the Scorzolettis was yet another example of a government agency that was running wild like a rogue elephant. Countless numbers of times over the preceding two and a half decades, the ire of conservative, patriotic Americans was raised by a federal government that began to resemble an elite ruling oligarchy that could trample on the constitutional rights of those it ruled over with impunity. Gone were the days where men of integrity represented the people of America as elected officials in the three branches of government. The political landscape was littered with one embarrassing scandal after another, particularly in the Senate, Congress, and Executive branches of the government. The Judicial Branch seemed more concerned with reinterpreting the constitution in a manner that diluted the moral fiber of the country, increased the power of the federal government, and usurped the liberty of the American people. The Senate and the Congress were two warring factions that were prone to throwing tantrums and disparaging the president with any number of frivolous and completely baseless allegations. Now it seemed like our elected officials were rulers and "we the people" were now the ruled class.

Finally, there were those who came to be known as "the alphabet army," of which the ATF was a charter member. They were the ones who acquiesced with the whims of the ruling elite and enforced their endlessly growing mandate of directives that increased their power while correspondingly decreasing the liberty of the American people. As time passed, Scorzoletti and his men would find themselves in the crosshairs of numerous agencies in the alphabet army, all of whom wanted to enrich the coffers of their agency's war chests and fulfill their own personal agenda of pride, perfidy, venality, vainglory, harlotry, and heroism!

A few days later, Scorzoletti's Nemesis Nine was in place and residing in Kenilworth. All of them had seen the video Scorzoletti had posted on YouTube before it was taken down. China, however, continued to run the video in English-speaking Hong Kong and even on the BBC news before the CIA prevailed upon them to cease their coverage of the event. The Australians, however, would not back down, and neither would mainland China. They continued running the video with corresponding interviews.

The Nemesis Nine needed no coercion to meet with Alvarez. They had all seen the video siege at Scorzoletti's home and willingly wanted to offer their services to their former comrade. They were brought to his home under cover of the night in pairs so as not to arouse any suspicions, since it was known that Alvarez rarely had visitors, and would certainly never have nine guys showing up at his door at one time. Alvarez would maintain the appearance he always had of being the only person in residence at his address, arriving or leaving the house only occasionally with a business associate or two accompanying him. Now, however, any departures would be made during evening hours.

It was a Friday evening when fuel would be added to the blazing fire that Scorzoletti's YouTube post had ignited. Another member of the alphabet army would enter the arena. They would begin chasing the usual suspects, unaware of the tactical sophistication, technical prowess, and sheer lethal power of their adversary. They were far off on one assumption—that they were looking for a team of two or possibly one perpetrator.

During the reunited camaraderie at the Alvarez residence in Kenilworth, it was decided that only two men would hit the pharmacy known as Sonny's. While Scorzoletti was writing the playbook on what would happen, the way it would happen, and all outcomes in the aftermath, the Philster acted as the mouthpiece for Scorzoletti. Now, while Philster often led and tried to dominate most conversations, the others would add points or counterpoints and the inimitable levity that only former military personnel who served together could add to any conversation.

"Listen up," began the Philster, speaking over the chatter and laughter pervading the room in the basement that came to be regarded as their command center. "First, I'd like to say it sure as shit is good to see all of you again...well, maybe not all of you," he said as he nodded toward Maxwell Peterson. He looked around the room at the others before carrying on. "Can you believe this Jimi Hendrix-looking dumbass actually became a doctor?" Philster laughed briefly. "I bet my left nut he's a gynecologist checking out pussy all day long."

Maxwell looked at Miles Sano and grinned.

"Sano, you still have that killing knife on you?" Maxwell asked

"All right, all right, so I was a little off. You're a proctologist. You spend all day looking at and smelling women's asses," Philster added quickly.

Sano threw a knife he extracted from its sheath to Maxwell, and Maxwell started walking toward Philster.

"I'm a board-certified family practice physician as well as a surgeon, and at least I didn't make my money selling twelve-year-old girls to traffickers, so it looks like you owe me your left nut, douchebag."

"Okay, enough fucking around!" Philster said with a serious demeanor. "What I really wanted to say is thank you all for walking away from your lives to hook up with Scorzoletti and me and right some egregious fucking injustices that each of us along with the American people have suffered. However, this isn't just about us! It's about every American who currently finds themselves at the mercy of our presently tyrannical government. A government, I might add, that can decide to deprive a person of life, liberty, and the pursuit of happiness whenever the fuck they feel like it!"

"So, when did you develop a conscience and start caring about the common good of the people, douchebag?" Max intoned self-righteously.

"When I learned that this very same government that I served was going to whack Scorzoletti because he had the guts and balls to shut down the heinous operation that I was a willing participant in…and their reason for deciding to take him out was predicated in greed, and greed alone! That fucking scumbag Pierpont thought all his ill-gotten gains were stolen by Sal, so he and Bickens devised a plan to stage a pre-dawn siege on his home for the sole purpose of finding out where the billions of dollars of funds went so they could divide the spoils.

"Pierpont didn't inform Bickens and his crew who they were dealing with because he was confident that a team of nine heavily armed ATF agents could easily subdue and take out one man. But as you all know from seeing the video, things didn't turn out quite the way they planned. They weren't anticipating other people there, but sure as shit as I'm standing here, they would have killed them all in a heartbeat if their itinerary went as they expected it to go!"

Philster walked right up to Maxwell and looked at him, his eyes blazing with rage.

"I got a conscience when I saw an innocent little girl die simply because her daddy stopped something that I was a part of. I should have been the one to die that night, not her. Then there's the matter of hundreds of thousands of innocent girls whose lives are forever fucked up because of me...that is, if they're even alive anyway! You want my left nut, Max? You can take it, because God knows my sins are worth more than just my left nut."

Seeing his contrite countenance, Maxwell just looked at Philster and tried to make light of a serious situation.

"I couldn't sleep nights knowing I took the left nut of a born-again douchebag. Besides that, you wouldn't be able to walk for a few days, and you have some risky business to do tonight."

"Indeed!" Philster said. "Fortunately for us, Alvarez tapped into their alarm system after closing this evening and turned it off. In addition, he tapped into their computer and got their inventory on all the schedule two and schedule four narcotics. They're all kept in one locked cabinet that's obscured from view. I was able to discreetly cast a mold of their back-door key, replicate it, and test it, so we are in tonight. The only thing we couldn't get was a schematic diagram of what shelves some of our other necessary pharmaceuticals are on."

Scorzoletti winced ever so slightly as he looked at the Philster and Alvarez before glancing over at Miles.

"That could just be the thing that turns this into a real disaster. Fumbling around in a dark store with a flashlight... I mean, it's not like cops have anything to do in this area, and all it would take would be one patrol car to pass by and see a light flitting around. Before you know it, you'd have six patrol cars there with officers drawing guns."

"That's not gonna happen, Sal," the Philster assured as he turned to Miles and nodded toward a duffle bag Miles had on the floor. Miles quickly extracted some military grade night vision goggles and tossed them to Philster. "I won't be needing any light with these, and since the pharmacy counter is in the back of the store and largely obstructed from view by the layout of the aisles in the store and the tall back counter, all I have to do is stay low, look up at the higher shelves, and grab the shit we need quickly once I spot it."

"Miles will be on the east bank of the Metra which has thick foliage and shrubbery he can hide in and yet still have a perfect view of the front of the store and streets to the east and west of it as well as the front. If he sees any patrol cars, he communicates that to me, and I lie low and stay still until danger is gone. Besides, I'll be exiting through the back door, and walking to another street where the car is parked. I'll pass through the gangway of the condominiums behind the place just like you advised when we did our recon."

Miles started laughing in the juiced-up manner typical of him when he was excited.

"This is gonna be great! Stealing about five thousand dollars' worth of pharmaceuticals and it all fits in a mid-sized gym duffle bag," he said, cackling once again.

"The old boy be whacko," Max said, shaking his head and rolling his eyes up. "Just don't go whacking off if you see any of those young Winnetka housewives out jogging in those Lululemon leotards that crawl up the crack of their asses."

"Man, I noticed that shit when we were heading up here," Gonzo piped in. "Man, those pants look like they're painted on those bitches. I tell you, man, if I had a woman that looked as fine as some of these moms, I sure as hell wouldn't let her be running her ass around like that."

"Yeah, isn't that the shit," Philster added. "They don't want to go working out in the gyms because they say all the guys just gawk at them like sex objects, but then they run around the streets of their neighborhoods like they're naked, wearing nothing more than fucking paint, as if nobody's gonna gawk at them like sex objects…go figure."

Philster took in a deep breath and looked at Miles as he exhaled.

"All right, Sano, it's game time."

With that, the Philster and Sano departed and carried out their mission so that none of the pharmacists or techs were aware that any-thing was awry the next morning until it came time to fill certain prescriptions that were entirely missing from the inventory. By mid-morning when all the prescriptions for controlled substances couldn't be filled, the pharmacists began to take an inventory as other orders were filled by the techs. The police were on the scene by 10 a.m., and the DEA shortly thereafter. Unfortunately, the first suspects were the pharmacists and the techs themselves, but after they were rigorously questioned by both the local police first and then the DEA, they were all cleared as subjects of interest.

The DEA began to widen their dragnet to the north, focusing on persons of interest in the lower income sections of Highwood and Waukegan as well as rural areas surrounding those neighborhoods that were economically depressed. While the DEA believed it was a one or two-man team that pulled the burglary off, they were stumped after that. Certain things just didn't add up. For instance, there was not a single print that could be traced to offenders in their dragnet. In addi-tion, there were no signs of forced entry, nor were there any signs that suggested the perpetrators feared they'd be caught; no anxiety-laden actions such as bottles strewn about or pills amiss on the floor. Finally, the DEA was most perplexed by the fact that the alarm never went off. Perpetrators who were so technically proficient and methodical in their ability to come and go without a leaving a trace of evidence would be better served by hitting a larger chain pharmacy where the payload of drugs would be much higher. So why hit a little mom-and-pop pharmacy in a community where the risk of getting caught was much greater than in a large city where police response time would be much slower and the case load much higher? Though it was a mystery initially, Special Agent Javier Contreras was determined that it wasn't going to become a cold case…not in Winnetka.

Contreras had worked out of the DEA's Chicago field office for three years, starting out as a field agent after he graduated summa cum laude with a degree in Criminal Justice from DePaul University. Thereafter, he would distinguish himself by completing a combined

JD/MBA degree at Robert Morris University while working as a field agent. Moreover, he completed every conceivable training offered by the DEA from Basic Agent Training to Forensic Chemist Training and Clandestine Laboratory Training and everything between, and he was the youngest candidate to be promoted to the position of Assistant Special Agent in Charge before being transferred to the Los Angeles field office.

Though he was immeasurably successful in coordinating attacks that crippled the drug distribution of the notorious Mara Salvador gang, better known as MSD-15, it was his brainchild, known as Project Cassandra, that targeted Hezbollah cells for drug trafficking to buy weapons and finance terrorist activities that would result in his promotion to Special Agent in Charge of the Chicago Field Office, winning the esteem of many within the DEA. Unfortunately, due to bureaucratic in-fighting, it seemed to put his career advancement on hold. FBI Counterintelligence wanted to take credit and jurisdiction of Project Cassandra, and they inveigled Principal Deputy Administrator Nathan Stubbs into acquiescing. The CIA also had a hand in stealing Contreras's thunder because they were deeply involved with Hezbollah in the Middle East, not to mention cultivation of FARC assets in Colombia.

So, once again, Contreras was going to think outside the box, but this time he would classify his information as secret using the DEA's Merlin file management system. There was no doubt that Contreras wanted to do everything in his power to bring the perpetrators to justice, but he justifiably wanted the recognition and career advancement that would be accorded with solving what looked like the perfect crime. It was not enough to just be good at what he did; Contreras had an unrequited desire to assuage the pain of his parents by resurrecting the honor of his brother, who died through drug violence. In fact, the very name he would give to this operation he was assembling in his mind over the weekend would betray this sentiment, and it would become his battle cry.

On Monday morning he stood before a room of silent agents with a very intent look in his eyes that suggested he would discern the mystery in Winnetka, but his briefing began in a manner that suggested they would arrive at the precipice of truth through methodical investigative work and due diligence. They knew what the briefing was about but were clueless about where Contreras began leading them.

"Tell me about Trier!" he began, almost as if he was continuing a briefing that had started on a prior occasion. The agents looked at him curiously. They were genuinely dumbfounded, but Contreras simply sat on the edge of the desk at the front of the room and waited for an answer.

"Excuse me, sir, but this is the first I am hearing about this person."

There was some murmuring in the room, and agents looked at each other before a few more piped in concurrently.

"Sir, we've never discussed this person. Where are we going with this?"

"Trier isn't a person?"

A flurry of new questions followed.

"Is it an organization?"

"A new cartel?"

"A Chicago gang?"

"A suburban gang?"

With each new answer, Contreras just nodded negatively, almost as if he were gravely disappointed.

"It might help, sir, if we knew where we're going with this."

Contreras stared at them with his jaws clenching and his head shaking.

"In other words, you're all telling me that you have no ability to think. Is this typical or is it just a Monday morning thing?"

A female agent cleared her throat and looked Contreras directly in the eyes as she spoke, taking a shot in the dark.

"Trier is the oldest city in Germany by the Mosel Valley, near the border of Luxembourg. Its home to Germany's oldest Christian church, and Roman emperors favored it as their place of residence. In fact, the Emperor Constantine made it the capital city of the Roman

Empire when it was in decline."

A few agents laughed at her.

"Fucking outstanding, Agent Carina!" Contreras thundered, much to the dismay of the other agents.

"I'm totally lost now, sir," another agent added

"The nice thing about being lost, Agent Nichols," Contreras began, "is that all roads will lead you away from the place where you find yourself lost, and one of them just might take you to the place where you want to be."

"Are you suggesting that our perpetrators in Winnetka were residents of Trier, Germany…that they were vacationing in the town of Winnetka and they decided to knock off a drugstore before they got out of Dodge and left the country?"

"No, I was simply giving our problem a name, and I wanted to fire up your critical-thinking skills."

There was a collective sigh of relieved chuckles.

"Our situation in Winnetka will be known as Operation New Trier because we are going to resurrect every possible event that took place in and around that drugstore for seventy-two hours prior to the discovery of the burglary, and we are going to put the spotlight on this town!"

As Contreras and his team worked tirelessly, interviewing the staff about every individual they noticed and interacted with, they also interviewed people who they noticed following patterns involving passing by that pharmacy at different times of the day. They were ordered to interview joggers, pet walkers, and housewives taking their infants on a stroll. Their intent was to determine from these individuals whether anyone was noticed in the area who looked like they didn't belong in Winnetka. If so, why were they in the vicinity? Had anyone been seen taking pictures of the store, or even taking seemingly random pictures near the pharmacy, and each morning they met to discuss progress and outcomes.

On Tuesday morning, the situation room briefing for Operation New Trier was filled with debating between the two investigative teams assembled to carry out the onerous assignment they were tasked with.

"All right, all right, which team is going to give me some good news first?" Contreras questioned.

"How about if we give you the bad news first?" Special Agent Nichols asked with a backdrop of laughter following.

"There's no such thing as bad news, Nichols. There are only facts, better facts, and the best facts. Which ones do you have for me?"

"I guess you could say I have the worst facts."

"Let's hear them, and I'll determine their value."

Nichols shook his head slightly and let out a frustrated gasp before he spoke.

"We interviewed everyone we saw engaging in the activities within our parameters. The runners all said everyone they saw during their jogging were the same people they usually see at those times: landscapers, women out shopping, people entering or exiting the pharmacy... we struck out!"

"Don't be so sure about that," Contreras said as he rubbed his finger under his lower lip.

Nichols raised his eyebrows and tilted his head slightly to the side as if asking Contreras to elaborate.

"When people go into a pharmacy, they often have nothing in their hands because a prescription can fit into a woman's purse or a man's pockets, but when they are exiting a pharmacy, especially a smaller one where prescriptions can be filled on the spot, they usually have something in their hands. They may even be reading the prescription information collateral attached to their prescription, or perhaps eating or drinking something they purchased. Did you happen to ask any of the people you interviewed whether they noticed one or two people leaving together with nothing in their hands?"

Nichols looked at his team to see if anyone asked that question, and they simply shook their heads to indicate that they hadn't. Then Nichols turned backed to Contreras with an uneasy look on his face and a defensive tone in his voice.

"None of us asked anyone that question, sir, and, forgive me for asking, but what relevance could such a thing have in our investigation? A lot of people go into a store and leave without buying something, especially women."

"That's when they go shopping for shoes. When we go to the pharmacy, we are going there with a specific intent to purchase something we need."

"Thank you, Special Agent Carina, and that brings us to two important points. First, if you did ask that question, you would have then had a chance to bounce that information off Special Agent Carina's team to ascertain whether there was any correlation between customers leaving empty-handed, and any unusual behavior exhibited by those customers inside the store. In the absence of surveillance cameras in that store, which is the current circumstance we find ourselves in, we have to look for patterns!"

"I can't understand why a pharmacy wouldn't have any surveillance cameras, not even in the controlled substances area."

"I wondered about that myself," Special Agent Carina interrupted, "but I found that they've been in business in Winnetka for almost eighty years. As far as safety, and lack of criminal activity in Winnetka, not much has changed in that regard over the last eighty years. The original owner, Sonny Walstein, knew all the neighborhood clientele by name, and was known to go into the store in the middle of the night to fill prescriptions for sick children in the neighborhood, and when he retired, he was very emphatic about the new owners carrying on in that tradition of excellent customer service. The current owners are a very congenial husband and wife team, both pharmacists who know their customers on a first-name basis in addition to knowing their family names."

"Here lies your reason for finding out whether any customers left empty-handed, and why the current owners didn't feel the necessity for surveillance cameras. Given what Special Agent Carina has just told us, wouldn't a family-run business with a small staff go out of their way to make sure that a new customer who they've never seen before didn't leave empty-handed? And if they knew all their clientele by name, or, at the very least, by appearance, wouldn't it be easy for them to spot someone they didn't recognize and find some memorable characteristic about them?"

"Yeah, when you put it like that…it makes sense," Nichols said, nodding in agreement.

Contreras rolled his head from one side of his shoulders to the other and faced Special Agent Carina.

"The ball's in your court, Carina. Tell me what you got."

"Well, we actually have to do a little more probing," Carina replied, seeming somewhat reluctant to confirm a hunch she had.

"Probing? Are we talking proctology here, Carina?" Contreras asked to ensuing laughter. "Just give me what you got so far, and I'll decide whether we need to bring in a proctologist."

"One of the high school part timers said this one guy kept walking around the store like he was looking for something, but when she asked him if he needed any help, he just shook his head without facing her, so she just kept putting products away and straightening up areas around them. Then a few moments later he asked if there was a bathroom, and when she told him there was no customer bathroom, he was rather emphatic that it was urgent."

Contreras slid off the desk for the first time as though he was extremely interested, and he walked over to the whiteboard at the front of the room.

"I have faith in you, Carina. You are gonna have my job before long! You've got the K-9 instincts," he said, smiling and encouraging her on, "so I am going to assume you already started questioning her for a description on him, didn't you?" Contreras put a dry marker to the whiteboard, showing her he was ready for the details.

"This is where we need to do a little more probing."

"I told you I have faith in you, Carina, so give me what you got from the girl. Let's start with the broad strokes first. What was his race?"

"He was white."

"Oh, that's a relief! At least you can still describe white perpetrators as being white and nobody gets their underwear in a twist," he said as he scribbled the word on the whiteboard. "How tall was he?"

"She was a bit indecisive about his exact height because she said he was wearing one of those hats like old guys wear…a Humphrey Bogart type hat. At first, she just said he was short, and then she said he was just a little bigger than her."

"Okay, so how tall was she?"

"She's about five feet, two inches."

"All right, and when we talk to someone, we essentially tend to address them at eye level whether we're facing them or standing to the side of them, so she could see the top of his head. So, if he was only one inch taller than her, wearing a fedora, she would never have perceived the difference. However, if he were two or three inches taller than her, that would be a readily discernable difference. Since the fedora would add about an inch to this man's height, we have to say that he would be between five feet three inches to about five feet five inches. Hair color?"

"She wasn't sure if it was black or dark brown because his hair was close cropped, and she was paying more attention to the hat."

Contreras turned and quickly scribbled "dark hair" on the board before turning back to Carina just as quickly. "What about eye color? He had to have faced her if he was insistent about using the bathroom."

"She said she couldn't tell what color his eyes were because he wore the brim of the hat in a way that obstructed her view of his eyes, and he looked down at the floor as he spoke, and he was gesticulating a lot."

Contreras looked around the room and bounced slightly on the balls of his feet as he questioned his agents.

"Avoids direct facial contact, makes use of a wide-brim hat, and looks down at the floor to conceal his prominent features. He also makes use of gesticulation to serve as a further distraction. He takes his time becoming familiar with the whole store from front to back. Is anybody else in this room starting to see a pattern here?" Contreras asked in a rhetorical manner. He didn't wait for an answer before continuing to question Carina.

"How about facial hair… Mustache? Beard? Sideburns, and, if so, were they dark colored, matching his hair color? The fedora suggests he is someone in his mid-forties, but I've known millennials to wear fedoras and have blonde facial hair and dark hair on their head or vice versa or even a shaved head under the fedora."

"He was clean-shaven."

"Is there any chance he had a five o'clock shadow thing going on that allowed her to see what color his facial hair would be if he grew it out?"

"No, she just said that he was clean-shaven, but she did say he spoke with an accent. She said she believed he was Russian."

"With all the things this girl wasn't sure of, how was she sure about his accent? Does she have a Russian accent?"

"No accent with the girl. She's first-generation American with a father of Russian descent, and her mother's Polish. Both spoke to her in their native languages, and her father always sang the Russian ballad 'Moscow Nights' to her when she was a girl, so the Russian accent made an indelible impression on her."

"Let's get back to the bathroom... Where is the bathroom in proximity to the back entrance, and did he use the bathroom?"

"The bathroom is on the back, south wall, behind the pharmacy counter near the west end of it. The back door is on the south wall, just two feet west of the bathroom entrance. The girl took him back to the pharmacists. The husband led the man to the bathroom."

"Tell me that one or both of the pharmacists can provide a clearer picture of this guy."

"I wish I could, but that's where the further probing has to take place. The wife was on the phone during that interaction, and today she was at a mandatory pharmacy seminar all day, so the husband was holding down the fort by himself. That guy didn't have a moment to take a deep breath much less talk to any of us."

"Pharmacists are definitely among the most hardworking professionals in the medical industry, so tonight, Special Agent Carina, you are going to take that man and his wife out to a quaint little fine dining establishment in Winnetka that is renowned for their exquisite cuisine and their exceptional array of fine wines. You will make it clear that no expense will be spared. They will be your guests tonight and they will be appropriately wined and dined through the courtesy of the DEA. After tomorrow morning's briefing, I want to have a sketch of this man ready for publication in all of the Chicago print and online media outlets, and I want him in every *Pioneer Press* newspaper they have from the Lakefront villages east, and extending in every direction. I especially want him to appear in 'The Winnetka Talk,' but we must make sure to refer to him as 'a person of interest,' and not a suspect!"

"Everything about this guy's behavior suggests he's a bona fide suspect," Special Agent Nichols asserted.

"And what would we claim we suspect him of?" Contreras retorted quickly. "The fact that he was wearing a fedora, had to use the bathroom, and didn't find anything he wanted to buy? Remember the phrase 'restraint of pen and tongue pays off' and remember what recently happened to our friends at the BATF because they went charging after someone like a bull in a china shop! We'll meet back here for morning briefing at eight o'clock. We are going to get the person or persons responsible for this! Carina, get on the phone and make a reservation at the Elegant Platter restaurant and extract every bit of information you can from our two pharmacists over a lovely dinner that leaves them feeling relaxed as opposed to feeling drained by a nonstop barrage of questions. Above all, leave them feeling good about the DEA."

Contreras swung his arm across the room and nodded at his agents.

"All right, dismissed!"

Contreras had no idea he was hunting for the same man the BATF was hunting for, and Philster had no idea that he and his associates were now being hunted by another, more formidable adversary. Contreras was not going to engage in any vulgar displays of federal power. Instead, he would rely on intelligence collection and analysis in which careful thought and planning would precede any actions. He was determined to hunt for his suspect as though he were playing a chess game. On the day of reckoning, his suspect would be backed into the corner of checkmate, with no options but to quietly surrender to justice.

Chapter 7
Man Up

Scorzoletti's Nemesis Nine were not ready to hear what he was going to tell them, and he could see it in their faces as he told them what they must prepare for next, and what the preparation would require. Now that Nemesis Nine had a cache of medicinal remedies for the tribulation of battle, they needed more lethal firepower than the agents who would oppose them. Fortunately, Philster's bombastic blustering dominated the conversation and added some needed levity to Scorzoletti's more sullen and serious manner.

"All right, listen up!" Scorzoletti began in a tone that commanded attention. "It's inevitable that we will have to leave our comfortable surroundings here if we are going to achieve our goals effectively. We must also acquire a taste for discipline and self-denial, especially you, Philster. I don't know how far you had to put your head up Uncle Sam's ass to get a new identity, credit cards, a car, and a job, while they were putting you up in the Palmer House, but all that's gone now."

For a moment, Philster squinted and dropped his mouth in a pregnant pause before he began to speak in his incessantly bombastic style.

"Are you kidding... You call a tin can KIA a car? I call it a piece of shit with a single coat of paint over some primer with a little chrome thrown in for laughs," he said quickly as he turned to Gonzo and asked him to throw his Chapstick over to him. Then he furiously rubbed some on his lips and licked them before continuing. "The first thing I noticed on that piece of shit car was a big M decal on the front window, so I said to Bickens: 'What the shit is with this oversized vehicle sticker? Does that indicate I'm mentally disabled or something? Or is that the vehicle sticker for Milltown, PA?' So, he tells me it's neither. It was for the job they secured for me as a rideshare driver with Mover, and I'm looking at him like…what the fuck? Then the prick said it's a perfect fit because I love to run my mouth."

"Well, you do enjoy talking, Philster," Scorzoletti said with a slight smile.

"Yeah, in a bar with some hotties, or with a lap dancer sitting on my crotch at the Admiral Theater maybe, but not with some jackass that thinks his shit don't stink. That's what you get when you drive for Mover around places like this up in Kenilworth, where it's safe and people are reasonably sane. Then there's places like Boy's town in Chicago, where you drive around asshole couples with blue mohawks and fifteen fucking earrings in each ear, and they giggle and shout directions at you like a couple of teenage girls. Sometimes you don't even know what the fuck you picked up because you'll get these freaky chicks that have the blue mohawks and fifteen earrings in each ear along with three fucking nose rings and a stud in their tongue; they also wrap their chests with gauze bandages so they can flatten their chest and look more masculine. You don't even know whether you're supposed to say good evening, ladies or good evening, guys. God forbid you should say the wrong thing in this fucking politically correct country we live in, and they could give you a rating of one bone… And that's another thing… They have this stupid rating system where someone can give you between one to five bones, with five meaning you're an outstanding driver, and one meaning you suck! And what the fuck do you think Mover expects? They think you should get five bones from every customer you drive! I think the CEO of Mover needs a bone! He needs a bone right up the ass for coming up with such a stupid rating system!"

Before Scorzoletti could reassert himself in the conversation, Gonzo and Max tried to further agitate Philster as they were prone to doing because they were amused by his face turning red and his bombastic demeanor.

"It's your own fault, douchebag!" Max chimed in while Philster paused to lick his lips. "You should have told them you wanted to be a flight attendant, you douchebag!"

The guys all laughed while Scorzoletti shook his head, knowing that once Philster got started, it would be hard to shut him down.

"Now there's a job for you..." Gonzo piped in. "Flying around the world with a crew of gorgeous babes, going to places like Thailand and the Philippines where you could meet more beautiful babes. Shit, I'd have me a mama in every part of the world the airline would fly."

"Yeah, flight attendant, and maybe I should have asked them if they could get me a job at the Admiral Theater fanning the farts from behind the strippers' asses! Why don't you make yourself useful and get me a beer!" he snarled at Gonzo before looking over at Max. "Being a flight attendant isn't a glamor job anymore with all these retarded new laws our politicians legislated the few days a year they actually do some work! I was reading the other day that there's a bunch of goofballs that use the disability laws to bring all sorts of different animals with them when they travel. They call it a 'creature comfort animal,' and they get psychiatrists to document that they have a mental issue that requires them to bring these different animals with them in order to feel comfortable when they're flying! Can you imagine that shit? Booking an extra seat so your rabbit or turtle or whatever fucking comfort creature you want to bring can sit next to you? I mean, isn't that the silliest fucking shit you've ever heard?"

"What a bunch of douchebags!" Max exclaimed with laughter. "What if the animals shit or piss on the seats? Do the owners have to carry a lawn bag with them and pick it up?"

"Are you fucking shitting me or something, Doc...a lawn bag? That law only applies on the ground where people have lawns which are considered private property!"

"Heads up," Gonzo shouted, throwing Philster a can of beer across the room as he returned from the kitchen.

"So, who cleans up the shit and piss?"

"The flight attendants have to do it after everyone leaves the plane."

"Oh man, that's messed up," Miles Sano said, laughing that zany laugh of his like he was jacked up on marijuana. "That's seriously messed up." Though he continued laughing a bit, he was nodding in disapproval.

"You think that's messed up? What do you think about this...? On this one flight that I was on, there was this guy from Arizona who boarded the plane with a diamondback rattlesnake, but nobody knew it until the plane was accelerating for takeoff on the runway and this guy starts to have an anxiety attack or some shit like that. Well, he took the snake out of the bag and plopped the fucking thing down on the seat where everyone could see it start to coil up and start shaking its rattlers."

Jake Poole, who exuded the persona of the standoffish, strong, silent type, became interested. "Is this shit for real?" he queried, with incredulity

"Hey, Jako, would I lie to a guy like you? For Christ's sake, you can kill a guy just by looking at him! Of course this shit is for real if I'm telling you!"

Everyone in the room including Scorzoletti laughed, and Max taunted him with a tone of incredulity.

"Oh, come on, you douchebag, how come this guy was able to handle a rattler without getting killed himself?"

"He was one of those Indian shamans...not one of those red-dot-on-the-forehead fucks from India, but a real Native American Indian, and he was bit so many times that his body developed a sort of anti-venom that rendered the snake's bite harmless. Hey, man, I asked the guy why he wasn't afraid of the thing and he told me, so it's for real! Now stop interrupting me, you Jimi Hendrix-looking motherfucker!"

"So, what did they do?" Jake asked.

"Nothing...I mean, what the fuck could they do? It's not like you can just roll down a window and throw a rattler out of a pressurized cabin while it's climbing to forty thousand feet at six hundred miles per hour. So, everyone just sat around him fucking petrified. The poor woman in the seat next to the snake pissed in her seat because she was afraid to pass by the thing or make any sudden movements."

"That's fucking harsh, man. She should have sued the fucking air-line for allowing that thing to have a seat booked right next to her like it was a person."

"So, what happened, douchebag? Did she get bit by the thing?"

"Well, most of the flight was pretty low-key after the initial shock the woman next to the snake experienced. The Indian just sat there petting the snake's head and singing to the snake in his language, and it seemed to fall asleep after a while. However, just as the plane began to descend for landing, the Indian had to take a dump. So, he left the snake there sleeping while he was pinching a loaf in the crapper, and what do you think happened?"

"The snake's eyes open suddenly, and it wakes up," Jake says as if narrating the story for Philster.

"Bingo!" the Philster shouted. "Not only does the fucking thing wake up, but now it decides to go for a walk to see where the Indian went!"

Immediately, everyone in the room started laughing and slapping their thighs or holding their stomachs to contain their laughter.

"Philster, you fucking douchebag," Max said, trying to stop laugh-ing. "Snakes can't walk."

"Well, what the fuck am I supposed to say? He went for a slither. Okay, he went for a slither! There, are you happy? Anyway, he's slither-ing down the aisle toward the crapper at the back of the plane because he can smell the Indian in there. Then one of the male flight attendants sees the thing coming toward him, and he screams like a fucking teen-age girl and throws a napkin at it."

"Did the thing bite him," Sano asked before beginning to shake his head while in a spasm of laughter.

Philster paused and looked at Max like he was getting a little frustrated.

"Hey, Doc, when did Sano become such a nutbar? I don't remem-ber him being like this when he was in the Navy."

"Hey, man, I'm sorry, Philster, go on man," Sano said, trying to keep a straight face.

"He's been this way since we ate too many magic mushrooms one night after we were discharged. The old boy went wacko that night, and he's been this way ever since, pretty much."

Scorzoletti shot a concerned glance at Max before looking at Sano, who was suddenly serious-looking.

"Hey, man, I'm sorry, Philster, it's just the way you were telling the story made me have this hysterical image of the super effeminate gay banger."

"Yeah, well, any guy that wants to make a career out of being an ass-kissing waitress at forty thousand feet probably is a super effeminate gay banger," Philster said with a smile coming back to his face. His voice started to rise again. "When he threw a napkin at that rattlesnake for God's sake, I even laughed myself! It had to be the single most ridiculously gay act I ever saw."

"He got bit, didn't he?" asked Jake.

"You know it, Jako! The thing struck him right at the ankle, and he fainted instantly and dropped like a gazelle struck by a tiger. Then the fucking thing bit him again in the ass once he was on the floor. I'll never forget the look on that snake's face...you know how they look when their mouth is slightly open...like they're fucking grinning or laughing to themselves. I swear, it was like he was saying to himself, 'That one in the ass was for good measure, so don't get up or I'll bite you again for throwing that napkin at me, you big sissy.' That's the way he looked. I could almost hear him saying it!"

Everyone was now laughing hysterically, even Scorzoletti, because everyone had a vivid picture of this villainous snake who possessed the rancor of an ornery old man that would strike at an effeminate young man if he felt like it.

After the laughter died down, Scorzoletti reasserted himself.

"On a more serious note, can I inquire about what happened to this unfortunate flight attendant?"

"Actually, he was fortunate because San Cristo Hospital was just five minutes from the airport, and they hustled his ass there ASAP, so he survived."

"Well, it's nice that the story had a happy ending, but we might not have such a happy ending unless we develop the ability to strike with the stealth and speed of your snake. I think the moral of your story is he who strikes first with deadly force wins."

"Hey, I can go along with that program. It's either that or resign myself to a life of servitude with that fucking rideshare company Mover, and Sal, let's face it, I'm not the type of guy who can be buckled into a seat by Mover for the rest of my life."

"That's for damn sure," Max concurred. "The old boy would be wacko after a few months."

"The only life for you is conceiving and planning ops or co-writing them with someone else," Gonzo added.

Jake had been sitting forward listening intently with his arms draped over his knees and his head dipped down slightly, but now he looked at Philster and smiled as he said, "Give me some targets."

Like Scorzoletti, Jake was phenomenal with a gun. He was a highly decorated sniper with more rapid-fire kills in Afghanistan and Iraq than anyone else across the five branches of the military, and his weapon of choice was a bolt-action Arctic Warfare Super Magnum rifle. Though he had a golden finger, he was dishonorably discharged for killing three nonessential civilian targets he accidentally sited who were raping a young girl, so he was more than willing to kill the remaining men who killed Scorzoletti's daughter as well as anyone else who was complicit in the deed. Moreover, he would kill anyone who replaced them or joined in with their ranks to assist them in their pursuit of Scorzoletti. Jake was a soft-spoken man. He was also a man of few words, but, as the guys in Nemesis Nine would say, he spoke loud through the barrel of his gun, and men took notice.

"You're going to get your targets tomorrow morning," Scorzoletti replied. "In fact, we will all get our targets tomorrow because tomorrow morning we will begin our field training in Fox Lake."

"Fox Lake," Philster mumbled to himself with a puzzled look. "What the fuck is out in Fox Lake?"

"A nice six-bedroom, five-bathroom home that Alvarez rented for us last week. It sits on twenty acres of secluded, wooded land with no neighbors close by, so we can do our shooting and training maneuvers without discovery. We all need to toughen up and become battle ready because I kid you not…Bickens and the ATF will turn this into a militarized conflict. I am an extremely high-profile, high-priority target. They will requisition all the military resources they legally can to acquire me."

"You seem pretty battle ready to me," Alvarez said somewhat timidly. He had never acquired the beefy bulk of most enlisted Navy men. He still had that lanky frame and geeky look about him, yet he could be more lethal than the sum of the Nemesis Nine with a computer.

"Yeah," Gonzo concurred, "you fucking killed half of a team that had the element of surprise and superior firepower, and, from the looks of that video, you could have easily killed them all."

"That was fucking awesome, Sal!" Sano said after laughing a bit. "You really fucked those guys up."

"Yeah, yeah, yeah," Max chimed in, "the old boy did a Billy-the-kid number on those douchebags."

"It was forty percent instinct and sixty percent adrenaline. I was drained afterwards. I couldn't have sustained that type of fight for much longer than I did. I just got lucky. They were less battle ready than me, and they made critical errors in judgment because they were acting on inaccurate assumptions. I'm sure next time I won't have that luxury."

"Hey, what about me?" Philster asked.

"What about you, douchebag? You're here to entertain us," Max interrupted, with laughter following.

"You're my silent partner," Scorzoletti added. "For now, the authorities think I whacked you, and it's best we keep it that way for your sake. You'll always have the freedom to disappear whenever you want."

"Fuck that disappearing act shit!" Philster countered. "I'm staying right here with you…all the way. It will be just like back in the day when I was doing the planning at ONI and you were carrying out the missions…like old times, only now we'll be shoulder to shoulder in the field as well. This time we'll be on the side of righteousness!"

"It's your call, brother, but the out is there for you any time you choose."

"What about you, Sal?"

"There's only one way this can end for me and we both know that."

"Well, fuck it then! We'll both go out in a blaze of glory."

"We'll all go out in a blaze of glory," Jake added, "but we'll kill a fuck of a lot of them first."

"Yeah, yeah, yeah…we'll do what Sal already did multiplied by nine."

"Nine squared if we implement technology effectively," Alvarez added.

"All right!" Scorzoletti slapped his hands on his thighs and stood up, making eye contact with everyone. "At zero one hundred, six of us will quietly leave in the van. It has tinted windows, so nobody will see how many people are leaving the house, if there should be any insomniacs on the street. Max, you and Sano will leave in the other car at zero two hundred. Alvarez, you'll wait here for Mohammed. He'll pick you up at zero three hundred and you two will join us. We had a Mover decal sent to his place, and he'll be putting that on his car. If anyone sees you leaving, they'll assume you're catching a red-eye flight, so wear a suit and bring a couple of your best laptops with you. Tonight, we clean this place out. No technology left behind."

"This place seems like it's out there in the sticks. How about Internet and Wi-Fi?" Philster asked.

"Alvarez took care of that last week. He also set up a shell corporation and got us nine new cell phones with one being listed to a phantom CEO and eight additional lines that are listed as simply employees one through eight, so we're anonymous."

By early morning of the next day, the Nemesis Nine were all in Fox Lake. It was secluded as Alvarez had said, and it put a good distance between them and Kenilworth. It was providential that they were there. While Bickens wallowed in the defeat of humiliation and men down in the line of duty as well as his confinement to a wheelchair, Contreras suffered no such constraints in the pursuit of their common prey.

Chapter 8

The Pursuit Grows

—⁓—

"Special Agent Carina, you are going to give us all some good news, aren't you?"

"Indeed, I am!" she replied unflinchingly. "Though the wife of the owner was on the phone most of the time talking with doctors and providers, she was alternately on hold…"

"Special Agent Carina, can you try for a moment to imagine you're an eighteen-year-old sex addict watching a porn movie and just fast-forward to the good part. The eighteen-year-old sex addict wouldn't want to listen to an intro with a lot of extraneous dialogue, and neither do we."

"Gotcha," she shot back, dipping her face with her lips drawn tight. "When the suspect…"

"Ah, ah, ah," Contreras interrupted. "Remember, he's only a 'person of interest' until we have something concrete to issue a warrant for."

"When our person of interest was coming out of the bathroom, the owner turned around quickly and began to extend his arm to a shelf behind him. At that very moment, our person of interest was approaching him, and the two bumped into each other. The hat fell off our person of interest, and the pharmacist picked it up, but before handing it back, he asked our person of interest if he was okay. They locked eyes and the pharmacist got a clear look at him. He could also sense a certain uneasiness in the eyes of our person of interest which led him to believe that something was not right, and he took careful note of our person of interest."

"And you got us a nice composite sketch of our person of interest, right?"

"My team did more than that, sir!"

"Oh my God, Carina, it's beginning to look a lot like Christmas! What else do you have? Give me all you got!"

"I'll let Agent Jikowski take it from here."

Jikowski paused for a moment as he thumbed through his notes looking for the sketch acquired by Carina.

"Well, come on, boy, we don't have all day...batter up!"

"Yes sir," Jikowski said as he stood up from the table. "When we were canvassing the area business owners, we spoke to a director at the Winnetka Center for Autism. It's located on a street south of the drugstore. Well, the director hadn't been out of the building during the time our person of interest was in the drugstore, or in the streets nearby, but she said perhaps her cleaning crew might have seen something on the night of the burglary."

"And you're going to tell me they did because Carina told me you guys had more, right?"

"Yes sir, you see, Agent Carina had a sketch artist meet her at our two pharmacists' home in Winnetka after dinner, and she distributed copies to all of us. Anyway, I was able to track down the polish maids last night and show them the sketch and ask them if they had seen our person of interest."

"And of course, they did!" Contreras said, sliding off the desk, laughing, "because my people are just so damn good at what they do! Keep going, Agent Jikowski."

"It turns out that our person of interest had cut through the alley behind the drugstore and come out from between the condo and a house that is directly across the street from where the maids were working. The one maid was putting some of the equipment in the back of the car with her back towards him, so she wasn't aware of him at first. At that same time, the person living in the home next to the condo was in her living room, and she noticed our person of interest staring at the maid's ass, presumably."

"Oh, this is getting so good…all right, what happened next."

"Our person of interest actually goes up to the maid and asks her if he could help her, but she says she's fine because our person of interest creeps her out due to the fact that he's wearing the fedora, a trench coat, and some tight black gloves. So, she puts her hands in front of her and waves them, indicating that she doesn't want any help, and then she shouts to her coworkers in Polish, who she hears coming toward her, that they need to hurry up because some creep is hitting on her. Well, it's possible our person of interest might speak Russian, but he damn sure doesn't speak Polish. Then the neighbor in the living room, perhaps sensing the girl might be having a hard time from what she saw and what she heard, activated her car alarm, and it startles our person of interest. So, he drops his bag, and the girls are all around him now. They noticed what sounded like a bunch of vitamin jars and pills shaking when he dropped the bag. At the time, they didn't think much of it because they thought he was just one of those health nuts going to work out because he had a Nike sports duffle bag…"

"Excellent!" Contreras thundered. "Now, where are we on getting those sketches in every media outlet in this area?"

"The wheels are already in motion, sir! *Pioneer Press* has the sketch, and it is being printed in every community newspaper printed."

"When can we expect to see that man's face displayed in the papers of every community on the North Shore?"

"Thursday, sir."

"Thursday! That's three days from now, Agent Carina! Three days from now this guy could be on the other side of the world!"

"Don't worry, sir. There's something called the Daily Digital Update. It's an online update of anything important happening in any of the *Pioneer Press* community distribution areas since the publication of their last hardcopy news edition. It's kind of like breaking news in the smaller communities. All Winnetka residents who read news online will see an alert of this in addition to the forthcoming print edition."

"All right, while we have a very solid lead here, we can't upgrade this man's status to a suspect until we find hard evidence. I know it's frustrating, but we have to consider the terrain we find ourselves in. This isn't Bumfuck, Iowa; it's Winnetka. Annual incomes on the low end here are close to a quarter million dollars a year, and it just goes up from there. There are CEOs of major corporations and self-styled entrepreneurs who live in these twelve-million-dollar estates and are making between twenty to thirty million dollars a year.

"If this guy falls in this category or is simply visiting someone here who's been seen in the company of this man, we could possibly open ourselves up to libel and defamation of character litigation. I don't want to go down those roads, so we are going to act with methodical discipline and restraint. Above all, we are going to conduct this investigation with the utmost of integrity. We are not going to jump the gun to satisfy our egos. Is that understood?"

Contreras looked around the room at each of his agents nodding in agreement with intense looks on their faces.

"I can't hear you guys."

"Yes sir," they responded in unison.

"All right, now that we actually have a face, we need to put a name to it and gather information. We need to work with local police departments and our dealers and druggies both inside and outside of the county lock-up and the state penitentiaries. We need to keep our search narrow at this point because time is of the essence. Connect with those individuals or groups that use or sell prescription pharmaceuticals. If you come up with a hit, call it in to me right away. It doesn't need to wait for the briefing. Okay, dismissed."

While Contreras made his reputation on integrity and solid investigative work, Bickens used whatever means necessary to make an arrest, and though Contreras was none too eager to jump the gun and tarnish the reputation of his agency, Bickens was only too eager to jump the gun. With his prime suspect and lead informant presumed dead, Scorzoletti's wife Julie was his only viable source of information at the time. While Bickens was consumed with self-pity, it didn't take the form of depression or suicidal thoughts. Instead, it took the form of anger and resentment, and he would vent it on Julie Scorzoletti.

Due to pressure brought on the ATF by the State Department, at the behest of the Chinese ambassador, Julie was not held in a prison. She was put up in a comfortable hotel outside of Washington, DC. While she was not formally charged with any crime, she was a veritable prisoner in the hotel. There was always an armed agent of the ATF outside her door, and all entrances of the hotel were under surveillance around the clock.

Julie could order food from the hotel or outside restaurants, but she could not go out. She could have books and magazines she requested brought to her room, and these things were all paid for by the ATF. She only requested one book: a copy of the New International Version of the Holy Bible in English and Chinese translation. She alternated between reading the Bible, watching faith-based programs on TV, and sleeping since her internment began. The men who questioned her and were keeping watch over her were not involved in the raid on her home, and having seen both video accounts of the massacre that ensued, they understood Bickens' animosity, but they also felt sympathy for this attractive, soft-spoken, and frail-looking woman who lost her daughter, her husband, and her routine way of life in one evening. As such, they were kindly disposed to her. Today, however, she would see Bickens for the first time since that fateful evening in her home. As he was pushed into her room in his wheelchair, the memories of that evening came back to her with crystal clarity, and her eyes began to well up with tears. Bickens put up his hand for the agent to stop pushing him, and the agent, seeing a tear roll down Julie's cheek, picked up a box of tissues to give to her.

"I'll take that," Bickens said, grabbing the box of tissue.

"Oh, that's all right, sir, I can give it to her."

"Give it to me," Bickens said with a genial smile, "and then leave the room. I'll call you when I'm finished in here."

"Very well, sir," the agent said, handing Bickens the tissue.

Bickens held on to the box until he heard the door close. Then, with rancor, he threw it against the mirror on the desk to the side of where Julie was sitting. When the box hit the mirror, Julie began to openly weep.

"Since this is the first time you're seeing me after your husband murdered my men and put me in this fucking wheelchair for life, I am going to assume your pity is for me and my men."

"Haven't you forgotten that you and your men murdered my innocent daughter, and tried to kill me and my husband as well?"

"All I seem to remember is that your husband opened fire on me and my men with a fully automatic weapon when we were trying to serve him with a search warrant."

Julie took a deep breath as her chest still heaved with sobs and she summoned all her courage to confront him with the truth as she knew it.

"All I remember is that you and your men threw explosives through our windows before you announced who you were or what you wanted. My husband had been in the military for many years. What did you expect him to do under those conditions?"

"Your husband is a murderer, and I assumed that he would realize he was in a no-win situation that would compel him to defer to our authority."

"I guess you assumed wrong when you failed to identify yourself or your men, and you handled things wrong because my husband is not a murderer and you didn't come to my home pursuing a murderer, and you know that!"

"I see, so I guess the United States government is wrong about your husband?" Bickens retorted in righteous indignation. "Well, let me tell you something, you little chink bitch, the United States government doesn't make mistakes!"

"They must have this time because my husband is not a murderer."

"Oh really, did he ever tell you about how he left the Navy after years of work as a trained assassin?"

"My husband didn't like to talk about his past service for your government, and he said that he couldn't even if he wanted to."

"He couldn't or wouldn't talk. There's a big difference. You see, your husband left the Navy as a disgraced man who was dishonorably discharged because he started killing foreign assets who were working for the United States government. I guess there weren't enough enemies of the state for your husband to kill, so he took it upon himself to start killing the good guys as well. Did he tell you how he ruthlessly murdered three ONI officers?"

"If that's true, why wasn't my husband put in prison?"

"Well, though the evidence surrounding his murder of foreign assets and Navy personnel was rather compelling, it was considered circumstantial. Like I said a moment ago, the United States government doesn't make mistakes. It also doesn't act on things that aren't verifiable facts, and so it chose to let a murderer go, but they relieved him from his service in the Navy with a dishonorable discharge and they abrogated his files."

"I don't know what that means…abrogated."

"It means that the United States Navy and the Marines destroyed all records of your husband having anything to do with US Naval command or military service for the United States government."

"Were you in the service with my husband?"

"No, fortunately I was not, or otherwise I might be dead as well."

"Then how do you know these things if all records of what he did were destroyed?"

"Because it's my job to thoroughly investigate people who go awry of the law, and I happened to talk with two people who were intimately acquainted with your husband's service history. One of them was a good friend of your husband. He went to prison on account of your husband's actions. His name was Steven…Steve Philster."

"Philster?"

"You knew him?"

"On that night…" Julie paused and just looked into Bickens' eyes as if searching for truth.

"What night?"

Julie felt as if she was being led into revealing things that might bring harm to her husband, so she decided not to divulge anything to Bickens.

"It doesn't matter," she said, stopping cold.

"No, I guess it doesn't really matter," Bickens said with a pretentious and disingenuous smile, "at least not where Steven Philster is concerned. You see, your husband murdered him. All we could find were different pieces of his belongings at two different ends of the city in Chicago. I suppose that might be your husband's humorous way of saying Steven Philster's body is spread out over the city of Chicago and we'll never find his fucking corpse to prove your husband murdered him!"

"Why do you keep talking about my husband this way? He is a kind and gentle man, and if he is all the things you say he is, why was he able to get a job working on the military base where we lived? You said the military wanted no association with my husband."

"There just happens to be a cadre of bleeding-heart liberals in this country who will allow the treasonous acts of traitors to go unpunished, or, as in the case of your husband, even rewarded. But your husband wasn't associated with the military. He was classified as civilian support personnel."

No sooner had Bickens finished his last sentence than the muffled voice of the agent outside the room called out to him from the other side of the door.

"What is it?" Bickens replied, annoyed.

"There are some men from the Chinese Embassy here to see Mrs. Scorzoletti," he said, opening the door slightly and stepping into the room with one foot. As Bickens looked away from Julie toward the agent addressing him, he saw a hand placed on the door above the agent's head, and it was pushed open wide enough for the three men outside to enter.

"Well, gentlemen, don't wait to be invited. No, of course not, just barge into the room where I am questioning a suspect. So, tell me, to what do I owe the pleasure of this most unwelcome visit?"

The men ignored Bickens' question and, looking at Julie, addressed her first.

"Zhu Li Xiao, this is Ambassador Li Xiao Jing of the Chinese embassy in Washington, DC."

The ambassador bowed slightly toward Julie. "It is most unfortunate that we must meet under circumstances such as these."

"To my left is Deputy Chief of Missions Minister Wang Zai Yan from our embassy in Washington, DC."

"Zhu Li Xiao, I extend my deepest and my most heartfelt sympathy to you for the loss of your daughter, Zhu Xiaoxiao." He also bowed to Julie.

"And I am Minister Cai Ko Pei of the Chinese Embassy here in Washington, DC. I am deeply grieved by the murder of your daughter through the unwarranted violence orchestrated against your family at the hands of Mr. Bickens." Cai Ko Pei bowed reverently and lower than the older men on each side of him.

"That girl's death was an unfortunate accident!" Bickens thundered back at the three men. "She was just a victim of circumstances! She was in the wrong place at the wrong time! It's called collateral damage!"

"Tell me, Mr. Bickens, where should a little girl be in the middle of the night other than sleeping in her bed, safe within her own home?" asked the ambassador. "Let me see if I understand you. It is your contention that she was in the wrong place at the wrong time because she was asleep in her bed in the middle of the night?"

"Are we to assume that you are saying it was wrong that innocent little Zhu Xiaoxiao was fast asleep in her bed during the middle of the night?" Deputy Chief of Missions Wang Zai Yan questioned in a pressing manner.

"In other words," the ambassador said, now with a tone of indignance, "it is your opinion that an innocent little girl who posed no possible threat to you or your men was responsible for her own death!"

"I said no such thing!" Bickens retorted angrily. "I merely meant to say that we had no knowledge that she or Mrs. Scorzoletti would be at that residence. We had no idea that our suspect had taken a wife and had a family."

The three men spoke amongst themselves in Chinese before responding to Bickens.

"You laid siege to an innocent man's home, using lethal force, without even knowing whether there would be other innocent people with him?" the ambassador railed.

"I can't understand why you would refer to a murderer as an innocent man, Ambassador Li, but then again, I wouldn't presume to say I understand the workings of the Chinese mind."

"You don't need to understand the workings of the Chinese mind. I am merely referring to your own American law. A suspect is innocent until proven guilty in a court of law. Isn't this correct, Mr. Bickens?"

"I am going to kindly ask that you address me as Special Agent in Charge Bickens."

"Such a title is partially fitting," the ambassador said, "for it does indeed take a special kind of an agent to murder an innocent little girl and then mistreat her grief-stricken mother for days on end. However, other than orchestrating violence against your own citizens, as well as foreign nationals from the People's Republic of China, I am not sure what you are in charge of."

Again, the three men spoke amongst themselves in Chinese, and upon cessation of the conversation, they looked at Julie Scorzoletti and told her to prepare her things for departure. She complied at once, pausing only when Bickens began to challenge the consular officials.

"I'm in charge of everything and everyone in this room, especially this woman over here, who needs to sit her behind right back down in this chair," he said angrily as he pointed at Julie and motioned her to resume sitting in the chair she had gotten up from. Julie, however, stood her ground as the ambassador began to speak.

"You are in charge of nothing here! You have absolutely no authority over us because we clearly identified ourselves upon entry into the room as consular officials of The People's Republic of China. As such, we are protected by diplomatic immunity, and the United States government abides by this law."

"Be that as it may, you have absolutely no right to come in here and remove an individual in the custody of the ATF who is an accessory to murder!"

"Since you insist on accusing Zhu Li Xiao of complicity in the loss of your men," Minister Cai Ko Pei began, "I'd like to ask you a few questions about a few routine procedures necessary to establish that conclusion."

"Bring it on," Bickens challenged.

"On the night of the siege…"

"It was by no means a siege," Bickens interjected. "Rather it was a peaceful and lawful attempt to serve a warrant to Mr. Salvino Scorzoletti."

"Ah, it was a peaceful attempt with no hostile intent," Minister Cai Ko Pei replied with derision evident in his voice. "So, I can assume that you or someone from your party of nine heavily armed men knocked on the door in the middle of the night when most people are sound asleep, and you clearly identified yourself and your purpose."

"Indeed, we did!" Bickens lied. "Since our purpose was to serve a warrant, we came to the front door."

"What did the court issue a warrant for?"

"Unauthorized possession of fully automatic weapons."

"But you stated earlier that he was a murderer. Why wouldn't your court have issued you a warrant to arrest him for murder, which is a much more serious offense than a weapons violation?"

"I was referring to murders at a prior time outside of United States jurisdiction."

"You are referring to when Mr. Scorzoletti was a Navy SEAL, and he terminated men who were trafficking young Asian girls, some of them Khmer nationals, to fund black ops for ONI and other intelligence networks that you didn't want your congress to have oversight of?"

"I have no idea what you're talking about, and I have absolutely no intention of entertaining your vulgar flights of fantasy, so just ask me what you want to ask me about the particular night in question that we were discussing."

"As you wish, Mr. Bickens. So, what happened next in this peaceful attempt to serve the warrant?"

"Mr. Scorzoletti opened fire on me and my men."

"Did your men breach the front door or did someone inside the residence open it?"

Minister Cai Ko Pei turned to Ambassador Li Xiao Jing and spoke with him in Chinese briefly about the contradictions in the answers being given and what the consular officials knew. The ambassador encouraged Minister Cai Ko Pei to continue his questioning.

"We didn't have time to breach the front door. Mr. Scorzoletti opened fire on us from inside."

"Very interesting," Ambassador Li Xiao Jing replied. "So, is that when you threw the stun grenades in the home?"

"Yes," Bickens said immediately, without giving it any thought.

"If all of you were in the front, as you said a moment ago, who threw the stun grenades into the back-bedroom window that killed Zhu Xiaoxiao?"

"When Scorzoletti began to fire upon us, I ordered men to the back of the residence because that's where he was firing from."

"So, if you and your men knew where Mr. Scorzoletti was firing from, why would any of your men throw stun grenades in rooms where there was no threat instead of the room where he was firing from?"

"Perhaps there was a miscommunication. I couldn't really say."

The men from the embassy continued to hammer Bickens with a flurry of questions in rapid succession.

"What type of weapon was Mr. Scorzoletti using when he fired upon you and your men?"

"He was using a fully automatic Thompson submachine gun."

"This was the machine gun your country introduced in World War Two and used also in the Korean War. It shoots forty-five-caliber rounds."

"That's correct," Bickens confirmed.

"And what type of weapons did you and your men have?"

"We were armed with semi-automatic AR-16 rifles."

"You didn't have fully automatic weapons?"

"We did, but I ordered the men to keep their selector switch adjusted to semi-automatic fire."

"That strikes me as curious, Mr. Bickens."

"Can I ask you fellas something?" Bickens said with a disingenuously puzzled look on his face. "Is my title hard for you to pronounce or are you just trying to annoy me? Because you keep addressing me as Mr. Bickens, which is the way some of my less than congenial neighbors address me."

"We have no desire to annoy you, Mr. Bickens; we merely believe there is no need to address you in an honorable manner since we find nothing honorable about your character."

Bickens laughed in a frustrated manner as he shook his head.

"Oh boy, I give up! You fellas are just too much! So, what strikes you as curious about me ordering my men to use restraint."

"It just doesn't seem plausible," Deputy Chief of Missions Wang Zai Yan said flatly.

"And why not?"

"Well, on the one hand, you're suggesting that you advocate the exercise of restraint with a weapon that has a more precise trajectory to its target, thereby increasing the possibility of mortal injury to the targeted individual and less likelihood of collateral damage. On the other hand, you show no such restraint in the act of allowing your men to throw more lethal explosive devices into all windows on every side of the house even though you claim you have already engaged the suspect and are aware of his location. In short, the threat is coming from one clearly identifiable location, yet your men were throwing explosive devices everywhere. What prompted your men to do so, especially when the primary use of those devices is in cases where you are relying on the element of surprise and specifically want to disorient your suspect to prevent the possibility of an armed response."

The ambassador spoke to the deputy chief in Chinese and then addressed Bickens.

"You had to have known that this man was a decorated Marine and a long-standing, highly decorated Navy SEAL master chief who remorselessly killed men who were helping your government, and he was also in unauthorized possession of fully automatic rifles that he was able to use with far greater precision than any of your men, yet you didn't seem to think it was necessary to use the element of surprise? Why?"

"Because he's in his mid-forties, and it's been a while since he was active. We figured he'd just as soon try to run out the back door."

Minister Cai Ko Pei looked at Bickens and shook his head in disagreement.

"Men like Salvino Scorzoletti don't run when their family is in mortal danger. They eliminate the threat to their family, or they die trying. And another thing, Mr. Bickens, when your agency killed a child who was a Chinese national, it was incumbent upon them to allow the Chinese government to examine the crime scene."

"The forensic evidence they established contradicts everything you've told us," accused the Chinese ambassador. "Entry was made from the back door first because AR-16 rounds went through the front door, which was aligned with the rear door, and they pierced the wood frame around the front door as well. The fire patterns are consistent with weapons fired on fully automatic selection as they start at a lower point and rise upward along the door toward the frame above it, corresponding to the recoil of an AR-16. No men were at the front door as you've indicated because if they were there, they would have been killed by their own team.

"Mr. Scorzoletti returned fire from behind a dishwasher in the kitchen counter that was on a thirty-degree angle from the open rear door's outside panel. We know this because forty-five-caliber rounds were hitting the lower outside panel of the rear door on a thirty-degree angle and moving toward the frame of the door on the side of the doorknob. So, Mr. Scorzoletti returned fire at your men, sweeping from right to left on a low level, hitting them in the legs."

"What an amazing conclusion you people have drawn to defend this ruthless killer..."

"Please allow me to continue," Minister Cai Ko Pei quickly interjected.

"Why certainly, I wouldn't dream of stealing your thunder, young man. You probably haven't had a chance to talk this much on anything of significance in your whole life, so you go right ahead."

"Only when your team of men entered from the front door did Mr. Scorzoletti initiate the firing, using your fallen men at the rear door as sandbags. There is not a single shot from a forty-five-caliber bullet in the panel of the front door because it was blown clean off by an explosive charge set by your men. Thereafter, Mr. Scorzoletti opened fire, taking direct aim at the legs of your men, and effectively incapacitating each of them. Being the last man alive and unwounded, you hoped to gain access to the room where his daughter lay dying or dead and lie in wait for him, but he heard you, and incapacitated you as well. Isn't that a closer version of reality for that evening, Mr. Bickens? Except for the stun grenades, which we believe you used before a single shot was ever fired, we feel that our version of what happened is the truth, while your version is a rather pathetic attempt to save your own skin."

"Well, I must commend you for your prowess as a storyteller, but I have plenty of photographic evidence that would thoroughly refute your hideously misguided version of events on that evening…"

Ambassador Li Xiao Jing cleared his throat and quickly cut Bickens off.

"We are aware of your photographic evidence. Unfortunately, your team arrived a day after our team to sanitize the scene and reconstruct it to be consistent with your version of reality. Doors were changed, walls were gutted and re-plastered, and a new series of shots were fired that would support your story."

Bickens looked at the ATF agent present in the room, and a smile began to stretch across his face.

"Are you saying that you or other people from the Chinese government were spying on us…committing espionage on American soil?"

"Not at all," Ambassador Li Xiao Jing said flatly, "but there are many in your country…I believe you call them right-wing fanatics and other such condescending names…many who have formed grassroots watchdog committees to provide your disillusioned citizenry with an alternate form of information than that available through your state-controlled media. That notwithstanding, we have every right to conduct independent investigations involving the death of our own foreign nationals. You see, Mr. Scorzoletti never wanted his wife or daughter to be granted citizenship for a reason precisely such as this."

"Well, isn't this like the pot calling the kettle black," Bickens said as he looked at the other agent. "I am being lectured by a representative from a state-controlled communist country that has an untold legacy of human rights abuses telling me that our citizens are disillusioned and in need of alternative forms of information. Now isn't that the biggest load of shit you've ever heard, Special Agent Wesley?"

Agent Wesley nodded nervously, not sure what to believe considering all that he had heard.

"What's the matter with you, boy? You look as though you just finished watching *The Exorcist*."

"I'm fine, sir; it's just that I've heard a lot of information I'm not sure how to process."

"There's nothing here to process, Agent Wesley. All you need to do is dismiss all their drivel as lies. Our forensic evidence represents the truth. Anything they say to the contrary is just wishful thinking on their part..."

Ambassador Li Xiao Jing raised his hand. "Excuse me, Mr. Bickens, but have you ascertained whether Mrs. Scorzoletti is capable of firing a handgun or handling a machine gun?"

"No."

"Did you test her hands, face, or clothing for traces of carbon that would be indicative of her having fired a weapon?"

"No, out of sensitivity to her emotional state at that time, we didn't. That doesn't eliminate the possibility of her firing shots."

"Mr. Bickens, Zhu Li Xiao was hiding underneath her bed in her bedroom. I don't think that would have been a good vantage point for firing at men who were coming in the front and rear entrances of her home. Moreover, not a single man on your team made it to the threshold of Zhu Li Xiao's bedroom door. Mr. Scorzoletti made sure of that. It was only after he was sure that all threats were neutralized that he retrieved her from where she was hiding to see their daughter."

"So," Minister Cai Ko Pei challenged, "you didn't establish forensic evidence to see whether she fired a weapon, you don't even know whether she's capable of handling firearms, yet you have held her for over fourteen days without formally charging her with any crime. You can only hold her for twenty-four hours if she is not formally arrested and charged with a crime."

"That's not altogether true, Minister," Bickens replied as he looked at Special Agent Wesley.

"You are correct," Minister Cai Ko Pei continued. "If a detainee is suspected of murder, you may hold her up to three days, and if a detainee is suspected of terrorism, you may only hold her for fourteen days, but you have not even conclusively proven this woman ever fired a single shot on the night you and your men laid siege to her home, much less established a credible case for her being an accessory to murder. Moreover, during the entire course of our conversation, you never once alluded to her husband or her being suspected of domestic or international terrorism, so you have no reason to detain her any longer."

The three consular officers spoke to themselves briefly and then Ambassador Li Xiao Jing spoke to Julie quickly and turned to Bickens with a stern look as he was finishing. She immediately began to gather what little she had and place it in a backpack.

"Forgive me, Minister," Bickens began, in a patronizing tone, "but I didn't study Chinese in school. I saw no use for it. So, now, tell me what you instructed the young lady to do because it looks to me like she thinks she's going somewhere."

"I told her to gather her belongings because she is leaving this place with us immediately! You have not charged her with any crime, nor are you able to do so, and, as such, you have absolutely no authority over her."

"Oh, I do have authority over her, and she is not leaving," Bickens replied. "Special Agent Wesley, please convince our disrespectful guests that I represent the power of the United States government and that Mrs. Scorzoletti is absolutely not leaving the premises under any circumstances with these men."

Agent Wesley backed away from the men, quickly drew his weapon, and then pointed it in their direction.

Julie looked on helplessly, frozen midway between the opposing groups of men, pleading with her eyes for an end to this confrontation, but the consular officers looked at her with reassuring calm.

"Agent Wesley, I would like to extract my cell phone from my coat pocket. If you mistrust me, you may come here and take it out for me," Li Xiao Jing said.

Agent Wesley looked at Bickens for guidance.

"What should I do, sir?"

"Ambassador Li, please remove your coat and toss it on the bed," Bickens replied. "Then I want the three of you to move away from the bed and stand facing the window. Special Agent Wesley, you keep them covered. Mrs. Scorzoletti, I'd like you to extract the cell phone from Ambassador Li's coat and bring it over to him so he can call the Chinese premier or whoever it is in China that he thinks will help him out of this mess he's gotten himself into."

Julie did exactly as she was told, but instead of resuming her position near her belongings, she stayed near the consular officers. In their presence, she felt safe for the first time since she was taken from her home the night of the siege. Ambassador Li dialed a number and then began a conversation with someone Bickens never imagined he would call for help.

"Hello, Director Snellings, this is Ambassador Li Xiao Jing from the Chinese Embassy in Washington, DC. I am at the DC Hilton with two of my consular officials being held at gunpoint by Special Agent Wesley under the direction of Special Agent in Charge Gary Bickens. I am hoping that you can persuade him to let us peacefully leave the hotel with Zhu Li Xiao. You are probably more familiar with her as Julie Scorzoletti. She has been held by the ATF for over fourteen days without being charged of any crime, and Mr. Bickens' account of what happened on the night of the siege at Mrs. Scorzoletti's home is egregiously flawed. Moreover, it seems that your agency lacks any tangible evidence to suggest that Mrs. Scorzoletti is anything other than a victim of your agency's deliberate malfeasance. While you cannot do anything to change the outcome of her daughter's fate, perhaps you can prevent any further violence from being perpetrated on Mrs. Scorzoletti by your agents. I am truly hoping that I do not have to contact President Courtland about this matter. I have no wish to embarrass your agency by escalating this to an international incident, but unless a more rational mind can prevail, I will have no choice but to contact the White House after our conversation."

As the ambassador was talking to Director Snellings, a quiet look of concern washed over the face of Bickens as he took several deep breaths.

"Ambassador Li, I can assure you that Special Agent in Charge Bickens is acting entirely on his own, and without the knowledge or approval of my office. Could you please give the phone to him?"

"Since we are being held at gunpoint, could I put the phone on speaker and have you address your agent holding us at gunpoint? I would much rather do this before I move anywhere near Mr. Bickens."

"Absolutely," Snellings replied instantaneously.

Ambassador Li placed the phone on speaker and informed the director.

"This is Director Sam Snellings of the Bureau of Alcohol, Tobacco and Firearms. Would the agent with the drawn firearm please identify himself?"

"This is Special Agent William Wesley, sir."

"Special Agent Wesley, is your finger on the trigger of that weapon?"

"No sir, it is not!" Agent Wesley quickly but discreetly and carefully slid his finger off the trigger and placed it on the side of the barrel.

"Very good! Now I want you to put the safety slowly and carefully on, lower the weapon, and holster it, understand?"

"Yes sir, understood."

Just then Julie let out a sigh as though she had been holding her breath the entire time, and she fainted into the arms of Minister Cai

Ko Pei. Hearing the ensuing response and activity, the director became alarmed.

"What's going on there? Somebody talk to me!"

"Mrs. Scorzoletti fainted, Director Snellings," the ambassador responded. "It must have been the shock of being held at gunpoint by men who seem to have the privilege of acting according to their desires with impunity! I am sure she will be okay in just a moment."

"Ambassador Li, could you please take the phone off speaker and hand it to Special Agent in Charge Bickens?"

"Of course, Director Snellings." Ambassador Li calmly walked over to Bickens and handed him the phone.

Bickens took the phone from the ambassador's hand with a look in his eyes that said he sensed defeat, but he wasn't aware of exactly what was coming.

"Bickens! Are you out of your goddamn mind!" Director Snellings began. "Where do you get off holding the ambassador of China and his consular officials at gunpoint? And when the hell were you going to tell me that you were holding Mrs. Scorzoletti?"

"Director Snellings, I know how bad this may look to you, but Mrs. Scorzoletti serves a very important purpose in acquiring Salvino Scorzoletti. Can't you understand that?"

"Goddamn it, Bickens! What I can't understand is that you not only kidnapped a woman who has committed no crime other than being married to a wanted man, but now you've practically admitted in front of the Chinese ambassador that you are also holding her hostage as a bargaining chip to acquire Salvino Scorzoletti. Have you gone completely insane?"

"Director Snellings, with Philster dead, what leverage do we have other than Scorzoletti's wife?"

"We have cooperating agreements with other agencies, and the most sophisticated intelligence-gathering apparatus in the world. You, however, may have a date with an early retirement on disability. Now you are to let them all leave that hotel. You tell the agent who's with you, and you radio that information to anyone you have on surveillance.

I don't want anyone following them, do you understand?"

"Can I ask them what their plans are regarding Mrs. Scorzoletti?"

"Absolutely not! There's no reason for it! Furthermore, I want you to apologize to them for what transpired! The last thing in the world that I need after the last incident you brought to our doorstep is to have the premier of China calling the White House and asking why the BATF was holding their ambassador at gunpoint! This has all the makings of an international incident, and that is something I absolutely don't want to happen. Isn't it enough that your last debacle down south, where you had no business being, I might add, has the Republican party calling our agency a rogue elephant running wild and trampling on the rights of American citizens? They're comparing us to Hitler's SS and depicting us as a bunch of jack-booted thugs, and I am sick of it! Now give the ambassador his phone back so I can speak to him! After he hangs up, you are to apologize to each of them before letting them go, and then you are to report immediately to me, is that clear?"

"Yes, sir…crystal clear." Bickens looked at the ambassador with a very subtle, sheepish grin and motioned for him to take his phone back.

"The director would like to talk with you for a moment, Ambassador Li."

A repugnant smile raised the right cheek of the ambassador's face with what was more like a sneer of victory than an amicable smile; the ambassador retrieved his phone just as calmly as he had surrendered it to Bickens.

"This is Ambassador Li."

"Ambassador Li, I want to first apologize for the behavior of Special Agent Bickens, but, more importantly, I want you to know that he was acting entirely on his own in this matter without either the knowledge or approval of the BATF's administrative command."

"Well, then I'd say your agency needs to task itself with a better system of monitoring what its leaders in the field are doing. We at the Chinese Embassy in DC have seen several other embarrassing spectacles of the ATF's untoward behavior in the not-too-distant past. It seems your agency is no stranger to these types of incidents. They are regrettable, but I believe they are entirely preventable with the proper type of oversight."

"You are absolutely right, Ambassador Li, and I can assure you that swift, corrective, and disciplinary measures will be taken to assure that Special Agent Bickens and those under his command are held accountable for their overzealous and thoroughly repugnant actions! The BATF simply will not tolerate rogue, independent action that is outside the oversight of administrative command's careful consideration of satisfactory actions and outcomes."

"I am quite satisfied by what I hear, Director Snellings, so I will say goodbye to you on behalf of the consulate and my colleagues who have joined me here."

With a tap of his finger, the conversation ended and Bickens dropped his head with a heavy sigh of what seemed like defeat and humiliation mixed with anger and frustration.

"It would appear that a more rational mind has prevailed in this matter," Ambassador Li said calmly to Bickens and the agent with him. "Perhaps you might want to consider retirement, given your current disability."

Bickens began to lift his head, but then paused for a moment, as though he was lifting a weight that was too much for his neck to bear, and then he continued until his eyes met Ambassador Li's, and each person after him who he addressed.

"Ambassador Li, Minister Cai, Minister Wang, and Mrs. Scorzoletti, I am sincerely sorry for my methods of operation, and I hope you will understand that my motives were born out of a desire to bring a violent man to justice, just as I know you would want to do if he would have killed colleagues of yours inside the People's Republic of China."

"Had Mr. Scorzoletti been sought by the authorities in China, he would not have had any guns in his possession with which to shoot them."

Bickens contained the anger that was rising from his chest into his throat and merely chuckled as he shook his head before responding with disdain cloaked in a feigned hospitality.

"Well, I guess there are some advantages of living in a country that isn't free. There's no such thing as a second amendment to the constitution. In fact, there's no constitution."

Ambassador Li also chuckled slightly, but he did not try to hide his disdain.

"Such a high price in human lives you pay for this so-called freedom you have. Now you can add the life of an innocent little Chinese girl to the price-tag of your freedom. How much of that freedom will you enjoy being confined to that chair for the rest of your life, Mr. Bickens? Was it worth the life of an innocent little Chinese girl? Does your constitution keep your women from being assaulted in their own homes? Does it prevent the racial discord that causes rioting and civil unrest, that destroys businesses and property of Americans who work to feed and house those who don't? Does it facilitate respect for mothers and fathers in the traditional family that extends outward to neighbors, authority figures, and government? We do not have a constitution such as yours or a second amendment, but we don't have any of the problems that you have here in America because of your freedom. Consider that, Mr. Bickens."

"Duly noted, Ambassador Li," Bickens replied before taking Agent Wesley's phone and calling down to his other agents. "Mrs. Scorzoletti will be leaving the building with Ambassador Li Xiao Jing and two officers of the Chinese Embassy. You are to let them go, and under no circumstances are you to speak to them or follow them."

Julie Scorzoletti quickly looked away from Agent Bickens and to the comforting eyes of Ambassador Li, who gently placed his arm on her back and bowed his head slightly toward the door, encouraging her to proceed out of the room. Julie glanced back at Bickens one last time. Though he was the one whose actions cost her the life of her daughter, he no longer seemed to be the imposing figure who lay on the bedroom floor near her daughter's bed. He seemed frail and appeared much older than he did that night, but where she saw some signs of remorse in him on that fateful evening, she now saw only bitterness and what she interpreted as a desire for revenge. It made no sense to her until she remembered what her husband told her…all the young girls who were sold into slavery. Julie paused for a moment.

"Now I understand why killing my husband consumes your being far more than remorse for my daughter's life."

"You don't have to talk to this man, and you really shouldn't," Ambassador Li consoled as he could see tears welling up in Julie's eyes.

She looked at Ambassador Li and spoke to him in Chinese, telling him that Bickens and another corrupt man in the US intelligence field planned the raid on her home because they thought her husband stole their blood money from them when he actually diverted the funds. Ambassador Li and the two other consular officials looked at Bickens with the malice that a heinous criminal deserved as Julie spoke one last time. Though her voice started out in a whimper, it rose to a powerful crescendo.

"If I knew where your filthy money was, I would have told you, but I can assure you of one thing…my husband doesn't have one filthy penny of that money that was amassed by stealing the innocence and lives of young girls and boys, with no feelings or remorse…just the way you took our daughter from us! I hope you live an awfully long life in that chair…until the memories of what you've done and the people you protected make you pray for death!"

Chapter 9
A Slight Indiscretion

Three days later Alvarez was reading the *Fox Lake Gazette* online when he came across the sketch of Philster and the corresponding tagline that he was a person of interest with the DEA regarding information about the burglary and theft of controlled substances at Sonny's Drugstore in Winnetka.

"Me-O-Man!" Alvarez bellowed from behind the screen of his laptop. "Philster, you're not gonna believe this, but you've been made in connection with the job you pulled over at Sonny's Drugs!"

"What are you talking about, you silly geek? We got away from that job clean! For Christ's sake, you took care of the alarm, and nobody saw us going in or coming out!"

"Somebody must have seen you…check this out," Alvarez said excitedly, motioning for Philster and the others to join him around his laptop.

"Oh my God, you douchebag…that sure as fuck looks like you! What did you do, ask some girl at the cosmetics counter where the condoms were?"

"This is not good," Jake said. "Now, in addition to Bickens, we've got the DEA on our ass."

Mohammed, who had just joined the crew in Fox Lake, looked at Scorzoletti and the Philster with a stoic smile and shook his head before speaking.

"I'd have a real tough time trying to get any group in the jihadist network to take responsibility for this one, guys. It just wouldn't have any credibility. I mean, think about it…a group of Muslims stealing a bunch of drugs that people are known to get high on?"

"He's right," Scorzoletti said, looking at Philster matter-of-factly. "Muslims may have a few other vices we tend to frown upon, but getting high on prescription drugs just isn't one of them; it looks like you're back from the dead, Philster, so you can't just walk away from this anymore. The good thing about this is that the only person here that Philster is a known associate of is me. Nobody even knows about our existence as a group, so the rest of you aren't linked to what happened at Sonny's."

"I should have worn a fucking turban on my head that night!" Philster exclaimed with agitation.

"I'm sorry, my friend," Mohammed said politely, "but Muslims just don't deal in drugs."

"Really, I happen to know a few who dealt in drugs big time. Those fucking sand niggers were purchasing and distributing massive quantities of shit to buy arms for their fucking jihad."

"They probably had their arms chopped off by now, my friend. Also, I would prefer it if you did not refer to me as a sand nigger. I have no African ancestry. Also, the Koran forbids the use of drugs."

"The Koran…give me a fucking break, Mohammed. It tells its adherents to marry eight-year-old girls, chop off the heads of infidels, and rape all women who are infidels. Oh, and by the way, guess who infidels are, Mohammed? Infidels are everyone in the fucking world who aren't Muslims. So read that from your Koran and tuck it up your ass," Philster said with a laugh. "If you didn't know so many whack jobs that hate Uncle Sam, I'd have nothing to do with you."

"Be that as it may," Scorzoletti interjected, "Mohammed's right. Knocking off a local drugstore doesn't fit the profile of the way terrorists finance their arms deals, and whatever other idiosyncrasies Mohammed has, we need him right now. Especially since you're back on Bickens' radar."

"Yeah, but he doesn't know about the rest of our group. I doubt that he even knows about me, Scorzo," Philster said.

"Why is that?"

"Because drug thefts don't fall under the jurisdiction of the ATF. That would be the DEA, and I doubt the DEA is going to share anything with the BATF, especially since the DEA must make their pursuit on a drug charge. Anything after that will be gravy for them."

While it was true for the moment that neither Bickens nor Contreras was about to let sleeping dogs rest, they would use any means at their disposal to snare their quarry. That, coupled with events that were about to transpire, would conspire against the group. Contreras spoke to his agents like a coach giving a pep talk during half-time to a team that had a small lead over the opposing team. Contreras was determined to turn a crime in the picturesque, sleepy Northshore suburb of Chicago into his opportunity to climb the ranks within the DEA. He was determined that he would not be passed over again. He also assumed that nobody above him would be interested in what happened in an affluent suburb of Chicago where there could be little chance of a connection to organized crime or large drug cartels. It was, everyone assumed, the work of a small-time drug addict or drug dealer…nothing that would garner national attention. Nobody except Bickens would think differently. Contreras, too, would take exception.

"Okay, people, we're trending in the right direction. We have a picture in the face of the public, and that's progress. However, it doesn't mean we can rest on our laurels. We can't sit back, relax, and think that the public is going to call in leads that are going to bring this case to closure. We must maintain our vigilance and we will nail this perpetrator!"

Before Contreras finished speaking, he was scanning the faces of his agents, sensing a certain resignation in most of them, as though their very eyes betrayed the thoughts that they had gone as far as they could go in the investigation. Then he stopped and scanned the face of Agent Carina, whose eyes seemed to be bulging from impatience.

"So, tell me some good news, people! What, if anything, have we heard since that sketch has been released."

"Are you ready to be blown away, boss?" Agent Carina asked coyly.

"I am hoping you're going to tell me that a number of leads came into your team that helped us identify this person of interest. That's the only thing that would blow me away."

"I'll do you one better, boss!"

"And how's that, Agent Carina."

"Well, at the time, I figured going this route would be an exercise in futility, but wanting to leave no stone unturned, I decided to give it a shot."

"Don't take too long getting to the point, Agent Carina."

"Okay, well, I know that Winnetka is not the city of Chicago, but I decided to inquire if they had surveillance cameras anywhere in the town."

"And you're going to tell me they do, and I am going to lift you right out of that chair and twirl around with you in ecstasy!"

"What they have is a set of photo enforcement cameras at two different intersections where they've had a lot of violations and a few accidents…"

"And…?" Contreras said.

"And a violation was photographed on the evening of the burglary at Sonny's Drugs. And believe it or not, we now have a photograph that matches our sketch, and we have a license plate of the car our person of interest was in on that night!"

"Oh Mother-of-God, I thank you for answering my prayers!" Contreras said, allowing his Spanish accent to surface as he broke into laughter before addressing his agents.

"You see what one determined woman can do when she wants her boss's job! This is phenomenal! This is beyond what I was hoping for! This will allow us to track him anywhere he goes within the state, or anywhere outside of it. All the tollways, bus stations, train stations, as well as Midway and O'Hare Airports, which have facial recognition software in their facilities!"

"And with the license plate we can find out who he is or who he's associated with," Agent Carina added.

"Don't you know it, señorita!" Contreras thundered jubilantly. "And with a little luck, perhaps our person of interest has a rap sheet or maybe even an outstanding warrant. Then he becomes our suspect! No more tiptoeing around affluent Northshore conventions!"

Contreras smiled and cupped his hands over his face; he shook his head as if to indicate his joy could not be contained, but after a moment he snapped back into a hunter mode, desperate to bring his team to victory.

"Okay! We need to get this photo to all the other federal agencies first. After that we issue a general APB, and last, but not least, we tighten the noose around this guy's neck by getting his photo to the local news media."

"What's our talking point on this guy with the media," Agent Nichols asked.

"At this point in time he's still a person of interest…at the very most he's been elevated to a traffic offender, but we're certainly not going to use either of these descriptions as our talking points. That's why the media is going to be the last leg of our offensive. We need to find some dirt on this guy or whoever was in that car with him… something that will allow us to stop talking about him as a person of interest and start describing him as a suspect that can be arrested, detained, and rigorously questioned! All right, people!" Contreras said, clapping his hands together in a quick staccato motion. "Let's start cooking with Wesson over a high flame!"

Like a team breaking after a huddle, the agents snapped into action, circulating the photo of Philster, in high resolution, to the FBI, the ATF, and the Illinois State Police. The license plate would have been yet another dead lead as Philster used one of the many aliases with a fake identity and address he created over the years with ONI, but when one of Bickens' agents saw the photo of Philster, the news for Contreras, which he welcomed at first, would become a double-edged sword.

Bickens, who was desk-bound in the Washington field office, saw his opportunity to get back in the field and, moreover, to pursue a nemesis who almost destroyed his many years of service with the ATF. Bickens knew that if Philster was alive, then he was invariably alive because Scorzoletti needed his connection to people in ONI and field operatives. Since his discharge from the Navy and the abrogation of all files and records linking him to the military, Scorzoletti had become a social pariah in that world, relegated to the service of a simple base mechanic with a civilian status. Bickens wasted no time waiting for Contreras to establish a connection with the ATF field office in Chicago.

"Special Agent Contreras, this is Special Agent in Charge Bickens of the ATF," Bickens said, in a pleasant manner that would suggest he and Contreras were old friends, though they had never met.

"The Chicago field office of the ATF responds more quickly than the boys at the Bureau."

"Well, actually, to be honest with you, I'm out of the Washington office."

"So, the Chicago office contacted you on the photo we put out?"

"Not exactly. You see, I've been monitoring the Chicago field office because your person of interest bears a resemblance to an ATF asset in a rather sensitive operation, and his last known whereabouts were in Chicago."

"I'm a little bit confused, Special Agent Bickens. Why wouldn't the Chicago office be contacting me about this man?"

"Because the op he was associated with, if your photo is our man, was handled out of my office. Chicago was out of the loop on this one."

Special Agent Contreras paused for a moment; his gut was telling him something was not quite right, but he continued as if he suspected nothing.

"So, what can you tell me about the man in the photo?"

"Actually, Special Agent Contreras, I was hoping that you would be able to provide me with some information on why he came up on your radar."

"Quite frankly, Special Agent Bickens, the reason we circulated that photo to agencies outside of the DEA is because at this point in time we can only classify him as a person of interest. We have some circumstantial evidence to suggest that he may be linked to the theft of a large number of controlled substances from a retail pharmacy in Winnetka, but we have no conclusive evidence linking him to the theft."

"What type of controlled substances?"

"Is that of some significance?" Contreras probed casually.

"No, just curious," Bickens said dismissively.

"It was a mix of schedule four and schedule two narcotics."

"Opiates?"

"Yes, every type they had in their inventory."

"Really? Just opiates?" Bickens questioned with a slightly rising intonation, knowing that Philster's drug of choice was Xanax.

"Whoever it was, they cleaned out everything from Vicodin to Oxycontin and Dilaudid tablets through the amphetamines of every type as well as all the benzodiazepines and other hypnotic sedatives… everything that has street resale value, with one odd exception."

"What's that?" Bickens asked with genuine curiosity.

"Among the inventory reported missing was antibiotics, saline, and glucose IV bottles, and the weirdest of all things…"

"What?"

"They took all of the Cyklokapron and Zoladex."

"I'm not familiar with those two drugs. What kind of high do they produce?"

"They don't produce any kind of high. They're used to stop bleeding and reduce blood loss. It doesn't make any sense given everything else that was stolen. Then there's the antibiotics. They have no resale value unless you're selling to a warlord in Somalia."

"Huh," Bickens responded, as if equally stumped, yet it would be perfectly logical if Scorzoletti sustained a wound that wasn't readily apparent to Bickens on the night of the siege. If this was so, it would also increase the likelihood that Philster and Scorzoletti were together. "Do you have any idea where he is?"

"We've run the plates on his vehicle with the DMV, and they're registered to a Florida address, just outside of Tampa, to a man by the name of Dexter Blithe. Is that the name of your asset?"

"No, but then again, our asset is a man of many names."

"What was his name when you were in contact with him?"

"I just knew him by a code name," Bickens answered deceitfully. "He was known as Lupe, or the Mouth."

"And I suppose this *Mouth*, as you call him, is also a man of many different residences as well?"

"You guessed it."

"Well, let me ask you this, Special Agent Bickens…why would somebody who looked like your asset come all the way up from Florida to commit a theft of pharmaceuticals up in Winnetka?"

"I didn't say he did. Your person of interest just bears a resemblance to our asset, that's all."

"That resemblance must be awfully strong for you to call this office within minutes after that photo went out. Does this guy have anything to do with that fiasco you were involved in down in Mississippi?"

"Not at all. The whole country knows who we're after regarding the Mississippi incident. My asset was in the Chicago area during the Mississippi incident, and was presumed dead. Our Chicago field office hadn't developed anything to refute that theory until I saw your picture bearing an extraordinarily strong resemblance to our asset."

"Well, let's say, for the sake of argument, that the guy my team is pursuing is your asset. Is he currently wanted by the ATF? Do you have something on this guy that would allow us to pursue him as something other than a person of interest, or a damn traffic offender?"

"I suppose you could pursue him as a traffic offender," Bickens said, beginning to laugh. "Why, hell, I don't suppose much else other than traffic offenses happen up in Winnetka."

"Very funny," Contreras replied, "but I hardly think I could muster the help of your agency, the FBI, or anyone else in law enforcement based on a traffic offense."

"No, I don't suppose you could, but the ATF could definitely be of assistance to you if it turns out that this is our man. Have you come up with any leads that might suggest he's still in the vicinity?"

"Unless he's hiding out in the sewer system, only coming out late at night to forage through dumpsters for food, I'd say it's highly unlikely. We've had a sketch of him out for over a week now, and nothing's come in except some information about him residing at the Palmer House hotel in the days prior to the burglary. So, we're going to hand that photo off to the local media as soon as we can get something from the FBI, seeing as how it looks like we've struck out with the ATF."

While Bickens' call to Contreras may have seemed to be immediately after Philster's photo was circulated, it wasn't before Bickens did some background research on Special Agent Contreras.

"You know, Special Agent Contreras, if the Bureau does have any information on your man, they're going to take jurisdiction over the case while you play second fiddle to them."

"Like hell we will!" Contreras shot back. "The FBI doesn't have a specific charter for drug enforcement! We do!"

"That's not exactly true," Bickens retorted, knowing he had touched a nerve from Contreras' past.

"How do you figure?"

"Well, your perpetrator has violated the Harrison Narcotics Act in their theft of schedule two narcotics, most presumably for interstate resale, since everything you have right now points in the direction of Florida. I'd say that gives them all the reason they need to come in and take charge. I've seen it done before…seen men lose the recognition they deserved as well as the advancement they had coming because the Bureau muscled in and took over an investigation that wasn't theirs to begin with."

"I appreciate the FYI, Special Agent Bickens, but that's just not going to happen here!"

"Javier," Bickens began in a cordial tone, deliberately dropping the formalities and addressing Contreras by his first name, "I've not only seen this happen before, but I've been a victim of it."

"And when was that, Special Agent Bickens?"

"Please, let's dispense with the formalities, call me Gary."

"As you wish…tell me when you've been a victim of the FBI."

"Well, I'm sure you heard about a little incident called Ruby Ridge, haven't you?"

"You know I have, Gary. I didn't jump into the game yesterday."

"That's good because then I don't have to tell you how that was entirely an ATF show. It was all about weapons. It wasn't an FBI matter at all, but they were the ones who came in and requisitioned military weaponry from the governor of Idaho, and it became an FBI show from there on in."

Contreras said nothing, so Bickens continued.

"And need I remind you of Waco, Texas, where the ATF sustained casualties in the process of trying to serve warrants at that compound. The FBI never had one man on the ground at the time, but once again, they requisitioned helicopters and tanks and it became their show. I certainly don't have to tell you what a nightmare that turned out to be."

"No, you don't," Contreras said, exhaling in disappointment. "And what about your nightmare in Mississippi? Does this man I am pursuing have something to do with that?"

"No, absolutely not," Bickens shot back quickly.

"You'll forgive me if I don't find you to be entirely forthcoming, Special Agent Bickens."

"Hey, look, if you can nail this guy and he does turn out to be our asset, I would consider that a win-win situation for both of us."

"I want him for a controlled substances theft, amigo, and that's quite clear. What's your interest in him?"

"Conspiracy to sell naval munitions on the international arms market."

"And this is someone you call an asset to the ATF?" Contreras replied with disbelief.

"Sometimes an asset plays both sides of the fence. You know that, Contreras. You've been around the block a few times. It just happens."

"Perhaps, but it's never happened to me."

"And I sincerely hope it never does, but if you're pursuing the man I think you are, you're going to need some help."

"Look, my friend, I have brought down some of the most danger-ous drug runners on the West Coast by myself. Are you suggesting

I need help to catch a cat burglar who knocks off a mom-and-pop drugstore? You don't think the DEA is capable of that, or is it my competence you're questioning?"

"I'm not questioning your competence at all. I just don't want to see you get the shaft again like you did on the West Coast if some political Pollyannas jump in the ring."

"And what do you know about the West Coast?"

"I happen to know that the best and brightest of the DEA's agents, a man with a degree from DePaul University and a doctorate in law, smashed the MSD-17 drug network on the West Coast, and then came up with an ingenious plan called Operation Cassandra that would kill two birds with one stone...drug traffickers and terrorists! Unfortunately, he didn't get the credit he deserved, which would have easily taken him off the streets and put him into an executive administrative post."

"You sound like a biographer speaking about me in the third person. I imagine that next you'll be telling me that if I share all my information with you, the circumstances of my destiny could change for the better, so how about if we just cut to the chase, amigo... Why should I trust you with my information?"

"How about this for a reason why... One of the people being targeted in Project Cassandra was neck deep in ONI, and he was none other than the man we're probably both pursuing. He gave the Bureau a bunch of terrorists without surrendering any of his ill-gotten millions, and he walked. So, the Bureau got the headlines, and we got the shaft."

"We got the shaft?"

"Yes, we...you and me...I was your silent partner in Operation Cassandra. I was using my asset to work the arms side of the operation while you were using Middle Eastern informants you turned to work the drug side of the operation."

"How did the Bureau take oversight of Cassandra? That's something that was never explained to me."

"It was never explained to you because it was above your clearance

132

level, and mine too. My asset was active ONI during the time he was double-dipping in drugs and arms, as well as a massive child sex ring in Southeast Asia. He was using the profits to fund black ops for the Navy so ONI could do things without congressional oversight since the money wasn't being allotted by Congress. He was also skimming a good deal of cream off the top of those profits for himself, and that money was never recovered. It wasn't until ONI got involved in cleaning house that this guy was sentenced to Leavenworth."

"So that's why you want this guy…it's a personal thing."

"Yeah, I guess you could say that, but it's no less a personal thing for you either. Project Cassandra was your baby, and the Bureau took it away from you because of the man we both have in the crosshairs of our sights. He was the reason that we only bagged a few drug-dealing terrorists before the operation was shut down."

"This is incredible, compadre! This guy was guilty of treason, and he walked?"

"He did do some time, but it was a walk in the park because he did even uglier things than that prior to Cassandra. As far as the Bureau was concerned, it was all done in the name of a greater good. It was sealed on grounds of national security."

Chapter 10
Taking Back What's Ours

———∿∿∿———

Scorzoletti and his men were training and honing their skills at gaining and taking enemy territory, defending against ambushes and initiating them, as well as flanking an aggressor. They also drilled rigorously in environmental deception so they could use the elements in any environment to aid them in escape and evasion, whether they were in a remote area or a crowded city. They all took turns keeping watch of their perimeter by day and night to prepare them for a lifestyle in which they would be actively tracked by a determined enemy. They deprived themselves of sleep, food, and water, and engaged in other oppressive training such as foraging through swamps and lakes and sleeping outside in wet clothing after swimming miles at a time. They engaged in every form of insufferable conditions and self-denial to give themselves the maximum advantage over their enemies who fought with creature comforts and returned home to warm, cooked meals and the love of spouses and families every evening.

As such, they were bonding cohesively as a team and growing in confidence of their ability to handle any situation, but Scorzoletti would always surprise them with tactics designed to humble them. He never wanted them to underestimate their adversary. He wanted them to develop cool composure under fire with the ability to rapidly assess a situation, coordinate a strategy, and execute it with precision. He called overconfidence the first enemy, and the one that always led to a fall sooner or later. As it was in SEAL training, any mistakes that were made were punished with more calisthenics, less food, and less sleep, and lengthy underwater swims in frigid water. Rather than punish an individual who made the error, Scorzoletti punished the whole team, and he made himself no exception to the rigors of the punishment. To everyone's surprise Philster complained the least, worked the hardest, and reacted with unusual stoicism.

On the evening that Bickens first reached out to Contreras, Scorzoletti would make a case in point about overconfidence. Four of the nine men were outside keeping watch of the perimeter while Scorzoletti, Philster, Jake Pool, and Jamal Nixon were inside discussing the necessity of using misinformation and disinformation as a part of their arsenal. Alvarez was trolling the Internet, monitoring police activity regarding the Mississippi incident and the burglary in Winnetka.

"Hey, Salvino, check this out...you too, Steven," Alvarez interrupted while they were talking.

"Steven," Philster repeated in a mocking tone as he shook his head. "What the fuck do I look like...your fucking butler or something? It's Philster, and Sal...or Scorzo, but not Salvino and Steven for Christ's sake!"

"Well, jeez, what are you getting so bent about? I mean, those are your names, aren't they?"

"Can you believe this guy" Philster asked, looking at Scorzoletti. "I swear, if this guy wasn't so good at pulling shit out of the ass of the Internet, he'd have absolutely no useful people skills whatsoever!"

As Scorzoletti and Philster approached Alvarez, Philster pointed his finger at him and began shaking it.

"You know, people like you are the reason why road rage exists!"

"What's the connection between road rage and your name? I don't get it," Jake said, wincing slightly.

"People who cause road rage irritate other people because they're insistent on following the rules of the road to the point of it being a fetish. They won't let people who want to speed pass them. They won't move out of their lane in traffic to let another car merge in...I could go on and on... Then you have this guy over here," Philster said, pointing at Alvarez, "who has to use the precise linguistic etymological derivation of my name to follow the fucking rules of grammatical etiquette and be polite."

"I still don't see what the connection is," Jake said with a subtle smirk.

"Forget it," Scorzoletti said in his subdued Southern drawl, swiping the air with his hand. He then turned to Philster. "And speaking of tranquilizers…it might be best if you took one. You seem a little edgy this evening."

"Look at this," Alvarez said to Scorzoletti, ignoring Philster's tirade.

"Oh, for the love of God!" Philster said, raising his voice again. "That motherfucking Bickens! Even in a wheelchair that cocksucker still has my ass in his mouth."

"This wasn't put out by the ATF."

"Then how did it go from being a goofy-looking sketch a couple of weeks ago to a glossy photo of me? I don't remember doing any autographed glossies for anybody before we left Kenilworth, so who put it out?"

"The DEA."

"Then Bickens had to be in on this."

"There's no doubt he's probably courting the DEA's attention like a teenage boy trying to score with the homecoming queen, but this photo was generated by a photo enforcement surveillance camera linked to the Winnetka Police Department at a no-turn-on-red intersection."

"Fucking Miles," Philster ranted, "always so fucking jacked up. I'm going to have a serious talk with that fucking nutbar…"

"Stop it right there, Philster," Scorzoletti interjected. "You both messed up because you were overconfident. You made yourself too conspicuous when you were casing the store, and on the night of the burglary, you stopped and talked to people who could identify you. Miles told me he wanted to up and leave your ass right then and there when he saw that, and that's more than likely why he wanted to get the hell out of Dodge so quickly. That's why he wasn't paying attention to the no-turn-on-red sign like he should have been. That led to your first critical mistake. Now Bickens knows you're alive."

"Still worse, now they're referring to you as a suspect rather than a person of interest," Alvarez said.

Philster and Scorzoletti looked at each other and nodded.

"The only reason my status would go from person of interest to suspect is if Bickens got involved and started talking with the DEA about something called Operation Cassandra."

"What's Operation Cassandra," Jake asked, sitting more upright and attentive.

"It was the brainchild of one of the DEA's crackerjack field agents," Alvarez answered. "He got wind of terrorists who were dealing drugs to finance their arms purchases. He's the DEA's SAC in the Chicago office now."

"I thought those guys were ascetics," Jake said. "According to Mohammed they pray like five or six times a day."

"Ascetics my ass!" Philster sounded off. "They have their women all covered up from head to toe with only their eyes showing, and some of them even put a porous band of linen like gauze bandages over their eyes so those don't even show. It's supposed to keep their men from worldly temptation, but then they'll go out and bugger a little nine-year-old foreign girl dressed in shorts and a T-shirt who's playing by herself in the park because that's okay...she's a foreigner, an infidel!"

"Man, that's messed up." Jake shook his head in disgust. "I sure as hell hope that Mohammed doesn't have any of those tendencies."

"Nah, he's good people," Philster said. "But there's a lot of those raghead pieces of shit that can justify all sorts of shit in the name of Allah." Philster stopped abruptly, as he was prone to doing, and shifted his attention back to Scorzoletti. "Anyway, what the fuck are we gonna do about this shit, Scorzo?"

"Actually," Alvarez interjected, before Scorzoletti could answer, "I'm not finished. There's more..."

"Oh, for the love of Christ, now what? Is Bickens initiating a law-suit against me to pay for his Pampers?"

"Depends," Jake added.

"Depends on what?" Philster asked.

"The diapers adults use are called Depends, not Pampers."

"Depends...Pampers...Huggies... Who gives a fuck?" Philster shouted at Jake before turning his attention back to Alvarez. "So, what else is there?"

"It's actually concerning Salvino...excuse me, Sal."

An expression of alarm enveloped Scorzoletti's usually calm demeanor, and he put one hand on Alvarez's shoulder and gently squeezed it.

"It's Julie, isn't it? Give it to me straight. Tell me what you know."

"Julie's gonna be okay, Sal." Alvarez patted Scorzoletti's hand.

"Come on, Alvarez, don't pull no punches with me."

"Look, see for yourself," Alvarez said, minimizing one screen and maximizing another that had live video streaming.

Scorzo could see his wife being led to a car by two men on either side of her and one in tow behind her.

"Who are those guys around her? How do you know she's okay?"

Alvarez paused the feed and placed his cursor and zoomed in on the three men one at a time, and then began identifying them.

"The one on her right side is Li Xiao Jing; he's the Chinese ambassador to the US. The one on the left is Wang Zai Yan, and the one who's a few steps behind them is Cai Ko Pei. His official title is Minister of Consular Affairs, but the truth is...the guy is as deadly as a heart attack."

"An assassin?" Scorzo asked.

"Yeah, and you can bet he's communicating with a team of confederates. Did you notice how he kept scanning the area side to side and front to back? Also, how he kept putting his hand up to his mouth as if he was clearing his throat?"

"Yeah," Scorzoletti replied blankly.

Alvarez backed up the stream and played it again at a slower speed.

"Here, look at the sides of his face. Notice how it looks like he's talking?"

"Yeah, yeah," Philster added.

"And also, Chinese men...especially young men, don't cover their mouth when they clear their throat. They typically clear their throat and spit anywhere."

"He's right," Scorzoletti said, looking at Philster. "I saw that all the time in China."

"How did you know that?" Philster asked Alvarez. "Whenever we docked at any port in Southeast Asia, you rarely came ashore. All the other guys were going to the brothels and getting laid, but most of the time you stayed on board the ship with your eyes glued to a screen. Shit, a lot of the guys thought you were a homo or something."

"I just got into trolling for information and seeing where it would take me. I was the one who discovered the presence of the dark web before it was ever heard of in the public."

"Yeah, that was one of the morsels I fed up the chain of command at ONI to get your ass out of a sling when you were caught smoking dope on the ship. They were so knocked out by that shit that they gave you a big-time pass, you pothead, computer geek motherfucker."

"All right, Philster, enough with the condescension...let's get back to my wife. Where do you think they're taking her?" Scorzoletti asked Alvarez.

"Probably to a safehouse," Philster said before Alvarez could answer.

"No, no way," Alvarez countered. "She's too high profile. Bureau counterintelligence is probably already watching her from the sky, so there's nowhere they could take her that wouldn't be known. No, they're taking her back to China."

"Can they do that?"

"Sure," Alvarez answered. "That's why the car they got in was from the embassy compound. That car is considered part of the embassy, and those three guys all have diplomatic immunity, which means they're untouchable even if they committed a crime."

"What about Julie?"

"Well," Alvarez began hesitantly, "the Bureau might try to play hardball at the airport to intimidate her, but legally they have nothing on her because she's still a Chinese national and they know it. More than likely, they'll revoke her green card, so her flight is a one-way ticket, courtesy of the Chinese government. That's the bad news."

"Well, at least she'll be safe, and she's got family back in China. At the end of the day, it's better for her," Scorzoletti said with a look of resignation in his eyes and the sound of defeat in his voice. He then turned to Alvarez and patted him on the shoulder. "Good job, Alvarez."

Philster nodded in agreement with Scorzoletti and gave Alvarez a soft swat on the back.

"Hey, I know I give you a lot a shit, but you're good people, Alvarez. You know that, don't you?"

"Philster, I don't think half the shit you be saying do any more than go in one that boy's ears and out the other," Jamal piped up.

"Oh, what do you know, you dreadlocked motherfucker."

"I know the best place for us to score a large cache of weapons and ammunition," Jamal countered.

"Yeah, so do I. It's the Hawthorne Army Depot in Nevada. That used to be Navy property until sometime in the late 1970s."

"Well, I guess if you want to get some major ass-whoop, that's the place to go because last I heard there be about six hundred marines guarding that place."

"No, no, no," the Philster said as he shook his head. "That was a long time ago. That fucking president who was a peanut farmer cut their numbers way down to a hundred and seventy-seven."

"So, what are you saying, Philster?" Jake sat up and asked. "Do you consider the eight of us plus Scorzoletti capable of taking on a force of company strength with no sweat?"

"No, I didn't say that at all, Jake! For Christ's sake, get the fucking wax out of your ears! I was just saying that's the best place to find a huge cache of arms and ammunition."

"If we can't get what we need and get out alive, it's no good," Scorzoletti said, looking at Philster. He turned to Jamal. "What did you have in mind, Nixon?"

"About an hour and a half west of here is a National Guard armory in Machesney Park. It's just a wee bit before Rockford, out in the middle of nowhere. And because it's out in the middle of nowhere, it's not heavily guarded."

"Oh yeah, and how do you know that, Doctor Dre?"

"Because I grew up in Roscoe, Illinois, about ten minutes north of there, and my pappy worked there all his life. I got a cousin who still works there."

"Philster, bring the guys inside. We all need to hear what Nixon has to say."

At once Philster was up and bounding up the stairs to retrieve the men outside. Once inside they retreated to the basement, where Alvarez had a huge mahogany table like one of those boardroom tables at a company. Scorzoletti seated himself at the head of the table with Philster to his right and Nixon to his left. When they were all seated and at attention with their eyes on Scorzoletti, he began to lay out their itinerary.

"In the few weeks we've been here, I've seen a vast improvement in our combat readiness, and now the time is upon us to do what we've assembled ourselves to do. Make no mistake about it, our mission is not one of revenge! Our primary objective is to return our country to a constitutional republic."

"Well fuck, Sal, there's nothing wrong with a little payback."

"Philster! This isn't a discussion. Right now, I'm doing the talking and all of you are doing the listening."

"Yeah, take a Xanax, you douchebag," Max said, smirking at Philster.

Scorzoletti immediately glared at Max and then raised his eyebrows, and the smirk disappeared from Max's face.

"Hey, man, I'm sorry, Sal…continue."

"Like I was saying," Scorzoletti continued, "if I had a mind for revenge, not one of those jack-booted thugs from the ATF would have lived on the night they laid siege to my home and killed my daughter. The truth is, gentlemen, what happened at my house that night was only a symptom of the disease that's consuming our nation, and revenge…huh, that would be like giving aspirin to a patient suffering from stage four cancer. And I'm not about to put all of you in harm's way on a quest for payback! My daughter's dead. No amount of human carnage we can produce will bring her back, nor will it reunite me with my wife, but we can strike at the cause of the symptoms that took my wife and daughter from my side. We can send a message to the bureaucrats in Washington that they've lost touch with the people of this republic and they no longer represent the will of the people, nor do they listen to the people or speak in the voice of the people! Moreover, we're going to send a clear message to them that we're their bosses; they're not our bosses!"

Philster kept shifting in his seat somewhat nervously until he finally spoke up.

"Hey, uh, Sal," he began somewhat hesitantly, "I don't mean to interrupt you, and I can agree with what you're saying, but, uh..."

"Go on, Philster, spit it out. You can speak freely," Scorzoletti encouraged.

"Well, uh, I could be mistaken, but it sounds to me like you're talking about a revolution."

"Well God bless you, Philster! At least I know you have ears that can hear."

"Hey, we might be able to wipe out a few offices of the ATF or blow up the theater of freaks..."

"Theater of freaks?" Miles said with a laugh.

Philster shot him a sharp glance. "That's the US Capitol building. I call it the theater of freaks because it houses a goofier bunch of motherfuckers than anything Hollywood can imagine."

Philster quickly turned his attention back to Scorzoletti.

"Sal, there's only nine of us in this room including you. There's no way we can take on the United States government!"

"If Washington would've thought that way, I believe we'd still be under British rule today," Scorzo shot back.

"Look, Sal, those were different times. We're not up against pirate ship cannons and soldiers using flintlock muskets. We're talking about fucking helicopters, tanks, drones, precision-guided smart bombs, satellite surveillance."

"Philster, I guarantee you that some of the people sitting at the strategy table with George Washington when he was talking about

142

taking on the British Empire felt the same way. Hell, think of it! At that time, in their day, the British Empire was the world's only super-power. Washington's army was outmanned, and outgunned. In fact, when they met the British forces in New York, they had to tear ass back in full retreat."

"Yeah, obviously, I know that."

"But do you know how they turned things around?"

Philster just looked at Scorzoletti blankly for a moment, and then looked around the table and shrugged until Scorzoletti saw Alvarez nod, and he motioned for him to speak.

"He left a group behind in New York that he called the Secret Six. Today they're known as the Culper Spy Ring. They gathered critical intelligence that turned the outcome of the war in Washington's favor."

"Yeah, but I can assure those six didn't have people like the DEA and the ATF on their asses like hickies," Philster countered. "They didn't stand out like we will. They could blend in with the crowd."

"As far as the British were concerned, everyone in the colonies was the enemy, so it's all in how you look at things. Think about it this way…when I posted what happened at my home after the ATF siege, why did it go viral?"

"Because people hate those fucking Nazi bastards at the ATF!" Philster said, beginning to raise his voice.

"Precisely! And what do you think that means?"

"I guess it means that the ATF has a fuck of a lot of enemies around the country."

"And what does that translate into?"

"A whole lot of people who would be willing to cover our six," Alvarez blurted out.

"The number of people who saw that and responded in a way that was favorably disposed to me was way more than enough just to cover our six. There's enough people to cover our six, nine, twelve, three, and every other position they could come at us from."

"I guess," Philster added hesitantly, "but how can you be sure they'll take up a fight that isn't theirs?"

143

"Because the responses I read to the video I posted tell me they will. Okay, let's fast-forward to the present day and lessons of history in modern warfare... Do you think the North Vietnamese army was any match for the technology and the firepower that we brought to the fight?"

"You know they weren't, Sal, but that wasn't a conventional war like we had always fought in the past against large, standing armies..."

"Did they win?" Sal interjected

"Fuck no! We fucking bombed their country back into the Stone Age! They were living off rice and rat meat after we pulled out of their country."

"Maybe so, but we didn't win either, you douchebag! We left, and the commies took over the whole country."

"Good, those fucking gooks weren't worth saving. They wanted to be commies, so they got the government they wanted in the end... Fucking Ho Chi Minh!"

"Actually, Philster, they got Le Duan. Ho Chi Minh died in 1969 before the war ended. But aside from that, you never answered my question," Scorzoletti asked calmly.

"Oh, Sal, we left their fucking country! What do you want me to say?"

"I expect you to say that since we went over to Vietnam to prevent their country from falling under communist rule, but we didn't succeed...then we lost."

"The same thing happened in Afghanistan with the Soviets."

"Yeah, the Soviets got a double dose of humble pie," Miles said with a laugh. "Those guys lost a war to a bunch of shepherds and cavemen."

"Oh, shut up, you douchebag! They weren't cavemen."

"Cavemen...cave dwellers... What does it matter, Max? They were primitives in battle compared to the Soviets."

"But the Soviets were never able to subdue them," Scorzoletti interjected above the growing clamor. "So, in the final analysis, there's more to waging and winning a war than superior fire-power. In both of those countries, the indigenous people used the lay of the land and

144

the enemies' own weapons against them. That's exactly what we're going to do."

"There's one thing you're forgetting, Sal," said Philster.

"What's that?"

"We're going to be fighting our enemy in his own territory."

"Only if we let him pick the battles, and that's one thing we're not going to do. We're going to hit and run. We're also going to use the anarchy so amply provided by our democratic traitors to hit and run. Our first objective is to get armed and supplied with plenty of ammunition. After that, we're going to start righting some wrongs in this country that should've be dealt with a long time ago, but first things first." Scorzoletti turned to Nixon. "What kind of inventory are we talking about at the Amory in Machesney?"

"You name it, brother, and they got it," Nixon replied.

"LAWS rockets?"

"They not only have LAWS rocket launchers; they also have Javelin anti-tank missiles. In fact, they even have the even more lethal F Javelins, but since those are assembled in Alabama, it's not certain how many they stock in Machesney."

"We have to be able to take out armor because it's sure they'll bring that to the fight. Hell, I'd even consider Howitzers if we had the logistical support."

"Who the fuck needs Howitzers when Alvarez can hack into weapons systems of ships anywhere off our shores and commandeer cruise missiles to strike at designated coordinates," Philster interrupted.

Scorzoletti's eyebrows rose as a smile slid across his face while he nodded.

"You can really do something like that?" he asked Alvarez.

"You bet your fucking balls he can!" Philster retorted.

"How come ONI never made a special home for him with that kind of knowledge?" Scorzoletti asked Philster with a pensive look.

"How come? How come?" Philster began excitedly. "I'll tell you how come..."

"Can you ever say something without getting a bunch in your

panties like a menopausal douchebag," Max interrupted with a smirk.

"Yeah, I was getting there, Brillo head, but it's frustrating to talk about someone who could've feathered my career nest, but, instead, wanted to smoke pot, spend his life playing video games, and live in fancy-schmansy Kenilworth…He could've been a fucking VADM with his knowledge and ability!"

"Why did you leave the Navy?" Scorzoletti asked pointedly as he turned to Alvarez.

"Sal, it just wasn't for me," Alvarez began sheepishly. "I wasn't a people person when I enlisted, and that never changed after eight years. In the final analysis, I was dishonorably discharged."

"Oh, Christ Almighty! You weren't a people person, but you fucking enlisted in the Navy straight out of high school? What, were you fucking high or something? Did you think military life was gonna be like living in a fucking monastery or something?" Philster ranted.

"No, I just thought it would force me to get outside of myself. You know, sort of lighten up and be one of the guys." Alvarez replied.

"Oh, for Christ's sake, Alvarez, you kill me! You should have just lived in your parents' basement and watched porn movies for the rest of your life." Philster said, turning red.

"Hey, douchebag, did you by any chance steal any Seroquel from that pharmacy?" Max asked.

"No, why should I?" Philster asked. "Nobody here is bipolar."

"You're about as close as it gets, douchebag. You could use about three hundred milligrams right in the ass. Chill you the fuck out."

"Oh yeah, I bet that would do it for you, huh? Looking at my ass would probably float your boat, wouldn't it, Doctor Deprave-o? That's probably why you enlisted for BUMED. You wanted to become a ship's doctor so you could harpoon all the guys in the ass when they came back from shore leave with the clap."

Philster turned to Miles Sano, who was just shaking his head and laughing.

"And what the fuck are you cackling at? Are you a fucking hyena or something?"

"Oh, eat shit, you douchebag," Max shot back. "I just wanted to become a doctor courtesy of Uncle Sam so I didn't have to go to medical school on the outside and graduate with a half-million-dollar debt burden. I got tired of NYU after a point."

Jake Pool, who had been reclining on the sofa with his hands clasped behind his back, finally spoke.

"Say, Nixon, you think they'd have any MK21 rifles or McMillan TAC-50s out at Machesney?"

Philster froze, then put his hands up in the air and shook his head with a bewildered look.

"What the fuck does that have to do with what we're talking about, Jake?"

"Nothing...absolutely nothing, but before you went off on a tangent, as you are frequently inclined to do, we were talking about the weapons inventory at Machesney," Jake said flatly. "A MK21 rifle and a McMillan TAC-50 are two of the best long-range sniper rifles."

"He's right, Philster," Scorzo said. "I'm a little concerned about your focus."

"There's nothing wrong with my focus, Sal! You were talking about Howitzers, and I brought up weapons systems that our resident geek Alvarez could requisition for us free of charge."

Philster looked around, first at Scorzoletti, and then Max before glaring at Jake as he resumed.

"What, aren't ship-to-shore cruise missiles weapons? How the fuck is mentioning something like that considered going off on a tangent? That's what I'd like to know!"

Philster quickly shifted his focus to Scorzoletti.

"And, Sal, you were the one who asked Alvarez why he left the Navy. That's what took us off topic! So how the fuck did I get us off on a tangent, huh? Can you tell me that? What's the fucking problem with my focus?"

Scorzoletti took in a deep breath and let it out as he rubbed his forehead.

"Look, just drop it, Philster,"

"I don't want to drop it! I don't want to drop it! Everybody's always on my case saying shit like 'You're like a menopausal bitch,' and 'Why do you always gotta be so hyper,' or 'You get more excited than a teenage girl at a lesbian pajama party!'"

A grin slid across the side of Max's mouth as he looked at Miles, who began laughing.

"How come nobody says anything about Miles always laughing like a fucking hyena all the time?"

"Because the ol' boy be wacko, douchebag, and, anyway, you know you sound like a fucking teenage girl on the rag too, so why don't you just go outside and suck on a tree stump."

Philster shook his head and started laughing as he looked at Scorzoletti.

"You see the kind a shit I have to put up with?"

"Look, you grew up in a big family. Didn't any of your brothers and sisters give you a hard time," Scorzoletti asked with a tone of genuine curiosity.

"Oh, Christ Almighty, don't even get me started with those retards..."

Scorzoletti inhaled through his teeth and put his hands up as if to physically prompt Philster to stop.

"Think of our crew as your family..."

"Every bit as dysfunctional as my own, so that should be easy."

"Be that as it may, we have to see each other as brothers and watch each other's six like we're as tight as family. We need to live like there was no past...no wives, girlfriends, mothers or fathers, brothers or sisters... all that's gone now. We are all each other has going forward. We are just like enlisted men going back into the shit all over again, and sometimes grunts and specialists alike are sarcastic with one another and give each other shit. At the end of the day, however, we all take it in stride because our mutual need to accomplish our missions and survive to see another day is greater than any petty little differences we have. Is that clear?"

Scorzoletti scanned the room and looked at each man, and they nodded in assent.

"With all that said, we need to be about the business of reconnaissance on the Machesney armory." Scorzoletti clasped his hands and rubbed them together. "Mohammed, I'm going to need you to go through your people and get us nine fully automatic HK416 A5s with thirty-round clips, eleven-inch barrel lengths, and sound suppressors. Top priority is to be for AK-47s with hundred-round boxes that contain armor-piercing tracer rounds."

"Look, Sal, I hate to steal your thunder," Philster interjected, "but why in the fuck would you want to use tracers that would give away our position?"

"Armor-piercing tracers won't give away our position because we're going to hit what we aim for, and our targets will be dead if we need to use lethal firepower. Our purpose here is to strike fear into the hearts of our adversaries and have them retreat while we advance on their positions. Now may I continue?" Sal turned back to Mohammed. "I want five thousand rounds of ammo for the AKs. In addition, I want nine fully automatic Glock 19s with hundred-round clips. We can't go purchasing that combination of weapons online or through traditional gun dealers without coming up on the ATF's radar. We're also going to need a large supply of armor-piercing ammo for both of those weapons, and a supply of incendiary rounds for the Glock 19s."

"Will that be all?"

"No," Scorzoletti continued, "I want nine AA12 fully automatic shotguns with thirty-two-round capacity drums. I also want three dozen high-explosive FRAG-12 grenades for them, and nine .300 blackout pistols converted to fully automatic fire with sound suppressors and folding stocks for dual use in distance and close-range kills—and mounted with laser sights. I want ten thousand rounds of 147-grain supersonic ammo for these babies, and last but not least, I want ten XM556 Micro-guns with 1,200-round boxes. I realize that last order might be a bit challenging, but it's the most imperative."

"Man oh man, you sound like a cat that be placing a special order at Burger King," Nixon chimed in. "You can get everything you mentioned from Machesney including the XM556 Micro-guns, but

1,200-round boxes are heavy as hell. If you don't mind me asking, why the hell are we gonna be hitting Machesney if Mohammed can get all this stuff for us?"

"Because the XM556s and the necessary ammo would be way too heavy to carry and transport."

"You said it, my friend," Mohammed replied. "The XM556 Micro's ammo would be cumbersome to say the least."

"With a cyclic fire rate of four thousand rounds per minute, we could put down an entire regiment in under one minute. All we need is one from Machesney to lay down cover fire while we're loading arms and getting out of Dodge. The hundred-round Glocks won't require a battery, they're handheld, and they can lay down an impressive amount of suppressive fire."

"Jesus H. Christ, Sal, you'd fire on our own military?"

"I was thinking more along the lines of CLM or AntiCap because they usually have assemblies of between six hundred to twelve hundred rioters, but if our troops or other federal agencies engaged us, I would definitely return fire. You men must understand something… when the military or federal authorities are taking orders from radical leftists, they're no longer our comrades. They're the enemy…plain and simple."

A pall of silence fell over the faces of the men as they looked at Scorzo before Mohammed broke the silence. Perhaps it was the first time that Scorzo's men understood that he wasn't looking for payback for his daughter's life. He was preparing to fight an enemy that had taken possession of his country's soul.

"Will you be needing anything else from me?"

"Well, actually, now that you mention it…" Scorzoletti added as he stroked the beard stubble along the sides of his face. "I'm also going to need a dozen black and white shemagh desert scarves, and two sherwani…"

"Scorzo, what the fuck are we preparing to do? Go trick or treating and waste anybody that doesn't have candy?" Philster said, scratching his head with a quizzical look on his face.

"No, these are things we need to misdirect our pursuers."

"Oh fuck, that's great…the fucking Muslim angle. Yeah, those motherfuckers need pursuing."

"You know, my friend," Mohammed said, ignoring Philster and looking at Scorzoletti, "you probably want to go with mid-length tunics instead of sherwani. It isn't easy to move fast when wearing a sherwani."

"Only two stationaries who are taking up perimeter positions will wear the sherwani. The rest of us who are doing the insertion will be wearing the tunics. By the way, the clothing will be the priority. We're going to need to be wearing that stuff night and day, so we get comfortable maneuvering in that kind of attire."

"Is that all, my friend?"

"No, Jake and Gonzalez are going to need some sniper recon clothing and gear, and, in addition, a nice drone so we can get pictures of this place and be familiar with the facility and the surrounding area. The people there know it well, and that gives them an unnecessary advantage. We can't have that, so we need to know the facility and the lay of the land as well as they do."

"Anything else, my friend?"

"I think my grocery list with you is complete."

Scorzoletti then turned to Alvarez.

"From you, I'll need the blueprints for the place with corresponding inventory locations for all the weapons, so hack into whatever place you have to in order to get me that. Finally, we'll need to rent a couple of trucks under an assumed name with government plates. That will get us past the entry without any shots fired."

"Consider it done," Alvarez replied.

"So, let me understand something here," Philster began. "Are you saying we have to wear those fucking jihadist rags until we actually engage our target?"

"You bet your BVDs we do. We have to be as comfortable wearing this type of clothing as a jihadist himself would be, so we're going to shoot, shit, sleep, and shave in this garb."

"What's next, Sal? Are we going to have to go to the mosque five times a day and read the fucking Koran?" Philster asked with annoyance. "And another thing...if we're wearing these turbans and tunics, what good will government plates do us?"

"No douchebag, just you," Max answered. "You'll wear a turban like an Ayatollah. We'll all kiss your hand when we're entering the compound," Max interjected with ensuing laughter from the others. "The guards will think we're Iraqi insurgents fighting for the US."

Scorzo laughed and shook his head in disagreement before speaking.

"Put a few copies of the Koran on my shopping list that can be left at the scenes where we engage the enemy. That would add some extra authenticity to our cover," Scorzoletti said, turning to Mohammed.

"Can I purchase them online, or does it need to be in-person from a retailer?"

"Neither. Anyone examining a site where one of those were left would see a brand-new, unread copy of the Koran as something deliberately planted. I need you to get me a few well-worn copies from amongst your contacts. If they're tattered and contain notes and pages that are bent at the corners, that's all the better...nothing online, and definitely nothing new."

"Okay, my friend, but that will not be easy. In fact, of everything you have asked for, that will be the most difficult."

"Mohammed, why the fuck would that be the hardest thing to get? I mean for God's sake it's just a fucking book! And it's a shitty one at that. Why would any of those pricks you know care about parting with a worn and tattered copy of the Koran? Can you tell me that?" Philster railed.

"Because it becomes like a sacred part of their faith through continual use and study. A Koran that is worn and marked with a lot of notes is a sign that the believer who possesses it has faith that grants him the favor of Allah. His focus is on the spiritual path to Allah instead of the evil ways of this world."

Philster rolled his eyes and began fidgeting with his hands and shaking his head. "Just offer them forty black-eyed virgins and they'll

152

all be running to a used bookstore if they don't want to give up their own copies. Either that or steal some from some local mosques."

"Oh, I couldn't steal copies of the Koran from mosques. That would be detestable. And if I should be caught, I could get my hands cut off."

"Oh God! Holy-fucking-moly! Those Koran-reading mother-fuckers are the ones who cause most of the evil ways of this world! The only reason those stupid fucks follow Islam is because their focus is on the path to pussy! Those bushy-bearded fucks couldn't give a shit less about the will of Allah and holiness. I mean, pussy is the only reason I can think of that would make a horny young mother-fucker strap a bomb to his body and blow himself up...he thinks he's gonna be put up in a mansion with forty black-eyed virgins who will satisfy his every sexual desire the instant he dies and goes floating up to Allah. If anyone catches you, just say you're evangelizing some filthy infidels for Allah."

"All right, give it a rest, Philster," Scorzoletti said abruptly as he looked at Philster and then turned to Mohammed. "Don't mind him, Mohammed; just do the best you can, okay?"

"Yeah, he's just pissed off because his mother was Muslim," Max added with a grin on his face that immediately created spasms of laughter in Miles. "He can't stand it that he's half Muslim." Max knew there wasn't a shadow of truth to his allegation about Philster, but he wanted to placate Mohammed, and at the same time he wanted to see Philster go off on another one of his tirades. An ominous glance from Scorzo laid the issue to rest, and Mohammed departed to fulfill Scorzo's order.

Chapter 11
Ghosts in the Machine

—ᴧᴧ—

As the weeks passed and Julie Scorzoletti adapted to her life back in China, her husband zealously took on the role of a SEAL team leader, and he trained his men harder than they would be trained if they were actively a part of the TEAMS. In his mind, they had to be faster, deadlier, and more knowledgeable than any force that would be brought against them. Everything he knew about weapons and tradecraft he taught them to shore up any deficiencies they had. He designated Miles as his instructor on hand-to-hand combat, with weapons and without them. Miles taught the others how to use common things they might find in a variety of environments as weapons, be they pencils, pens, a serrated bottle cap, or a tie on someone's neck. Scorzoletti wanted each of his men to be a weapon, every bit as lethal as if they were armed. So, it came to pass when September arrived, Scorzoletti and his men were well trained and sufficiently armed for their siege of the Machesney Park armory.

It was a warm, cloudy evening on September 11 when Scorzoletti and his men headed toward the armory in three special vans that had been modified with armor plating, bulletproof windows, and 426 Hemi engines to provide power and speed as well as compensate for the added weight of the armor plating. They were also clad in the clothing that made them appear to be Islamic radicals, but their license plates were government issued. Their adrenaline was high, their senses acutely attuned to their environment, enhanced by dextroamphetamine tablets fifteen minutes prior to their arrival.

At the same time Scorzoletti and his men were undertaking their siege on the Machesney Park armory, Contreras was probing the mind of Bickens in the DEA's Chicago field office regarding Philster. It didn't make sense to Contreras that Philster left the safety of the Palmer House and surfaced in Winnetka. Moreover, the fact that he would risk committing a crime that would land him back in a federal penitentiary seemed even more illogical. As such, Contreras was resigned to the fact that he needed to work with Bickens and share whatever information he and his team could gather through their contacts on the streets and in prison that might explain the motive for Philster's actions and what his next moves were likely to be. Bickens assumed a posture of collaboration with Contreras, but he felt no inclination for mutual reciprocity concerning the flow of information. Neither man held a high enough security clearance for securing direct access to information on Philster, but Bickens was connected to Philster's world through ONI's Deputy Commander Richard Pierpont. That, however, was something he had no intention of divulging to Contreras. It was his intention to come off as clueless as Contreras was about Philster's motives.

"Now that we've confirmed the man we captured on photo surveillance in Winnetka is indeed your asset Steven Philster, what are your ideas as to why he would leave the comfortable and protected lifestyle you set up for him?"

"Well, our extension of protection was without limits, but the comfortable lifestyle had limits. He had to become self-sufficient within ninety days," Bickens stated deceitfully.

"That doesn't make any sense," Contreras retorted, as the lines on his forehead rose upward. "If that's true, why would he leave a posh dwelling at the Palmer House Hotel, dispense with his credit cards, and abandon his car? It doesn't add up."

"It doesn't add up if your assumption is that he did these things of his own volition, but I think there were other reasons that prevailed upon him."

"Such as?"

"Such as the fact that he had some vices which led to his hasty departure. His room looked as though an altercation had taken place."

"Yet the people at the front desk and one of the women on the floor from housekeeping all confirmed that the last time he was seen leaving the hotel, he was by himself. Moreover, the woman in house-keeping said that he appeared clean-shaven, well groomed, and well dressed. There was nothing disheveled in his appearance nor indicative of an altercation even though his room was in disarray."

"You mean your people interviewed personnel at the Palmer House?" Bickens asked.

"Yes, of course."

"Why didn't you just ask me if you wanted information regarding Philster's departure from the Palmer House? Did you think I wouldn't be forthcoming with information?"

"Not at all, but some information is better when you get it first-hand from the source."

"Agent Contreras, I am the source when it comes to information on Steven Philster."

"Yes, of course," Contreras began in a conciliatory tone, "but you know how witnesses can be. Initially they tell an investigator what they believe is all the information only to remember some other details at a later point in time. I'm sure you've had that happen in your career."

"No, no, I don't believe I have. I do a very thorough job in my interviewing and crime scene investigations, so I can't recall that happening during my career."

"Getting back to this issue of Mr. Philster's vices. What kind of vices are we talking about?"

"He loved his hookers and loved tranquilizers…benzodiazepines. Xanax, ground to a powder and added to Coca-Cola, was his favorite."

"Xanax was among the controlled substances stolen from Sonny's Drug, but, as I've told you, there was quite a large inventory of controlled substances stolen from Sonny's. Moreover, I'm puzzled why this guy took the risk of engaging in a burglary up in Winnetka, of all places, when he could have easily acquired some Xanax with a visit to any doctor near the Palmer House."

"You're right, and I don't have any logical answers for you. I can only hazard a reasonable guess."

"Okay, I'm all ears."

"All right… He connected with a hooker on the evening prior to his departure. In addition to sex, he also wanted tranquilizers. Being unfamiliar with the area, he asks the hooker if she can provide him with a connection. She makes a call to a dealer she knows, and he or she arrives with benzos. The dealer and her see a guy who's alone, apparently well-to-do, and an easy target to roll. So, they slip him a few bars of Xanax in his champagne, unbeknownst to him, and before long he's comatose. Naturally, at that point they grab his wallet and steal all his cash and credit cards that are readily available, and then they ransack the room in search of any other hidden money or jewelry. A little later they slip out one at a time. The next morning Philster realizes what happened and embarks on a quest to turn things around."

"Why wouldn't he just inform you of what happened? Why take flight when he has you as a safety net?"

"I don't presume to know what's in the minds of men like that, but the facts we're left with is that he shows up on our radar in Winnetka on the same night a pharmacy there is burglarized. The burglary is executed exactly the way someone with his background would pull something like that off."

"Well, I guess we'll just have to wait until we catch him before we can unravel that mystery. Since you know this guy, where do your instincts tell you we should go from here?"

Bickens thought he knew exactly where Philster wanted to go, but he wasn't about to share that information with Contreras.

"Well, seeing as how we have a license plate from the photo-surveillance picture in Winnetka, I think the best way to use your team would be start following that lead. Perhaps that may tie into something that makes sense about Philster's actions and his movements."

"What about your team?" Contreras asked.

"Well, it seems that the only thing we can presently do is continue to follow the course of your investigation of him."

"What about his transfer of illegal weapons?"

"That's ancient history. He gave up people who led to convictions and he served some time. The same way he did this time. So, we only want him for information. There's nothing we have on him presently...well, except for the possible theft of narcotics, but that's within the charter of your agency, not mine."

"Then you don't believe he's with your shooter in Mississippi?"

"No, that definitely wouldn't be a wise choice of travel companions. It would be like travelling around with a big neon sign saying 'fugitive...call 911.'"

"If he isn't with your shooter from Mississippi, why would Philster know his whereabouts or anything else about him?"

"Because Philster is like a dandelion."

"I am not a botanist," Contreras replied with a chuckle.

"A dandelion is a resilient, nasty weed, but it has a deep root. You can yank out the portion that's visible, but if you don't get the whole root, it just grows back. Our friend Mr. Philster provides authorities with the unsightly things we see, things he's associated with, but he's never rooted out of society by justice. He disappears for a while only to reappear again."

"Well, unfortunately, Dexter Blithe, the man associated with the license plate on their vehicle, was found dead at his residence, so that's another dead-end."

"Not necessarily—the DEA needs to drill down deeper. Interview anyone associated with him in the area. What seems like a dead-end may turn out to be a treasure trove of information."

"You will be returning to Washington then?"

"No, I will be doing a parallel investigation that will involve teamwork between both of our agencies, so I will be working out of the Chicago office for now," Bickens replied.

"What kind of parallel investigation?"

"An investigation searching for arms purchases in exchange for drugs. With his credit cards gone, and his ATF funds frozen after his disappearance, he would need some other form of capital. In the black market, drugs are a form of collateral that's just like money, especially pure pharmaceutical-grade drugs."

"Why would Philster want to purchase arms with these drugs instead of just sell them for cash?"

"Cash can be used for any purpose with anyone that might give our mutual friends up," Bickens suggested. "Drugs, however, limit you to criminals who aren't eager to seek out police with information. Moreover, drugs can only be sold one time for a single use. Guns can be sold multiple times, so they have a higher resale value than drugs."

"I didn't consider that," Contreras replied with a sound of naivety.

"That's understandable," Bickens said in a conciliatory tone, "your market in vice is always a one-time sale and one-time consumption, unless, of course, you're talking a larger scale distribution. But the result is always the same...once the supply is gone, so is the opportunity for profit. In our world, there can be multiple sales of arms shipments to many opposing groups of people who initially use the arms and then sell them to another group for a profit. You can't do the same thing with drugs. Once they're sold and consumed, they're gone."

"That makes a lot of sense," Contreras conceded.

"Of course, that's why it's the most likely scenario. It was the same thing with the human trafficking he was involved in. Human beings who are trafficked, regardless of the form of slavery they are sold into, will continue to yield profits for those who control them, and they can also be resold multiple times for a profit. Our friend Philster always deals in vices, and black-market commodities that have high resale value yielding continuous streams of income."

While Bickens' explanation did make logical sense, he didn't believe in the scenario he offered Contreras. It was no more than a clever ruse to convince Contreras that the two men and their agencies had a common goal while Bickens pursued another path that he had no intention of sharing with Contreras. Bickens' goal was to leech any information from Contreras that would be useful to the ATF while giving no useful information in return.

Just as Bickens was about to turn to Richard Pierpont for information that would have been detrimental to Scorzoletti and his team, news came out of the Chicago ATF office that a daring arms theft had taken place at the Machesney Park armory while Bickens was busy offering his logical cover story about Philster to Contreras. Interest in Philster and Scorzoletti was immediately supplanted by the events that transpired at the Machesney Park armory for two reasons.

First, this was a major event within the jurisdiction of the ATF. Secondly, it bore resemblance to Contreras' Project Cassandra, so it commandeered the full interest of Bickens and Contreras. The media, however, was not reporting information that Bickens and Contreras were privy to. The media only divulged that a large cache of weapons was successfully stolen during a daring, precision strike on the armory by an unknown group of perpetrators. When journalists on the scene were questioned about the identity of the group, they offered the tentative theory that it might possibly be white supremacists or some faction of a neo-Nazi group since they often have military backgrounds and they are prone to stockpiling arms and ammunition identical to that which was stolen during this heist. This was offered up for public consumption even though military personnel who engaged the perpetrators provided a description of them as radical Islamic militants. They were dressed like Islamic militants, they were armed with AK-47 fully automatic weapons, and they were shouting "Allahu Akbar." Moreover, the event took place on the anniversary of 9/11.

Contreras and his team continued to pursue what they believed to be legitimate leads on Philster, while Bickens requested approval to work with the Chicago ATF field office, suggesting that the attack on the Machesney Park armory could possibly have been orchestrated by Philster or may lead to him because of his background of dealing in arms and also working with certain Middle Eastern militias when it served the interest of the US. Like Contreras, he bought in to the information provided by troops at the scene that it was Islamic jihadists, especially since the media was avoiding the implication of Islamic terrorists like the plague.

As both Contreras and Bickens treaded down different paths pursuing a connection to Islamic jihadists, Scorzoletti and his men felt the spoils of victory in an operation that achieved exactly what they planned. Philster was gregariously lambasting a media restricted by political correctness upon return to their compound at Fox Lake.

"Are we fucking good, or are we good…huh, Sal? I told you the media was gonna come up with some bullshit coverage to convince the public that the Machesney Park operation was anything but Muslim extremists! Didn't I tell you?"

"You did at that," Scorzoletti agreed with a smile. "That's why I made us all prepare for it by living in those clothes. We not only looked the part, but I'm sure we smelled the part as well."

"Man, I swear, Sal, those fucking globalists that control the media will do anything to protect those fucking Muslims! Their politically correct agenda is fucking unbelievable!"

"You know, that's something I couldn't understand in the Navy, and I still can't wrap my arms around it," Alvarez said. "Why? Why would they want to protect our enemies?"

"Because they're a mobile army that can be used by the wealthy elite to incite chaos and discord that plays into the globalist agenda," Philster shot out immediately. "And not only that, but we actually have those motherfuckers in government now! Did you hear what that bitch in Congress from Ohio said, 'It doesn't surprise me that the prevailing racism and xenophobia in this country would give rise to such incredulous lies.'"

"I think you've been watching too many YouTube videos, douchebag!" Max said as he and the others looked to Scorzoletti.

"I have to agree with him, gentlemen. He's on the money with that idea."

"How so?" Jake asked.

"Case in point, Afghanistan… We used indigenous Muslims in that country as freedom fighters against the Soviets when they invaded that country. We trained them, armed them, and supplied them. Most important, we sold them on the truth, which was that the Soviets would crush Islam and deny Muslims of their ability to worship Allah. The extinction of their religion became more important than economic, political, or cultural differences. Islam was and always has been at the heart of their identity. They were willing to die for the cause of Islam. In fact, that was the conflict that gave birth to suicide bombers."

"Yeah, but that was during the Cold War," Gonzo added. "Since then, they've always been our enemies."

"Not true," Scorzoletti continued. "Remember when the Philippines requested our help in Mindanao? Muslims there wanted to break free of the archipelago and become an independent Islamic nation? So, we recruited and imported Shia Islamic fighters that were opposed to the Abu-Sayyaf, who followed the Sunni branch of Islam. Now make no mistake about it; those Shia Muslims were never crazy about us, but they just happened to hate the Sunnis more than they hated us."

"Can you believe that shit!" Philster half shouted. "Not only do those idiots hate all non-Muslims, but they even hate each other! I swear, those people have shit for brains, and that bitch in Congress had the opportunity to grow up here and go to college and become an elected official in our country and she fucking hates America and Americans."

"Maybe so," Scorzoletti countered, "but sell them on the idea to fight and point them in the direction of their newest enemy, and they'll go into the fight using their own body as a bomb if it's the only way to kill their adversary. It doesn't get more lethal than that. Especially when you consider that our strategy is always to go into a fight and come out with as little loss of life in our numbers as possible…"

Philster paced around the room as Scorzoletti was talking as though he couldn't wait to add a counterpoint. Finally, he just blurted it out.

"There's only one cause that those rag headed jagoffs fight for, Sal, and that's pussy! Well, with the exception of that bitch in the state of Ohio. I'd like to place a bar of c-4 under that turban she's always wearing."

"They're not all suicide bombers," Jake said. "I remember being in a firefight with some Abu-Sayyaf and we were taking some heavy fire, so this Filipino Muslim I had trained threw himself on top of me to cover me from incoming fire. It doesn't get more righteous than that."

"Yeah, the guys that worked with us in Mindanao only had the arms we supplied them with, and they never engaged in any panic fire," Gonzo added. "It was basically one shot, one kill as far as they were concerned. Muslim or not, they were some good boys. I didn't see any suicide bombers over there."

"Oh my God, you guys are naïve!" Philster exclaimed. "They don't need to visit Allah's shop of pleasures to have sex with virgins. They just rape virgins in the locations where they're fighting. Remember when Iraq invaded Kuwait? The first thing those horny pricks started to do wherever they assumed control was rape any female they saw. Kuwait was the place where they developed a strong liking for Filipinas because there were tons of Filipinas over there working as nurses and in other service industries like housekeeping for hotels. For some reason or another, they seemed particularly fond of sodomizing their Filipina captives. Maybe that's the way Allah tells those fuckers to rape infidels, who the fuck knows! And what about the Abu-Sayyaf who kidnap visiting tourists with MILFs and young daughters. You think they build a campfire and sit around reading their captives the Koran and try to convert them? Fuck no, they rape the shit out of them and then sell them to traffickers."

"No, it's more likely that Allah forbids them from engaging in that type of activity with Muslim women because it's unclean," Scorzoletti countered. "They probably rationalize that since infidels are dirty, Allah will give them a pass for engaging in sex acts like that with non-Muslim women."

"Sal, you give those bastards too much credit for integrity!" Philster continued to pace around the room. "Don't forget the Anfal campaign in which Saddam's forces tried to wipe out the Kurds. Even though there was a religious mixture of faiths amongst them, most of them were Muslim, and all the women amongst them took it up the rear from Saddam's troops! What about that, huh?"

"Okay, calm down, douchebag!" Max piped in. "So, Muslims enjoy doing girls dirty…but I bet you do too!"

"Yeah, yeah, yeah," Philster responded, amidst the laughter of the guys before abruptly changing the direction of the discussion. "Hey, anyway, the feds are going to be chasing their tails looking for Islamic extremists while everybody else in the country will be inundating their offices with bullshit leads on white supremacists and neo-Nazis! We're too good to be true!"

"Hey, Philster, remember that pride goeth before a fall," Scorzoletti warned.

"Ah come on, Sal, let's take credit where credit is due. The idea of masquerading as Islamic jihadists was pretty fucking good!"

"Duly noted, Philster, but let's not get swelled heads. It was a successful red herring that bought us some time, but we'll have to successfully piggyback on that operation for our next move. Our next move will be fraught with difficulty, so we need to maintain perspective on our capabilities. Most of all we need to stay humble. Another thing we need to make happen immediately," Scorzoletti said with emphasis as he turned to Mohammed, "I need you to have one of your people in ISIS contact the ATF and a few conservative news networks and take credit for the theft at the Machesney Park armory."

Chapter 12
The Circle Widens

Scorzoletti's admonition to his men and his use of misinformation was prudent. He knew that his itinerary would bring a formidable force against them. In fact, as Scorzoletti began to discuss his plans to rob the Federal Reserve Bank of Chicago, President Courtland called on General William Seaquest, a brilliant leader who Courtland served under during the conflict in Vietnam. Courtland had previously been briefed by Brandon James, the director of Counterintelligence in the FBI, but the president neither liked nor trusted him. James gave his loyalty to the progressive, democratic socialist party, and the president suspected him of leaking sensitive information to the press as well as forming and funding the group named the Anti-Capitalists, better known as simply AntiCap.

General Seaquest, on the other hand, embodied everything that President Courtland respected. Seaquest was a highly decorated general who was conservative, patriotic, and an ardent opponent of groups like AntiCap. He saw AntiCap as nothing less than a group of communist thugs who resorted to violence and terror tactics to suppress the voices and opinions of patriots who wanted to take their country back from career politicians leading America down the path of socialism. Both men were opposed to the vast influx of Muslim migrants during the previous administration of President Allen Sayed Osama. Both men mutually agreed that Islam and Western society were fundamentally incompatible. General Seaquest was also a man who was deeply knowledgeable about the Koran and Islamic culture. That was another reason why President Courtland wanted his opinion on the Machesney Park armory theft.

"General Seaquest, I trusted you on the battlefield in Vietnam, and I presently find myself on another battlefield as I sit in the Oval Office. This time the enemy isn't firing bullets at me. They're waging a war of words against me and I'm surrounded on all sides."

"President Courtland, you have my undying loyalty and steadfast allegiance. I'm always at your service, sir; I think you know that. So, how can I help you."

"Well, I'd like your opinion on the theft that occurred at the Machesney Park armory. As you know, the media reported a cover story that indicated the culprits were either white supremacists or neo-Nazis because it's not politically expedient these days to implicate Muslims in anything controversial, especially since this took place on 9/11. Your boots on the ground, however, stated that it was militant Islamic jihadists, but something just doesn't sit right with me on either alternative. You went there, and you talked to your men. I'd like to get your input on this, so give it to me straight, General."

"Well, while Islamic militants would certainly have a motive for pulling something like that off, they'd also have no reservations about coming in with guns blazing and taking out as many of our boys as possible. Killing infidels is something that Islamic extremists believe is a service rendered to Allah."

"Exactly! I heard that they relied completely on non-lethal weapons throughout the incident, even though James over at FBI counterintelligence contradicts that. He states that the terrorists spent over a couple hundred rounds of ammo as they engaged our boys."

"Not true," General Seaquest replied flatly. "Though they did expend a couple hundred rounds of ammunition, they fired into the air or at the ground in front of our boys. They never aimed at our boys and engaged them."

"That doesn't make sense at all."

"Nothing about this incident does, Mr. President. When they arrived at the armory with a caravan of three vehicles, two men came up from the rear of the caravan and subdued the guards with Tasers. Then they bound their wrists and ankles and gagged them but left them where they were unharmed. When they encountered other personnel, who were out of range for using a Taser, they resorted to the use of a laser diode."

"What does that do?"

"It interferes with the electrical circuitry of the brain and essentially renders individuals non compos mentis, so they are neutralized as a threat. It can also cause blindness if it is aimed directly at the eyes, but this didn't happen during the incident. The laser diode was used by our forces in the Middle East because it has a ten-mile range of effectiveness and it only requires minimal exposure to achieve its goal."

"What else did James and our media fail to report?" the president asked.

"Aside from shouting Allahu Akbar, there was no verbal communication between these guys. Everything was communicated through hand signals and nods. That's the strangest thing about this incident."

"Do you think they were trying to maintain silence in order to minimize the amount of personnel they would have to engage?"

"No, that can effectively be ruled out," said the general. "Whether they were shouting directives to others within their group, or they were as quiet as church mice, our personnel heard the shooting and commotion of our own men as the group was leaving. That was their call to action, but the problem was that by the time it was clear that there was a problem, these guys already had a massive amount of ammunition and arms and they were on their way out of the facility."

"So, general, what are your ideas about this very unusual incident?"

"There are multiple scenarios, all of which are valid. They could have indeed been Islamic jihadists with limited firepower seeking to avoid a protracted firefight against overwhelming forces with superior firepower. It's a matter of simple common sense."

"Why would they dress in a manner that clearly identifies them as Islamic extremists? They must know that we've infiltrated various cells in the US, and they can't just roll up in any neighborhood with a caravan containing a huge number of weapons and ammunition, especially when they're dressed like Islamic fundamentalists. People are going to notice something like that."

"You're correct! Indeed, they would. That's why I suspect that they chose a remote, rural area where there's no neighbors to notice them or their activities. It might be close to Machesney Park. That may be the reason they targeted that particular armory."

"Okay, give me another scenario."

"They could be preppers or militia groups who assumed the appearance of Islamic fundamentalists to portray Muslims in a negative way and generate hatred toward them. It's no secret that most militia groups and others on the fringe right hold Muslims in contempt for their refusal to assimilate into the culture of countries they migrate to while demanding that host countries accept their ways. Simply put, they see Islamic ideology as a direct threat to their existence, and if they can direct large-scale animosity or even violence toward them, they believe that the Muslims will back down with their vocal protests and complaints of racism and Islamophobia."

"Given the way they behave, that scenario makes the best sense yet," President Courtland declared.

"Well, there's actually one more scenario that's even scarier. The heist on Machesney could have been pulled off by friendlies."

"Friendlies? Who would that be?"

"Current military personnel or recently discharged military personnel."

"Why would members of our own armed forces do something like that?"

"Their motives are questionable, but they sure carried out the heist with the precision of a special forces unit. They knew their terrain well, they managed to carry out their objective without being detected until they were leaving, and they used non-lethal weapons against our boys. Any Muslim terrorist group would have killed as many soldiers as possible."

"I appreciate you raising all the possibilities, General, but I'm not willing to accept that members of our own military are behind that theft."

"I didn't say they were, President Courtland. It's merely a possible scenario. In any event, sir, you can't stay silent on this forever. You are the commander-in-chief, and an incident like this is a matter of national security that you'll have to weigh in on with the press."

"The only credible source of information that I have at this point are the eyewitness accounts from personnel at the armory. That's what the press will be given."

"You know what they're going to say since they've already created the narrative that the suspects are likely white supremacists or neo-Nazis?"

"Yes, they're going to say I'm a racist who's sympathetic to ultra-right fringe groups. So, what else is new?"

"Your assessment is on point, and boy, I'm sure glad I don't have to walk in your shoes."

"Ah, it's not all that bad, General. Truth and due diligence to our leftist controlled media is like a foreign language. They just don't understand it. It will be easy to accuse them of irresponsible journalism on this one in light of the firsthand eyewitness accounts provided by armory personnel."

The president decided he would hold a press briefing at the White House at midday regarding the Machesney Park armory theft. Fortunately, news outlets began releasing information that ISIS was claiming responsibility for the theft, and videos of those reports had already made their way to social media. While the president usually faced a hostile media on most subjects, he was fortunate to have information in circulation that substantiated his views on the Machesney Park armory theft. So, with corroborating evidence, the president was able to stroll out to the press corps with confidence in his statements.

"At this time," the president began confidently, "I would like to announce that the terrorist group ISIS has claimed responsibility for the brazen theft of arms and ammunition at the Machesney Park armory." As members of the press tried to interrupt with questions, he continued with the power of a train speeding through an intersection. "Earlier, unsubstantiated reports that this was an act carried out by white supremacists, neo-Nazis, or any other ultra-right fringe groups have been proven to be false. Brandon James, the director of FBI counterintelligence, has informed me that the FBI field office in Chicago received a call originating from the northern area of Iraq near the city of Mosul. He also reported that further corroborating evidence was found on the Amaq News website, which is a source of information on ISIS activities. These are very credible sources, so we are going to be pursuing this line of investigation as we move forward and determine what our options are in responding to this threat. This is what we know at this point in time, so I will now take a limited number of questions from the press."

A chorus of shouts called out to the president in unison as members of the press also raised their hands. The president chose one of his most fierce adversaries in the mainstream media, a young, attractive Muslim journalist from the Socialist News Network known simply as SNN. The combination of her given name and surname, Zara Abdullah, meant princess and servant of God. While her attractive appearance was certainly deserving of the title princess, she was anything but a servant of God as far as President Courtland was concerned. He felt that if he could respond to any of her questions to her satisfaction, everything else would be easy.

"I'll take the first question from Zara."

"Mr. President, why did the initial reports about the attack on the Machesney Park armory indicate that the perpetrators were members of an ultra-right conservative group—the type of group that your administration has been remiss in their criticism of and response to in light of the detrimental effect they are responsible for when it comes to bigotry, racism, and Islamophobia?"

"I think it's time for a reality check, Zara!" the president began with power and authority as his face turned red. "First of all, SNN, which is your news outlet, provided the first report about the alleged identity of the perpetrators, so if anyone could shed some light on that question, you'd be in a better position than I would. I don't make up information to fit a political narrative that makes my life easier… but SNN could just as easily be named DNN as the Duplicity News Network!"

"Mr. President," Zara interrupted defensively, "I wasn't on the scene when the incident occurred, and the press wasn't allowed to question personnel at the compound. It was the FBI that provided our information."

"Isn't that amazing, the FBI briefed me on the attack as well, and while they didn't definitively confirm any specific group, they did say that a high-ranking member of ISIS claimed responsibility for the attack. The FBI simply offered a possibility of which group could have been responsible, but you took their speculation back to the newsroom and SNN reported speculation as fact! I, on the other hand, gather all the information on an event and report the facts so the press and the citizens of our great country have the truth. This is something known as due diligence! I think you folks at SNN need to look up 'due diligence' and start exercising it! SNN's inability to deliver news that is both relevant and factual is inexcusable and shameful. The disgraceful thing is that you people have no shame about your lack of integrity!"

After the president finished verbally hammering Zara, her lips tightened and her jaws visibly clenched as she scribbled some notes on a small pad of paper. President Courtland immediately proceeded to the next question.

"Jim Kibitzer, KBS news."

"Mr. President, unlike your predecessor President Osama, who enjoyed a warm relationship with Muslim Americans, how do you feel about the opinion that your anti-Muslim policies may have played a part in triggering this attack, and subsequently, how does distrust of you within the Muslim community hinder Muslims from being forthcoming with information that would facilitate a successful outcome in this investigation?"

"Well, Jim, if you're talking about Islamic extremists, I would have to agree with your opinion that President Osama enjoyed a warm relationship with them. His thoroughly irresponsible immigration policies allowed Muslim extremists to set up shop in our country and purchase land in remote areas where they could train to carry out activities like the raid on the Machesney Park armory. Why wouldn't our enemies have warm fuzzies for our former Muslim president, who provided them with the ability to enter the US undetected and plan acts of terrorism within our borders? As for my anti-Muslim policies, I'm not sure what you're talking about..."

"Mr. President, I'm specifically referring to your Muslim travel ban that was recently passed," Kibitzer quickly interjected.

"There's no such thing as a Muslim travel ban, Jim!" the president retorted vehemently. "We recently passed a travel ban that restricts travel for people from countries we have identified as active sponsors of terrorist groups, so it is targeting terrorists, not Muslims. If you believe in the ridiculous idea that restricting the flow of people entering our country from terrorist-sponsoring countries is the cause of the attack on the Machesney Park armory, you might want to consider a career change. Your logic is more deficient than someone who's mentally challenged, and that doesn't facilitate good journalism. Furthermore, I have great faith in the Muslim community who have demonstrated their love and allegiance to our country by cooperating with law enforcement on all levels..."

"Are you denying the large-scale protest by Muslim Americans on your travel ban, and the role it's played in creating divisiveness and Islamophobia that promotes a hostile environment for Muslims?"

"Neither the travel ban that my administration drafted, nor any other legislation implemented to protect American citizens has created divisiveness. The truth is the false narrative created and perpetuated by irresponsible journalists who function like agents of propaganda in their zeal to demonize this administration is creating divisiveness! The incorrigible bias with which you people present news pertaining to this administration, as well as the way in which you suppress news that doesn't support your narrative, is the greatest threat to unity and diversity within our great country!"

Once again, a slew of hands shot up and there was a cacophony of shouts seeking to gain the attention of the president, but he raised his hands and offered a tight-lipped smile for rapid snapping of cameras as he backed away from the podium with parting words.

"That's all the information we have for now, and when we have more details surrounding this attack, that information will be forthcoming," the president said quickly as the press continued to hurl questions at him unabated despite his clear announcement that the briefing was over.

Chapter 13
We the People

The press conference was the first one in three years where it seemed impossible for the press to crucify the president for what had happened at Machesney Park and the responses he gave the press regarding it.

"This is the first time I can remember, since he took office, that the press wasn't able to bust the president's balls," Scorzoletti said with a satisfied grin.

"Yeah, I actually got a woody from the way he responded to that bitch Zara."

"You got a woody just by looking at her," Max added, much to the delight of everyone else, especially Sano, who doubled over with laughter.

"Hey, all kidding aside," Scorzo said, "I think we actually did the president a favor, even though that wasn't my intention at the time. Honestly, he's the first man to hold that office who hasn't been a career bureaucrat concerned with political longevity longer than the pant legs on a Brooks Brothers suit."

"You ever hear of the Twenty-eighth Amendment?" Philster queried.

"There are only twenty-seven amendments, you douchebag!" Max shot back.

"That's because the Twenty-eighth Amendment has never been ratified, nor will it ever be," Jake said, coming to the Philster's defense. "Lobbyists, bankers, Big Pharmaceutical companies, and Big Money from any source will always control our country. There's no such thing as 'We the People.'"

"Jake and the Philster are on point about that, Max," Scorzo piped in.

"So why hasn't it been ratified?" Max said, raising his eyebrows at Philster.

"Tell him, Jake," Scorzo said, looking at him with a knowledgeable grin.

"The Twenty-eighth Amendment states that Congress shall make no laws for the people that do not equally apply to the Congress and the Senate. That's basically what it says in a nutshell, but what it means is that they can't have any of the special privileges they currently have because we the people don't possess them, and it means that they can't vote exorbitant salary raises for themselves like they currently do because essentially they work for us, and since we can't show up for work and demand that our bosses give us exorbitant raises, they shouldn't be able to do that either. They can't have immunity from criminal conduct and prosecution because we don't have that privilege, and the list goes on and on. So Max, if you had all those privileges and many others, do you think you would vote for them being taken away?"

"Fuck no!"

"Thank you, Jake," the Philster said, nodding with satisfaction.

Just then Sano looked at Max and started laughing, much to Philster's chagrin. "What's gotten into you now, ya fucking hyena?"

"I was just thinking of all the things that Max would amend to the Twenty-eighth Amendment, like permissible sexual harassment of hot-looking interns, drinking while on the senate or house floor, swearing during speeches..." At this point Sano and Max as well as the others doubled over in laughter at the insanity of these propositions, but with the realization that many, if not all of them, happen during the course of business in the halls of congress and the senate anyway.

"Well, I don't think President Courtland is your typical politician," Scorzo said, bringing the conversation back to him. "And the Twenty-eighth Amendment is exactly what my agenda is...not revenge."

"Of course Courtland's not," Philster added. "The guy is loaded, so he's immune to bribes, kickbacks, and corruption from foreign governments. That notwithstanding, he isn't a Washington insider, so he doesn't have to play that game of 'if you want to get along, you have to go along.' The only thing Courtland has to do is please the base that voted him into office."

"As far as I can tell," Scorzo added, "he's done a pretty damn good job at that."

"Damn straight!" Philster shouted. "He's the first president I've voted for since the 'Great Communicator.' And that was a long time ago. Good old Reagan. I remember when he was interviewed on Johnny Carson's show, and Johnny asked him if he thought more government was the answer to the country's problems. I'll never forget when Reagan looked him straight in the face and said, 'No, people have the misguided opinion that government is the answer to their problems, but government is the problem, not the solution.'"

Jake looked up again with a serious expression as he spoke to both Philster and Scorzo.

"You guys do realize that what we're planning to do in hitting Federal Reserve banks will put us at odds with the president we admire, don't you?"

"How do you figure?" Philster began in a rhetorical tone. "President Courtland didn't have anything to do with the creation of the Federal Reserve system. That was an un-American behemoth created offshore at a place called Jekyll Island in the 1920s. There's ab-so-fucking-lutely nothing Federal about the Federal Reserve bank. It's a completely private bank that is run by unelected elitist officials who make policy completely outside the oversight of any branch of the government. The Federal Reserve banking system has created every recession and depression this country has ever had, and it has looted the Social Security system amongst other things and it's complicit with the Treasury Department in looting the working poor taxpayers. So, tell me how President Courtland has anything to do with the Federal Reserve?"

"Isn't he compelled to protect it by virtue of his office?" Nixon asked with naivety clearly evident in his tone.

"That's the job of the Federal Reserve Police, but they're only about a thousand members strong, so you can believe the FBI and the Treasury Department would join the circus as well," Philster responded. "All the president is compelled to do is make a statement condemning the thefts. He's not going to get personally involved in something that has thousands of tentacles all over it. Besides, there's nobody more astute than him regarding what a bunch of thieving vermin dwell in the halls of the Federal Reserve banks."

As if he was in his own private reverie, Scorzo just listened to the talk about President Courtland. He didn't like casting aspersion on Muslim citizens, but casting aspersion on a president whom he admired and saw attacked daily was even less appealing to him. As if coming out of a trance, Scorzo suddenly looked at Philster.

"Philster, do we currently have any DI shell corporations with the Chicago Fed Reserve?"

"Yeah, of course we do. Shit, you know how corrupt Chicago is, Sal. They use the OCC, commonly known as the Office of the Comptroller of the Currency. They were created in 1863 as an independent bureau within the Treasury Department."

"Who appoints the comptroller of the OCC?" Sal asked.

"The president."

"Jesus," Sal said pensively. "No wonder why they want to get rid of Courtland. He's trying to decentralize the Fed."

"Yeah, in a manner of speaking, that's exactly what he's trying to do," Philster said. "Quite frankly, I'm not sure why they haven't pulled a Kennedy on him yet."

"They're not gonna get that chance because we're going to start hitting the Federal Reserve banks, but we're gonna need a little more help from Mohammed."

"Oh, shit, Sal, we're not gonna have to go knocking off Federal Reserve banks wearing fucking dresses and hajibs?"

"No, but we're gonna have to recruit some females wearing dresses and hajibs because we aren't knocking off the local savings and loan. We're going to be stealing billions, so we're going to need multiple female personnel with large enough DI currency deposits to buy us the logistical time we need to carry out our operation."

"Definitely, we can't pull this off without a distraction. We're going to have multiple associates assuming multiple roles. All that logistical support requires time, so our DI's currency deposit must be large enough to give us the necessary time to set up our logistical support. This is not going to be a smash-and-grab 40K heist. We're talking billions here, so we need to turn off the security cameras, secure the vault and the loading dock, position armored vehicles, control traffic in the surrounding areas, and handle any resistance we're going to meet."

"Forgive me for questioning you, Sal, but are you suggesting we're going to pull this off in broad daylight with female Muslims yelling Allahu Akbar?"

"No," Sal said, shaking his head. "That's only part of the plan. Three of us will enter the bank dressed as Muslim women wearing dark-tinted contacts, which will be the only thing visible on our body. One of us will ask to use the restroom, which just happens to be near the vault. I already secured a Federal Reserve uniform and two jackets from the Bureau along with three uniforms from the Chicago police. Our first Muslim will join the two uniformed feds, who are Jake and Max. Our uniformed Federal Reserve cop (Sano) and I will be loading what is designated as unfit currency into the trucks. Our first Muslim Nixon will peel off his gear and drive off. I will ensure that all trucks have ease of access from the dock as I will be dressed as a uniformed CPD officer stopping traffic. Our second Muslim will be Philster. The other women will be decoys keeping the other tellers busy verifying the DI's."

Scorzo immediately looked over at Philster, sensing he would meet with resistance from him on his role, but he put his finger up to Philster's lips and shook his head negatively, and Philster smiled wryly but said nothing. "You will excuse yourself to see what's taking the other woman, Nixon, so long in the can. But, like Nixon, you will proceed to the loading dock and drive off in the second armored vehicle. Seconds later, I will signal a car alarm that will give Alvarez an excuse to briefly leave the premises to turn off his car alarm. You will then board the third vehicle that has been loaded and head to our prearranged location.

"This part of the heist should go smoothly. The part where it will get tricky is if a CPD cruiser passes by while I am stopping traffic. Or a cadre of Bureau boys decide to stop and ask the Federal Reserve cop on the east side of building why a CPD officer is stopping traffic instead of him. Even though Jake will have an official Bureau jacket and Sano will be wearing a Federal Reserve officer's jacket, there's always the possibility we'll be made in a heartbeat, so our option will be limited to immediate lethal force since the people inside will already know by then that they were scammed. Our escape and evasion in the event of a shootout is via the Adam Street sewer to lower Wacker Drive, where we have a car with tinted windows waiting. Prior to the op going down, we will set up a Streets and Sanitation tent covering the sewer. We got all the schematics on the bank from Alvarez; my only question to you, sir," Scorzo said as he looked at Alvarez, "is how does the escape and evasion plan look?"

"Without seeing the schematics myself, I'd say you couldn't have picked a better tunnel than if you had worked for Streets and Sanitation. Adams has dozens of ancillary tunnels, many coming up in Grant Park, and even two coming up in the underground parking garage under Grant Park. If anyone saw you go down on Adams, that's the most logical place the Feds and the CPD would stake out because of the certain possibility of a waiting getaway car. They would never think you'd run a half mile away. The most logical assumption if they acted on that route is that you were going to one of the train stations, which would be stupid because of all the surveillance cameras. The Grant Park garage would be a no-brainer for any cop or Fed. But honestly, with a Streets and Sanitation tent up by the Adams Street sewer, I don't think they're gonna have a clue as to your escape and evasion plan. They're going to be looking for suspicious people with large cases on foot or cars with out-of-state plates that have four or five people in them, but it's all gonna come down to whatever looks suspicious above ground.

That's just the typical way bank jobs are pulled off. Since we'll be loading Brinks trucks on the docks, nothing will look out of the ordinary."

"Okay, then it's set. We hit the Federal Reserve Bank next Friday," Sal said with firm conviction. "Our objective is not escape and evasion, but driving those armored vehicles to waiting C-130s at O'Hare airport."

"Why Friday, Sal?" Philster spoke up. "Why not first thing Monday or mid-week?"

"Because every Friday they have tours of the Federal Reserve that are open to the public. Not only will this add to our own distractions, but it will also minimize the possibility of a deadly firefight. Neither the CPD nor the FBI will want a bunch of civilian casualties. Since half of our crew will be gone before the bank knows what hit them, escape and evasion for four guys using the sewer system, where we will have a man working tent setup, will leave them scratching their balls wondering how we got out of Dodge in burning daylight with billions of dollars, especially when Brinks trucks are everywhere downtown on Fridays."

Chapter 14
The Best Laid Plans

Every detail of Scorzo's plan seemed to be going exactly as planned, yet as it is said, "The best laid plans of mice and men often go awry." Four armored trucks and six accomplices careened away from the Federal Reserve bank of Chicago unnoticed, but it would not be so with the last three men. It was a sunny and pleasantly warm Friday morning, so the Federal Reserve officers who usually sat in their car decided to engage in some uncommon foot patrol around the perimeter of the bank. Scorzo saw the first officer rounding the southeast corner of the bank. He quickly backed into the alley and signaled for the others to get inside the bank.

"Tell me there's no trouble," Jake said, looking at the sweat beading on Scorzo's face.

"There's trouble! Mr. Federal Reserve Officer decided he wanted to enjoy the fresh air and he's coming this way…now! We have to assume the other one is coming from the opposite direction rather than sitting in the car playing with himself."

"Fuck, Scorzo, what's our out now?"

"Take my Thompson and put it against Sano's back. He won't be able to see what type of weapon it is until it's too late. All he'll notice is your official FBI jacket. I'll use the Glock if anybody else backs him up. It's filled with armor-piercing rounds and it's set on full auto so I can take out a small army with one magazine. Exit the door slowly. We are going to claim Sano is an imposter so we can try to get the other guy to lay down his weapon."

As they opened the door slowly, the Federal Reserve officer already had his weapon drawn and pointed in their direction.

"FBI, drop your weapon," Jake yelled authoritatively. "I'm not gonna ask you again. This man in uniform is not a Federal Reserve officer. He's an imposter, so I need you to put your weapon on the deck slowly!"

"Fuck that!" the officer yelled back. "Why didn't the CPD officer brief me about that? Why did he go back into the building with you?"

"He was following my directive. I am calling the shots here now, Officer."

Suddenly Scorzo grabbed Sano by the collar and shoved the gun up against his head and pulled him out of Jake's line of fire. Immediately the Thompson unleashed a torrent of fire blazing at the wildly flaying officer as Scorzo turned and opened fire on the stunned officer approaching them from the rear. Neither of the officers had a chance to fire a single round before they were riddled with bullets. Though their bodies convulsed to the cacophony of automatic fire, they were dead before they hit the ground. Without a moment's hesitation, Scorzo's weapon was put in what looked like a tool bag along with the Glock. The three descended into the street below, following their predetermined run to lower Wacker Drive. The car was there as planned, and they drove up and entered the expressway at the Randolph Street entrance.

Once again, the Nemesis Nine eluded their adversaries, and their only calling card were two dead officers and bank personnel who relayed information about three Muslim women who acted rather suspiciously about a seemingly legitimate account, but then disappeared without receiving the verification of the DI's they provided. Still more curious was the fact that the bank could not account for more than forty billion dollars that disappeared and two dead officers who were riddled with so many bullets that somebody should have heard, yet nobody did because the weapons had suppressors affixed to them, greatly reducing the sound.

While the media provided coverage on all Chicago news outlets at five, six, and 10 p.m., there was no mention of Muslim perpetrators who entered the bank at exactly the time that the death of the Federal Reserve officers was determined and the missing money was discovered. The consistent narrative was that the mystery heist must have been the coordinated effort of southside gangs using social media to orchestrate their flawless robbery and stealthy getaway.

Back in Fox Lake there were mixed emotions on the events that transpired because the spoils of their victory were loaded on cargo planes about twenty-five miles away.

"Scorzo, you look like you just got kicked by a horse," Philster said. "We succeeded, baby! We're rich and retired now!"

"It's not about being rich for me, and we killed two innocent men."

"Hey, look, Scorzo, it was either us or them," Jake rationalized. "You had to think quick, and that's what you did. I gave that guy the opportunity to put his weapon on the deck, but he wouldn't because he knew his partner was behind us."

"He's dead on," Sano added, "And the fact that the guy in front of us was looking at his partner was sheer idiocy on his part. It was like he was clearly telling us we were in a no-win situation, so what choice did he leave us? It was either waste them or surrender."

"Well," Scorzo began with a sigh, "I just hope neither of those poor sons-a-bitches had wives or children, and I hope nobody goes sniffing around our C-130s."

"Look, Scorzo, we all knew there was a possibility of casualties, on their side or ours," Philster consoled. "If they had stayed in their car, like they did whenever we cased that bank, they'd still be alive today." Philster patted Scorzo on the shoulder and started to walk toward the refrigerator for a beer, but then he stopped dead in his tracks and pointed his finger at Scorzo.

"And one more thing…nobody on the news has mentioned a word about fucking Muslim bitches being in that bank, so if you ever ask me to demean myself like that again, I'll slip a roofie in your beer, shave your head, put lipstick on you, and post your picture on Facebook as a gay SEAL."

"Deal," Scorzo said, shaking his head glumly.

Alvarez took a rare break away from his computer monitor and sat next to Scorzo.

"Sal, did what we do get us closer to accomplishing your ultimate goal?"

"Well, what it did was get the attention of the movers and shakers that stand in the shadows of our government and make things happen through our politicians."

"So, the two guys that got wasted today…"

"The two guys that got wasted today had nothing to do with our goal, Alvarez. They were simply collateral damage. And I don't like what happened to them any more than you do. That's why I want to rely on your skills as much as possible so we can avert those types of tragedies. If you hadn't provided us with the underground schematics for our escape and evasion plan, I can assure you there would have been a hell of a lot more collateral damage. Probably a lot more of them would have been women, children, fathers out with their families. You did real good, Alvarez. You just keep doing what you're doing and don't pay attention to Philster. Think of him as the big brother that loves to pick on you."

"So, what's next," Alvarez questioned. "I mean, forty billion divided nine ways gives any of us more money than we will need to survive for this lifetime."

"We take more. That's what's next. Then we give it to people in need…like the families in the impoverished region of the Appalachians. There's a Christian Food Pantry Project there that could use a good portion of that money. The pastor there, Al DiSoto, has a heart of gold and he'll make sure that all the money we give will go directly to the people in need. He's incorruptible…a modern-day Moses.

"Those people slaved their lives away in the filth and darkness of those dangerous mines, making the owners very wealthy men, but when they got sick or the mine ran dry, do you think the wealthy gentry cared about them, paid their medical bills, gave a severance to their widows when men were buried alive in those mines? And what about the Detroit auto workers. Their companies sold them out by using slave labor from other countries that didn't have to pay union wages, provide medical coverage, or offer pensions. That money is gonna benefit the people it was stolen from…the working-class American people."

"Excuse me for saying so, but how can we right all the wrongs in our country by simply redistributing the wealth? Isn't that what communism is based on…wealth redistribution? Look at their legacy of failure."

"In a manner of speaking, I guess you could say that, but I also want to eradicate those who have grown ill because of their disproportionate measure of wealth. That's something communism didn't do. Communism fattened up a small cadre of wealthy elites while it enslaved and controlled the rest of the population. We're going to take away from the haves and give to the have-nots. That's not communism. If you have to give it a name, I would prefer the Robin Hood Monetary Fund… We take from the robber barons and give to those they stole from."

"Excuse me, Mr. Boss-man." Nixon sauntered toward Scorzo, slightly inebriated. "Are you sure you aren't half nigger somewhere in your linage? Because if I'm hearing you correctly, you seem to be talking about reparation payments."

"Oh, blow me," Philster chimed in. "If he was talking about reparation payments, you moolies would be getting four goats and ten acres of land each. That's what you were supposed to get after the slaves were set free."

"Hey, Scorzo, take a look at this," Alvarez called out from his desk. "You just made the top of the FBI's most wanted list."

"Jesus Christ, how did that happen? We got away clean today. No witnesses whatsoever," Scorzo said, shaking his head in disbelief.

"It wasn't about today. They still have their heads up their asses on that one. In fact, the socialist media is still trying to entrap President Courtland into implicating the Muslim disguises we used to turn him into a divisive Islamophobic."

"So, what then?"

"Four of the nine ATF agents you fired on died of their wounds… massive blood loss before they could be treated. Bickens no doubt passed that on to Pierpont, but I'm sure he isn't happy about the Bureau's involvement now. However, since they were Federal agents, you just made the FBI's most wanted list. They also gave you a new name."

"Well, that was bound to happen sooner or later," Scorzo said with a sound of resignation in his voice, "but I felt more pity for those two officers we killed today than any of those ATF agents. They got what they deserved. They killed my daughter and separated me from my wife! Those stupid fucks! All I wanted was to be left alone to enjoy the rest of my life with my wife and daughter!" Scorzo turned to Alvarez with a quizzical look and asked, "What's the bit about the new name?"

"They're calling you Machine Gun Scorzo."

Jake came over and sat on the armrest of the couch next to Scorzo, offering him a beer. "You know we're all with you, Sal. That was a real shit sandwich Pierpont dealt you after all your distinguished service in the teams. And now…to make the FBI's most wanted list…what a crock of shit!"

"Well, our next strike is going to hit really close to home for him."

"How so, brother?"

"Remember how he had his ass covered by Senator Lacey Nervosi in the aftermath of Operation Lotus Blossom? She fucking buried that investigation and Philster became ONI's patsy because they couldn't find corroborating evidence for what I did."

"But Sal, Lotus Blossom was Philster's brainchild."

"That's all it was…his brainchild, and, admittedly, not a good one at that, but Pierpont authorized it, and when Nervosi, who he answered to, somehow got wind of it, what do you think happened?"

"She tried to shut it down and go public?"

"Not on your life, Jake…not a fucking prayer! The fucking bitch wanted a cut of the action. And it wasn't just her. Congresswoman Lakes of former bank fraud fame wanted a piece of the pie too."

"You can't be for real, Sal. I mean, she's not the sharpest tool in the shed, but she's not that dumb."

"No, Jake, but she was that greedy! How do you think she ended up living in a 2.4-million-dollar estate with a net worth of fourteen million dollars, especially given that she came into public office two years prior to declaring bankruptcy? No, she's not dumb at all! She's a shrewd and calculating bitch who made her fortune off the bodies of innocent boys and girls in Southeast Asia! And so did that viper Lakes!"

"I never could stand those cunts!" Philster added, moving closer to Sal. "Every time they questioned me, they had this look on their faces like they were driving stakes into my body. The thing that really killed me was being questioned and cross-examined by a bitch who was more complicit in the op than any of the people in ONI. She was providing protection for the whole op from beginning to end. Lakes was just a tailgater."

"I don't even want to know any more than I already know, Philster," Scorzo said with disdain.

"But you need to know because she was the reason why Pierpont and Bickens decided to come after you. That greedy bitch wanted all the funds you siphoned off. She was the one that put that idea in Pierpont's head, but Pierpont had no reason to come after you. He didn't want to tarnish the image of the SEALs. That's where Bickens enters the story, and she's the reason why the DC office of the ATF led the siege instead of the Mississippi office, as it should have been."

"I did find that rather curious, to say the least."

"And that notwithstanding," Philster continued, "why weren't any of the local authorities informed of the op as they were supposed to, given it was their jurisdiction. They weren't even allowed to do a forensic examination of the crime scene. And get this, the Chinese came in to provide oversight because of the fact that your wife and daughter are both Chinese nationals, and after they did their investigation, the ATF entirely refurbished the place. Rumor has it from the local authorities they went on a shooting bonanza from the inside of your home using none other than a Thompson submachine gun...the same weapon you used to defend yourself. Then they fired a limited number of shots from the outside of your house using their weapons to make it look like you were the aggressor."

"Oh, fuck me." Scorzo shook his head in disgust.

"Hey, if it's any consolation," Max said, "you absolutely did the right thing by leaving your wife behind. I know it's not easy on you, but she fared a lot better because the Chinese Consulate got involved. If there's one thing Washington didn't want on their hands, it is an international incident. They had to treat her with kid gloves and let her go because we're always accusing China of human rights violations, so they played that same trump card with us where your wife was concerned."

Jake took his beer and bumped it up against Scorzo's.

"Not to make light of your pain or change the subject, but we got into this while talking about our next strike. So, tell me, what *is* our next strike?"

"Forget it, Jake. I'd actually rather talk about something else anyway."

Chapter 15
Public Enemy

"Our next strike is actually two strikes. We're heading to San Francisco."

"San Francisco! Shit, Sal, why don't we just head out to Hawaii while we're at it?" opined Philster.

Max spoke up. "Because there's no Federal Reserve bank in Hawaii, you douchebag."

"Why not St. Louis?" Philster asked. "That's a hell of a lot closer to where we are now, and we've got a buttload of cash here in cargo planes that we have to deal with."

"First off," Scorzo began, "we're going to dispose of most of that cash to people who really need it...to people who can't even put food on their tables."

"Sal, how are we gonna do that?" Philster asked, seemingly annoyed. "We can't go flying around Appalachia in C-130s dropping pallets of cash down with notes that say, 'Hi we're from the Publishers Clearinghouse and you've just won a shitload of money to the tune of twenty million dollars.' I mean, come on, Sal, really, how are we gonna pull that off?"

Scorzo swiveled around to Alvarez

"Is there a way to move the amount of cash we have in a discreet manner?"

"Article 4A of the Uniform Commercial Code would make that pretty much of an impossibility here in the States. Besides that, all banks have to report cash deposits over ten thousand dollars by virtue of the structuring laws. Another thing, I wouldn't be surprised if every bank in the tri-state region was issued a warning on cash deposits as soon as we hit them. By now, every institution in the USA is on notice."

"So, what's our option?" Scorzo asked, tightening his lips.

"We need a C-17A Globemaster III to get that cargo out of the country and convert it to a digital cloud platform such as Currencycloud. com. After that, we can slide that money around like hash browns in a well-oiled pan anywhere we want to. On the other hand, we could visit some areas on the south and west side of Chicago and start our own little propaganda campaign against CLM. We make a quick announcement that CLM doesn't care about the plight of Black lives, but the Robin Hood monetary fund does. Then we simply load up one of the Brinks trucks and abandon it. And with Mayor Leadfoot ordering the police to stand down in the midst of civil unrest, you know the police won't go there."

"Everything after the first sentence sounds beautiful, but how the hell are we going to requisition a C-17A Globemaster? That's like a flying aircraft carrier, for Christ's sake."

"Hey, don't look at me, Chief," Philster said, shaking his head negatively. "I can fly one of those, but I sure as fuck can't steal one! Then there's another problem. The weight capacity for a C-17A is a little over 170,000 pounds. Do you have any idea how much forty billion dollars weighs?"

"Not really," Scorzo replied.

"Assuming we're talking about denominations of hundred-dollar bills, it would be 800,000 pounds. That means five flights from and to the US."

"Then we'd have to go with a C-5M Super Galaxy. They have a payload capacity of slightly over 285,000 pounds. That means we only need two trips out of the country, and we could distribute the rest here in Chicago and in the Appalachians, where people need it and where we could inflict a lethal propaganda war against CLM. After all, we're going to need ammunition and logistical supplies, and the people we're going to be dealing with love cash and don't ask questions."

"You got it all figured out, huh, Chief?" Philster said with a sarcastic grin. "What about C-5Ms? Where are we gonna get those...pull them out of Doctor Brillo-head's ass?"

"Eat shit, you douchebag. At least I was a doctor during and after I served. I didn't end up in the big house like you."

"Can I make a suggestion, Scorzo," Alvarez interrupted. "You said our next strike is in San Francisco, and I presume you're talking about the Federal Reserve Bank of San Francisco, right? And we also happen to need a plane that can carry a substantial payload, right?"

"That's right, keep talking."

"Well, Travis Air Force Base has C-5M transport planes, and, moreover, it's only about an hour's drive by car to San Francisco."

Scorzo looked over at Philster, shaking his head disapprovingly.

"And I thought you said this kid didn't have any common sense. How come you didn't think of that, Philster?"

"Because we're civilians, Scorzo, and you happen to be number one on the FBI's ten most wanted list. What are we gonna do, dress up as Muslims again and hijack a C-5M? They'd scramble a pack of fighters to shoot our asses down as soon as we took off."

"May I," Alvarez asked Scorzo tentatively.

"Absolutely," Scorzo responded with authority as he looked around the room at the others. "Everyone in this room keep their mouths shut and listen! Go ahead, Alvarez."

"All I need to do is produce paperwork and a corresponding electronic transmission through COMSEC authorizing the requisition of two C-5Ms from TAFB to Sano and Max because they can fly them. Philster, you're grounded on this because you're already too high profile, and Mohammed, you don't have the requisite skills for this mission. Nixon and Jake, you're both qualified co-pilots. I can serve as one of the flight engineers, and, Gonzalez, you've got the qualifications for that too."

"Outstanding, Alvarez!" Philster bellowed. "You see what you're capable of when you're not puffing the magic dragon all day."

"I didn't finish, Philster. We still have a problem. We still need two more flight engineers and six loadmasters to fill the bill for an appropriate flight crew."

"Maybe now would be a good time for you to puff the magic dragon," the Philster said with a smile. "Maybe you could get a little imaginative and create eight imaginary crew members."

"I've got a better idea," Alvarez suggested. "How about if you think of eight people you know with flight backgrounds who were discharged for PTSD or battle-induced depression."

"Section Eight terminology is no longer politically correct, so the military now uses medical terminology? Oh, fuck me," Philster said with exasperation. "Section Eight, PTSD, mental retard…why in the fuck would we want to use people like that?"

"Because their civilian opportunities are severely limited, and they'll keep their mouths shut at the chance to do something that will pay them more than panhandling, dishwashing, or drying cars at a car wash. Do you think you can handle that?"

"Yeah, as soon as we're into ONI's database, it's as good as done."

"Say, Alvarez, I trust you can create the paperwork that will get us our equipment, but what about the credentials? How are we going to get fourteen people cleared to get those planes off the ground?"

"I am going to create TS/SCI clearances for them with a SAP directive. Trust me, no one's going to question a SAP. And I'll postdate them going back about five years."

"Hey, Sal, didn't I tell you this kid was a virtual disaster," Philster boasted. "Didn't I? Didn't I call it right?"

"Yeah, Philster, but I'm gonna make this even more challenging."

"Sal, come on, man, you've already got me trying to find eight retards, and two of them with flight engineer backgrounds. What else do you want?"

"I want them to be Middle Easterners."

"Oh, don't tell me we're gonna have to dress up as Muslim bitches again!"

"No, not women, but we're definitely going in as Middle Easterners. It's an important part of our distraction for the second strike. At some point, the media is going to have to admit there's a Middle Eastern threat because too many of the alternative news sources are playing that up twenty-four/seven."

Philster glanced at Mohammed and put his palms up and outward in an apologetic manner.

"Don't get the wrong idea, Mohammed, I think you're a real stand-up guy, but I just don't understand the people of your culture, and I hate having to dress up and pretend to be one of them. I mean, I'd rather throw on a wig, a bra, and a tight dress and prance around in a bar full of bull dykes than dress up like a Muslim."

"It's that bad, my friend?"

"Yeah, basically."

"Let's get back on point, Philster," Scorzo interjected. "I don't want just any eight guys. I want eight guys from three different crews. I want you to recruit from the USS *Pasadena*, the USS *Annapolis*, and the USS *Alexandria*."

"Those are all subs, Sal. The need for the planes is obvious, but subs? What the fuck do we want with subs?"

"Alvarez is going to use them to send some special delivery packages to some good friends of yours by the name of Senator Lacey Nervosi and Congresswoman Nadine Lakes."

"Oh, that's sounding real good, Sal, and I hope those packages contain all the things you're supposed to answer no to when you're sending a package at the post office."

"You think you can fill that order for me, Alvarez?"

"Yes, sir!" Alvarez replied in military fashion.

"That's good because there's another package I want her to receive just in case she happens to be at her vineyards out in the Sonoma Valley. I also need a package delivered to one Representative Nadine Lakes in South LA, and last, but not least, we will need to deliver a package to the Federal Reserve Bank of San Francisco after we make a massive withdrawal and clear all of the bank personnel out of the facility. I don't have any beef with the people who work there; I just can't stand the people who own it. We're going to hit Lakes and Nervosi first to create confusion and chaos that will facilitate our mission at the

Federal Reserve Bank. Then we deliver our final package to the bank so the crime scene is obliterated. We must accomplish all our logistical ends in five days. That's when the House and the Senate will recess, and our targets will be back in their districts."

"You know, Sal," Philster began, after taking a deep puff off his cigarette, "I'd almost like to show up at Nervosi's house dressed like a Muslim bitch wearing a thong and say, 'Trick or treat' about two minutes before a Tomahawk slammed into her palace...just to see the look on that old battle-axe's face, and to have the knowledge that my face, which she hates so much, would be the last one she'd ever see."

"Well, you'll have to get your woody over her in the distance," Max said with a laugh. "We won't have time to indulge your perverse geriatric fantasies."

Scorzo laid out the duties and responsibilities of each man, and they went about their mission with military precision. Philster and Alvarez scoured the ONI database for section eight discharges of Middle Eastern crew members on the aforementioned subs. Jake purchased a premium semi-tractor cab and an adjoining trailer. There would be no time for loading and moving multiple vehicles, no Reserve Bank Museum tour to add distraction as there had been in Chicago, and no decoys assuming to make a protracted transaction.

Considering this, the thought of civilian casualties weighed heavily on Scorzo's mind. He and his team would study the bank like a chess board, trying to assume the actions of all involved before a single move was made, but there was always at least one guard, if not more, who was ready to put up resistance to stop a perpetrator or group of marauders and heroically do their duty. As Scorzo gazed off into the distance of the fields outside, he thought how stupid it was for any guard to want to be a hero. Why would any man want to die protecting the money of a rich dynasty whose money was insured anyway? They wouldn't lose a penny of the pilfered profits whether the guards fought valiantly or hid in a corner so they could go home to their wife and children at the end of the day.

It was all so senseless, but then that's because we are taught from an early age that the lies of the rich are true. The very name of the Federal Reserve bank is a lie. There's nothing federal about it. It doesn't belong to the government or to the people of the government. It belongs to age-old dynastic families who have owned it and controlled it through their proxies for generations. It has the power to inflate or deflate monetary value and it can seize or steal property or estates as it deems fit. Yet no one dares call this establishment a thief or an enemy of the state and its people.

Instead, it garners the respect that alternates with fear of its awesome power, and men will die unjustly to protect its interests. Its interests are not federal, and its reserves are of value to only a few privileged elites. But Salvino Scorzoletti was beginning to lift a veil that obscured the vision of the forgotten Americans. He had not only seen the perversity that great wealth brings in impoverished nations, but he came home to see a country he no longer recognized. He came to the inescapable conclusion that America was now a country that consisted of a ruling class and the ruled. Politicians no longer sought to serve limited terms of office for the purpose of serving the people of their country. They were instead career bureaucrats whose chief goals were turning people of the republic upon each other and creating civil divisiveness as well as fomenting partisan political discord, so the masses were distracted from how little they accomplished and how vast their net worth grew during their political tenure.

Then a single thought pervaded Scorzo's mind. He remembered how his embattled commander-in-chief said of the democratic party, "They're not coming after me; they're coming after all of you. I'm just standing in their way right now!" He felt a love and admiration for his president like no one before him, but his admiration was dissipated by a sullen sense of grief because he knew that he would be fighting the men and women who President Courtland had to protect and defend as well as appease. For Salvino Scorzoletti, there would be no such reserve. There was only the sheer determination to win using the art of war. It was what Salvino Scorzoletti knew best.

Philster and Alvarez had actually produced fifteen candidates to winnow out the wheat from the chaff so to speak, and as Alvarez occupied himself with the business of backgrounding these candidates and producing falsified COMSEC orders and TS/SCI and SAP credentials for their crew, Philster walked over to Scorzo, noticing him in a rare pensive mood. He gave him a light smack on the shoulder and handed him a beer.

"You're thinking about your wife and daughter?" he queried softly.

"No, I was actually thinking about us and the challenges we're going to be facing this time."

"Hey, come on, Sal, you're the best, and you got us all walking in lockstep with you, so what could go wrong?"

"A lot could go wrong. We're taking on eight new guys that were section eight for one reason or another, and you don't know anything about them. That's a big difference from the crew you put together for us back in Chicago."

"We'll put them through hell week just like you did to us. Well, shit, you put us through hell year in the course of a few months."

"That's my point, Philster. We aren't going to have three months, three weeks, or much more than three days with these guys, and that worries me."

"Look on the bright side, Sal; these sons-a-bitches are all Middle Easterners, so they've probably been using AK47s since they were eight years old, and that's exactly what we're going to be using on this op…AK47s."

Sal turned away from Philster and glanced over at Alvarez, who was busy clicking away on his keyboard.

"Alvarez, I need you to get me detailed schematics of the Fed in San Francisco, and I want close-up satellite imagery of all sides of the bank and the surrounding streets. Most important, I want to know what streets are off-limits to semi-trailers. I don't want any unnecessary traffic stops that result in us wasting an innocent cop."

"I already have the bank schematics, street photos, and our route from the Fed to the US Air Force recruiting base down I-280. Oh, and another thing, Sal, I narrowed our fifteen candidates down to eight."

"Give me the lowdown on these eight. Why them?"

"In a nutshell, they were all section eight because they wouldn't follow objectionable orders."

"Such as?"

"Not killing civilians who had been raped by a squad, and not participating in the activity, or insubordination to a CO for stuff like prayer breaks."

"All right, all right, enough. So, we know they have a conscience, but what we're asking them to do also falls outside the pale of the law. How do you know they will buy in to our mission?"

"Because six of the eight served time with no crimes committed. They were set up simply by virtue of being Middle Easterners. They were made to look like they were compromising the mission by refusing to kill a foreign national that was tracking and transmitting their movements to indigenous hostiles."

"And the other three?"

"We really lucked out on the other three."

"How so?" Scorzo asked. "We don't even know who the fuck they are."

"All three live in San Francisco with no family, no relatives in the States, a past association with ISIS predating their immigration and citizenship in the US, and all three of them drive for Mover, so they know the city well."

"Jesus Christ, Alvarez, how do you find all this shit out?"

"The dark web...anything you want, you can find it there, and lucky for us, I was the one who sold the Navy on that platform for its black ops using a virtual box I set up."

The Philster started waving his hands and gesticulating.

"Hey, hey, wait just a minute there, Alvarez, I was the one who sold high command on the idea of the dark web to keep your dope-smoking ass out of the clink."

"All right, all right, I can give credit where credit is due, but you only brought me to their attention. I was actually the one who set up ops for them so they couldn't be found. I still know to access them too."

"Something I'm a lot more interested in…" Scorzo began as he rubbed the side of his forehead. "…Launch codes for the weapons systems on these subs. Can you access them, and initiate firing?"

"Hey, Scorzo," Philster interrupted, "didn't I tell you this kid could do that?"

"I'm not asking you, Philster. I'm asking him."

Alvarez looked at Scorzo first, nodding affirmatively, and then at Philster.

"Since we have the precise locations of all four targets, direct hits will be like child's play for me."

"That's what I wanted to hear." Scorzo patted Alvarez on the back with a sigh of relief.

Chapter 16
Dead in the Water

With two federal police murdered in the Chicago Reserve bank robbery and no substantive clues as to the whereabouts or actions of Scorzo and Philster, the FBI formally announced their entry into the case and their jurisdiction over it. This was announced at a midday briefing that took place at the White House. The FBI cited the absence of explosives in the raid on the Scorzoletti home, nor was there any indication of automatic weapons present despite allegations that hundreds of rounds had been fired at ATF agents.

The refurbishing of the Scorzoletti home was not done until after the FBI's Mississippi field office visited the scene and noticed only a small number of forty-five-caliber rounds fired. While they could have indeed come from a Thompson submachine gun, they could have come from a number of other semi-automatic weapons that could have easily inflicted the casualties on ATF agents by a highly trained soldier. In any event, the FBI dismissed the idea of a Thompson being used against the ATF agents due to the sparsity of collateral damage to the inside structure of the Scorzoletti home. And since Scorzoletti's current whereabouts were unknown, the FBI stated in the briefing that they would welcome the assistance of the AFT, but jurisdiction was now clearly in the hands of the FBI counterintelligence division. They saw no connection between the siege on the Scorzoletti home and the incidents at the Machesney Park armory and the Federal Reserve bank of Chicago. "I find it highly unlikely that two high-profile fugitives on the run would be able to pull off the Machesney Park Amory assault, and much less so, the daring robbery of the Chicago Federal

Reserve bank," announced Derrick Panetta, special agent in charge of the Chicago counterintelligence division.

Added to this was the photographic and video evidence provided by the Chinese consulate in Washington that directly contradicted Bickens' assertions of damage caused by massive amounts of fire from a Thompson submachine gun, an obvious source of embarrassment to all federal agencies including the ATF. Bickens was furious that his agency was being told to stand down by the FBI, while the DEA was still being allowed to be a working counterpart of the operation due to the types of narcotics and medical supplies that were stolen in proximity to both crimes.

While President Courtland himself was not taking questions, he did allow the press to ask questions of the respective agencies present, represented by Bickens, Contreras, and Panetta.

"Special Agent Bickens, why was the Washington office of the ATF involved in a matter that was clearly in the jurisdiction of the Mississippi ATF office?"

"I'm not sure where you're getting your information from, but the Mississippi ATF office was most assuredly involved in the investigation of Mr. Scorzoletti."

With that, Bickens shot a furtive glance at the special agent in charge from the Mississippi office, who nodded in agreement with Bickens smiling in approval.

"The next question is for Special Agent Panetta... Sir, why would the DEA continue to be involved with this case when the ATF is being asked to stand down?"

"Perhaps you misunderstood me. The ATF will still have an investigative role since the Machesney armory theft would fall squarely into the line of criminal activity they pursue. However, with that said, the only concrete lead we have on the known fugitive Steven Philster resides with the DEA, who are currently pursuing him for a separately related narcotics theft in the Cook County area. We have no leads on the Machesney armory theft or the robbery of the Federal Reserve bank in Chicago."

"Special Agent Panetta, Zara Abdullah of SNN... Why hasn't there been discussion of the identity of the perpetrators in these two incidents where it was claimed that Muslim extremists stormed the Machesney compound, and three Muslim women who disappeared without a trace were seen at the Federal Reserve bank at the time of the robbery?"

"That's an excellent question, Zara, and the reason why we have not made any definitive pronouncements regarding race, affiliations, and a definitive composition of our perpetrators is twofold. First, it appears at this point that these two events have nothing in common with each other, and, second, we can't just assume that three women of possibly Muslim descent have anything to do with an unprecedented scale of bank theft just because they happened to be present at the time and then left. Our video surveillance shows the women entering a Checker taxi and entering a subway at Randolph and State. Nothing in their actions is indicative of a crime or even complicity in a crime. The fact that they left the bank during a robbery where there was actual shooting suggests nothing more to me than that they left out of fear."

"I guess what I'm getting at, Agent Panetta, is why weren't they mentioned given the fact that they began a rather large transaction and never completed it?"

"For the same reason that other patrons of the bank who engaged in similar actions with similar outcomes weren't mentioned. Now if you'll excuse me, that's all we have currently. As more information becomes available, you'll get it as soon as we get it."

In a gesture of amicability, Special Agent Panetta clasped the handles of Bickens' wheelchair and attempted to push him off the ramp of the platform. It was an awkward moment as both men assumed the cameras and video sound were off, but they weren't.

"I can handle this goddamn chair without your help, Panetta! Just like I can handle this case without the goddamn Bureau bustling in like a bunch of headline-grabbing pricks!"

As the cameraman came closer with Jim Kibitzer of KBS news closely in tow, Panetta cupped his hand over the camera and thrust it in a downward motion that caused the cameraman to fall forward; Panetta grabbed Kibitzer's microphone and threw it about twenty feet from them before looking at both of them with obvious rancor and shouting, "What does 'that's all we have at this time' mean to you?"

"Does freedom of the press mean anything to you, Special Agent Panetta?"

"It sure does when it's exercised properly."

Bickens left Panetta as soon as the altercation began when he saw other journalists take notice of it; he wanted to extricate himself from the adversity unfolding. He was hoping it would prove to be an embarrassment to the Bureau and their heavy-handed tactics with respect to everything they do.

Meanwhile, Contreras was relieved that no questions were directed at him. He was quite satisfied that Agent Panetta addressed the question involving his agency's involvement. However, the fact that Panetta seemed to let him off the hook in the press briefing didn't keep him from catching up to him and quickly trying to strike up a quick rapport.

"Special Agent Contreras," Panetta called out, chasing after Contreras. "I know we haven't met officially, but I really wanted to thank you for your restraint and diplomacy in that briefing." He extended his hand. "I'm FBI Special Agent Derrick Panetta. I head up the counterintelligence division at the Chicago field office. You can address me as Derrick. I see no need for formalities. We're two guys hunting an elusive pair of enemies, and I want to think of us as having a friendship based on that, and one that will last long after that."

"I'm flattered, Agent Panetta," Contreras responded.

"Please," Panetta said, giving Contreras a soft pat on his shoulder. "It's Derrick."

"Okay, but tell me how a new guy like me garners more respect from you than a seasoned veteran like Special Agent Bickens?"

"Because your reputation precedes you. I heard about Operation Cassandra. That was an amazing piece of work!" Panetta said enthusiastically.

"But that operation was credited as the Bureau's brainchild, not mine."

"According to Bickens, right?"

"Yes, how did you know?"

"Bickens was working with an ONI asset who your team identified as Steven Philster. Bickens wasn't using Philster as an asset to bring down some dirty operatives along with cartel leaders. Bickens was in bed with Philster, profiteering off of everything from drugs to guns to human trafficking. That's why jurisdiction was taken away from him and given to the Bureau."

"And what about my career? Why wasn't credit given where credit was due?"

"It was done for your protection. You were a single man who was able to put all the pieces together on his own. If that were made common knowledge, you would have had a bullet in your head faster than you could have read the headlines of your victory. Just between you and me, the reason why you received what you thought was an undeserved promotion to the Chicago field office as SAC was because of my call to Chief Ruther at the DEA in Washington."

"How do I know you're not just blowing sunshine up my ass?"

"It would be no problem for me to arrange a sit down with Ruther so you can hear it straight from him."

"How about you just call him and put him on speaker?"

"Come on, Contreras, don't be childish. It would be easy enough to find out whether my story is bullshit or real through other sources, but if you choose to go through Ruther, he's probably going to give you a bit of a song and dance because he still wants Bickens, and so do we."

"Okay, Derrick, for now I will take what you're saying at face value."

"Can I count on you for all the information your team assembles?"

"You can count on it," Contreras replied, but in the back of his mind he looked at Panetta as the lesser of two evils, knowing what he had been told about Bickens. The only problem, as far as Contreras was concerned, was how much of what Panetta told him was credible. Did he owe his promotion and his very life to a man who lived in the suspicion world where lies were told as truths, and truths were fashioned with lies to serve what was always called a greater good? It was something Contreras pondered on into the morning.

Upon entering the DEA briefing room, Contreras looked at his team and asked a single question.

"Who are we, people?"

His team looked first at each other and then stared blankly back at him.

"This isn't a trick question, people. Who are we?" he asked with greater fervor rising in his voice.

"We're the DEA," Agent Carina said confidently.

"Oh, Christ almighty! I have only one female in the room, and she's the only one brave enough to answer the question."

"Well, she's the only one dumb enough to answer such an easy question," Agent Nichols responded to a chorus of laughter.

Contreras pressed his hands downward as if to suppress the laughter in the air with his hands.

"Since you all like to pick on the only agent in the room who gave us our first solid lead, I'm not even going to ask you what the DEA stands for. Then you'd all be dummies because I don't think one of you would think that's a trick question. However, what I want you to consider is what the DEA is going to represent in our minds."

Once again there were glances at each other around the room, and Agent Nichols even raised his eyebrows at Agent Carina while shrugging his shoulders at the same time. After a few moments, all eyes were back on Agent Contreras, who possessed a look of deadly seriousness.

"Every single morning, I want you to look in the mirror and say to yourself, 'I work for the DEA…the Deadliest Enterprise Around.' And when you come back home at night, I want you to go to that mirror again and look even deeper into your eyes than you did in the morning and say, 'I work for the DEA…the Deadliest Enterprise Around.'

"The ATF believes our case is dead in the water. The Bureau, as always, is so full of themselves that they want all our information so they can reap a public relations coup. However, while the ATF has been busy licking their wounds, and the FBI has been busy talking about how they're going to run this show despite how little they know, the Deadliest Enterprise Around knows that this case is far from dead in the water."

Contreras scoured the room in an almost menacing way before his eyes settled on Agent Ariana Carina.

"Stand up, Agent Carina, and inform the Deadliest Enterprise Around what new developments we've made while Mr. Bickens was busy trying to jerk our chain."

"I have a friend who studied digital forensic photography at Columbia college in Chicago. Using satellite imagery, she was able to turn the car so that we could see the back side. She then digitally enhanced the license plate to visibility that allowed us to get a reading of C45 6938."

"Fucking A," several members of the team murmured supportively.

"Oh, don't stop there, Agent Carina; remember, you're talking to a room full of men. When they get excited, they expect the payoff, if you know what I mean."

"Yes, of course," Agent Carina laughed, "I wouldn't want to deprive them of that." Then she donned a more serious demeanor and began with a firmer tone. "The license plate is registered to Jerry Alvarez, who lives at 135 Kenilworth Avenue on a spacious lakefront estate in Kenilworth, Illinois. He also happens to have served in the Navy during the time that Steven Philster was serving, and his Kenilworth residence is about a mile southeast of Sonny's Drugs."

"Well, men, I could say this to Agent Carina, but I might find my-self in some difficulties with HR, so I'll say it to all of you... Well, fuck me! Is this woman good or is she the best we got!"

"When do we saddle up and go to Dodge?" one of the agents asked Contreras.

"As much as I would like to do that ASAP, we have to involve the Bureau."

"What for?" Nichols yelled out in objection. "This is our collar. This twit knocked off a drugstore. That's purely a DEA matter."

"You're forgetting something, Agent Nichols…Steven Philster is still only a person of interest for us, but he's got a file with the Bureau that's like the Chicago Yellow Pages, and if they can bring him in, we have carte blanche to question him about the theft at Sonny's. Remember, at this point it's all circumstantial. If we can get him talking, it's our collar. Another thing to consider, with what I ascertained from Bickens, is that where Philster is, we may also find Mr. Scorzoletti."

"How do you figure?"

"Because Philster was the one who gave Bickens information that allowed him to track Scorzoletti to his home, where Bickens and his team killed Scorzoletti's only daughter and separated him from his wife. That notwithstanding, he, along with Jerry Alvarez, also served in the Navy with Philster at the same time. So, if Scorzoletti is not actually travelling with these two, he's not too far in the shadows behind them."

"But, boss," Agent Nichols objected. "Philster is all we have!"

"Wrong, we have Alvarez with aiding, abetting, and maybe even playing an active role in the theft at Sonny's. The Bureau's primary concern is Philster because they feel they can get to Scorzoletti through him. That's their payday…Salvino Scorzoletti. They couldn't care less about Alvarez. That's a bone they'd be more than willing to throw our way. They take custody of Scorzoletti, and we bag Alvarez. And, between the two of them, I think Alvarez is far more likely to give us bona fide information. I mean, consider this…look at how botched up the raid on Scorzoletti's place went given the information Bickens had from Philster."

"So, what's our plan on this," Agent Carina inquired.

"We share what we have with them tonight, and it will be their call if they go in tonight, or whether they wait until first light tomorrow."

"So, it's their show," Agent Wilkens said with dissatisfaction clearly evident in his voice.

"As far as Philster goes because he has a special relationship with Bickens that makes him a person of interest to the Bureau. We let them make the entrance and serve the warrant on Philster, but the collar for the narcotics theft is attached to us. Since the Bureau didn't find any weapons or explosives at Scorzoletti's residence, Bickens doesn't have a leg to stand on."

Contreras threw his hands up and smiled as he lifted himself off the desk.

"Come on, what is everybody looking so glum about. The FBI is going to do all the work, and we're still going to get our man and the recognition for it."

"No other agency gets recognition for something the Bureau gets involved in," Agent Nichols said.

"That's for damn sure!" Wilkens added. "In fact, if I were you, Carina, I'd be piss pot angry. If it weren't for you, the Bureau wouldn't have a toilet to shit in!"

"I hear you guys!" Contreras said with righteous acquiescence. "But my instinct is that Philster is far more valuable to us than Scorzoletti, so in my opinion the Bureau is getting the shitty end of the stick here. As for now, I want you all to focus your sights on finding out everything you can about Philster, Alvarez, and Scorzoletti, both while they served in the military and what, if any relationship, they had after they got out."

After dismissing his team, Contreras made the call to Special Agent in Charge Derrick Panetta of the Chicago counterintelligence division. The conversation was brief and informal as Contreras remembered Panetta impressing that upon him when they spoke in Washington. Contreras gave Panetta the address of Alvarez's home and suggested that the best procedure would be surveillance beginning during the middle of the night so as not to attract neighbors, and an early morning breach of the premises.

Contreras also advised Panetta to inform the Kenilworth police what was going down because it would be very unlikely for any of their officers to see two or three cars with dark tinted windows parked on that street with men sitting in them. They would most certainly call for backup and turn on their flashers, thus tipping off Philster and

Alvarez. Panetta thanked Contreras for his cooperation and assured him that Alvarez would be the DEA's suspect and taken into custody by his team. In response, Contreras asked only when the warrants would be served, and promised that only he and one other member of his team would be there to take custody of Alvarez. Panetta stated that the surveillance would begin at 11 p.m., and the home would be breached at 7 a.m. if nobody responded.

As the night of surveillance began, several lights alternated between going off and then turning on until 11:30 p.m., when all the lights went off. The Bureau agents waited patiently until Contreras arrived at 6:30 a.m. with Agent Carina. Contreras parked at the very edge of Kenilworth Avenue, overlooking the beach. He appeared to be a photographer taking early morning pictures of the sunrise with his wife. He had no visibly discernable weapons and neither did Agent Carina.

Six of the eight agents from the FBI's Chicago office took up positions in the rear and on the sides of the house, obscuring themselves in the shrubbery so as not to attract the attention of any neighbors who might be out running or walking their dogs. At precisely 7 a.m., two agents rang the front doorbell twice and waited a moment before ringing it again.

They radioed agents in the back to check on any movements from the rear, but it was negative, so the order was given to silently breach the back entry with the six men entering through the rear. At the same time, two agents would enter from the front with one agent extending his arm inside the open door as if shaking Mr. Alvarez's hand. The agents proceeded from room to room with their guns drawn, but it became clear from the lack of furnishings that Alvarez and Philster weren't present. The lights they saw were merely lights set to go on and off to give the appearance of residents living there. Unbeknownst to all the agents present, they were actually being watched and listened to remotely by Alvarez, who called Scorzo and the others.

"Fuck!" Panetta shouted. "They've probably been gone since they pulled that job at the drugstore! Go tell Contreras and his partner we're fucking dead in the water!"

Chapter 17
Legend or Reality

With the COMSEC paperwork completed and the falsified credentials made, it was time to head to California. There was a small airport just northwest of Glenview where Alvarez had a small jet that could fly the nine out to San Francisco. He had already rented a spacious home in a wooded area of Fairfield. Gonzo would purchase two large vans with tinted windows that would be used for the additional men as well as the Nemesis Nine when they got to San Francisco. Since three of the eight men had experience as drivers with Mover, they were designated drivers of the two vans, and the third would ride shotgun with Jake, as he was the only one who held a valid CDL and was capable of navigating a semi in any kind of traffic condition. But a GPS was no match for a human being who knew the alleys, dried-up ravines, and sidewalks that were as wide as streets, all of which could be used to a driver's advantage when attempting to escape and evade a determined pursuer.

Drivers with as little as two years' experience could outmaneuver a cop with decades on the force who only knew the roads and the alleys of a given jurisdiction. Cops never have the pressure of being told to get somewhere fast in heavy traffic. They simply turn on their lights and siren and people move for them. Anyone who worked for Mover had to know how to "move around" traffic, so they learned every possible angle that existed to reach a destination as quickly as possible while remaining calm and pleasant. They were the ideal getaway drivers.

Gonzo and Jake would go into the bank on four different days under the aegis of setting up additional accounts for currently existing

CIA shell corporations. In doing this on different days at different times, they could observe the volume of people and the number of guards and when they changed shifts for lunch or to replace a part-time guard. They also ascertained vital information about the age of the guards, which would make a significant difference in reaction time, with older guards being slower and less inclined to take life-threatening actions toward perpetrators unless it was called for in their own self-defense.

With Alvarez providing schematics of the first and second floors and Jake and Gonzo providing the location of all the guards who were visible, Scorzo and his crew relentlessly grilled the five new recruits over and over again in an abandoned two-story building that had approximately the same square footage and a similar layout. Since time was limited, with only three days remaining before the Senate and Congress would recess, it meant their packages would be in place in four days. This would be an essential part of the success of this mission.

Using 300 blackout pistols with sound suppressors, stable and moving target practice took place all day long, stopping only at night so the muzzle flashes couldn't be seen and once during the early morning of the third day. Practice was going as usual until four cars pulled up next to the building and fifteen young African American men exited the vehicles and headed toward the building.

"Jake, Gonzo, Sano, and Max," Scorzo whispered quickly, "go and plant yourself at the bottom of the stairwells on both sides of the east side of this structure. If they come up, as I believe it's likely they will since they have these luxury furnishings," Scorzo said, pointing at some old couches and aging La-Z-Boy chairs, "Jake and Gonzo take the two west stairwells. Sano and Max, stay planted at the bottom of the east stairwells. We'll drive them down to you.

"The rest of you stay up here and get behind these pillars around the perimeter of the floor. I'm going to stay out and draw fire."

"Why do you want to take the risk of being shot at?" one of the Middle Eastern men whispered.

"I'll tell you later," Scorzo whispered.

When the group of youths entered the second floor and saw Scorzo leaning against a pillar on the perimeter of the room, they looked at each other and laughed. Then the one who appeared to be the leader spoke.

"What the fuck are you doing up in my building, bitch. This is the property of the Wharf Sharks, and we ain't never jumped in any white bitches to our club. So, I'm gonna ask you again, bitch...what you doing up in here?"

Scorzo put his hands out as if he were ready to embrace the first person to come near him, though they were about fifty feet away from him. Then he smiled a very genial smile.

"Now I didn't know this property belonged to the Wart Sharks."

"It's Wharf Sharks bitch, not Wart Sharks."

"Wart Sharks, Smurf Sharks, who gives a shit. Look, my nigger, I'm just a slumlord real estate agent who buys aging shit like this and turns it into luxury loft condos..."

"I don't believe this motherfucker. Did you hear that?" the leader said, looking at the other young men assembled around him. "This motherfucking white bitch just called me his nigger." He pulled a younger looking youth from behind him. "Dingo, shoot this motherfucker! My bullets be too valuable to waste on this bitch."

The young man shot and clearly missed Scorzo, but before going for cover Scorzo quickly pulled his 300 blackout from the back of his belt and shot the leader dead center in the forehead. The other members looked on with incredulity as their leader fell face forward, and Scorzo simply smiled again.

"Well, it looks like you're the new leader, Dingbat."

"It's Dingo, bitch."

Scorzo shot him in the neck and the head and ran for cover of the pillar nearest to him. As the youths raced toward him with guns blazing, Scorzo yelled for the others to open fire. The gang members were picked off like sharks in a shallow pond as they were in the center of the floor with their only protection being the couches and chairs that had no effect in stopping the armor-piercing bullets. The few who managed to escape to the stairwells were effectively cut down by Jake, Gonzo, Sano, and Max. Not one of them was alive after the firefight ended.

"So, tell me the reason you wanted to draw fire from them," the Middle Easterner who had previously inquired of Scorzo asked again.

"Because those gangbangers can't shoot worth shit, and I wanted them to expend enough rounds to make it look like two rival gangs went at it. You see, we're going to be using different guns tomorrow, but we now have four cars we can use that belong to them. By the way, you guys did a terrific job in a live, close quarters combat situation, but don't let it go to your heads. Our adversaries tomorrow will know how to shoot what they aim at. We will have three principal advantages. First, and perhaps most important, we will have an element of chaos existing thanks to our friend Mr. Alvarez. The second advantage will be full body armor protecting both our torsos and our legs. Third, we will be using fully automatic weapons equipped with hundred-round magazines filled with armor-piercing bullets. Since head shots on a moving target are the hardest shots to land, they'll be going for body shots, which we'll be impervious to. They, on the other hand, won't have that advantage."

According to plan, the vans with tinted windows were parked a half mile away from the bank near the onramp to I-280, where the team would head southwest toward US Air Force Recruiting Base at Skyline Plaza. At exactly 10 a.m., the bank surveillance cameras were disabled by Alvarez. A minute later Jake backed his semi-trailer up to the loading dock of the Federal Reserve Bank of San Francisco. At the same time, the first Tomahawk cruise missile slammed into Senator Nervosi's home, killing her and her husband instantly. Now Alvarez entered the launch codes initiating a hit on her other home and then on the bank. These targets would be hit in precisely thirty-five minutes. A fourth and final launch would hit Congresswoman Lakes' home in a little less than five minutes.

The vault was accessed easily enough because the majority of the first-floor guards were confused by the thunderous explosion so near to the bank, but one of the guards nearer to the freight elevator noticed one of the Middle Eastern men with an AK-47 and ordered him to halt. The man shouted as Scorzo instructed him earlier: "Allahu Akbar, you pig," and he opened fire on the guard, killing him instantly. Other Federal Reserve guards rushed to his defense and returned a flurry of shots in his direction, but the unwitting guards had been flanked on both sides and were massacred in a torrent of automatic gunfire. This was all according to Scorzo's relentless drills and instructions up to and including the incessant shouting of "Allahu Akbar!" while firing their weapons.

The plan played out like a video gamer's dream. There were no surveillance cameras to record the activity. No silent or audible alarms could go off because Alvarez had disabled them all. Police cars and emergency vehicles that raced by were unaware of what was happening in the second largest bank in the USA. Federal Reserve guards were either dead or quickly dying, but the greatest threat was from the inbound Tomahawk cruise missile that would strike the bank in approximately fifteen minutes. Around twenty billion dollars in currency on fiberglass pallets had been loaded on the truck, but Alvarez said they had to leave immediately. The gold bullion was a luxury they didn't have time to secure.

Alvarez's orders were carried out immediately. Jake put the forklift in the back of the rig, slammed the door down tight, and then locked and sealed it with a US government seal that Alvarez provided. No state, county, or municipal officer could break that seal and examine the contents of the truck. Moreover, not even a federal officer could inspect their cargo once the COMSEC papers were shown to them and Jake presented his credentials. It was like having diplomatic immunity.

Minutes after Jake and his shotgun driver pulled away, the men inside the bank ordered everyone outside.

"Go far from this den of Satan, for Allah will rain down fire on it!" The patrons and bank personnel seemed shocked and confused, not knowing whether it was best to remain lying on the floor or follow the instructions they were now being given. The men started firing up at the ceiling and yelling, "Go now, run far from this building! Allah will soon rain fire down on this den of Satan! Stand over on the hill and watch the will of Allah!"

The people began running away from the building as Scorzo and his entire crew exited the rear of the building and piled into the cars they had obtained from the gangbangers the previous day. They quickly made their way to the I-280 onramp, where the vans were waiting for them. As they made their way onto I-280, they heard the thunderous explosion of another Tomahawk slamming into the Federal Reserve Bank of San Francisco. Only moments prior to that, a fourth Tomahawk missile slammed into the opulent residence of Nadine Lakes and her husband, who were lounging by their pool, sipping margaritas. It would be the last drinks they would ever have and the last moments they would share in the bastion of wealth they had acquired through ill-gotten means.

The naval command was at a loss of understanding of how Tomahawk missiles were launched within minutes of each other with no on-board personnel entering target coordinates, launch codes, and no CO authorization for the strikes. This would throw the vindictiveness of Bickens to the wind, the Bureau's need for jurisdictional oversight into a thousand shards scattered in the wind. A small robbery in Winnetka seemed to pale in comparison to what transpired in California, but Contreras held on to the idea that his team had the only concrete leads of an elusive and most likely very dangerous man who might have something to do with all of these things. Moreover, he had no intention of sharing what his team had gleaned.

Scorzo and his team of men presented their paperwork at the airbase entry gate, and two C-5M Super Galaxy transport planes were being started for immediate takeoff to O'Hare International Airport. By the time their cargo was loaded and they were airborne, the crew began to monitor police and news airwaves to glean information on media narrative of the day's events.

Flags throughout the country were lowered at half-mast to mourn the slain politicians from California, but that would not be without incident as well. Patriots and others from the militia movement who considered Senator Nervosi and Congresswoman Lakes to be virulent forms of radical leftist ideology that was ruining the last bastion of a free and great America were raising the flags that had been lowered to half-mast positions. Because there were so many red flags with the current succession of events, the ATF's crusade against Scorzoletti was buried amidst the headlines and broadcasts of the fallen politicians and the corresponding aura of insurrection occurring simultaneously throughout different regions of the country.

Philster looked over at Scorzoletti and shook his head with a half-hearted grin. "I never thought I'd see the day when you would start a revolution in our own country."

"I started insurrections and counterinsurgencies in a lot of places our country had no business being in, but I never started a revolution in our own. You can thank those bureaucratic pricks in Washington for what's happening right now. They came to my home to pick a fight and go about the business of thieving as they usually do, but things didn't go as they planned."

"I had your back, Sal... You know that, right?"

"You called me. That's what I know. That's why I don't believe you were in league with them, and that's why you're riding shotgun with me instead of in lying in a cemetery."

As the vans pulled off of I-294 to head back to their Fox Lake retreat, they passed a post office where the flag was at half-mast.

"Hey, pull over, Sal, I have to take a leak," Philster said with a feigned air of tension. When he jumped out of the car, he retrieved an AK-47 and began shooting at the flag, slicing it off the mast. He then jumped back into the car and grinned at Scorzoletti as the flag dropped to the ground. "How's that for shooting, huh, boss?"

"Are you fucking nuts? Shooting a flag in front of a government installation?" Scorzoletti replied. "You're going to draw the federales right to us!"

"Nah, our place is about nine miles west of here. They'll never find us. It's too remote, and, besides, those guys working with Bickens are some of the dumbest apes on the planet."

"The problem with your thinking here is that you're underestimating the capabilities of our adversaries and how many of them want a piece of our ass. The only thing we have going for us presently is that they haven't connected all the dots yet. Right now, it's only Bickens and the DEA that officially want us, but that will change quickly if you do any dumb shit like you just did back there near the post office."

"All right, Sal, I promise...Scout's honor," Philster said, raising up two fingers and grinning.

"Scout's honor...you douchebag." Max began laughing. "I could just imagine the den master straddling your ass over a big old log in the forest and hosing you up the ass." With that, everyone started laughing as Philster tried to rebut Max.

"I was an Eagle Scout before all the den masters became peter-pumpers. I was a Scout before being gay was like a fucking badge."

"Yeah," Max added, "then you and one den master changed the world. You started getting merit badges quid pro quo by soliciting other young nubiles into the Peter-Scouts."

"Oh, eat my shit, you Brillo head!" Philster retorted. "When I was growing up, being gay was listed as a mental illness in the DSM, so even guys that felt gay got married and had kids. Now granted, today, if a kid is even remotely intrigued with his best friend, the schools are saying it's okay to be a peter-pumper or labia-licker and he and his or she and her best friend should explore their sexual boundaries. They teach kids about condoms and safe sex in grade school, for Christ's sake, so now if a boy or girl feels gay when they're twelve years old, the Scouts are a natural choice for them because all the butt-bangers and labia-lickers gravitate towards those organizations now."

"He's right," Scorzoletti interjected, "and it's not just about facilitating a kid's feeling of comfort about their sexual orientation. The schools today are promoting homosexuality as an acceptable norm. In fact, doesn't that high school you attended have a gay club now?" Scorzoletti asked Alvarez.

"Indeed, it does," Alvarez replied. "They had to change the school's name from the Indians because they were afraid that would be offensive to Native Americans, but they could give a shit if anyone finds a gay club in the school offensive."

"And you know what?" Philster chimed in. "I bet there was never even one Native American Indian that ever attended that school in its entire history."

"I couldn't say it for a fact," Alvarez replied, "but it's more than likely true."

"And another thing," Philster added, "if the reason gay people call themselves gay is because they're so fucking happy about their lifestyle, why do they commit suicide in much higher numbers than straight people? Can anybody tell me that?"

"Yeah," Max began after he had laughed for a moment, "it's because only ugly douchebags like you are all they can find to bang."

"Look, I ain't no peter-pumper, Brillo head!"

"Hey," Jake suddenly interrupted, "did you get high when we touched down at O'Hare? You were in the crapper for quite a while back there."

"No, why would you think I got high?"

"For one thing," Sano interjected, "you control all the pharmaceuticals and you're always popping pills or encouraging us to do it."

"I don't give a shit about that," Jake countered. "I just wondered why he's always going on these fucking rants that have nothing to do with anything that matters."

"What rants are you talking about?" Philster asked.

"Well, last time you were complaining about people bringing comfort animals on a plane, and now you're going off about the gays... How do you go off on these tangents?"

"Ask Brillo head over there," Philster said, motioning back toward Max with his thumb. "He started it all by conjuring up images of me getting buggered by my den master when I was an Eagle Scout. All I said was 'Scout's honor' to Scorzoletti, and Brillo head went off on the tangent."

217

"He's right about that," Scorzoletti said, wincing and nodding his head affirmatively as he glanced at Jake in the rearview mirror.

"Well, I think you should take a few of those Xanies and chill out, Philster, because nobody thinks you're gay, and nobody would really give a shit even if you were."

Philster looked at Scorzoletti, who nodded at him and said: "That's not a bad idea."

Philster opened a Coca-Cola and threw a bar into his mouth. As he was wafting off into a comfortable reverie, events were unfolding that would start to break the links in the group's carefully crafted legend, and the reality would seem stranger than fiction to Agent Contreras and his team.

Chapter 18
Your Bird Is Green

The mood in the DEA briefing room was somewhat glum as Agent Contreras looked at his team, nodding his head with a slight smile.

"All right, boss, what's up?" Agent Nichols began. "Are you going to rub our noses in the fact that the lights were on, but nobody was at home at the Alvarez estate?"

"No, I am definitely not going to do that."

"So, you're just grinning like a Cheshire cat because you're so happy? We arrived at another dead end, and you're smiling...it sure doesn't seem like we're the deadliest enterprise around. What is there to smile about?"

"There's two reasons," Contreras began. "First, Agent Carina and Agent Nichols used the McDonald's formula again with success, and Cassandra came back into my life."

"Excuse me for being a bit raunchy, boss, but how does Micky D's and some broad you're banging turn our situation around? I mean, don't get me wrong, burgers and broads are particularly good and satisfying... But how does that erase the fact that we're still dead in the water on this situation with Sonny's Drugs and a connection to Bickens' man Scorzoletti?"

"Agent Carina, would you enlighten us on what the McDonald's formula is?"

"Sure, you find a model that works, and you replicate it in different locations and situations."

"So, what was the model?"

"Remember how our first lead came through a traffic surveillance camera?" Carina said, after which everyone present nodded affirmatively. "Well, Agent Nichols and I checked the iPass database to see if Alvarez used that in any of his vehicles, and it turns out he uses iPass in both of his vehicles…and neither vehicle was at his residence at the time we came up dead in the water at his place."

"Keep going," Contreras encouraged.

"Well, we just found out today that a week ago, when Alvarez put his estate on the market, both his cars travelled north on I-94 to the west ramp spur, where both vehicles passed the iPass at almost identical times. Then they headed north and exited at the 120-toll collection point, which leads into Lake Villa and Fox Lake, where they have photo-enforced speed restrictions due to construction. Fortunately for us, they ignored the signs and were ticketed in both Lake Villa and in Fox Lake before the trail goes cold."

"Nice," another agent said, looking at Contreras and smiling.

"For us, yeah, but not for them," Contreras agreed. "Because now, we have a specific vicinity to search, and we can use satellite feed to track them to a specific location. All we need to do is key in the time and location where we want to start tracking them and then sit back and follow them with the eye in the sky."

"What about this broad Cassandra? Where does she fit in, boss?"

"Cassandra wasn't a woman; Cassandra was an operation, and one of the bit players in that operation was a local San Francisco gang that went by the handle of the Wharf Sharks."

"How does this tie in with what's happening here?"

"We all know about what happened this weekend out in San Francisco with the Federal Reserve bank, Congresswoman Lakes, and Senator Nervosi…"

"Yeah, of course, but what does that have to do with Steven Philster and Jerry Alvarez?"

"A lot," Contreras replied pointedly.

"How so?"

"A couple of things connect them, and it ties in with other things that happened besides the burglary at Sonny's."

"I'm lost. The stuff out on the West Coast and the robbery at the

Fed here in Chicago are tied into Muslim extremists. What does that have to do with Philster and Alvarez?"

"Let me enlighten you. In the intelligence world there's a term… it's called a legend. It's basically a contrived life that is crafted to be a reality. What we have here is a group legend rather than an individual legend…a group posing as something they have nothing to do with. They're especially convincing because they actually have some Middle Eastern confederates working with them."

"I've heard you're good, boss, but how do you know all this? Is it just speculation, or are there facts to back it up?"

"Definitely facts to back it up! That's where Cassandra comes in."

"All right, let's hear about the mystery woman."

"As I said earlier…when I was previously working Operation Cassandra, I became familiar with certain gangs that were involved in drugs for arms deals with Middle Eastern terrorist groups. One of those gangs was a group out of the San Francisco Bay area called the Wharf Sharks. This weekend I got a call out of our San Francisco office because there had apparently been a hit on this group."

"A hit on an entire gang?"

"Well, while it appeared that way, there was one lone survivor who confirmed otherwise. He wouldn't talk to anybody except me because I had a previously established rapport with this guy. He was spooked into silence, but he opened up to me because he confirmed this wasn't DEA, and it wasn't any rival gang in the area."

"If it was a rival gang and it wasn't anybody on our side, that leaves the case a little cold, wouldn't you say?"

"Not at all," Contreras replied definitively.

"How did this lone survivor live through a massacre to tell the story?"

"He was literally getting his joy-stick pleasured in an adjacent building."

The room descended in laughter.

"Who said there was no value in the joy-stick?" Agent Wilkens shouted out.

"You guys are impossible," Agent Carina said, shaking her head with a wry smile before Contreras hushed them up.

"Anyway, he hears all the shooting going on, so he cowboys over to the window after it stops to see a crew coming out of that building that consists of some Middle Easterners and a bunch of other guys.

"After the heist on the San Francisco Fed, I faxed over pictures of Alvarez, Philster, and Scorzoletti to the San Francisco field office and reconnected with my contact there. While he wasn't one hundred percent sure, he said the photos bore a resemblance to a few of the guys he saw there."

"What if he's just jerking your chain for protection, boss?"

"That might wash, if there was no other corroborating evidence to back up what he was laying down, but after the heist on the San Francisco Fed, things got a little more interesting."

"As in..."

"As in some video surveillance evidence."

"I thought you said there was no surveillance footage available for the San Francisco Fed heist."

"Correct...there was none available from the bank, but there was a video camera across the street that captured images of perpetrators leaving the scene that were taking off their head wraps as they were entering their vehicles."

"Why would they do that?"

"Because it was hot, and they didn't want to look the same in transit as they did in the bank. In any event, they did what they did to our benefit."

"Damn straight!"

"Anyway, when we used some high image resolution, it was clear that Philster and Scorzoletti were among this group of Middle Easterners that had been shouting Allahu Akbar."

"Well fuck me," Agent Wilkens retorted.

"No, fuck them!" Contreras spit out quickly. "They were really good on the Chicago job, but they got a little sloppy on the San Francisco job, or maybe just arrogant."

"What do you attribute that to? I mean, Philster, Alvarez, and Scorzoletti are all ex-naval intelligence operatives...the consummate professionals. Why would they get careless?"

"Because they're not acting as intelligence professionals anymore. They're acting as common thieves."

"Is Bickens aware of this, and are we sharing it with the Bureau?"

"There's no need for that right now, but that doesn't go out of this room...is that understood?"

Everyone present acknowledged the directive affirmatively.

"Even though there are violations that concern multiple agencies, our angle is the drug connection here, and the Wharf Sharks were definitely all about that. As far as anybody is concerned, we are only in pursuit of suspects wanted for questioning in connection with a burglary. The fact that they are wanted for the murders of Bickens' men and bank robbery is incidental to our pursuit."

Unfortunately for Contreras, the DEA field office on the West Coast had no personal interest in Philster, Alvarez, and Scorzoletti for anything other than the drug offense, and since their whereabouts were presently unknown, they shared information with the Bureau's West Coast office. Word quickly travelled back to the FBI's Chicago field office, and the loyalty of Contreras's team was a moot point.

Since the Bureau was leading their investigation as if Scorzoletti and his group were acting like domestic terrorists, the Bureau's Chicago counterintelligence division chief quickly paid Contreras a visit. It was not a cordial visit of interagency cooperation either.

"Special Agent in Charge Contreras, do you want to tell me why in the fuck you would withhold information on a group of federal fugitives wanted for murder, weapons violations, and bank robbery of not one, but two major banks in the Federal Reserve banking system?" Counterintelligence Agent Brandon James huffed angrily.

"Agent James, you need to bring me up to speed on what you're talking about, because I am only concerned with perpetrators who do the aforementioned things while in commission of crimes associated with my jurisdiction."

"Don't give me any of that Mexican monkey bullshit, Contreras! You know damn well that a subject of interest you are pursuing merely for questioning is somebody who has already murdered federal agents and committed armed bank robbery that resulted in the death of more federal agents as well as bank personnel guards. Would you like me to relieve you of your shield now for aiding and abetting a federal fugitive?"

"The fuck I was aiding and abetting federal fugitives!" Contreras retorted angrily. "I allowed the information to be passed along to the bureau in the appropriate jurisdictional manner! Our San Francisco office was under obligation to pass along information about criminal activity related to your jurisdiction in the San Francisco area, and they did just that! So, fuck off with your aiding and abetting bullshit, cabrona!"

"I'm gonna bring you up to speed real fast, hombre! Either you give me everything you have on Philster, Scorzoletti, and their crew, as well as everything you learn going forward or I will have your Chicano ass drummed right out of the DEA!"

"I wouldn't think of doing things any other way than that! Unlike people in your agency, who consider everyone the enemy, I can see the good from the bad…and I definitely see which camp you're in!"

"What the fuck's that supposed to mean?"

"You can take it whatever way you want it!"

"I'm gonna take it to mean that you feel my foot so far up your ass that you can taste the shoe polish on my shoes! You'll give the Bureau your full cooperation or you can join the rest of the sorry-ass Americans in the unemployment office!"

The two men stared at each other momentarily in a brief, but heated standoff. James possessed an impassioned hatred of the explicit insubordination apparent in Contreras, and Contreras hated the express domination exhibited by James. Much to his chagrin, Contreras felt it necessary to share some information with James. The information he shared, though, was dated and of little value to the Bureau's Chicago field office as Contreras only shared information about the

Nemesis Nine's activities in the Bay area. Anything they gleaned from recent work was not shared with the Bureau. The Bureau and Bickens remained in the dark about the Nemesis Nine's arrival in the greater Chicago area.

Meanwhile, Contreras was tightening the noose around the Nemesis Nine after securing satellite imagery live feed that picked up Scorzoletti's loosely travelling caravan. From the moment they passed through the I-294 north tollway near O'Hare Airport at Touhy Avenue, they tracked the lead car straight to the Fox Lake retreat they had purchased through Alvarez. Those of the Nemesis Nine thought their legend remained intact. They were clearly unaware that Contreras was now aware of the reality, so they planned on leaving O'Hare in the loaded transport planes the following Monday.

Chapter 19
Sunday Bloody Sunday

—✺—

Amidst the bombs bursting in the sky and a cacophony of noise that sounded like automatic machine gun fire, the Nemesis Nine discussed their carefully planned retreat from their Fox Lake base of operations.

"Fuck!" Philster suddenly shouted, grabbing a vibrating beer bottle off the coach-side table. "What the fuck's going on?"

"Sounds like an aerial bomb that cooked off before launch."

"That was no aerial bomb," Scorzoletti replied. "That was one of the trip-wire claymores that I set around our perimeter! It will be followed by a series of louder explosions closer to us! Take action!"

Immediately the men went into action to retrieve a variety of weapons they needed for what appeared to be an imminent assault. Contreras, emboldened by the certain knowledge that his subject of interest was also a federal fugitive, didn't wait for the Bureau or the ATF to join forces with him. He requisitioned military aid that included two helicopter gunships and one tank along with thirty-six heavily armed DEA agents. Using the protocol of loud, distracting music as a psy-ops form of weaponry in assaults, Contreras had one of the gunships play the song "Sunday Bloody Sunday" by U2, as he clearly expected to wipe out the Nemesis Nine if they posed any opposition to his assault.

Though Contreras was clearly expecting to face automatic fire from his adversaries, he had not yet received information on the type of munitions that had been stolen in the Machesney Park Armory theft. He was caught by surprise by the claymores that instantly took down sixteen of his thirty-six-man team as well as the AT-4 anti-tank weapon that would disable the approaching tank a few short moments later. The thought that all this was playing out against the backdrop of an anthem protesting violence was surreal.

"We've got to knock out those gunships quickly, but we've got to watch our three, six, nine, and twelve! We have to assume that they are advancing upon us from all sides!" Scorzoletti shouted to his men. He quickly sent the Middle Eastern team to head off the approaching team with M-60 machine guns and Javelin anti-tank missiles since Contreras was transporting some of his team in armored personnel carriers. He would then split his crew into three-man teams on each side with Javelin anti-tank missiles, grenades, and AK-47s. His objective was to annihilate the rear forces and disable the side perimeter forces so they could flank the frontal assault team.

The rear assault team, which was the lightest, was neutralized in short order by Scorzoletti, Gonzo, and Jake, with the XM 556 micro guns that rained down a hailstorm of bullets cutting through foliage and trees as well as any other cover the rear advancing team could use. After they had taken out the helicopter gunships that posed the greatest danger to the Nemesis Nine, their XM 556 micro guns had cleared a large, unmanned area for escape. Contreras stood in awe that all his heavy military equipment was taken out quickly and more than half of his assault personnel lay dead or dying since he was unable to maintain radio communication with them. Alvarez provided remote support to the east and west flank teams through the use of a predator drone. Clearly, this was not the type of resistance that Contreras anticipated encountering. Added to that, Carina, the first female agent he ever had under his command, was missing and assumed dead. At ninety-eight pounds and twenty-four years of age, she was a petite waif of an agent and the youngest agent under his command. He felt an almost paternal responsibility for her.

Contreras believed that he would be encountering men who were caught off guard due to confidence in the belief that their legend would conceal them. He believed that he had requisitioned what was more than sufficient military hardware and personnel to bring in what he estimated to be about ten heavily armed men. What he didn't anticipate was how heavily they would be armed. He never imagined that they possessed arms that would be able to take out tanks and helicopter gunships.

He also couldn't see that the Nemesis Nine weren't a desperate group of men who were aligned with a federal fugitive. Rather, they were a group of men running toward an objective instead of a cowering group running away from an adversary. They were warriors of battle ever ready to bring a fight to the politically correct majority who they believed hijacked the freedoms and liberty of the common American, those who had now become the silent and forgotten Americans. The class of people who were ruled instead of empowered.

Scorzoletti bore no personal animosity toward Contreras, but during this siege he thought his real adversary was Bickens. Working on the assumption that he was fighting Bickens made Scorzoletti more determined to inflict as much damage as he could on the advancing enemy. Though Contreras and his forces saw Scorzoletti as an enemy of the state, Scorzoletti saw the men advancing on him as the enemy of the people. As such, he and his like-minded comrades fought with more ferocity. This was something that Contreras was clearly not counting on. He had been emboldened by the thought that he had the element of surprise with his ambush-style pitched battle against Scorzoletti. He suddenly found himself unprepared for a group that was always ready to fight for the ideals they believed in.

For men like Contreras, Bickens, and James, the only ideals to be adhered to were those that offered opportunities for advancement in their career path. That was simply a matter of pursuing those who opposed the charter of their specific agency. At the end of the day, nothing mattered other than how close they came to achieving that objective. Scorzoletti, on the other hand, no longer had a job, and the one he previously had wouldn't have led anywhere meaningful anyway. Like so many Americans, his job was one of basic subsistence. He worked simply to pay his bills and keep food on his table. This was the price he paid for taking the moral high ground at a pivotal point in his career and doing what he considered right instead of doing what was considered a greater good as Steven Philster had done.

When Contreras retreated from battle to call in reinforcements, the Nemesis Nine fell back to the house to resupply and escape. However, they were met with a surprise. Half of Scorzo's men entered through the front and the other half through the rear.

"Freeze, DEA!" Agent Carina shouted at Scorzoletti, who was the first in the front door. She pointed her weapon straight at him. "Drop your weapons now!"

Jake entered first from behind her very quietly, aimed for her forearm, and fired. His direct hit caused her to instantly drop her weapon.

"Why didn't you finish her!" Philster shouted, pointing his gun at her.

"We may need her as part of our escape and evasion. She's wired, so we can monitor her people, and she's also a bargaining chip that can buy us time if things get hairy."

"Besides, killing in self-defense when under attack is different than assassinating a federal agent in cold blood when she is outnumbered and outgunned. Now get something out of that bag to ease her pain and slow down the bleeding. We're gonna have to move her fast. She's going with us, and we probably only have a ten- or fifteen-minute reprieve before they come back at us in overwhelming force."

"She's a fucking enemy combatant," Philster argued, as Scorzoletti scooped her up and carried her to the couch. "Why should we waste any of our supplies on her."

"It's like Jake said…she's an asset, not a liability. She's hit two fucking times. She poses zero threat to us and can be of maximum benefit in our escape and evasion." Scorzoletti turned up her radio monitor and heard what he had assumed. Contreras was calling in reinforcements and had merely fallen back to regroup.

Philster produced narcotics to dull Carina's pain, and had Max remove the bullet from her right thigh while applying dressing to her forearm where the bullet had gone clear through.

"What's your name?" Scorzoletti asked.

"Ma Qing Xu," she replied, using the family name her mother had given her instead of her legal name from her father. She felt that this would garner more influence over Scorzoletti because his wife, whom he was separated from, was Chinese. She had already decided to act in a cooperative rather than adversarial manner with her captors, hoping to be of some use in bringing Scorzoletti and the Nemesis down. She was far cleverer than her youthful appearance would attest to, and her mother's Chinese influence gave her a keen insight into what Scorzoletti needed most in a woman after having lost his wife and daughter.

"That's curious," Scorzoletti began. "Your skin is very light, and your accent suggests you grew up and were educated here in the States, yet you have a full-blooded Chinese name. *Ni shi wu sui dui ma?*"

"*Shi de,*" Agent Carina replied, agreeing with him, unaware that he was asking her if she was fifteen. She replied with one of the few words she knew in Mandarin, believing she had a fifty-fifty chance of correctly answering what she believed was a yes or no question, so she replied yes.

"I don't think so," Scorzoletti retorted, searching for some identification from her pants, which had been removed to treat her wound. "So, Special Agent Carina, the DEA doesn't hire fifteen-year-olds, much less use them in heavily armed assaults. Why didn't you tell me your real name? You had to know that I was gonna find out sooner or later."

"I was scared. I thought you were going to kill me," she said in a woozy voice.

Scorzoletti looked at her for a moment and saw the fragile countenance of his wife. This was exactly the sentiment that Agent Carina was seeking to arouse. She was well briefed on his background through information Contreras gleaned from Bickens. She knew the only advantage she would have with him was if she could get in his head, if not his heart.

Max finished up tending to her wounds, and Scorzoletti prepared her for evacuation.

"Lift up your feet, princess," Scorzoletti instructed Carina as he assisted her in putting on some clean battle fatigues. "These are going to be a little big on you, but loose is better than tight in your condition."

Carina nodded, trying to peer directly into his eyes with as much warmth and compassion as she could muster in her narcoticized state.

"Thanks," she said softly, noticing that he continued to fix his gaze upon hers as he helped her put on her pants. Though she was Amerasian, she had dominantly Asian features, especially her dark, almond-shaped eyes and the low bridge between her nose and forehead. She believed that this had already yielded its advantage as she was aware that Scorzoletti had always referred to his now deceased daughter as "princess." She summoned her emotions to sadness so that her eyes would well up with tears.

"I don't want to die," she said with a slightly quivering voice, even though she knew she wasn't in mortal danger. She never allowed herself to drift into sleep even though the effects of the narcotics were strong. She kept her gaze steadfastly locked on Scorzoletti's eyes as a tear rolled down the side of her face.

"You're not going to die, princess…not under my command," Scorzoletti assured her, wiping the tear from her cheek.

The other men were too busy loading the cars and carrying out the orders Scorzoletti had given to notice what was playing out between him and Carina.

"Scorzo, we're ready to roll," Sano yelled, standing at the rear door.

"We're leaving?" Carina asked.

"It's the best plan of action since we have adequate transportation. Your lead agent isn't too bright. If I was him, my first order of business would've been to disable our vehicles so we had no route of escape other than on foot. I guess he thought we wouldn't be leaving here, huh?"

"I guess, but he is really sharp. I think he just underestimated you guys."

"That was his first mistake."

"Yeah, we all thought it was a no-win situation for you guys."

"All right, princess, up you go." Scorzoletti heaved Carina over his shoulder and headed out to the vehicles. The door of a waiting SUV was open, and he carefully laid her out in the back.

"*Resta con me, papa. Sono spaventato*," she asked with pleading eyes, speaking to him in Italian, which she had learned from her father.

Scorzoletti paused for a moment, locking onto her gaze.

"I can't stay back here, princess, but there's no need to be scared. You're going to be fine," he answered, taking her radio from her vest. Scorzoletti took the wheel in the lead car. They drove off-road through a semi-wooded area without detection until they reached a main road. This had all been planned in advance.

The Nemesis Nine made their way to I-94 heading south toward O'Hare Airport. The entourage left before police air support could arrive to track them from above. Scorzoletti removed the iPass transponders from all the vehicles so there would be no electronic trail of their escape through the toll collection points, but he knew that there was a possibility they could be tracked through Carina's radio. Scorzoletti made one brief communique to Contreras, deceptively claiming to still be at the house, before flinging her radio into a roadside swamp about five minutes from the house.

"Special Agent Javier Contreras, this is Salvino Scorzoletti. We have in our entourage one Special Agent Ariana Carina. If we are not allowed to leave the house unimpeded by your forces, Agent Carina will not live to see her twenty-fifth birthday, and that would be a damn shame. Her blood would be on your hands!" Scorzoletti handed the radio to Philster, who was riding shotgun, and it was promptly thrown out of the passenger's side window into the water. Scorzoletti didn't wait for a reply from Contreras.

"Fuck!" Contreras shouted as he looked at the house through binoculars for the first time. He was now forced to call in the FBI HRT group because he wrongly believed he would have to negotiate the release of Carina. Such a ruse was a credible threat; there were no eyes on the rear perimeter to report that there were no cars in the back of the house. The fact that he could see no movement of anyone at any of the windows on the front side of the house also seemed logical since men with Scorzoletti's training would stay away from all windows. "All forces stand down," Contreras said over the radio with resignation apparent in his voice. "We have to wait for the FBI HRT team to come in."

Contreras and his arriving reinforcements waited for twenty minutes to hand over jurisdiction to the FBI HRT team. First on the scene, and much to the chagrin of Contreras, was special agent in charge of the Chicago field office, Derrick Panetta.

"So, what did we have here, Agent Contreras? Your showdown at OK-fucking-Corral? It's plainly apparent that you totally fucking disregarded my orders to cooperate with us regarding this interstate fugitive, and now it has resulted in more loss of life and a hostage rescue situation with one of your own agents! I guess playing Lone-fucking-Ranger was much more important to you than teamwork!"

Contreras took the berating with no argument. His chief concern at this point was the life of Special Agent Ariana Carina, who he believed was being held hostage in the house occupied by the Nemesis Nine. It would be another twenty minutes before the FBI would have a subsequent team at the rear of the house when negotiations would commence.

"Salvino Scorzoletti! This is Special Agent in Charge Derrick Panetta of the Chicago FBI field office. You are going to be talking with Special Agent Louis Freemont of our hostage negotiations team. He will be facilitating the safe surrender of DEA Special Agent Ariana Carina as well as you and your men." With that announcement, Panetta passed the bullhorn over to Freemont. "Okay, Freemont, do what you do best."

As helicopters whirred overhead, and the engines of armored personnel carriers hummed in the background, Freemont stepped behind an armored shield to begin what he believed might be a protracted process of negotiation. He began by addressing Scorzoletti on a first-name basis.

"Salvino, this is Special Agent Louis Freemont of the FBI hostage rescue team. I'm going to be very honest with you from the outset. There will be no surprises, so you can completely trust me. I say what I mean, and I mean what I say. I would be remiss in this regard if I didn't start out by informing you that we have set up a perimeter completely surrounding you. In addition, we have coverage of the sky above you, so you have absolutely no recourse but to work with me on a safe surrender of everyone in that structure.

"You can communicate with us using Agent Carina's radio until we set up additional open lines of communication with you. I will wait five minutes for your response. If I don't hear from you within that time, I will pursue additional communication as well as other measures to ascertain the well-being of Special Agent Carina and the safe surrender of your men. I also want to let you know that we will take into consideration the past service in the armed forces of you and your men. We want to provide every opportunity for you to be treated with respect and fairness, and without further loss of life for all present."

During the five minutes that elapsed, Scorzoletti and the Nemesis Nine started to taxi down a runway at O'Hare International Airport. They were bound for Switzerland, where Philster and the other members of Nemesis Nine would set up a multitude of private accounts over the course of several weeks for the massive amount of money they had. When they were safely airborne, the fruitless negotiations were about to get underway again after five minutes of total silence. Just before they resumed, though, Agent Freemont received communication from the rear perimeter.

"Agent Freemont, did Special Agent Contreras remove any vehicles from outside the structure in his initial assault?"

Freemont turned to Contreras, who heard the question radioed in from the rear.

"Well, what about it?"

"No, we neither disabled nor removed any vehicles from any area surrounding the structure."

Panetta glared at Contreras. "Oh, that's just fucking great! Can somebody get me some thermal binoculars!"

The rear perimeter radioed again.

"One of our agents who moved up closer just noticed tire tracks from the back of the house leading into the woods in a northwest direction."

Panetta and Contreras both heard the information and Panetta shook his head in disdain as he glared at Contreras.

"Terrific! Just fucking terrific," Panetta said, placing the thermal binoculars up to his eyes. "Not a single heat signature in there of a live body! Freemont, give the orders."

"All agents proceed with extreme caution in taking the structure. There may be booby traps. I repeat, take the structure but exercise extreme caution once inside."

Agents moved in slowly from all sides and breached the structure. Once inside, a laser-detonated explosive device was activated and nine men inside the house as well twelve agents surrounding it were instantly killed. All of this served only to slow down pursuit of their adversaries and widen the distance that separated them.

What Contreras hoped would be a bloody end to a group of fugitives that three federal agencies were pursuing ended up being a well-publicized bitter defeat for the DEA. The DEA, ATF, and the FBI were all smitten with rage that the siege at Fox Lake turned into a disaster worse than Ruby Ridge, Idaho, or Waco, Texas. Perhaps the only thing favorable in the outcome was that it was as swift as it was violent. It didn't drag on to become a media spectacle for all the agencies involved, but it assumed the proportions of a club big enough for democrats to bludgeon President Courtland with. Three local news networks erroneously reported the incident as another ATF siege gone tragically awry in the attempt to capture the elusive Machine Gun Scorzo, as he was now being referred to.

Scorzoletti and the Nemesis Nine, while relieved at their newfound independence wrought out of the Fourth of July siege in Fox Lake, were hyper-vigilant in their cautiousness and preparedness to repel any subsequent assaults wherever they may arise. While it was safe to assume that the dragnet for their capture was currently limited to the USA, they were now in the CIA's backyard and ran the risk of drawing them into the web of agencies in pursuit of them.

The risk of this was particularly high in Switzerland, where the CIA had numerous accounts at different institutions for various covert operations around the globe. It was no less the same with ONI, so this limited the number of institutions they could use for storing the huge sums of money they had accumulated.

"I can't believe we're flying in a plane with pallets of hundred-dollar bills stacked to the ceiling," Philster said ebulliently.

"That's the worst of our problems, because the safest place to store it is where the CIA and ONI have most of their offshore accounts… in Switzerland."

"It's actually not that big of a problem, Sal," Alvarez said.

"Why's that?"

"Because the company and ONI use either the top-tier Swiss banks or the incorporated banks of Switzerland. They never use the family-owned Swiss banks, which leaves us a lot of options for storing cash, but there's also another option that we can leverage."

"And what would that be?" Scorzo asked.

"Have you ever heard of something called Currency Cloud."

"Something like an iCloud?"

"It's roughly the same principle, but instead of storing your money in a bank or iCloud computing system, you actually become your own bank. You have the capacity to store as much money as you want, and you can digitally transfer it to any other bank in the world with no traceable destination because the money is stored in numbered accounts, the same way some Swiss banks work. Moreover, you can send and receive thirty different types of monetary funds with SWIFT. So, some of the money can be stored in numbered Swiss accounts, and much larger sums can be stored in Cloud Currency Spark Banks that we own and operate."

"From this point on," Scorzo said, pointing his finger at Philster, "I don't want to hear any more references to this man as a pothead. His technical proficiency is resolutely more kick-ass than all the firepower we can summon. Despite the inherent dangers posed by what we've already done, Alvarez has a mind that can pull off our next two targets and have the bad guys shooting at each other instead of us."

Scorzoletti reasoned that it was not enough to merely steal from the premier thief who had siphoned off tens of trillions in wealth from the common, working-class Americans. He also wanted to send a message to the corrupt federal institutions that were usurping the liberties and freedoms of the common Americans...those who President Courtland called the "Silent Majority."

Chapter 20
Princess or Judas

"How are you feeling, princess? Any pain?" Scorzo asked Carina as he placed his hand on her forehead.

"*Sto bene, papa*," she replied, telling him she was okay in Italian.

"Why do you keep speaking to me in Italian?"

"You remind me of my father. He was Italian, and he liked to speak in Italian to me from the time I was an infant, so I just picked it up. I guess he thought it was cute to have a little girl who looked Chinese running around the house speaking in Italian."

"Well, there's something you have to understand."

"What's that?"

"I'm not your father. In fact, I may just be the one to put a bullet in your head if you try to compromise us in any way. I could never have a daughter that consorted with a bunch of gestapo thugs that murder innocent little girls in their sleep."

"That was Bickens' crew, Salvino. The DEA had nothing to do with that. For what it's worth, I give you my heartfelt condolences."

"You're running a fever," Scorzoletti said, turning away from her gaze. "Philster, get some antibiotics to Agent Carina so we can start an IV drip. Max, you redress her wounds. Philster, get her some glucose as well. She hasn't eaten in a while."

"Hey, why don't we take her to a hospital where we can all stand around her bed praying for her too," Philster replied smugly.

"Do we have to keep reminding you that she's worth more to us alive than dead?" Jake piped in.

"Do I have to keep reminding everybody that this bitch was part of an assault team that tried to wax our asses?" Philster retorted. "We should've just put two in her head in Fox Lake instead of bringing her along with us and baby-sitting her."

"That's enough, Philster," Scorzoletti said, as his eyes shifted between Carina to Max, who was attending to her.

"Make no mistake about it, Sal," Philster continued, "this bitch would have had no reservations about taking you or any of us down in Fox Lake if she could've. These fucking alphabet cowboys love to play Wyatt Earp and go into every situation with guns blazing! Tell me something, sweetheart," Philster asked, looking at Carina, "what the fuck was the deal with the helicopters, armored personnel transports, and the tacky music by U2 all about. It was a bit of overkill, don't you think? Fucking psychological warfare, that's what it was! Disorient and overwhelm your adversary with immense firepower!"

Carina didn't answer Philster. Instead, she fixed her gaze on Scorzoletti's eyes as if to seek refuge therein.

"Typical! Typical! Typical!" Philster ranted at her. "No fucking answers! No fucking bravado when they're not backed by a few dozen foot soldiers covering their asses."

"Hey, douchebag, didn't you put any Kotex in that doctor bag of yours?" Max said, speaking up for the first time.

"What? Are you telling me it's that time of the month for this bitch!"

"I wasn't inquiring for her. I was thinking of you. It sounds like it's that time of the month for you."

"Oh, real funny, Brillo head."

"Do me a favor…if you have one, stick it in your mouth."

"Sure, after I shave your head, you fucking sheeny."

"How about if you wash down a chill pill with some of that fine German beer we have. It sounds like you've been hitting the Dexedrine."

"Max, give her a little more Oxy for the pain and some Tylenol to bring her fever down," Scorzoletti said, intermittently making eye contact with Carina, who never took her eyes off him. "Alvarez, I want you to sit next to her while the rest of us meet in the front of the plane."

"Roger that, boss."

The guys moved to the front of the plane and Scorzoletti convened the meeting.

"All right, we've been made, so we can dispense with the legend now. The FBI, ATF, and the DEA know we're not Muslim extremists..."

"Which means they're not going to be dragging their heels anymore in their pursuit of us," Philster interjected. "They don't have to worry about the liberal fucking media calling them racists anymore, so they're going to go full throttle."

"Absolutely right," Scorzoletti concurred. "More than likely, they will brand us domestic terrorists who have a white supremacist of Neo-Nazi orientation...either that or an anti-government group out of the militia movement."

"It's going to be textbook disinformation and misinformation using every media platform they can to rally public opinion against us and justify any means necessary to kill us," Philster began. "It's not about catching us anymore. Those days are over. We represent a clear and present danger to the corrupt intelligence community and everyone they serve, so they'll go to any lengths to permanently silence us."

"So how do we roll with this?" Jake asked, exhaling with a sigh.

"We do what they will least expect," Scorzo said flatly.

"Which is?" Sano asked.

"We go for the motherload. We hit the Federal Reserve Bank of New York City in a few months from now after we've banked all of our current cargo..."

"Forgive me for saying so," Max interrupted, "but that's insane. I mean, realistically speaking, it will take us weeks if not months to get all of the cash we have in private Swiss accounts and Cloud Currency."

"We aren't going to bank all that cash in Swiss accounts. Mohammed is going to get some of his Middle Eastern connections to exchange money for arms since we had to leave most of what we had behind in Fox Lake in the interest of expediency. They're also going to help us bank some of that money in the Middle East within their organizations in exchange for a percentage of the cash. Philster, remember that Jew from the Mossad, Ariel Aronstein?"

"Yeah, a real mover and shaker when you needed to make anything happen with Israel. I used him a lot when I was with ONI, but they never knew anything about him. He was an asset I cultivated myself, and he knew how to keep his mouth shut. He never worked for anyone else in ONI or the CIA."

"That's exactly why we want him. He's going to move a huge chunk of our change into protected Mossad accounts that he'll set up for us because he can requisition transport planes and everything else necessary to accomplish those ends. Finally, the remaining portion of our gains is going to be distributed to accounts we'll set up for people who were part of the Cassandra network. That's where Carina is going to help us."

"How's that?" Nixon inquired.

"She worked with Contreras, and Cassandra was a pet project of his that nailed high-level drug kingpins and arms dealers. It was one of the greatest coups of the DEA, and it should have propelled Contreras to a top-level administrative post within the DEA. Unfortunately for him, the Bureau's counterintelligence division usurped jurisdiction from him, and he was totally passed over. The glory went to the Bureau, specifically a guy by the name of Brandon James. At the time he was only a SAC working for the Bureau in DC. Now he's the Bureau's director of counterintelligence."

"So why do we want to get involved in the politics of the Bureau and the DEA?" Nixon asked.

"It's a red herring," Scorzoletti replied. "You see, we're going to use Agent Carina to offer up this morsel to Contreras as a connection to us, and naturally he's going to bite hard because this was his brain-child, and the Bureau stole his thunder. After his humiliation at Fox Lake, this is going to be like redemption to him."

"Isn't this going to allow them to get a fix on us?" Jake asked.

"Yes, and no," Scorzoletti replied. "Knowing who we are, the Bureau has, without a doubt, enlisted the help of the NSA, which monitors every call that is placed around the world. They would have the voice prints of all of us through our past military service, and also Agent Carina's through her work with the DEA."

"It clearly looks like yes," Sano interjected. "How do you figure it's also no?"

"Because none of us are going to do the talking. Agent Carina is going to help us by passing along the information to Contreras when our asses are just about to be airborne back to the States. We then resume radio silence just as we have since we arrived. This all fits in perfectly with the whole anti-government militia narrative that they themselves will believe in because they're the ones that are going to be perpetuating it. And, since it's coming from Agent Carina, it will be very credible to Contreras and all parties listening in; the Bureau has no doubt already wire-tapped and bugged his office."

"How can we assume Agent Carina will cooperate with us," Max asked. "Maybe she won't agree."

"She's alone, she's been away from her team, her family, and her country, and she will believe she's providing information that will help her boss. She knows the history of Cassandra and what happened to Contreras. They're very tight… His personal appeal for her safe return in yesterday's press conference was the first time I ever heard a supervisor do something like that.

"Meanwhile, the Bureau and Contreras will be at each other's throats because he knows the drill. Despite his blunder in Fox Lake… overall, he's a sharp agent. I'm sure that he's more than aware that his office is already bugged and wire-tapped, so he's going to be operating under the radar with all his information. The Bureau will find that getting his cooperation will be harder than pulling teeth from a pregnant horse. Mark my words, when Agent Carina calls in, he'll request that she give him a call-back number that he can contact her at in about five minutes so he can get out of the office and use a clean line."

"Won't he know it's a set-up since Carina is our prisoner?"

"No, because Carina is going to make him believe that she has escaped, and that will be very credible because she's going to identify a

DEA safehouse for us where she will make both the calls from. That will be more than sufficient reason for him to believe what she says."

"You know, Sal, I get what you say about her emotional state of mind," Max countered, "but why are you so sure she's going to cooperate with us given how we decimated her team in Fox Lake and also shot her ass up?"

"You ever hear of the Helsinki syndrome?"

"Yeah, a psychological condition where a captive begins to identify with her captors and turns against state authorities. But hey, I don't think we've impressed upon her the idea that we're altar boys."

"Not in Fox Lake, we didn't. But we've treated her well, and we're going to bring her into the fold. She's going to be re-educated, as it were, and made privy to us setting up accounts for charitable and humanitarian organizations. She's going to be convinced that the money we looted from the Federal Reserve banks in Chicago and San Francisco is being used for a greater good, and that our use of the Casandra network is for the purpose of righting a wrong done to her boss. Can we all agree on that? In short, she's going to be politically corrected."

One by one all the men nodded affirmatively. It made sense logically and it appeared to have a very plausible rationale for eliciting the desired emotional response from Agent Carina.

"Immediately following this meeting, we are to begin treating her with compassion and respect as if she were one of our team. We are never to address her as Agent Carina. We will address her by her first name, Ariana, or Carina, because she is merely a woman in our group and not a DEA agent. Any time she suggests that we give her up and surrender, we gently counter her requests with what our mission and purpose are. She has to be convinced that we aren't a group of cowboys that are knocking off Federal Reserve banks to become filthy rich.

"Instead, she must be made to understand the inherent futility of what she once did because of the corrupt men that are the ringleaders of the cesspool circus the alphabet agencies operate in. This girl is a go-getter…an idealist, so our task in these next few months is to help her see the lasting good in our ideals over the futile and transient ideals of waging a so-called war on drugs that can never be won, or a promotion that can be usurped by corrupt, politically connected superiors to suit their own hedonistic and self-serving ambitions."

"Are you going to keep calling her princess?" Philster asked with a smug smile.

"Probably, she's such a petite waif, but my point is that we totally stop referring to her as an agent of the DEA. That identity has to go."

Scorzoletti called out to Alvarez and motioned him to come up front after the men had all exited. He briefed him on their agenda and started to plan their future itinerary back in the United States as their plane touched down.

While the Nemesis Nine carried out their task of disbursing their large cargo of cash into a multitude of different sources that they kept secret from Ariana, they allowed her to see them funneling cash into organizations that fought the scourge of human trafficking, as well as a variety of other humanitarian organizations. They even enlisted her help in identifying entities that could be considered useful to victims in the drug war without directly financing what they considered the useless war on drugs. While she initially disagreed with their premise that the war on drugs was an exercise in futility, she saw the logic in them wanting to focus on the victims rather than doing battle with the cartels.

Ariana supplied names and contacts of grassroots organizations that helped farmers transition from growing coca to other crops such as coffee to support them. They also funneled money to officials who would protect the farmers because it was in their financial interest to side with the farmers instead of the cartels. Ariana appreciated Scorzoletti's logic of dealing with poverty and bureaucratic corruption, the root problems fueling the drug trade.

"You know, Scorzoletti, I don't like your methods or means for dealing with the world's evils, but I have to admit I admire the ends you are trying to achieve. It's just a shame that you couldn't use your intelligence and your resourcefulness to achieve these ends legitimately through legal means."

"What? You mean like lobbying Congress to support impoverished farmers in Latin America or dismantle the infrastructure that allows human traffickers to operate on a global scale with impunity?"

"Yeah, why not work within the system instead of breaking the laws and killing people to effect a change?"

"Come on, princess, wake up and step out of the ivory tower. Do you think American congressmen or senators give a fat rat's ass about what happens to illiterate farmers in Latin America? Hell, they don't even give a shit about their own constituents right at home in America. And as far as human trafficking is concerned, our senators and congressmen are the biggest consumers of goods and services rendered via trafficking networks. So, they're not going to come within a country mile of shutting down that shit! Christ's sake! They even protect it. The Navy was even selling children in Cambodia for profits to finance black ops so they wouldn't have to go to Congress and be hamstrung by congressional oversight."

"Is that why you got out?"

"I didn't get out. I was forced out because I shut the operation down."

"Wait a minute, you're saying that trafficking in children was a Navy operation?"

"Yeah, a highly classified operation... Isn't that just peachy?"

"So, you were retaliated against for being a whistle-blower?"

"Whistle-blower, ha! If he had tried to go that route, he would've been dead before his information jumped up to one person in the chain of command," Philster interjected. "Every motherfucker involved in that op was as serious and lethal as a heart attack."

"If you weren't a whistle-blower, how did you shut the operation down?"

"I sent a message that spooked the locals and cut the head off the dragon," Scorzoletti said flatly.

"Yeah, he sent a message all right," Philster chimed in. "He killed a fleet admiral and two high-ranking ONI officers with a signature style of killing that only he and one other individual could execute. The other individual was on the other side of the world at the time, so that left only my friend here as the likely culprit."

"You assassinated US military personnel?" Ariana said with a sense of astonishment.

"Assassinated! Assassinated!" Philster cried out in his typical vitriolic manner. "He blew the top of their torsos clean off their fucking bodies before their dead carcasses could hit the ground and bleed out! But they could never pin it on Scorzo, so I ended up being the patsy that had my ass shagged into the big house! Meanwhile, all the other fucking pricks associated with the op were never touched! All thanks to Senator Nervosi, with a little help from that bank-embezzling sleazebag Congresswoman Lakes!"

"You'll have to forgive the Philster. He gets a bit testy whenever he talks about Operation Lotus Blossom."

"You'll have to forgive the douchebag every time he opens his mouth," Max said, to the amusement of the other men.

Ariana smiled faintly and then looked back at Scorzoletti inquisitively.

"So, you were never implicated or charged with anything?"

"No, but my actions weren't without consequences. I was relieved of my command, stripped of my rank, and my service history files were totally abrogated, creating this huge black hole that became a sizable impediment to becoming gainfully employed as a civilian. You see, I could no longer tell any employer that I spent most of my life in the military because there was no longer any record of that. If it hadn't been for a colonel who had hired me as a civilian mechanic, I would probably have ended up as a homeless street person when I came back to the US with my wife and daughter."

"And that wasn't the end of it," Jake said as he stared at Ariana coldly and spoke in a low, flat tone. "ONI Deputy Commander Richard Pierpont and ATF SAC Gary Bickens figured on taking ill-gotten gains from Operation Lotus Blossom as their personal booty. They wrongly assumed that Scorzoletti had shut the operation down for the purpose of siphoning off all the funds procured through Lotus Blossom. That resulted in the siege at his home and the death of his daughter. And that, in fact, is why we are all here."

Ariana looked at Scorzoletti with a mixture of compassion and subtle grief as she stared into his eyes.

"I'm sorry about your loss. I assumed your daughter's death was entirely your fault because you drew first fire on Bickens' team."

"Of course you assumed the death of my daughter was my fault. Do you honestly believe you were going to be briefed on the reality of the situation?"

"That greedy motherfucker Bickens was there because he believed he was going to get information from Scorzoletti that would build him an early retirement nest egg," Philster opined. "Once he had that, he would have whacked Scorzo and his wife...you know, dead men tell no tales."

"This is a lot to swallow."

"You're lucky you didn't work for that hopped-up twit Bickens, or swallowing would've been the only way a peach like you could've climbed the ranks."

"Keep it clean, Philster," Scorzoletti said, rolling his eyes upward. "She's a lady."

"I'm the only female in the Chicago field office, so I'm used to the banter of the guys, but thanks anyway," Ariana said with a slight smile as she reached out and lightly put her hand on Scorzoletti's wrist. "Scorzo, even though I understand why you're doing what you're doing, I still don't approve of it. I don't think you're going to live long."

"Everybody has to die some time," Scorzoletti said, gently pulling his wrist away from the warmth of her hand. "I just might surprise you though. God has a strange way of exacting retribution on scumbags."

"But the wages of sin are death," she replied softly.

"Yeah, and since we're all sinners, princess, we're all going to die at some point. That's the inevitable and unavoidable fact of life, but if we can do some good in spite of that fact, maybe that's the most meaningful thing we can derive from the circumstances in which we find ourselves."

"Hey, Ariana, don't you just love this dago motherfucker," Philster said with a brief chuckle. "He can make a pile of shit smell like a dozen roses."

"He definitely has a way of finessing light out of the darkness," she replied.

"You'd never know he was so intelligent owing to his lack of social conviviality."

"I guess some people put more stock in action rather than words. Contreras is a lot like that. He's really big on accomplishments rather than talk."

"Ouch, Operation Cassandra must have been a real kick in the balls for him. The fucking Bureau boys stole his thunder on that one. Is that why he had such a hard-on for us back there in Fox Lake?" Philster asked.

"Hey, Philster, let's not go there. It's over and done with. We came out unscathed and Contreras's team got hosed. Remember what we just talked about?" Scorzoletti said, raising his eyebrows. "That agency doesn't exist as far as we're concerned."

"I must be missing something. Why doesn't my agency exist?"

"It doesn't exist for you anymore. It's over for you."

"Are you trying to tell me in a roundabout way that you're going to kill me?"

"Ariana, this guy doesn't do anything in a roundabout way," Philster said. "He's like a fucking hurricane that slams into shore head-on."

"If I wanted you dead, I would have just put two in your head at Fox Lake and called it a day. What I wouldn't have done if I wanted you dead was take you with us and nurse you back to health. That would be an unnecessary waste of time and resources, don't you think?"

"I guess," she replied tentatively.

"Do you know any of the agents that died in Fox Lake?"

"Only two of them mortally that were wounded. I saw Steve Huskers take a head shot. The back of his helmet disintegrated like

248

shrapnel and he fell. Graham Nuesam was in front of me. He took two direct hits in the chest and collapsed back into my lap. I had fallen because one of the rounds went straight through his body armor and hit me in the leg. He died in my lap. He was only twenty-eight and he had two young children. A tear fell from his eyes and he asked me to tell his wife that he loved her and would always be with her in spirit. After that I just saw men falling as your people advanced on us. I stayed really low and made a beeline to my right to avoid the advancing line. I was separated from the others. That was how I made it to your house."

"That's some sad shit, Ariana," Sano said, patting her on the shoulder.

"That's the sad thing about death," Scorzoletti added. "We live our lives in the present thinking of all the things we want to do, or we believe we will do, but we never know when death is coming."

"Yes, it was very sad, but it was very quick."

"Death in our line of work often is," Jake said.

"I can still see his vacant eyes when the life faded out of him. I can remember feeling so angry. I hated all of you so much that I didn't even feel the pain of my own wound. I wanted to kill as many of you as possible."

"Well, that was the whole point," Scorzoletti said as a smile cracked the corner of his mouth. "That's why your boss brought so much firepower to the siege. He didn't expect to bring us in. We were a thorn in the side of too many people's asses. He just wanted to exterminate us."

"You must have hated us too."

"I was concerned with self-preservation and the survival of my team. We didn't have any time to think or hate. We just reacted to the threat. Besides, I never killed a man I hated. They were always just targets in a particular mission. The only person I think I can say I truly hate is Special Agent Gary Bickens of the ATF. That's why I didn't kill him."

"You wanted him to suffer for what he did?"

Scorzoletti sat next to Ariana and looked at her as if he was teaching her when he spoke.

"I wanted him to remember what he did for the rest of his life, and that wheelchair will remind him of what he did to my daughter. You're incredibly young, so I don't expect you to understand that. As the British would say, you're a noticeably young bird...green too, but you'll learn."

"And you're going to teach me?" Ariana said, somewhat sarcastically.

"We're all going to teach you."

"Why not just let me go? You guys got away clean. I'm no longer any use to you."

"Sorry but we can't do that. You know way too much about us, and you're also the only one who's heard me openly admit to shutting down Operation Lotus Blossom through the assassination of US government personnel. You also know I ordered the assassination of Senator Nervosi and Congresswoman Lakes in addition to robbing the Federal Reserve banks of Chicago and San Francisco."

"I understand why you did it, and maybe I would've done the same thing if I was in that position."

"No, you wouldn't have done the same thing I did. You would have tried to go through the chain of command, and you would have ended up dead."

"Maybe."

"No, for sure," Scorzoletti said with a smile as he patted her shoulder and moved off the couch.

"I guess you're right. Sometimes I think with my heart as much as I do with my head."

"It's an admirable quality, but it can also be a serious liability in the intelligence field."

"There's no place for heart in our field," Jake added, "only cold, methodical, calculated precision."

"Damn straight," Sano said.

"Tell me something," Ariana said, looking at Sano. "Were you carrying a sword during our assault or was I just imagining that."

"The old boy be wacko," Max said with a laugh. "He thinks he's Genghis Khan or something whenever he goes into battle. It's in his

250

DNA from his mother's side."

"Your mother was Chinese?"

"She is Chinese. She's still alive."

"Well, we have something in common. My mother is Chinese too. Do you speak any Mandarin?"

"My mother had me go to Mandarin classes when I was a child, but I never cared for that stuff. I just wanted to fit in with all my classmates. As far as I was concerned, I was American, but when I was in second grade, I saw a Bruce Lee movie for the first time, and I was fascinated. Then there were all the Steven Seagal movies, so I was hooked on martial arts and eventually became a master in both kung fu and aikido by the time I was twenty-one. Then, after I finished college, I enlisted in the military and became a SEAL."

"So, you're a very dangerous man."

"I'm a teddy bear, you'll see," Sano said, starting to cackle in his zany manner.

"He's also a douchebag too," Max said with laughter as Philster said "douchebag" in unison with him. He knew Max's verbal repertoire. "The old boy ate too many mushrooms one night, and he hasn't been the same since."

The innocuous banter continued throughout the evening with each man letting Ariana get acquainted with his history. It would continue as the days became weeks and it was time for her to be initiated into the fold by making a call to Contreras. Prior to that, however, she helped the men set up foundations that would issue annuities to care for the family of Nuesam and her other fallen comrades in the DEA. When Carina questioned why Scorzoletti wanted to help the families of people he deemed government thugs, he said pointedly: "Maybe I think with my heart sometimes too. Besides, spouses and children are innocent, just like my daughter was." Ariana was touched, but she didn't say it. It was a secret she kept within herself as her heart moved farther away from the DEA and closer to the Nemesis Nine.

Chapter 21
Public Enemies Number One

—⁓⁓—

As the weeks passed and there was no trace of the Nemesis Nine, tempers began to flare within the Bureau, and suspicions grew that Contreras might be withholding more information from them. Similarly, Bickens was at odds with the Bureau for entering what the ATF started and had every intention of finishing, but his hands were tied just as were those of Special Agent Contreras. Though the two would not renounce their vows for vengeance on the group that had caused them so much private and public grief, they were ordered to stand down and cooperate with the Bureau. From now on, the FBI would be the public persona representing the forces of good that would pursue these public enemies to their eventual demise.

On a sweltering August afternoon, Brandon James and the acting director of the FBI, Joel Weinstein, met with President Courtland in the Oval Office to discuss the threat posed by Salvino Scorzoletti and his Nemesis Nine, and how they would neutralize that threat. Until now, President Courtland had little to say on the matter, but the Bureau wanted that to change. They wanted to rally the president's conservative, patriot-loving base to their pursuit of the Nemesis Nine by getting the president to publicly acknowledge that they were a malevolent force of evil in the United States whose wantonly ruthless acts endangered the well-being and lives of all Americans.

"Mr. President," Weinstein began in a cordial tone, "the FBI feels it would be in your best interest to make a public statement regarding the heinous acts of Mr. Scorzoletti and his reprobate group of men to unify public opinion on their malevolent nature. We would also like you to invoke the Insurrection Act of 1807, and the Bureau would like to call on you for Title 10 deployments of the military."

"I'm not sure I understand why it would be in my best interest to get involved in something that is a police matter," the president replied. "I have never made any public statements with regard to others who committed criminal acts during my term. This is a matter for the FBI to resolve. It has nothing to do with the executive branch of the government, and I will absolutely not use the Insurrection Act of 1807 or Title 10 deployment of the military for the capture of one man and a few of his criminal associates! The mere thought of it is patently ridiculous and I am adamantly opposed to it!"

"Let me put it another way, Mr. President. The Bureau believes it would be prudent for you to do this, since our counterintelligence division, under the leadership of Mr. James here, has clearly established the possibility of these men being directly involved in the deaths of Senator Nervosi and Congresswoman Lakes. He was likely responsible for the deaths of Senator Nervosi and Congresswoman Lakes. These were sitting members of the Senate and the Congress for Christ's sake! This amounts to nothing less than a direct attempt to overthrow the powers of the United States government!"

"Mr. President, we believe these men are nothing less than a well-disciplined group of domestic terrorists," James added. "That's something which definitely concerns the executive branch of government. Moreover, they are responsible for the theft of munitions at the Machesney Park armory. That's a military installation. You are the commander-in-chief of our nation's military, so that should put these men directly on your radar, and, as such, the counterintelligence division of the Bureau believes it imperative that you weigh in on this group with a public statement about pursuit of this group as well as decisive military plans to counter their threat. Consider what these men did in Fox Lake! They took out a force of heavily armed, militarized DEA agents like they were playing a quick game of chess with a child."

"I think the both of you need to stand corrected on a few facts," the president rebutted. "First, it hasn't been clearly established who committed the theft at the Machesney armory. Second, it still remains a mystery to everyone in Naval Command how those missiles were launched that killed Senator Nervosi and Congresswoman Lakes and then destroyed the Federal Reserve bank in San Francisco. Finally, the siege at Fox Lake was a sloppy, carelessly executed raid on men with special forces training who were probably expecting a confrontation!"

"Mr. President, we've obtained video surveillance footage of these men exiting the Federal Reserve bank in San Francisco only moments before a missile slammed into it…the exact same kind of missile that destroyed the homes of both Senator Nervosi and Congresswoman Lakes."

"All that substantiates is that they were at the Federal Reserve bank. There is no surveillance from inside the bank, and the bank personnel can't identify the perpetrators of the bank robbery because their faces were covered. Moreover, your own counterintelligence division briefed me on the fact that they were shouting Muslim epitaphs during the robbery and as they exited the bank just as witnesses had attested to in the robbery of the Federal Reserve Bank of Chicago, so we're right back to Muslim extremists and not home-grown domestic terrorists."

"Excuse me, President Courtland," James said, "but what you weren't briefed on was their connection to the murder of a San Francisco-based gang that was associated with arms dealing and drug running."

"Actually, I was briefed on that by the DEA Chief of Intelligence Bill Ruther. The Wharf Sharks dealt with Middle Eastern terrorists, so once again everything points back to Muslim extremists. Unless you people can prove to me beyond a shadow of doubt that we are dealing with home-grown domestic terrorists, there's no way I am going to go making statements that color Muslims as terrorists in one broad stroke. I am going to continue to look at Mr. Scorzoletti and his group as being separate from those individuals who attacked the Machesney armory and the two Federal Reserve banks until I have reason to believe otherwise."

Director Weinstein shifted in his seat and cleared his throat and then spoke in a tone that was an imploring call to action for the president.

"President Courtland, even if we forget all about Machesney, the two Federal Reserve banks, as well as Senator Nervosi and Congresswoman Lakes, we are still left with the inescapable facts that Mr. Scorzoletti himself is responsible for the death of four ATF agents attempting to serve him with a search warrant at his home. In addition to that, he and his men are responsible for the deaths of more than a dozen DEA and FBI agents in Fox Lake who subsequently attempted to serve him and Steven Philster with warrants for questioning in conjunction with a narcotics robbery in Winnetka, Illinois, and the massacre of the Wharf Sharks in San Francisco."

"As I understand it from Chief Ruther, it was only Steve Philster who was wanted for questioning, and he was considered only a person of interest. In all my years as an American citizen, and during my three and a half years as the President of the United States, I have never heard of using helicopter gunships and armored personnel carriers to bring a person of interest in for questioning."

"Mr. President, the Bureau's counterintelligence division established the fact that Steven Philster was traveling with Scorzoletti. The ATF can back that up with the necessary facts. Agent Contreras of the DEA has a source that confirmed the massacre of the Wharf Sharks at the hands of Scorzoletti and his group. In light of these facts, I think the trail of bodies, both Federal agents and civilians, definitely merited the resources that Agent Contreras brought to the scene in Fox Lake."

"Those are details I was never briefed on."

"Oh, and I almost forgot to tell you that now Scorzoletti and his men are wanted for the kidnapping and likely interstate transport of DEA Agent Ariana Carina as a hostage."

"What's being done to secure her release?"

"Nothing."

"Nothing! Why nothing?"

"Because we've lost Scorzoletti and his group. We don't know where they are. Moreover, neither the DEA nor the Bureau negotiates ransoms for hostages."

"Well then, I think the declaration of Agent Carina as a hostage is a bit premature. It's probably more accurate at this point to assume that she's a casualty."

"Mr. President, we aren't prepared to inform her family that she's deceased until we have confirmation of loss of life. The last communication on her was issued by Scorzoletti's group. They specifically stated that they would be removing her from the location to ensure unimpeded transit."

"She may have been brought with them, then killed and disposed of in a manner that would leave no trace. After all, FBI on the scene confirmed that vehicles were not present at the house and it had been vacated prior to the beginning of hostage negotiations, correct?"

"That is correct, Mr. President."

"Well then, rather than trying to goad me into making a public spectacle of myself by jumping into a quagmire of political quicksand, I think your first order of business should be to locate Agent Carina's body and locate this group of fugitives. Then start pursuing leads that are based on what is known about Mr. Scorzoletti and his group rather than generating a narrative that is based on circumstantial evidence and conjecture. I don't have to lecture either of you on how far the latter will get you in court, but the fact that he and his group have killed federal agents is thoroughly substantiated, so pursue that angle."

"We are all over that, Mr. President, but we would also like it if we had your approval to use a strategy that was used with great success by Mr. J. Edgar Hoover himself."

"And what would that be?"

"We'd like to resurrect the moniker of 'public enemy number one' for these men, and shorten Mr. Scorzoletti's name in addition to attaching an actual symbol of violence to his name."

"Director Weinstein, don't take me for a walk in the woods. Be a little bit more specific."

"Well, specifically we would like to start a media campaign that refers to him as Machine Gun Scorzo instead of Salvino Scorzoletti. We've been referring to him that way amongst ourselves, but we want citizens to think of him as Machine Gun Scorzo, public enemy number one. The machine gun is a symbol of destructive fury, and we want to evoke that image whenever we mention his name. I would like your explicit approval to use the media in the implementation of this strategy."

"Since when have you people and the media ever looked for my blessing on anything?"

"Mr. President, we believe that national unity about the perception of Salvino Scorzoletti is central to bringing him down. That unity begins with you and filters down to the common American throughout the States. We want Salvino Scorzoletti to become a social pariah instead of the folk hero that some patriot groups as well as some of the nation are starting to consider him."

"Mr. Weinstein, I can assent to the change of his name and using the media to garner public support in his capture, but I want to strongly caution you against associating him and his actions with patriotic Americans."

"If I may clarify, Mr. President," Director James began, "in the world of counterintelligence we use the term patriot groups to refer to the fringe right radical groups that are militantly anti-government, yet they position themselves as patriots."

"Make no mistake about it, President Courtland," Director Weinstein added, "these people are by no means patriots in any sense of the word."

"Again, I am going to remind you gentlemen," President Courtland warned, "by no means are you to use the term patriots or patriot groups. The average American doesn't think of patriots or patriot groups as radical anti-government fringe groups. Just stick with the facts! Scorzoletti is wanted in connection with the death of federal agents and should be considered armed and extremely dangerous."

"We'll stick with the facts, and in return we want to be able to call on the military for assistance in his apprehension."

"No deal! I am not going to allow the use of the military on US soil in the apprehension of an American citizen, even if he is a dangerous fugitive. I will not cross that line and start that kind of precedent!"

"Mr. President, I have made you aware of what he did in Fox Lake! This man is a longtime master chief SEAL team commander, and those others with him that we have been able to identify are all military special forces veterans. They may even have confederates inside the military that are assisting them!"

"The idea that they actually have people inside our military assisting them is nothing short of wild conjecture."

"Sir, those precision-guided munitions were fired from subs somehow."

"Until it can be conclusively proven that Scorzoletti and his group did that…and I don't see how they could have, we are not going to go there with public statements to that effect. In the meantime, I suggest you make use of other agencies like the US Marshals as additional resources. You can even use the CIA if you believe they are operating outside the country. I will not, however, approve the use of the military in any capacity for use in the capture of these individuals. Is that clear?"

"Crystal clear, Mr. President! We villainize Scorzoletti based on facts. What we know so far is damning enough!"

"I'm glad we understand each other, gentlemen. If there's nothing else for now, I have a meeting I need to get to. Please keep me abreast of any new developments in this situation."

Though the FBI director and his director of counterintelligence agreed with the president's verbal directives, they were not completely on the same page with him. A phone call to the FBI director a few days later would lay bare the cunning duplicity that was at the heart of many of the Bureau's public relations triumphs.

"Director Weinstein, good afternoon. This is Richard Pierpont, deputy commander at ONI. I hear your request for military support in the apprehension of Salvino Scorzoletti didn't go over so well with the president in your meeting with him a few days ago."

"I wasn't aware that news of the president's decisions traveled to so many different places."

"Well, I happen to have a particular interest in the apprehension of Salvino Scorzoletti, and the Office of Naval Intelligence is privy to information on the president's briefings whenever he consults the joint chiefs for any matter at hand."

"So, you're interested in Scorzoletti because he was a SEAL?"

"Yes," Pierpont replied deceitfully. "It would be an embarrassment if one of our own elite members was known publicly as a lowly, treasonous bank robber gone rogue."

"So, what can the FBI do for you?"

"Well, I'd like to see this situation as one where we could do something for each other."

"Well, Deputy Commander, I am all ears. How can we help each other?"

"You need military assistance that I can provide."

"And you naturally want something in return."

"Actually, I want a couple of things in return. First, I don't want you to disclose Scorzoletti's history with the SEALs to the media. In fact, I don't want the background of any of his confederates disclosed to the media."

"And if the media should get wind of his history?"

"There's no way they could, because he no longer has a military service record. He can't even go to the VA, for Christ's sake. The only way the media could get wind of his history is if a credible source such as the FBI leaks information...and you're going to make sure that doesn't happen. Control the narrative on Salvino Scorzoletti and his wayward comrades. The Bureau is very good at that. It's what you guys do best!"

"What's the second thing you want in return?"

"The second thing is very simple. I want you to allow Special Agent Gary Bickens of the ATF to be a part of your counterintelligence task force to apprehend Scorzoletti."

"You do know that Bickens is in a wheelchair, don't you?"

"I am aware of that. I'm not asking that he actually participate in the physical capture of Scorzoletti. I am just asking that you allow him to participate in the investigation headed by your counterintelligence division."

"I can agree to that, but he has to come in with the understanding that the Bureau has full jurisdiction in this situation now. I will not allow his desire for retribution to justify including the ATF in a joint effort to apprehend Scorzoletti."

"Yes, of course. It's the Bureau's ball game all the way."

"Any particular reason for wanting him involved?"

"We have a history together that goes back to college. I also feel terrible about what happened to him. I know he feels a personal obligation to his men to have a hand in bringing Scorzoletti in, even if it's in an investigative role in his capture. It's the least I could ask for an old friend who will have to suffer for the rest of his life because of Scorzoletti.

"He's also familiar with Scorzoletti's background and other crimes that amount to high treason. These crimes are not a matter of public record. They are classified and sealed indefinitely. They are crimes that Scorzoletti was never brought to justice for. ONI couldn't touch him after he was discharged from the teams, but Bickens was able to legitimately pursue him for federal firearms violations. Bickens and his men didn't deserve what happened to them, but the Bureau can right that wrong."

"I can definitely agree to your terms, but how can you provide military assistance to me when the president has made it absolutely clear that he will not allow any military engagement in the pursuit and apprehension of Scorzoletti? He was most emphatic about that."

"Well, that's the beauty of the SEALs. Nothing they do ever exists. They are ghosts hovering over the face of the earth, righting the wrongs that are never adjudicated in the courts or punished by a jury. Owing to plausible deniability, the president is typically never informed of their presence in an operation, and this will be no exception."

"Pierpont, we definitely have an agreement. Bickens will be part of our task force."

"Very well, I will reach out to Bickens and establish clear parameters for his involvement with your counterintelligence team. This way there will be no misunderstanding about who has jurisdiction in this matter. You can subsequently brief him as well regarding his role within your team. Oh, Director Weinstein, I won't be communicating with you on this matter again. At such time in the future when you need my SEALs, you simply let Bickens know. He will direct the SEALs to work under the Bureau's command in the apprehension of Scorzoletti."

"Incidentally, we are no longer referring to Salvino Scorzoletti by his legal name. Going forward, he will be known to the public as Machine Gun Scorzo, public enemy number one."

"I like that. It's sort of like Machine Gun Kelly from the 1930s. Referring to him as public enemy number one also evokes an image of him as the most dangerous menace to society that America faces."

The two men chuckled and said goodbye with the tacit understanding that each man would help the other to get something that both men wanted. However, while Director Weinstein was looking to add another public relations triumph to the Bureau's long-standing history, Pierpont and Bickens were looking for something completely different.

"Good afternoon, this is Special Agent in Charge Gary Bickens."

"Bickens, it's Pierpont. I've got great news! We are going to get our retirement, and we are going to take care of Scorzoletti as well."

"How are we going to do that now that the Bureau's counterintelligence division has taken jurisdiction and told everybody else to fuck off?"

"I made a little deal with Director Weinstein, and as of now you will be a part of the counterintelligence task force to pursue and apprehend Salvino Scorzoletti, aka Machine Gun Scorzo, Public Enemy Number One, as the Bureau is now referring to him."

"But apprehending him was never a part of our plan."

"It's still not a part of our plan. Extracting information and terminating him was and still is the plan. Moreover, the pot has gotten a lot sweeter since our initial plan."

"How so?"

"The Bureau has connected him to the robbery of the Federal Reserve bank in San Francisco. As such, it's highly likely he's also connected to the robbery of the Federal Reserve Bank of Chicago as well, and knowing the way Scorzoletti stole and concealed all the funds from Operation Lotus Blossom, it's a sure-fire bet that he's done the same thing with the mother-lodes from Chicago and San Francisco.

"That's most likely why he's vanished without a trace…even the NSA hasn't heard so much of a word uttered by him within the trillions of calls they have been monitoring globally. He's been operating under the radar now for over six weeks, so he's probably already distributed that cash into accounts all over the world by now."

"So, what's my role within the Bureau?"

"How does the title 'information troll' grab you?" Pierpont chuckled. "You're simply going to glean as much information as you can from the Bureau and give them nothing in return. We will then use all the intelligence they have to direct a team of SEALs to acquire our package without the help of the Bureau. After that we can use all means necessary to extract information on our funds as well as funds he and his group have recently acquired and thereafter discard of the package."

"What's our cover story going to be?"

"The unexpected."

"The unexpected? I don't understand."

"Yes, the unexpected. We were fully prepared to assist the Bureau with a predetermined date to apprehend their Machine Gun Scorzo when he and his group suddenly, and without notice, attempted to flee to countries that have no extradition treaties with the United States. We just didn't have time to wait for the Bureau. We had to act or Machine Gun Scorzo and his posse would have gotten away! We couldn't let that happen, now, could we? After extracting all the information from our package, we simply discard him and turn the others over to the Bureau."

"But say the others try to cut deals and provide information to the Bureau in return for leniency?"

"Think about it… If you had a cut of billions of dollars waiting for you upon your release from prison, would you compromise that by trying to cut a deal for leniency that might not be any better than a full sentence? Need I remind you what happened to the DEA agent that was prosecuted for skimming millions of dollars from the Cali cartel in Colombia? He never talked, and the money was never recovered, so after two years in prison, he was freed to become a rich and retired DEA agent."

"In ten or fifteen years, though, these guys are going to want to make bank, and what's going to happen when they find their booty is gone?"

"What's going to happen? Well, for starters, they're not going to ask the FBI to help them find their stolen money, are they," Pierpont said, and began to laugh.

"These aren't the kind of men to let something like that slide. All of them are hunter-killers."

"I don't think they'll possess the same physical and mental prowess after fifteen to thirty years in a federal penitentiary. They'll be happy to sit in a peaceful retirement home and play checkers during recreation time."

Bickens began to laugh at the thought of such a scenario, and his apprehension dissipated. "That's a happy ending I can live with," he said, still chuckling.

"You, me, and the Bureau."

"How do you figure the Bureau is going to be happy?"

"Because they're going to get all the credit for bagging Machine Gun Scorzo, public enemy number one, and all of his cohorts. They get a hard-on about shit like that, and they have been looking for a public image makeover ever since they were embarrassed by that shit they were involved in during the 2016 election. We're just going to be their silent partners who bag all the money."

Both men had a laugh before saying their goodbyes and hanging up. They felt proud of their resourcefulness, and envisioned a better life awaiting them at the conclusion of the plan they would execute.

Not more than a week had passed before the DEA's chief of intelligence, Bill Ruther, got wind of Bickens' role in the Bureau's counterintelligence task force. He wasted no time in contacting Director Weinstein.

"Can you tell me why the ATF is involved with the Bureau's task force, but the DEA has been hamstrung with orders to stand down on this investigation and pursuit of Scorzoletti?" Ruther asked.

"Because the DEA is the weakest link in the trail of evidence that would lead to the apprehension of Machine Gun Scorzo, that's why!"

"The weakest link! Are you fucking kidding me, Weinstein?"

"What have you produced other than a tenuous case regarding Steven Philster as a person of interest in a burglary of a small pharmacy in Winnetka?"

"It was intelligence gathered by Special Agent Contreras and his team that identified Scorzoletti and Philster in the massacre of the Wharf Sharks. A member of their gang who survived also clearly identified them as the perpetrators of the Federal Reserve bank robbery in San Francisco and the slaying of four Federal Reserve police at the scene. It was on that basis that the FBI was able to begin pursuing the actual perpetrators of the robbery instead of chasing their tails for weeks on end!" chief Ruther thundered.

"And Agent Contreras thereafter continued pursuing them within a jurisdiction that was outside of the DEA charter! Since when does bank robbery fall within the jurisdiction of the DEA?"

"Contreras wasn't pursuing them for bank robbery. He was pursuing them in connection with the possible robbery of narcotics for the Wharf Sharks and their subsequent massacre! Most likely to exchange for arms! You may remember something called Operation Cassandra, which was the sole effort of Agent Contreras before the Bureau took jurisdiction of it and shut Agent Contreras down.

"He was told to cooperate with the Bureau, and he and his team withheld evidence from us before going off on his high horse and engaging the suspects in a siege at Fox Lake that was both a media spectacle and a public embarrassment for the Bureau as well as the ATF."

"Maybe if the Bureau and the ATF would have shared information on who Contreras was contending with, Fox Lake might not have become the debacle that it was. Contreras and his team had no idea they were up against a veteran SEAL team commander and a bevy of special forces experts. Besides, the DEA took full responsibility for what happened out there in Fox Lake."

"But at the end of the day, the photos that ended up in papers and on social media were of my agents from the Chicago field office, not to mention more bad press for the ATF. I'm sure you've heard of the saying that a picture paints a thousand words. Well, pictures of my agents from HRT, counterintelligence, and bank robbery division were front and center in those stories, so who the hell cares what the DEA accepts responsibility for behind closed doors!"

"Look, Contreras may have acted a bit presumptuously..."

"Presumptuously! That's the understatement of the century! He acted with wanton disregard to any sound protocol for apprehending a group of suspects like Machine Gun Scorzo and his group. He went in with guns blazing, which is exactly what men like Machine Gun Scorzo and his group are trained to repel at a moment's notice. He acted with sheer stupidity when he went in the way he did without first coordinating things with the Bureau's Chicago field office. Had he done so, Machine Gun Scorzo would likely be in custody right now instead of God only knows where!"

"You can hardly blame his overzealousness given what the Bureau did to him on Operation Cassandra. His work on Cassandra was nothing short of genius, but did he get any credit for it?" chief Ruther argued.

"Very little of Cassandra had anything to do with drug cartels. The Bureau took jurisdiction from him because Cassandra was about international arms dealers and a few gangs that were trading drugs for guns."

"That's a bunch of bullshit and you know it, Weinstein! The Bureau wouldn't have had anything if it wasn't for Contreras. He put all of his time and effort into identifying a labyrinth of bad guys who were operating right under the Bureau's nose, and then the Bureau steps in and takes the glory!"

"Think what you want and say what you want, Ruther, but Contreras's preemptive siege tarnished the Bureau's image as well as the ATF's and allowed an extremely dangerous fugitive to take more lives…lives of your people in the DEA, I might add. And he allowed public enemy number one and his band of mercenaries to vanish without a trace!"

"Look, you're allowing Bickens to contribute to your team, so why can't you let Contreras join the team? He's a good man."

"We have our reasons for allowing Bickens to act in a consultant capacity to the Bureau, but we have absolutely no reason to let Special Agent Contreras join us, given the way he withheld information from the Bureau that could have led to the arrest and capture of Machine Gun Scorzo and his gang."

"Well, what are your reasons?"

"Our reasons for allowing Bickens on our task force are disseminated on a need-to-know basis only, and you don't need to know, Chief Ruther."

"So, it's like that, huh? The old Bureau two-step to contain information, huh?"

"Believe whatever you want, Chief Ruther, but Contreras and the DEA are out on this one."

"I'll remember this the next time the Bureau needs information from our people!"

"Watch it, Chief Ruther, you're treading down a precarious path when you say things like that."

"I'll tell you what's precarious, Weinstein…precarious is when an agency's ends justify the means, no matter what the cost to decent people within it or around it. Right now, I have more respect for the mafia than I do for the Bureau. You know, speaking of the mafia, I wonder why it took the Bureau so long to even acknowledge the existence of the mafia much less investigate them. Funny, but wasn't it until sometime after Mr. Hoover died that the Bureau decided it was time to get out of bed with them."

"Good day to you, Chief Ruther. I'm going to forget you said that."

Though the DEA's chief of intelligence was stonewalled by Director Weinstein, Ruther didn't consider that Weinstein had the last word on the subject. While Contreras wouldn't be privy to information produced by the Bureau's counterintelligence task force, Ruther gave his tacit approval for Contreras and his team to continue their pursuit of Machine Gun Scorzo and Steven Philster.

Chapter 22
Will to Power

—◁·▷—

As the FBI unleashed its media narrative against Machine Gun Scorzo, the Nemesis Nine began to prepare for their departure from Switzerland. In the weeks that had passed since the Nemesis Nine left the United States, American citizens became aware of Machine Gun Scorzo, the ruthless outlaw and his renegade compatriots whose signature style of murder was with a machine gun. They were disparaged as being an organized group of men adhering to the ideals of Nazism, white supremacy, and radical anti-government militia groups.

As Americans digested a daily consumption of information intended to thoroughly villainize Salvino Scorzoletti, public debate centered on how and why such a dangerous individual who allegedly wreaked so much havoc could possibly remain at large for so long, and why he donated massive sums of money to charities and impoverished Americans while publicly deploring the lawlessness of groups like CLM and AntiCap that sought to overthrow the American way of life and usher in an era of socialism within America, while seeking to build vast financial war chests for themselves.

Director Weinstein, however, made sure that his training in escape and evasion from the SEAL teams was undisclosed. Similarly, the military background of those who had been identified by the Bureau was carefully concealed so no journalist seeking sensational headlines could cast aspersion on any branch of the military, particularly the special forces. But for every piece of disinformation spread to villainize Machine Gun Scorzo in the mainstream press and media, there were stories hailing him as a champion of America's silent majority in alternative media platforms. Particularly damning to the mainstream media was a story run in an alternative publication called the *End Times,* which ran an exposé on the illegal hierarchy of the Federal Reserve banks and the reason why Machine Gun Scorzo was targeting them and redistributing their ill-gained funds to charitable organizations for victims of human trafficking and impoverished inner-city neighborhoods that CLM, AntiCap, or BOB, the Brotherhood of Blood, did nothing to empower.

"Alvarez, what's happening stateside?"

"You are one hot potato, Scorzo. The Bureau has headed up the investigation now, and they are referring to you as Machine Gun Scorzo, public enemy number one. We also share that title with you on an individual basis. They also put a cash bounty on your head of $500,000 for information leading to your arrest."

"Machine Gun Scorzo…public enemy number one, huh?"

"Yep, and according to the Bureau, you're a career criminal who went bad at the tender age of thirteen, when you killed a man with a machine gun who had raped your sister. Oh, and the rest of us are a bunch of racist, anti-American Nazi sympathizers who you manage to retain a Svengali-like control over. Moreover, we're seeking to overthrow our government. The flipside of that coin is that there's a growing number of alternative media outlets that are extoling you as a modern-day Robin Hood stealing from the evil cabal that runs the Federal Reserve banks and giving to the disenfranchised poor."

"Is that true?" Ariana said with a subtle tone of surprise in her voice.

"The second part of it is…that is, what the alternative media outlets are reporting," Scorzoletti replied nonchalantly. "The Bureau has followed the Satanic blueprint of mixing truth with lies."

"So, what's the truth and what are the lies?"

"I had access to and knew how to fire machine guns when I was younger than thirteen, but killing a man who raped my sister is fiction. They probably used that age because kids younger than fourteen can't be tried and punished as adults. Also, that particular story leaves the door wide open for a lesser charge than first degree murder, and an early release from a juvenile detention facility by age eighteen so I could begin my life of debauchery and crime, leading to my current status as public enemy number one today. They probably intimidated my sister into silence, so she won't refute the Bureau's claims to the media."

"I must say, the Bureau is imaginative."

"Imaginative!" Philster suddenly cried out. "The Bureau fucking imaginative? Don't make me laugh! The only time those guys are imaginative is when they're watching porn and jerking off! They just superimposed the legend of Billy the Kid on Sal, and they resurrected the image of Machine Gun Kelly from the fucking 1930s and threw that in for good measure. Now suddenly, he's the elusive Machine Gun Scorzo...public enemy number one! The Bureau! What a fucking joke!"

"I guess I'm glad I didn't work for them."

"Hey, hey, Ariana...newsflash, the people in the DEA aren't altar boys either. During the height of the Drug Wars, two DEA agents robbed the entire contents of the evidence property vault at one of the West Coast offices, and I'm sure your boss would know about that, even though it was before his time. It was the stuff of legends. Those two pricks were living the life of Riley. They profited over two million dollars over the course of a couple of years!"

"Is this for real?" Carina asked, looking to Scorzoletti.

"What are you looking at him for? I'm not shitting you! Then! Then, in the 1990s, the DEA ran this scam on Colombian Narco-traffickers called...get this..." Philster paused to laugh before looking back at Ariana. "...the operation was called Operation Princess."

Scorzoletti shook his head and Philster continued to laugh before looking first at him and then at Ariana.

"Sal, I think you better stop calling Ariana princess."

Philster rubbed some Chapstick on his lips and stood up from the couch, clearing his throat. Max and Sano looked at each other and smiled.

270

"Oh no, here it comes," Max said.

"Keep quiet, Brillo head. Anyway," Philster continued, "these fucking scumbag DEA agents railroad a Colombian airline stewardess with two children and a clean record into working as an agent provocateur for the DEA because her husband had ties to the drug trade. They fucking threatened her with prosecution if she wouldn't cooperate with them and pose as a money launderer. She was never involved in the drug trade and she wasn't guilty of shit!"

"I don't know if I want to hear any more," Ariana said with a sigh.

"Of course you do; it gets better." Philster started out again, in a more impassioned tone. "Because the fucking DEA agents are so fucking inept when it comes to cash-seizing operations, in addition to the fact that they're skimming and pocketing cash, they blow this poor woman's cover."

"Was she killed?" Ariana asked with bated breath.

"Oh no, she wasn't killed…she was kidnapped by the Colombians because the stupid DEA sent her right back into the fray of things after her cover was blown. She was then held hostage for over two months because the fucking DEA wouldn't pay ransom for her. They said they didn't want to negotiate with terrorists or some bullshit like that, ha!"

"Well, what happened to her?" Ariana asked with anticipation clearly visible in her face.

"You'll never guess."

"Tell me," Ariana goaded.

"While the fucking DEA takes the moral high road as their agents are pocketing millions of dollars, one of their other informants negotiates her release using his own money! How the fuck do you like that?"

"I think the DEA was just following protocol while some of their agents, on the other hand, went rogue. That's what I think."

"Oh my god, you are so naïve, Ariana! No wonder why Scorzo calls you princess. I think if the DEA was following protocol, there would have been a plethora of DEA agents arrested and prosecuted for corruption, but after a four-year investigation only one DEA agent was ever charged, and he only did about sixteen months' time…a fucking slap on the wrist if you ask me!"

"Well, at least there was an investigation and justice was eventually served," Ariana offered somewhat sheepishly as she looked around the room at everyone present.

"Justice was served!" Philster bellowed animatedly. "Are you fucking kidding me, or what?"

"Come on, Philster, lighten up," Scorzoletti said.

"Lighten up nothing," he said, looking at Scorzoletti before he turned to Ariana and continued. "Over sixty million dollars was laundered by the DEA, and to this day twenty million dollars has never been recovered. It just vanished…gone into thin fucking air! And you honestly believe that one fucking agent took all that money and hid it up his fucking ass or something before he went to the big house for a little over a year?"

Ariana felt uncomfortable and began to blush as she felt Philster and everybody else expected her to answer.

"Heads up, douchebag," Max said, finally breaking the silence as he entered the room and threw a beer at Philster. "Why don't you take a couple of tranquilizers and chill. You're acting like Ariana was complicit in the whole operation or something." Max grinned and shook his head dismissively, then looked at Ariana. "Don't listen to this douchebag."

"You'll have to forgive him," Jake added. "He tends to get his underwear in a twist about things like this because he ended up as a patsy in the aftermath of Lotus Blossom being shut down."

"I guess I can understand given what I now know about a few things."

"There, see, she understands, Brillo head," Philster said, turning to Ariana and smiling cordially. "I just wanted you to know a little bit about the history of the shysters you worked for. You ought to read some Nietzsche when we get back to the States. He laid it out perfectly when he said that for the most part, groups in power are always trying to increase the sphere of their power. Say, can I get you a beer, kiddo?"

"Sure, why not," Ariana said with a somewhat resigned smile.

Philster began to head toward the kitchen before Max intervened.

"I'll get her a beer, douchebag. You sit down and don't start going off about Nietzsche now," he said to Philster authoritatively. "I don't want you putting anything in her drink and trying to pull a Nietzsche on her," he said with a mischievous laugh. The others present laughed and encouraged Ariana to feel at ease.

"Philster's always going off on someone in the group about something. It's nothing personal, Ariana," Sano assured her.

She smiled, and genuinely felt a sense of comradery with the men of Nemesis Nine. She didn't see herself so much as a hostage who was in danger anymore. Instead, she began to look at the men as fellow Americans who she got caught up with under the wrong circumstances. She reasoned that their macho banter wasn't unlike that of the guys in her former DEA unit. Who knows, she thought to herself, any one of them may have even come to work for the DEA themselves had certain circumstances prevailed. They seemed like basically decent guys who had ended up on the wrong side of the law through either circumstance or providence. Who was she to determine which it was?

She began to think of these men as guys who had served their country and, on a personal level, even fought in God-forsaken places to defend the liberty and freedom of her and her family while she was yet unaware of it as she grew up. She also began to feel a certain respect and subtle affection for Scorzo because of their mutual upbringing with Italian fathers. She also felt a certain heartfelt compassion that none of the humanitarian battles they engaged in around the world would ever be known to the public or anyone else for that matter.

She was surprised that Scorzo and the men lived rather monastically, with most of the money they acquired going to charitable and humanitarian organizations after they purchased food, supplies, and weapons. They also treated her with kindness and tenderness as she was recovering from her wounds and accorded her the dignity of a human being rather than the disdain of an adversary. They even kidded about setting her up in business and buying her a nice house and fancy cars. Indeed, in some ways, they didn't seem that much different from Contreras and her former colleagues in the DEA.

As Ariana felt the warmth of a second beer wash over her, Scorzoletti brought the focus back to their impending itinerary.

"Mohammed, I need you to connect with your people stateside via email, using a VPN. There's a company in Spring, Texas, called Empty Shell LLC. We can purchase more XM556 micro guns from them. They'll have to be set for a cyclic rate of four thousand rounds a minute. We'll absolutely need a tremendous amount of firepower. We need ten of those along with a shitload of ammo to use them effectively."

"Four thousand rounds per minute," Ariana said with astonishment. "That's enough suppressive fire to put down an entire platoon. What are you planning?"

"More like a fucking company or a small battalion," Philster added.

"We're going to take the Federal Reserve Bank of New York."

"What about all the civilian casualties?"

"Ariana, let me educate you on something..." Philster began.

"Hey, Philster, hold up a minute. Allow me, okay?" Scorzoletti asked.

"Yeah, we don't want you going off again on another one of your rants, douchebag."

"Oh, muzzle it, Brillo head. I don't even know how you became a doctor with your limited vocabulary."

"Ariana, the Federal Reserve banks are like a cartel," Scorzoletti explained, "only they're not a cartel whose interest is in drugs...it's in currency. The Federal Reserve system was established by an act of Congress; however, it is not a government bank. In fact, the Federal Reserve cartel is controlled by very wealthy and powerful families and individuals such as Marcus Goldman, Samuel Sachs, Abraham Kuhn, Solomon Loeb, the Rothschilds, the Warburgs, and a few others."

"So, you're telling me that the money in the Federal Reserve banking system is theirs?"

"Essentially...and the reason that hitting them through the federal system hurts them is that the sum of their money can't be insured against loss. However, they don't typically put all their currency reserves in banks anyway. They invest in stocks, bonds, municipal securities, mutual funds, and US treasury securities. But these things aren't insured, so if they lose them, they're wiped out."

"I think the probability of your success in looting the Federal Reserve Bank of New York is slim to none, regardless of how much firepower you go in with. You got lucky in Chicago and San Francisco, but New York is an altogether different situation.

"First of all, the vault holds over four hundred billion in gold and over three trillion in assets which are eighty feet below the basement level of the bank. The entrance to the three-story vault is protected by a nine-foot-tall ninety-ton steel cylinder that's housed within a 140-ton concrete and steel frame. Trying to transport heavy gold and pallets of currency to the street side docks would not only be a logistical nightmare, but it would also be onerously time-consuming. It would probably take over a week for nine guys to clear out even if you were all working around the clock every day. No amount of firepower could keep local and federal forces at bay for that length of time. It's suicide, Scorzo!"

"That's where you're wrong," Philster suddenly barked, no longer able to restrain himself.

"Why attempt it? Do you guys have a death wish? You'd need a miracle to get in there, clean house, and then get back out of there and get away with your lives. In fact, you'd need more than a miracle."

"No, we don't have a death wish," Philster continued. "We're going to clean them out all right, but we're not going to set foot in the facility."

"So why all the firepower?"

"Because on the very day we plan to hit them, those stupid communist fucks that call themselves CLM, along with their deranged cohorts AntiCap and BOB, are going to stage a 10,000-man demonstration at the New York Federal Reserve Bank. They got the idea that if we could do it, so could they."

"So, you're going to coordinate your efforts with them?"

"No, Alvarez is going to digitally clean every last penny of the cash out via wire transfer; CLM and AntiCap will be left with the back-breaking and labor-intensive work of loading the gold into armored trucks that are going to be conveniently lined up around the entire building the night before."

"Won't that seem a little bit suspicious?"

"Not at all," Philster piped in. "Since the stupid fucking mayor of New York defunded the NYPD and ordered them to stand down in the wake of all these riots, those trucks are simply going to appear as for-tification to protect the bank. Police cars can be tipped over, but gold transport armored cars can't, no matter how many of those fuckers you have pushing on them."

"So, let me guess...you guys take the bank through cyber theft?"

"Bingo!" Alvarez chimed in.

"And you don't think they have security in that area as formidable as the security for an actual physical breach of the facility? It would probably be every bit as impossible to compromise them electroni-cally. If it could be done, others would have already tried it."

"It's already been done, Ariana, and successfully I might add at that," Alvarez said with a sense of pride.

"Really?" Ariana replied with apparent surprise.

"Yes indeed, they hacked into the SWIFT system, which is used by banks to transfer money, and they successfully made off with over eighty million dollars. They could've made off with an additional twenty million if it hadn't been for a spelling typo that raised a red flag."

"They weren't caught?"

"Nope, they got away clean...just like we're going to. I've got the necessary codes for all the transfers, so we are going to hit them like a thief in the night."

"I give you more than a miracle...I give you Jerry Alvarez," Scorzoletti said, smiling as he waved his hand toward Alvarez. "Machine Gun Scorzo will be nowhere to be found on that day. Even the gold will be hijacked en route to various locations by members of New York's crime syndicate that Philster recruited to pose as AntiCap sympathizers. They'll get a generous cut and the rest will be loaded on the docks to finance mercenaries that will shut down sex trafficking hubs and whack the movers and shakers that are financing the destruction of our country. The mafia will be armed with the XM556s, and they'll cut down as many of those CLM, AntiCap, and BOB motherfuckers as they can. The police will be more occupied by dealing with the casualties and the wounded CLM, AntiCap, and Bob civilians than they will be with the actual looters."

"So, if none of you plan to actually be at the site, and you don't expect any heavy resistance from the police, why is all the firepower necessary?" Ariana asked.

"Well, you don't expect us to let ten thousand communist insurgents knock off the New York Federal Reserve Bank and get away with it, do you? Besides, probably the only people who hate those fuckers more than we do are the members of organized crime. We hate those fuckers for political reasons, but the family hates them because all the looting and rioting they did took a huge chunk of change away from organized crime. It seriously disrupted business as usual."

"Did you ever hear of the malevolent midgets?" Philster asked.

"Malevolent midgets? Who are they?" Ariana asked.

"Not who…what. It's a video game…one of several that our boy here created and marketed for millions," Philster said, nodding his head with a smile as he looked at Alvarez.

"So, you're obviously not with Scorzoletti for the money?"

"No, absolutely not. Honestly, even though I'm good at creating video games and it allowed me to live a comfortable life, there's no ultimate purpose to it…nothing to believe in. It's probably also the reason why most kids don't even possess the slightest bit of critical-thinking skills and common sense. In fact, my video games have probably contributed to a large part of the school and public shootings."

"So now you have something to believe in?"

"Yeah, I absolutely have something to believe in. I mean, you see what we're doing. Don't you think that's something to believe in?"

"Like I said before, I believe in the ends you are trying to achieve, but I don't believe in the methods you guys employ to achieve those ends."

"Ariana, come on already!" Philster suddenly barked. "Do you really believe that in this day and age the world can be changed through governments and political maneuvering?"

"It's served us this far."

"Oh my God!" Philster bellowed as he threw his hands up in the air. "Are you kidding me? Man is constitutionally incapable of ruling himself. That's why all those fuckers like Nervosi and Lakes were on the take. For Christ's sake! That's why those two idiots along with all the other democrats were pushing for open borders and voting rights for illegal aliens in the United States! They just wanted to garner as many votes as possible so they could stay in office and get richer! Do you honestly think that those two hags cared anything about representing the people of the United States? Look at the state of things in their respective districts while they were alive!

"Consider their net worth at the time of their deaths. Nervosi was worth eleven million plus and Lakes and her husband were worth more than seven million! I read that the governor of Illinois has a net worth of about 3.5 billion. Now how in the fuck did they accumulate that much net worth on 175K and 255K salaries? Can you tell me that?"

"Maybe investments?" Carina suggested.

"Investments my ass!" Philster barked.

Max and Sano both looked at Ariana and chuckled while shaking their heads and looking at her as if to assure her there was no need for her to feel intimidated by Philster's bombastic manner.

"Her investments were about 350,000 dollars of her husband's stock in First United Bank! Well, guess what... In 2008, First United was going under and that stock would have been worthless! So, in comes Congresswoman Lakes and facilitates the bank's application for TARP funds from the US Treasury that provide the bank with twelve million dollars in relief. Everybody here, probably except for you, knows that the Treasury Department doesn't really have any money. All they do is issue fucking promissory notes and securities that are simply backed by the US government's word. The real money comes from taxpayers like you and me!

"We aren't as fortunate as Nadine Lakes was. Her fucking house alone was valued at somewhere between two and a half to four million dollars. I wonder how many other working-class people that make 150K live in four-million-dollar homes! Fucking investments...I'll tell you how she got rich! She fucking greased the palms of corporate fat cats on the West Coast while ignoring the plight of residents in south central LA, which she supposedly represented, yet she didn't even live in her own fucking district!

"After thirty-seven years in politics, what do the Black residents of south-central LA have to show for her so-called concern for the downtrodden Black masses?" Philster bellowed excitedly as he looked at Ariana.

Ariana looked at Philster and merely shrugged her shoulders, knowing that any answer she gave would probably be met with a heated rebuttal.

"I'll tell you what the fuck they've got! They've got record unemployment, fucking record poverty, rampant gang violence, and they're worse off now than when she took the US House seat for their district in 1991! But hey, what the fuck did she care! She didn't even live in her own fucking district! Guess where the fuck the Pied Piper of racial division lived?"

"I have no idea," Ariana said softly, again shrugging.

"She lived in a fashionable, exclusively white, gated community in Peacock Hills! How's that for a crackpot scenario? She fucking hated white people and blamed President Courtland and all his white supporters for every issue of alleged oppression that Black people faced, but she didn't want to live anywhere near her suffering and oppressed Black brothers and sisters! Instead, she chose to live in the midst of rich white people that she claimed were the source of every evil in

American life! How the fuck do you like that, Ariana? Are you starting to get the idea of the way things really work in the real fucking world, princess?"

"I think it's messed up. I'm starting to see things I guess I really never paid attention to before. I feel bad."

"Don't feel bad, Ariana. Like most folks who work for a living, you just didn't have time to pay attention to what fuckers like Lakes was doing, and if, by chance, you did tune in to the news, all you heard was the fucking socialist narrative that every media outlet in America pushes!

"I'm glad you agree with me. Now maybe you can see why our methods justify the ends when it came to a racist fucking hypocrite like her! She was beyond redemption! The only way to end her legacy of corruption and hatred was to do exactly what we did to her. Maybe now her district can get somebody to represent it who actually cares about the residents who live there!"

"What can I say other than amen to that?" Ariana said, wanting to placate the Philster so a lighter mood could prevail.

"And don't even get me started on that old hag Nervosi! She's over eighty years old and most of the time she's fucking incoherent and stumbling over her words between her fucking highballs and martinis! That old girl needs to check herself into the fucking Betty Ford center ASAP!

"When you listen to her press briefs or read her tweets on social media, it seems like her full-time job has more to do with waging war on President Courtland than anything remotely concerned with representing the needs and the will of the American people."

"I don't think anybody has or needs to get you started on anything," Scorzoletti said in a calm, straightforward manner as he gave Ariana a pat on the shoulder, presumably for tolerating Philster with such reserve.

"Yeah, sometimes you're like a freight train rolling. You just keep hurtling through one subject after another without slowing down or stopping," Jake added.

"Indeed, that he is," concurred Max.

"Anyway, we need to move on to other business. Alvarez, how are we doing with real estate on the Eastern Seaboard, preparations for Jake to take out Jurgen Morros, and our departure?"

"Funds were wired to a proxy that purchased Beacon Rock, a mansion in Newport, Rhode Island, and get this... It was originally built for JP Morgan and once owned by a naval admiral. It's like a fortress sitting on a bluff that overlooks the Atlantic on three sides, so only the north side of our perimeter is accessible to ground forces. On all other sides they would have to approach from the sea and scale the bluffs. No local police force or federal agency is prepared for that kind of stuff. If they want to hit us on any other side than the north, it would either be from boats or the air. In either case they would be like sitting ducks given the arms we're going to have to repel any force striking us."

"Excellent work, Alvarez!" Scorzo said before turning to Mohammed. "Mohammed, how are we doing on arms?"

"We have ten XM556 micro guns with 50,000 rounds of ammo, twenty javelin missiles, fifteen HK416-A5s mounted with laser optics and fitted with suppressors along with 10,000 rounds of ammo for them. I've also bought ten M249s with 20,000 armor-piercing rounds for sustained cover fire on the western perimeter of our headquarters, and twenty Javelin anti-tank missiles to neutralize Apache helicopters and any armored ground vehicles. Tonight, an intermediary associate will be delivering a McMillan TAC-50 A1-R2 sniper rifle for Mr. Jake to handle our friend Jurgen Morros."

"Jake, Nixon will be your spotter," Scorzo declared. "He was one of the best in Afghanistan. The two of you will have rations for two days only. That's all the time you have to terminate Mr. Morros. After that our planes can no longer stay at Dubendorf."

"Alvarez has had satellite imagery on his residence since we got here." Jake added. "We've been aware of his comings and goings from his estate, so that's not gonna be a problem. Don't be surprised if we send word that the job is done by the end of the first day."

"Isn't he the billionaire philanthropist who helps refugees?" Ariana asked. "Why would you guys want to kill him?"

"Oh Jesus, Ariana, don't you follow current world events?" Philster suddenly blurted out. "That fucker is busing illegals and terrorists by the thousands up to our Southern border!"

Scorzoletti looked at Philster sternly and put his index finger over his lips to indicate he wanted Philster to be quiet. Philster obeyed but paced around the room seeming to be in anguish because of his silence.

"Suffice it to say, that man uses his money and logistical resources in every conceivable way to cause as much chaos as he can in our country."

"He's so old though…over eighty or something, isn't he?" Ariana asked.

"He's seventy-nine to be exact, but evil knows no boundaries in time. Don't be deceived by the seeming frailty that his age would lead you to believe. That man is personally responsible for the suffering of millions of people around the world. We want to make sure that he doesn't touch the lives of millions more innocent people."

"Besides that, he's a fucking hypocritical coward!" Philster barked, unable to contain himself. "The motherfucker and his family fled the Nazis to avoid persecution by Hitler and the SS. Then he fled the Communists and came to the US, where he was educated and made his fortune! Now he wants to destroy the US with his fucking open society bullshit and Marxist ideology! But do you think he practices what he's preaching to the masses? Alvarez, let her see the monitor you have queued up to the satellite imagery of his estate. That guy lives in the lap of fucking luxury, but he wants to promote universal basic income for everybody else on the planet, except for him and his rich cronies that rule the world!"

"I guess you have to educate me on that subject. I'm not familiar with universal basic income."

"I didn't expect you would be because you work for a living! So did your parents. You didn't grow up in a family that looked for fucking government handouts! The premise of universal basic income is that the government provides every family with an income without anybody working."

"Well, how much, and how is that possible?" Ariana asked.

"Fucking peanuts...maybe one thousand or two thousand a month. Now since the government really has no money...only debt, they have to get it from somewhere, so they confiscate working people's property and assets and redistribute it."

"But then wouldn't the wealth of Morros be redistributed as well?"

"Oh no, that motherfucker will continue to live like King Farouk! You see, the super-rich elites are exempt from the tyranny of governments. They always have been, and they always will be! They're the fucking puppet masters for the useful idiots! It's people like you and your family that will suffer!"

"But given our situation, isn't it an unnecessary risk to take him out now? What if you get caught?" she asked, looking at Jake. "Sniper rifles are loud. What if somebody hears you?"

"I'll be shooting down at him from a remote area where there are no people. And my weapon will be fitted with a suppressor."

"But what if you miss, and he hears you? There's a chance you could be caught, isn't there?"

"People like Jake never miss what they aim at," Nixon said in a matter-of-fact manner.

"Most definitely," concurred Gonzo.

"First of all, I'm not going to be shooting him from the perimeter of his estate. I am going to be taking my shot from about a half mile away from him, but the bullet will be traveling at supersonic speed, so he'll drop to the ground with a hole in his chest about three inches in diameter long before even the remotest sound will reach him."

"I wish I could be standing next to that miserable old fart to see his fucking evil heart being blown right out the back of his torso," Philster said, nodding at Jake and grinning maliciously.

"The deed will be done, make no mistake about that," Jake assured Ariana dispassionately.

"Good, you and Nixon will head to your destination this evening," Scorzo instructed. As soon as you have completed your mission, you two will leave Dietlikon and head to Bassersdorf, where Alvarez has booked you a room at the Hotel Postli for three days. When you arrive, you are to give the desk clerk on duty this number. Tell him to call your friend and let him know you have arrived. The friend is an associate of Mohammed's who will relay the message to another associate of Mohammed who is near us. He will personally come by and deliver the message that you are in Bassersdorf. This way, none of us has to break silence until Ariana makes the call to Contreras from the DEA safehouse in Wallisellen. Immediately after her call we head out to pick you and Nixon up in Bassersdorf."

"What about our flight crew," Gonzo asked.

"They leave tomorrow morning. Alvarez has them booked at Dolder Grand, which has a direct route to the airbase about fifteen minutes away. We'll use Mohammed to connect with our intermediary in Bassersdorf just prior to Ariana's call to the States. He, in turn, will contact our flight crew at the Dolder Grand, which will be the signal for them to head to the air base and have our planes ready for takeoff. The planes will be fueled and ready to taxi for takeoff as soon as we all rendezvous. Any questions?"

"What about all the weapons you've requisitioned? Won't it be hard to conceal that kind of activity, and won't it be especially risky after the Morros assassination?" Ariana asked.

"It certainly would be risky; that's why none of those supplies are being delivered here. Most of the supplies are being loaded on a fleet of surplus patrol boats that will be waiting for us by a small tributary along Pan Am Road at JFK. We will board those and make our way into Jamaica Bay, where we will then proceed into the Atlantic and head up the coast north to Rhode Island. The rest of the supplies will be ferried in over a period of days via a surplus CH-47 Chinook that Philster picked up for a cool three million."

"How is all that going to happen without anyone noticing?"

"Let me ask you something, Ariana. If you were going about your daily assignments in Chicago and you noticed a fleet of Navy patrol boats heading from the Chicago River out into the open waters of Lake Michigan, would you make any attempt to go down there and stop them to check them out?"

"No, I wouldn't."

"Why? What would your thoughts be? Wouldn't that seem unusual to you?"

"It certainly wouldn't be a usual sight, but I would probably assume that they had some business in the South Chicago docks and were heading back to the Great Lakes naval base north of the city. It wouldn't concern me."

"It's the same principle here. Anybody that sees us will make a similar assumption because the vessels will arrive just minutes after we land, and we will depart quickly. Even law enforcement will assume the presence of the boats has something to do with a transfer of materials from the airport. They don't involve themselves in military operations because it's way out of their league."

"But the CH-47 Chinook will be coming and going for a few days, landing at a residential address. Won't that be rather imposing to other residents in the area?"

"When Alvarez bought that property, he had that in mind. The Beacon Hill estate sits on ten acres of wooded land, and the nearest estate to it is over three miles away. So, while some folks will hear our bird flying overhead, they won't see where it's landing, and the heavily wooded landscape will act as a sound buffer. Besides, there's a naval air base just five miles northeast of us. Any more questions?"

"What about us and the supplies coming by sea, and isn't that base closed?" asked Ariana.

"I'd bet my left nut on the fact that nobody in the area knows." Philster replied.

"That's another reason why Alvarez chose the Beacon Hill estate." Scorzo added. "On the northwest side of the estate, there's a deep-water dock that will accommodate all our boats. There's a trail that can accommodate golf carts leading from the dock up to the estate. Those carts have been modified to pull a small train of carts behind them that will carry our equipment from the dock to designated points on the estate."

"So, who's doing all this for you guys while we're here...buddies from the military?"

"Jesus, Ariana, you sure ask a lot of questions," Philster said.

"Sorry, it's just that I've never been involved in something like this. This is the kind of thing you only see in movies. I'm just curious."

"No, we're not using former or current military personnel. Most of them drink too much and talk too much. We can't have that. We're using Mohammed's connections. They've been led to believe that they're working for the cause of Allah, and they know how to keep a secret."

"Besides that, the Bureau never touches Islamic extremists," Philster said smugly. "Those motherfuckers have training camps all over the US, but the Bureau never raids them...go figure! They probably made a deal with Director Weinstein! If he stays away from them, he'll get forty black-eyed virgins to fuck his brains out in paradise after he dies."

Max and Sano burst out laughing and were joined by everybody else present, including Ariana.

"I think you've been hitting the amphetamines again, you douchebag," Max said.

"Hey, hey, hey, wait a minute," Philster blustered over the laughter. "Do you think FBI directors are above bribes and blackmail, Brillo head? Is that what you're telling me?"

"No, I'm just saying you're an overly imaginative douchebag."

"What about J. Edgar Hoover?" Philster implored. "Why do you think that prick never investigated the mafia, huh? It's because they had pictures and videos of him cross-dressing and having peter-pumper parties long before that kind of shit was acceptable! If he would have made one move against the mob, his entire legacy with the Bureau would have been destroyed, and he knew it! So, he kept his fat fucking cross-dressing mouth shut, and he continued to enjoy his peter-pumping parties with that other butt-banger who was his assistant and constant companion!"

Ariana doubled over in laughter on the couch as the rest of the men laughed with her. When she resumed an upright seated position, she began laughing again and continued while leaning up against Scorzo.

"Oh my God, Philster…cross-dressing, peter-pumping parties; you're incredible," she blurted out, unsuccessfully trying to contain her laughter and amusement.

"Man, that girl be busting a gut, Philster, you better stop," Nixon said.

"Well, it's the truth, you Snoop Dogg-looking motherfucker," Philster replied innocently.

"Snoop Dogg-looking motherfucker!" Ariana cried out, looking at Nixon and then back at Philster as she doubled over again in an uncontrollable spasm of laughter.

"What? What did I do?" Philster asked innocently as he looked around at everyone laughing. "All I said was Snoop Dogg-looking motherfucker. I mean, with those dreadlocks and all…you look like a dead ringer for Snoop Dogg. In fact, I'm surprised the Bureau hasn't arrested him yet and tried to pin the heist of the Federal Reserve bank out in San Francisco on him. Those incompetent motherfuckers!"

Scorzoletti softly rubbed Carina's back until her laughter abated.

"You know, you're good people, Philster." Ariana smiled at him as she resumed an upright position.

"Thanks, kiddo. It's nice to see you laugh. You know, you look cute when you're laughing."

"Shit, she looks hot even when she's not laughing," Gonzo said.

"Amen, amen to that," Nixon added.

Ariana blushed and looked at Scorzoletti in a somewhat shy manner. Scorzo smiled and nodded his head in assent.

"It's true, he's right about that," Scorzo said, looking directly in her eyes.

"Yeah, the douchebag is on point about that," Max said.

"Girl, if I didn't know better, I'd say you're one of those good-looking shy girls," Gonzo added.

"It's just that none of the guys in my office ever talked like this about me."

"What did you expect, Ariana? Those guys are probably all a bunch of closet peter-pumpers," Philster said, with laughter ensuing again.

Just then an unexpected knock came at the door and the room fell silent. Mohammed prepared to answer the door as the others dispersed into other rooms. Mohammed's courier had arrived early with the rifle for Jake, and after he left, the others reconvened to watch as Jake examined the rifle.

"My God, that thing's a monster," Ariana said with a look of awe.

"Yeah, and with armor-piercing rounds, it'll go through him like a hot knife through butter and cut him in two. It will even go through anyone standing behind him. He'll be dead before he's even aware of what's happened to him," Jake said in a tone that almost seemed consoling.

"All right, if there's no other questions, I'm going to go next door and brief our flight crew about their itinerary," Scorzo announced. "Mohammed, I forgot to tell you earlier...I want you to add one hundred claymores along with motion detectors and laser sensors. We're going to have to make sure that no formidable ground force can breach our western perimeter at Beacon Rock."

"Scorzo, my friend, if you set up trip wires, you run the risk of the claymores being detonated by small animals roaming around," Mohammed cautioned.

"We aren't going to wire the claymores. We'll set them for command detonation. The motion detectors and sensors will be interfaced with cameras that we can monitor from a command center that Alvarez will set up."

"You think of everything, my friend."

"Yeah, that's what I was paid to do most of my adult life."

As night fell, Sano, Max, Gonzo, and Scorzo kept watch on the streets below as Jake and Nixon departed and the others slept. Jurgen Morros was completely unaware of the destiny awaiting him, and the Bureau wasn't any closer to locating their prey despite all the resources they enlisted, their massive manhunt, and the accompanying propaganda effort they hoped would mobilize the help of citizens throughout the United States.

The more they used the media to disparage the man they now called Machine Gun Scorzo, public enemy number one, the more the alternate presses and conservative social media platforms extolled the virtues of his philanthropic endeavors with American farmers, poor Appalachian rural families, and victims of sex trafficking; plus the enormous, untraceable donations of protective equipment for police departments in California, Chicago, and New York along with a barrage of television ads that supported police and portrayed the democratic leadership of those cities in a negative light that suggested they were directly responsible for a dramatic rise in crime in those cities.

Despite their best efforts to portray Machine Gun Scorzo as public enemy number one, patriots and the silent majority of Americans along with alternative media sites began to champion him as an American folk hero who was turning the tides against the cancel culture of political correctness and anti-American sentiment. Moreover, he brought to light the nefarious machinations set in motion against working Americans by backdoor legislation consisting of thousands of pages of laws in the federal register that no working citizen had either the time or the inclination to read.

With the aid of Alvarez, Scorzo was able to disrupt the socialist narratives of primetime news broadcasts with special reports that interrupted their broadcasts as breaking news stories. He railed against senators and congressmen who engaged in the unconstitutional practice of exempting themselves from laws that applied to ordinary citizens while at the same time allowing themselves unfair privileges such as voting pay raises for themselves and guaranteed full-salaried lifetime pensions even if they only served a two-year term in Congress or a six-year term in the Senate. Machine Gun Scorzo was succeeding in raising the ire of the country against its politicians and federal agents far more successfully than they were casting aspersions on him and his comrades.

Chapter 23
Xiexieni (Thank You)

—◦—

Under the cover of night and with the aid of Dexedrine that Philster had provided, Jake and Nixon assumed their position on a hill surrounded by a desolate, but pleasant meadow that reminded Jake of the countryside in which he grew up. As the sun rose, there was no sign of them, for they had seamlessly blended in with the earth which they seemed to be a part of. Nixon provided the essential "dope" for Jake to account for windage, elevation, temperature, and MOA. Jake was ready for a moment that he knew would come at about 07:15.

He had patiently watched Morros every day prior to this point in time from the monitor that Alvarez had set up which provided real-time satellite imagery of Morros as he enjoyed coffee with his wife on the patio at the back of their estate every morning starting at 07:15, give or take a few minutes. He and his much younger wife would enjoy the view of their lush green lawn and the abundance of beautiful flowers as they engaged in leisurely conversation. It was no less the same on this beautiful summer morning.

At exactly 07:17 Jurgen entered the patio with his wife from the large sliding door at the back of their home. They seated themselves at a small bistro-style table, and a servant poured their coffee. Jake had precisely sighted his target for a direct hit in the chest. He began breathing deeply and slowly; his heart was beating slowly and calmly as if his fixed gaze on Morros was a form of meditation. He placed his finger and was about to pause his breathing when his heart rate suddenly began to increase.

As if from nowhere, Jacob Morros, the younger of his two sons from a previous marriage, made his entrance from the sliding glass door. It was usual for his son Abraham to arrive at 08:00 on Tuesday mornings, but Jake had never observed Jacob at the estate during the prior weeks while he had Morros under satellite surveillance. Jake took a deep breath and began to relax again.

"Adjust for target standing to the right of Morros with wind coming from the left," Jake said softly and calmly.

"Why not take the primary first," Nixon said after providing new dope for Jake.

"Because our new secondary is younger, with faster reaction time, and he's standing up. He may just decide to make a run for it. If he gets away, he'll alert the police and his brother Abraham. We can't have that. We need Abraham to arrive as he usually does today."

"Why are we taking out his sons?"

"Because we don't want them taking up the work of their father. Abraham is already the chairman of Jurgen's Freedom Society Foundation. He arrives every week on this day to brief his father on the foundation. He's integrally involved in his father's work, and though Jacob isn't, at this point, he would be the most likely successor in the event of Abraham's demise. We can't take that chance, so he must go."

"Why didn't you tell Scorzo or me? This changes everything."

"You and Scorzo didn't need to know because it doesn't change anything other than the number of targets I need to neutralize. I need you to prepare dope for me on the southeast corner window of the coach house."

"Roger that," Nixon replied obediently as Jake sighted Jacob and made necessary adjustments to his scope.

Jake placed the crosshairs to the left side of Jacob's chest just below his shoulder to provide extra compensation for windage. Again, he was breathing slowly and relaxed as he brought his finger up to the trigger; upon pausing his breathing, he slowly squeezed the trigger. As soon as he released the trigger, he calmly and mechanically pulled the rifle bolt back and then slid it forward, ejecting the spent shell and chambering a new round. Less than two seconds after squeezing the trigger, the round made impact directly in the center of Jacob's chest just above his abdomen. The round completely severed his torso. His upper body fell forward onto the table, and his lower body fell back toward the house.

Jake had already sighted Jurgen, who was sitting wide-eyed and stunned. He squeezed the trigger a second time, and as the round made impact with Jurgen, he was slammed backward in his chair. When he hit the patio deck, his body bounced upward about a foot in the air before descending into a pool of his blood that splattered onto his wife's white blouse. Nixon could see a mixture of shock and terror in her eyes as she looked upon the ghastly sight of mangled corpses who were once her family.

Jake moved his aim to the southeast corner of the coach house awaiting a scream from Jurgen's wife that would summon their driver to the window. As he expected, she let out a blood-curdling scream after her hands had dropped from her mouth. They could only see her mouth widen, but they were too far away to hear the sound she emitted. Seconds later the driver had appeared in the window to see what was happening. He looked down at the scene below him in stunned silence, giving Jake the window of opportunity he needed to squeeze the trigger yet a third time. The glass shattered like shrapnel, showering the driver as his body fell backward after impact from the round.

Jurgen's wife, who had been kneeling over her deceased husband, now stood up and looked in the direction of the driver. This provided Jake with a clear shot that would enter her back. He already had her sighted, but he waited until she turned to such a degree that she provided maximum target exposure of her back. At that precise moment Jake squeezed the trigger again, silencing her forever before she could scream again. He quickly pulled the bolt back and slid it forward one last time and fixed the crosshair of his scope on the sliding glass door. As soon as the servant appeared behind the glass door looking out on the patio, he squeezed the trigger before she could open the door. He didn't want any more screams. As he gently exhaled, he felt a sense of relief that silence would prevail until Abraham Morros appeared.

Though it seemed like hours had evaporated in the course of suppressing the five targets at the Jurgens' home, it was 07:25. Only a few minutes had elapsed from the moment Jurgen was initially sighted until the last round had been fired. Though Jake had done contract work for the government that required suppressing civilian targets after he left the military, Nixon had never provided dope for any targets other than enemy combatants during his tours of duty. He felt uncomfortable and wanted to talk, especially in the wake of seeing Jurgen's wife put down.

"Man, this be some cold shit we just did. I ain't never killed a civilian before, especially not a young woman or some innocent servants."

"Everybody's a civilian, Nixon. It's just that some are wearing uniforms and others are not. Be that as it may, you have to see this man for exactly what he was…"

Nixon stared into the cool, dispassionate eyes of Jake as he spoke. The Dexedrine dilated his pupils to the extent that Nixon only saw lifeless black orbs like those of a shark that has no compassion for his prey as he closes in for the kill. There was no guilt or remorse in Jake's eyes, only a dull glare as he looked at Nixon.

"This man was a clear and present danger to the peace, stability, and sovereignty of our country. In fact, he was more dangerous than all the enemy combatants in uniform that you helped suppress in the service of our country. His civilian clothes allowed him to commit egregious acts around the world with impunity, and today we put an end to that."

"Yeah, but I wish the driver would've taken the wife's ass out shopping or something. I could take comfort in knowing that she was out buying Gucci purses and spending the old man's money while we were busy blowing him away."

"For what it's worth, Nixon, I wish the scenario had played out like that too. You know as well as I do that in situations like these there's always the possibility of the unexpected variables and additional collateral damage."

"Yeah, I guess when you put it that way, things that took place make more sense. At least I can rationalize it now, even if I have some misgivings."

"Enough said. We need to remain focused until Abraham arrives. There's no telling how he will react, and what he may do when he arrives."

"Roger that…understood."

As the sun rose, the two men waited still and quiet, speaking not a word to each other for what seemed like hours, although it was only thirty minutes before Jake saw the silhouette-like figure of Abraham standing next to the bloodied and lifeless body of his father's former servant. Nixon could see that he stood looking down at her for a few moments, almost if he didn't want to see what he clearly expected to see next. Jake fixed the crosshairs of his scope on Abraham's chest as Nixon watched him begin to raise his foot to cross the three or four inches of shattered glass that was still intact on the bottom of the door. Before his foot would reach the ground, a round had slammed into his chest, sending him flying backward and landing directly on top of the servant.

Jake exhaled and looked at Nixon with a surreal sense of calm given all that had happened. To Jake's way of seeing, he simply neutralized threats to the United States with minimal collateral damage. All things considered; it was a highly successful morning as far as Jake was concerned. He took a few minutes to remove the firing pin from the weapon thoroughly clean it to ensure there wasn't a trace of prints on it.

"All right, Nixon, the mission is accomplished, buddy. We're out of here."

"We're not bringing the rifle with us?"

"Not a chance…there's too much ballistic evidence in the home of Morros that leads straight to this weapon. Taking this thing with us would be like tethering a ball and chain to our necks. It stays in place. When the authorities do discover the remains of Morros and the others in his household, they're not going to immediately start searching a half mile away from the house for a weapon and other clues. They're going to start interviewing neighbors and turning over every stone in immediate proximity to the house."

Jake and Nixon shed their sniper cover and carefully placed it over the gun so that it appeared to be nothing more from a distance than a small mound of grass slightly protruding from the hill. They retrieved cameras from their backpacks and hung them around their necks to appear like sightseeing tourists. They quickly made their way to the hotel in Bassersdorf and had the desk clerk call Mohammed's contact as previously instructed.

At 10:15 Scorzo motioned Mohammed to answer a knock at their door. It was Mohammed's connection. He came to inform Mohammed that Jake and Nixon were already at the Postli hotel in Bassersdorf. Scorzo and the others, except for Ariana, knew that Jake had put down more targets than Jurgen Morros. They had watched the termination of Jurgen Morros and his household on live satellite feed as it happened while Mohammed kept Ariana busy in the kitchen on the pretext of teaching her how to make a delicious Middle Eastern breakfast for the group.

"All right, everybody, it's time to call it day here and be on our way. After Wallisellen, we pick up Jake and Nixon in Bassersdorf and we are homeward bound," Scorzo announced. "Ariana, are you ready?"

"I'm ready," she said, with a solemn look.

Scorzo stood before her and placed his hands on her shoulders firmly.

"You know, I've never depended on anybody the way I'm depending on you right now. In fact, none of us have. We either depended upon our own skill, methodical precision, and resourcefulness or we depended on the guys with us that we just assumed were covering our six."

"Scorzo, why are you trusting me like this?" she asked softly.

"Because I don't want your parents and the people who love you back home to live in torment thinking you're dead. I guess maybe I'm thinking with my heart instead of my head. All right, people, let's giddy up!" Scorzo said as his hands slid off her and he broke eye contact.

The entourage departed in three separate cars, somewhat enjoying the pleasant scenery on the short drive as they were en route to the DEA safehouse in Wallisellen, but their tension mounted upon arrival at the destination. Ariana felt the premises would surely be vacant, but Scorzo didn't want to leave anything to chance venturing into the unknown. Armed only with concealed pistols, they were by no means prepared to engage DEA agents and reinforcements they were sure to summon in a protracted battle.

Upon coming to their destination, Scorzo looked at Ariana with more intensity than she had seen since they first met. He spoke in a profoundly serious and sobering tone as he stared into her eyes in an almost hypnotic manner. Mohammed got out of the car and quickly told the other two cars to drive to the rear of the house before returning to the driver's seat.

"All right, here's the drill, kiddo. You are going in alone to establish whether the location is secure. If the house is empty, you come to the window and beckon us in. If it's not, you come to the window and wave goodbye. We'll be crouched down, so if anyone is with you, they'll only see Mohammed, who presumably just waited to see that you made it inside safely. We will then drive around to the rear and Mohammed will wave the others on, alerting them that we need to get the hell out of Dodge quickly. That's when you'll part ways with us because I have to assume you'll give us up. But for God's sake at least wave us off so there's no gun battle. I don't want you to get hurt, Ariana; I don't want anything to happen to you."

"You know what Contreras always used to say when any of us used the word assume? Whenever you assume, you make an ass out of U and Me."

"Yeah, I've heard that one, but I'd much rather make an ass out of myself acting on an assumption that might save my life rather than going to the grave as a trusting soul."

"I'm not going to give you up, Scorzo; I'm finished with the DEA. I can't go back to that life."

"Look, whether you tender your resignation inside there or stay with the DEA, you open yourself up to charges of aiding and abetting a federal fugitive."

"Don't you understand, Scorzo," Ariana pleaded. "I don't believe in them anymore. I don't believe in the whole goddamn system anymore!"

"Ariana, you have to go in there now."

"I don't want to go in there. Why can't we all just leave now, and I'll make the call when I get back to the States?"

"Because the whole reason for you making the call from here is to make them believe that we're out of the country when we're actually coming back home. That way, they start wasting their time looking for us overseas while we're fortifying our headquarters at Beacon Rock... *capisci?*"

"*Capisco lo,* Scorzo," she replied in Italian, affirming that she understood. "*Ci vediamo dentro.*"

"Yeah, if the house is empty, I'll see you inside. Now go."

Scorzo watched Ariana enter the house and then crouched down as all the other occupants in the car were. He could feel the sweat beading on his forehead. Several tense moments passed by before she appeared in the window and signaled Mohammed that the house was empty.

"Okay, my friend, you can get up. Everything is all right."

Upon hearing this, it seemed that everyone in the car let out a collective sigh of relief.

"All right, Mohammed, you go around the back and let the others know that I will let them in through the rear entrance. Sano, you and I will go in first to meet Ariana. Max, Gonzo, and Philster... you three enter the foyer and stay put there until it's absolutely clear that we're good."

"Come on, Scorzo, don't you think you're being just a little bit paranoid. The girl gave us the all-clear signal. Besides, I think she's falling for you, Scorzo. Haven't you noticed how she looks at you."

"She might be a good actor. Look at it in these terms... we took out a platoon-strength assault group in Fox Lake that was using helicopters and armored personnel carriers, and we got away clean. Then we vanish sight unseen for over two months. Now a frail ninety-eight-pound female agent single-handedly leads our whole posse into arrest and capture, and all by herself. She totally upstages the DEA, the ATF, and the Bureau…can you imagine what a coup that would be for her? Given how the Bureau has villainized us, she'd be nothing less than a national hero."

"All right, okay, we play it your way for a possible double cross, but I still think she has the hots for you, paisano," Philster said with a grin.

"All right, let's move out."

They proceeded into the house cautiously with Scorzo and Sano approaching Ariana while Max, Gonzo, and Philster remained in the foyer by a staircase that led up to the second floor.

"Hey, why are you guys all standing by the door looking so nervous?" Ariana asked with a comfortable smile. "We're all good."

"Let's go and let the others in at the back door." Scorzo placed his hands on her back and elbow, turning her gently.

"Sure," she replied compliantly.

As soon as her back was turned on the three, Scorzo looked back and gave them a signal to proceed upstairs and check out the second floor. When all the men had come in and it was established that there were no hostiles among them, they quickly went about the business they came for.

"All right, Ariana, there should be a clean phone for establishing secure communication with your team. It's either in the main room or beside a bed in one of the bedrooms upstairs."

"Oh Jesus!" Ariana replied with sudden alarm. "I didn't even check upstairs, Scorzo. I just called out, and there was no answer."

"Don't worry, they did," Scorzo said, motioning with his thumb back toward Max, Gonzo, and Philster. "It's all clear; we're good."

"I didn't notice any phone down here."

"Gonzo, go upstairs and check the bedrooms."

As everyone gathered in the main room, Gonzo bounded up the

stairs and retrieved the phone. Upon entering the main room, he stood before Ariana silently for a moment. He then looked first at Scorzo before panning around the room looking at everyone else who stood in silence before he looked at Ariana.

"Well, this is the moment," Gonzo said solemnly before handing the phone to Scorzo so he could provide last-minute instructions.

"All right, this is it," Scorzo began. "Dial his personal cell number first and have him call you back on a secure line because the Bureau as well as the NSA are certainly intercepting and listening to all the calls on his personal cell by now. He's a SAC, so he'll have a clean, secure, alternate means of contacting you whether he's at home or in the office. It's 11:30 here now so it's 18:30 Chicago time now.

"You need to keep it short and sweet. Your conversation needs to focus on your condition to the extent that Contreras isn't even concerned with our whereabouts. His main concern should be getting you home for a face-to-face debrief rather than traumatize you further by interrogating you over the phone. If he asks anything about us, distract him. Ask him where the wall safe is because you have no money. Ask him if he has any contacts at the embassy in Bern...anything to keep him focused on your needs and not us. Got it?"

"Capisco," she replied and took the phone. She stared into Scorzo's eyes for a moment before looking down at the phone and dialing Contreras's cell number. The phone only rang two times before he answered.

"Contreras here."

"Contreras, it's me," Ariana said in a weak voice.

"Ariana! Are you okay? Where are you? Do they still have you? Are you alone? Can you speak freely?" Contreras asked in a staccato flurry of questions.

"I need you to call me back on a secure line."

"Yes, sure, okay, let me get this number off my caller ID."

Contreras quickly scribbled the number down.

"Okay, got it!"

Ariana disconnected the call and exhaled deeply just before her phone rang.

"Ariana, it's me. You sound so weak. Where are you? Are they still holding you?"

"No, I'm not with them. They didn't hurt me, Contreras. They treated me well."

"You're calling from an international location."

"I'm in Switzerland at our safe house in Wallisellen."

"They brought you there? They knew about our location in Wallisellen?"

Scorzo scribbled down some information and held it up to Carina.

"No, they brought me to the University Hospital of Zurich after we arrived. I was released from the hospital after a few days."

"Why didn't you contact us?"

"There was only one English-speaking doctor and one nurse who oversaw my care. Nobody else except the people at the reception desk spoke English. I asked them if I could call you, but they couldn't allow me to call the US."

"Why didn't you get to the embassy?"

"I didn't have any identification, no passport, no money, and I was alone. The staff there probably would have assumed I was a prostitute because of the condition I was in."

Sensing that she was losing control of the conversation, Scorzo once again quickly scribbled some information on a notepad that was lying on a table and he handed it to her.

"When I was released, I was lucky enough that they directed me to a place where I could stay that didn't require money. I stayed at a Salvation Army shelter for women in Zurich. I actually had to work in a small pastry shop they owned to get money to make it here to Wallisellen."

"Oh Jesus, I'm sorry, Ariana, but you're okay now. You're safe, and I'm going to get you home."

"Javier, there's a safe here at this location, right?"

"Yes, in the Wallisellen location the safe is in the basement on the west wall. It may be exposed, or it might be behind a picture or some other type of furniture obstructing the view of it, I don't know that for sure, but it's on the west wall. I need to look up the combination... give me a moment."

"Javier, please tell my family I'm all right, okay?" Ariana asked as Contreras scrolled through a database containing all the safehouse combinations. "I don't want them to worry about me. They must be going through hell right now not knowing whether I'm dead or alive."

"I've been in contact with them every few days or so over the past few weeks trying to comfort them and reassure them I was doing everything possible to locate you."

"Thanks, boss, I appreciate that so much."

"Okay, here's the number to that safe. It's two turns to the right stopping at thirty-two, then one turn to the left stopping at eight, and then directly right to the number four. Inventory shows that there's ten thousand dollars in US currency and a little under five thousand in Swiss francs available. That will be more than enough to get you some new clothes, transportation to the embassy, and then a flight back to Chicago."

"It'll be nice to get a new change of clothes. I've been wearing the same ones since I arrived at the Salvation Army. I've lost weight; I look like shit, and I feel so weak."

"Don't worry. I will contact our field office in Vienna and have an agent come to assist you at the embassy in Bern. Everything's going to be all right. Is there anything else you need? Is there anything else I can do for you for now?"

"Yeah, I want you to get those guys that did this to me."

"We've been ordered by the Bureau to stand down on our pursuit of Machine Gun Scorzo and his group after the incident in Fox Lake. Besides, nobody even has a clue where they are. Right now, I'm more concerned with just bringing you home safely."

"I have a clue where they are. At least, I heard them talking about a possible location while we were flying to Switzerland. They were talking openly because I was out of it. They were giving me meds for the pain and I was sleeping a lot. They were talking about the Philippines. I guess it was because it's an English-speaking country where they had connections. I'm sorry I couldn't get anything specific, but I was fading in and out. I was in pretty bad shape."

"You always come through for me, Agent Carina. Don't be sorry. You've given me more than anyone else has right now. The Bureau still thinks these guys are stateside. They're now referring to him and his crew as the Machine Gun Scorzo gang." Contreras paused for a moment and Carina thought the call was dropped.

"Are you still there, boss?"

"Listen, I don't want you to share anything with our office in Vienna, okay?"

"Yeah, sure, I won't say anything to the Vienna field office."

"Also, when you get back to Chicago, the Bureau is going to debrief you. Don't say a word to them, understand? You were wounded and they drugged you. You were unconscious most of the time, and when you were awake you were non compos mentis. You had lost a lot of blood, you were dehydrated, and traumatized by the fear that they were going to kill you, and they kept you bound, gagged, blindfolded, and totally isolated during the entire time they held you, understand? When you finally came to in the hospital at Zurich, you didn't even know where you were or what happened to you, understand?"

"Yes, I understand. I won't give the Bureau anything. You're going to get him, boss. This time they won't be able to take it away from you."

"My Lord sweet Jesus! Thank you, Agent Carina, thank you!"

Carina ended the call and looked at Scorzoletti and all the others who stood looking at her in silence that gave way to smiles of relief.

"Well, it wasn't short, but it certainly was sweet. You didn't have to do that, Ariana; you know that, right?"

"I know, but I wanted to," she replied, gazing intently into Scorzo's eyes.

"Thank you, Ariana, thank you," Scorzo said humbly as he placed his hand palm down at arm's length in front of Carina. She put her hand on top of Scorzoletti's, and one by one all of the men placed their hands on top of hers and thanked her. When they were all finished, Scorzoletti smiled and looked at Sano.

"Hey, Sano, do me a favor and queue up that Chinese song you were listening to after Ariana sacked out last night." Sano queued the song and handed his phone to Scorzo, who then handed it to Ariana as the song started playing. Again, she stared intently at Scorzo seemingly oblivious of everyone and everything else in the room as it played. Though she couldn't understand what the words meant, the rhythm and the beat of the song felt like they were pushing her heart closer to Scorzo.

"I love it," she said after listening to it. "I know Xiexieni means thank you very much in Mandarin, but what is he talking about?"

"He's talking about a very beautiful girl who he admires, and he's thanking her for her presence in his life."

"It's his girlfriend?"

"Well, that's a little ambiguous. The wording suggests that he might only be imagining what he wants to have with this beautiful girl, so it's not clear. In any event, he's incredibly grateful for her presence in his life."

"It's so touching, but why did you play that particular song for me?"

"Well, it's my way…our way of saying thank you for what you just did. You've been through a hell of a lot, yet you never caused us any grief. Right here and now you could have run outside with that phone and started spilling everything to Contreras, but you didn't."

"How could I cause you guys any grief when you saved my life, took care of me, and nursed me back to health? You treated me better than any of the guys in my own unit, especially for a group as notorious as you guys. They've named you the Machine Gun Scorzo gang."

"At least we're not a bunch of fucking peter-pumpers. Shit, those guys were probably all hoping you'd turn butch dyke one day and show up with a buzz cut so they could tell dirty jokes, talk about sex, and watch gay porn videos at their work stations without worrying that you would rat them out to HR!"

Ariana looked at Philster and immediately started laughing. She no longer felt that his caustic manner was intended to intimidate her. She knew that it just meant that he considered her one of the group.

"I don't think I've ever met anyone like you, Philster," she said, struggling to regain her composure.

"Yeah, nobody else has met a douchebag like him either," Max said to the ensuing laughter of everyone else. "The old boy's one of a kind."

"Yeah, yeah, so are you, Brillo head," Philster replied. "The same goes for that nutbar over there who thinks he's Genghis Khan or something." Philster pointed to Sano.

"All right, everybody, that's enough," Scorzo said, bringing their itinerary back into focus. "We need to get our asses out of here and over to Bassersdorf ASAP to pick up Jake and Nixon before we high-tail it to the air base in Dubendorf. Mohammed, call your contact and have him go to the Hotel Postli and tell Jake and Nixon to be outside waiting for us. We'll be there in about ten minutes. Then call our flight crew at Dubendorf and tell them to get those planes ready to take off twenty minutes from now. Hotel Postli is only a little over five minutes from the air base."

"I'm all over it, my friend," Mohammed answered as he dialed his phone.

"Okay, let's giddy up!"

They quickly made their way to the Hotel Postli, where Jake and Nixon were waiting for them outside the entrance. As previously planned, Alvarez had booked an additional three days for them, so they didn't check out as they were leaving. Scorzo wanted it to appear that they were still in Bassersdorf long after they had left the country.

When the group arrived at Dubendorf Air Base, they saw the planes running and awaiting their arrival. Once inside the planes, they waited somewhat anxiously until they had clearance for takeoff. They received clearance at 11:27 and left the ground at 11:31 When they were finally airborne, they changed into military

304

uniforms so they would be in character with their cover upon arriving at JFK. Their estimated flight time to New York was close to eight and a half hours, so this would have them landing at approximately 20:00 hours. Scorzo felt that the early evening was by no means the ideal time to land, but they didn't have the option to stay in Switzerland any longer.

Chapter 24

The Sacrificial Lamb

"IRS, Lisa Ramirez speaking, how can I help you?"

"Hi Lisa, it's Javier Contreras."

"Well hello, stranger, how have you been? I was worried about you after I saw that stuff that happened out in Fox Lake."

"I'm fine. Hey, can I come upstairs and see you?"

"Yeah, sure, I'm free, but what's up?"

"What's up…can't an old friend drop in on you and take you out to lunch?" Contreras asked, knowing that his call was being monitored.

"Are you buying?" Ramirez asked in a jocular manner.

"Yes, of course, I would never let a pretty lady buy."

"Well then, get your butt up here, Special Agent in Charge Contreras."

"Okay, see you in a few minutes."

Contreras quickly made his way to the elevator without telling anyone in the office where he was off to, and upon arriving upstairs at the IRS office and meeting Ramirez, he took control of the conversation.

"It's such a beautiful day. Are you up for a place we can walk to?"

"Sure, what did you have in mind?"

"I'm feeling in the mood for German, and Berghoff is just around the corner."

"I like their food, especially the wiener schnitzel, but it's always so busy."

"True, but we're early, so we'll beat the long lunch line. We can eat in the basement restaurant and come upstairs and have a drink at the bar afterward," Contreras said, leading her in a brisk pace toward the Berghoff.

"I only get an hour, Javier. I'm not a high-profile DEA supervisor like you."

"Hey, if your supervisor gives you any shit, just call down to me and I'll get my high-profile ass in his face."

"It's her, not a him. Not all supervisors are male, you know."

When they reached the Berghoff, Contreras took control once again as they approached the host.

"We'd like a table in the far north side of the lower level, preferably the last table in the northeast corner."

Since they were early, the table that Contreras requested was available. Upon being seated, Contreras extended a folded twenty-dollar bill to the host.

"I would appreciate it so much if you could avoid seating anyone at the table in front of us. You know how noisy it can get during lunchtime."

"That's really not necessary, sir," the host said, looking at Contreras and declining to take the bill from his hand. "I'll be happy to seat people away from you, but if it gets really busy, I can't promise nobody will be seated next to you. The floor manager would be all over me if there were patrons waiting and I had an unoccupied table that was set."

"I'll tell you what...take the bill and if it gets really busy, you send the floor manager over to me and I'll deal with him."

"Oh, the floor manager is not a man. Well, biologically she's not a man, but she identifies as a man, so she insists on being called sir. She's transgender."

"Okay, if it gets busy just send her...I mean, him over here and I'll deal with things for you, so take the bill...really, I want you to."

The host took the bill and nervously placed the menus on their table. He quickly dispatched the waiter over to their table, hoping they would eat and leave quickly before the restaurant became crowded.

"You see, Contreras," Ramirez began, "you have to stop assuming all people in positions of power are men. That's the problem with

Spanish men...they all suffer from machismo."

"But I was correct," Contreras said, grinning with a sense of triumph. "The floor supervisor wants to be recognized as a man, so we have to recognize her as a man despite her biology."

"Yeah, well, personally I don't believe in this current trend. You can't change what you are biologically just by claiming to be the opposite."

"Hey, who knows, maybe even your supervisor is really a man who just hasn't come out about it yet," Contreras teased.

"I doubt that. She sleeps around, even with guys in the office, and I've never known her to be interested in women or trying to look like a guy, so I don't think so, dude."

"Well, just between me and you, I don't buy in to any of this politically correct bullshit either, but you can't challenge this publicly. These people are serious as a heart attack when it comes to their alleged gender identity. They've taken employers, restaurants, and a bunch of other institutions to courts and sued them for discrimination...and won!"

"Do you two need a little more time, or are you ready," the waiter asked cheerfully upon approaching their table.

"We're ready to order," Contreras said, looking at the waiter and tipping his hand to Ramirez.

"I'll have the wiener schnitzel and the creamed spinach and roasted Brussels sprouts as my side dishes."

"And for you, sir?"

"I'm going to go with the sauerbraten along with a potato pancake and spätzle for my side dishes. Also, we'd like two glasses of a nice Riesling wine while we're waiting. What would you recommend?"

"We have a nice dry Spatlese Riesling that would go perfect with your meal."

"All right, let's do it," Contreras said, handing the menus back to the waiter.

"All right, Javier, I haven't seen you since the day before never, and suddenly you're wining and dining me in the middle of the day. So come on, dude, what's up?"

"Can't a guy just want to get out of the office and have lunch with a pretty lady?"

"Yeah, sure, if he isn't a guy that works in a DEA office. I mean, you guys are like packrats or something. You guys only do things with each other all the time. Now, suddenly you jump ship and want to have some interagency companionship. I don't think so, so just tell me what's up. We're old friends. If you need something, just come out and tell me and I'll help you in any way I can."

"All right, I do need your help."

"Okay, shoot, what can I do for you?"

"Can you access bank accounts?"

"Sure, tell me who we're talking about and I'll go to work on getting you the information."

"You've heard of Machine Gun Scorzo, I assume."

"Of course I have. I don't think there's anybody in the country who hasn't. He's the guy who's hit the Federal Reserve banks in Chicago and San Francisco. They made off with over four hundred billion in assets between the two banks."

"Could you check into accounts in the Philippines?"

"Yeah, sure, but I'd need a name and a social security number. But you got two problems. First, there's no way this guy would be opening accounts over there using his real identity. He's way too high profile. The BIR in the Philippines would certainly contact authorities in the US. Second, he wouldn't want to bank his money in the Philippines because it would be taxed at a rate of six percent. So, if we use the figure of four hundred billion, he will lose twenty-four billion right out of the gate. I don't think he's going to want to take that kind of a hit. It's much more likely he would park his funds in Switzerland, where he didn't have to pay taxes to their government or ours."

"All right, then let's focus on Switzerland because I have it from a reliable source that he and his group were there. But that stays between you and me, understand? Even though we have a history with each other, I'll deny I ever said that if you let word out to anybody."

"The problem with Switzerland is that while they are now CRS members and FATCA compliant regarding sharing information with the USA, Swiss accounts are still anonymous in respect to numeric identifiers used for account holders rather than names and social security numbers. So, while we're no longer shut out by article forty-seven of their banking secrecy code, we need to provide the number of the individual that we want information on or we can't get anything."

"Oh shit! Can't you just request information on recent large accounts that were opened?"

"No, but even if I could, there are thousands of countries and wealthy individuals opening accounts there all the time. There's no way they would start divulging information on hundreds of thousands of accounts without specific identifiers and valid reasons."

"How about the fact that this guy and his partners have killed over a dozen federal agents and robbed two major government banks for valid reasons?"

"FYI, I'm going to tell you a little secret, but if this gets out, I'm going to deny it even though we have a history. The Federal Reserve banks aren't federal like their name implies. They're private banks."

"Yeah, so I've heard," Contreras said with frustration, as he quickly shoveled food into his mouth.

"I know this isn't what you want to hear, but I don't want to bullshit you. Given what I know, I could almost guarantee you that this guy had corporations and shell accounts which he banked this money in that have absolutely no ties to him or any of the people he's running with. Think about it, Javier… If he was good enough to pull off these kinds of robberies and get away clean, then he definitely knew what he was going to do with that money afterward so he wouldn't lose it."

"So, essentially, you're saying there's nothing the IRS can do to throw more light on where the money is and where Machine Gun Scorzo is?"

"Sad, but true, that's where it's at unless you can provide me with more specifics."

Three men wearing suits who were sitting a few tables away from

Contreras and Ramirez all stood up at once and casually walked over to Contreras's table. To the less astute observer they could have been Chicago businessmen out to lunch, but there was something uniquely imposing about their presence as they stood before Contreras.

"Special Agent Javier Contreras?" one of the men asked, even though he clearly knew he was addressing Contreras.

"Do I know you gentlemen?" Contreras replied, quickly noticing that there were weapons concealed under their suit jackets.

"I am Derrick Panetta, special agent in charge of the FBI field office in Chicago. To my left is Special Agent Tim Braeburn, FBI Counterintelligence, and on my right is Special Agent James Stone, FBI Counterterrorism."

"How can I help you gentlemen this afternoon?"

"Could you please stand up, turn toward the table, and place your hands behind your back," Panetta said in a low tone.

"You as well, Ms. Ramirez," Agent Stone added.

"This is insane—what are the charges?" Contreras asked through clenched jaws.

"Javier Contreras, you are formally charged with harboring an international fugitive from justice by willfully concealing information that would assist in his capture and arrest."

"I don't have anything to do with this," Ramirez protested. "I am literally out to lunch. Is that what I am being arrested for?"

"You're being arrested as an accomplice of Mr. Contreras."

"An accomplice! An accomplice of what? Going out to lunch with a friend who works in the same building as I do?"

"Ms. Ramirez, you will be questioned, and if we determine that you are not complicit with Mr. Contreras, you will be released. We would appreciate if the both of you cooperate with us and surrender peacefully. We don't want a scene, and we don't want anybody getting hurt. I'm sure you can appreciate that, Mr. Contreras." Panetta turned to Stone and Braeburn. "Discreetly take the firearm from Mr. Contreras as well as his shield and cuff them both."

"You keep calling me Mr. Contreras. I am DEA Special Agent in

311

Charge Javier Contreras of the Chicago field office."

"Not anymore," Stone said as he fastened the cuffs around Contreras's wrists. "Javier Contreras and Lisa Ramirez, both of you have the right to remain silent. Anything you say can and will be used against you in a court of law. You have the right to an attorney. If you cannot afford an attorney, one will be provided for you. Do both of you understand the rights that I have just read to you? With these rights in mind, do either of you wish to say anything to me?"

"This is bullshit! We're friends, and I was only telling…"

"Lisa, don't say anything," Contreras quickly interrupted in a firm and authoritative manner.

They both fell silent and so did the normally noisy room as other diners had become aware of the scene and looked on with curiosity. Contreras was led out of the dining room in total humiliation, with many thoughts racing through his mind as he ascended the stairs to Adams Street, where cars were waiting to take him into custody.

Did Agent Carina betray his confidence while she was in Switzerland? Did the trauma in Fox Lake and her ensuing experiences in Switzerland cause her to break down and talk with an agent in the Vienna field office about Scorzo? Perhaps it was at the embassy in Bern, where FBI counterintelligence agents were stationed. *Why haven't I heard from her, and why hasn't she arrived in Chicago since her call. Is she being held in FBI custody for debriefing? What has she said and how has she implicated me? Carina has always been a loyal agent who would never compromise the unit, much less me. What's changed?*

Before Contreras could make any sense of what had happened, he was stripped of his rank and position with the DEA and brought to the FBI field office on the west side of Chicago. He was allowed to make one call before an attempt at interrogation was made. He chose to call DEA Chief of Operations Wil Bryant, who he knew would be much more accessible than Bill Ruther. He had also worked with Bryant in California and believed his impeccable moral standards would garner the sympathy and aid of Bryant.

While Bryant was sympathetic to the plight of Contreras and

assured him that he would send legal counsel and rally the full support of the DEA behind Contreras, he encouraged Contreras to cooperate with the FBI. The Bureau had elevated anything surrounding Machine Gun Scorzo to a level of their highest priority. Anyone who dared to oppose the Bureau's investigations on any aspect of information related to Machine Gun Scorzo was analogous to a man standing in front of a speeding steam roller on a fresh pavement. This was precisely the analogy that Bryant used when encouraging Contreras to cooperate with the Bureau and be forthcoming with what he knew and his motives for concealing it. Contreras held out hope that Ruther, who instructed him to continue with his work investigating Machine Gun Scorzo, would soon come to his aid and negotiate some type of agreement with the Bureau that would allow Contreras to be reinstated in his role within the DEA. Instead, Ruther disavowed any knowledge of encouraging Contreras to continue investigating Machine Gun Scorzo, and he distanced himself from Contreras.

As the evening approached on the day Contreras was arrested, things took a turn for the worse. The Bureau's counterintelligence division leaked word to all the major media outlets that Contreras was in custody for aiding and abetting Machine Gun Scorzo in evading capture in Fox Lake as well as in Switzerland. While the Bureau refused to openly comment publicly on the allegations they leaked to the media, they made reference to the fact that Javier Contreras was also being investigated for criminal complicity that involved taking a payment from Machine Gun Scorzo in exchange for tipping him off about the siege at Fox Lake that resulted in the death of sixteen DEA officers, four paramilitary personnel, and the hostage kidnapping of Agent Carina.

All the cable and major news networks followed the same damning narrative regarding the activity and character of Contreras. Without the benefit of a trial, it appeared as though Contreras was guilty of complicity with Public Enemy Number One before the verdict was even in. Moreover, because he invoked his Miranda right to remain silent until he had counsel, the Bureau held him at their Chicago field office without providing him with food or water for over twenty-four hours. In addition, he wasn't even allowed to use the bathroom. His only solace during the gross abuse the Bureau subjected him to was that maybe Agent Carina had fared far worse at the hands of the Bureau. Maybe it was the reason she divulged information to them.

After twenty-four hours had passed with different agents using good cop/bad cop tactics on him, he was transferred to the Metropolitan Correctional Center in downtown Chicago, where he was placed in solitary confinement after he was processed. He was given his first meal after a full forty-eight hours had passed, just shortly before his attorney arrived to see him. His attorney was the first person who treated him with warmth and respect since his embarrassing arrest at the Berghoff restaurant. Contreras had always thought that those doing solitary did easier time than those in the general prison population because they were segregated from all the uncertainties and danger inherent in prison life. Now he realized that there was nothing easy about solitude and segregation from all human contact. He wished that he could reach through the thick glass that separated him from his attorney so he could shake his hand, but it was not possible.

"Special Agent Contreras, my name is Charles Hanson and I'm your attorney. Please feel free to call me Chuck."

"It's been forty-eight hours, Chuck, and I haven't been arraigned. Why is that? What's happening? I was told that the formal charges against me stem from harboring an international fugitive and preventing his arrest and capture. Where are they getting ridiculous bullshit like that?"

"May I call you Javier?"

"Yeah, sure, it seems as though I'm no longer a part of the DEA."

"All right, look, Javier, that isn't true. The reason why I am here is because of Wil Bryant. He wouldn't have retained me on your behalf if you were no longer a part of the DEA, but you have to play ball with these guys."

"Chuck, you know as well as I do that it was my right to remain silent until I had legal counsel."

"That's absolutely true, but they have irrefutable evidence that you

314

knew Machine Gun Scorzo was outside the US, and that you withheld that information. In addition, you wouldn't cooperate with them before you were placed here. That doesn't put you in a particularly good light as a DEA SAC."

"How could they have irrefutable proof? Did they debrief Agent Carina?"

"Nobody has seen Carina since Fox Lake. It's presumed that she remains a hostage of Machine Gun Scorzo and his gang."

"I don't believe it. I spoke to her, and she told me that she was dropped off at the University of Zurich hospital by Scorzo. She mentioned overhearing their plans to leave the country, possibly heading to the Philippines."

"An NSA analyst working as a surface warfare officer with the navy intercepted your conversation with her. Your voice print and hers were a direct match with the profile they have on both of you. That's their irrefutable proof."

"Jesus, Mary, mother of God."

"It gets worse."

"How could it get any fucking worse, Chuck."

"The Bureau checked out her story, and none of it was true. She was never at the University of Zurich hospital, and she was never at the Salvation Army shelter. The NSA analyst used software to detect stress and deception and saw all the indicators of deception in her conversation with you. In short, it's presumed that she was coerced into providing misinformation specifically intended to mislead authorities that are searching for them. Currently, it's assumed that she's still very much a hostage of Machine Gun Scorzo's gang and actively assisting them to evade capture."

"Hey, I know her! Agent Carina would never willingly do anything to help him! It was her efforts that first led to the identification of Steven Philster in the theft of narcotics in Winnetka after the ATF lost track of both him and Machine Gun Scorzo. Hell, up until that point Bickens and his team thought Philster was deceased."

"Yeah, and then she was responsible for homing in on Scorzo and his group again as they proceeded north on I-294 to Fox Lake, but again the DEA shared nothing with the Bureau until lives and billion-dollar equipment were lost. Can't you see how this looks from the Bureau's perspective?"

"I'm not the first person in the intelligence community to sit on information and I won't be the last."

"It's not just about withholding information that could have led to the capture of Machine Gun Scorzo. The current media narrative is that you're a dirty agent on the take…that you deliberately botched the capture of Machine Gun Scorzo…that you deliberately waited until he left the scene with a hostage before calling in the Bureau."

"That's a bunch of bullshit! I lost men out there that day!"

"Large amounts of money can cause a man to change in strange ways."

"So, you believe I'm guilty of these totally fabricated and wholly unsubstantiated allegations?"

"I didn't say that, but you know the DEA's history with agents siphoning off massive amounts of money from Colombian cartels in the 1980s and '90s. Need I remind you of Juan Gustavo in 2020? He was the DEA's poster boy. He was everything an agent could aspire to be until he was assigned to work in Bogota, where he diverted over six million dollars in cash to a shell account he created for his personal use. That's not that long ago."

"Okay, I'll admit it's an embarrassment for the DEA, but what's that got to do with me?"

"The both of you worked together, assisted each other at times, and you both had the same superstar status within the DEA. Moreover, you learned how to set up shell accounts from Gustavo and you used that to your advantage in Operation Cassandra."

"First, I had nothing to do with Gustavo once he was assigned to Bogota. Second, the shell accounts and shell companies I set up during Operation Cassandra were fully transparent to the DEA, and they were dismantled after the operation ended."

"To the Bureau's way of seeing things, the parallels between you and Gustavo are disturbing, given the DEA's history of corruption from the 1970s up until the present time. The reason your agency got involved with these guys in the first place was due to a burglary involving narcotics. Who's to say these guys aren't involved in the drug trade?"

"Hitting a small suburban pharmacy in Winnetka hardly provides a profile of individuals with a link to major cartels and the drug trade. In hindsight, it's more likely that they stole pharmaceuticals they might need due to the nature of their work. In addition to pain relievers and amphetamines, they also stole Cyklokapron, which is used to stop bleeding, as well as antibiotics. I know that Agent Carina was wounded, and she said they cared for her. It's highly likely that they used the antibiotics, narcotics, and Cyklokapron to stabilize her and anybody else in their entourage who was wounded."

"There are a lot of unknowns with these guys, but given their high-profile notoriety, along with the enormous amount of cash they've amassed and successfully concealed, it's not unthinkable that they would bribe someone hot on their trail to back off in a manner that cast no aspersion on their pursuer. Aside from that, you have to consider that these guys have become classic anti-heroes as far as most Americans are concerned."

"That's ridiculous, Chuck, and you know it! If I agreed to stage a gun battle with him that would ultimately lead to his escape, why would he need Carina as a hostage?"

"He wouldn't, but if she wasn't complicit in this with you, she simply became a victim of circumstances."

"That's a load of crap and you know it, Chuck! These guys wouldn't have hesitated to put her down just like they did to over a dozen other agents and assisting personnel."

"What you aren't considering is that these guys are all highly trained special forces operatives. They saw Carina as a valuable intelligence source they could glean information from. She has no training on how to defend herself against highly skilled special forces operatives who are deadly assassins much less neutralize a threat consisting of nine of these men."

"Look, how about discussing our strategy to get me out of here so I can pursue these guys."

"That's not gonna happen, Javier. At least not any time soon."

"Why's that?"

"Because you have nothing to offer the Bureau. The only thing you had going for you is something they've already discovered on their own without your help…or, rather, despite your refusal to help. Now you're only a nuisance that they want to eliminate. To their way of seeing it, you aided and abetted a federal fugitive on the top of their most wanted list along with his confederates."

"What exactly do you mean when you say eliminate?"

"Frankly speaking…they want to bury you."

"With what? I didn't share information with them. I kept secrets. This type of thing has been going on between the Bureau and the CIA for decades, and it's never resulted in personnel on either side being arrested and charged."

"It's also never resulted in the deaths of federal agents, senators, congressmen, civilians, and the unauthorized use of military arms."

"All of those events happened prior to the siege in Fox Lake."

"Well, like it or not, the Bureau is trying to wrap all of those things around your neck."

"Why? How can they do this?"

"It began when you started pursuing a man who was wanted in connection with the death of four agents from the ATF."

"My pursuit began with Steven Philster for the theft of controlled substances in Winnetka. He had nothing to do with the murder of those agents. Moreover, Bickens didn't share anything about Philster being associated with Machine Gun Scorzo. He didn't share anything about that with me, and neither did the Bureau. I didn't know anything about him until the Bureau approached me after San Francisco. Even then, I wasn't certain that he was going to be in Fox Lake because we tracked him through the iPass transponders associated with Jerry Alvarez."

"Jerry Alvarez is another enormous problem."

"How so?"

"He was a surface warfare officer in the United States Navy. He's said to have a genius level IQ and extraordinary proficiency in electronic warfare capability, and the ability to breach the most complex security in onboard weapons platforms and thereby hijack them."

"The Tomahawk cruise missiles that killed Senator Nervosi and Congresswoman Lakes in addition to destroying the Federal Reserve Bank of San Francisco were initiated by Alvarez?"

"The NSA analyst is saying that those weapons were controlled from a land-based mobile operating system in San Francisco, so the Bureau is laying the blame for the deaths of Senator Nervosi and Congresswoman Lakes at your doorstep. Given the case that the Bureau is trying to build against you, it will be a miracle if I can get bail for you."

"This is unreal," Contreras said, shaking his head in defeat. "This can't be happening."

"Unfortunately, Javier, it's very real, and it is happening. The Bureau has created this larger-than-life supervillain called Machine Gun Scorzo, and now they need to show America that they can slay the beast which nobody knows they created. They've had nothing for over six weeks until now."

"So, I'm the sacrificial lamb?"

"I couldn't have put it any better myself, Javier."

Chapter 25
When Right Is Wrong

The arrival of Machine Gun Scorzo and the Nemesis Nine at JFK airport was without incident. Initially, the Bureau was monitoring all civilian ports of transit out of Switzerland after they became aware of the call between Contreras and Agent Carina, but they weren't focusing on military aircraft inbound to the USA. Alvarez had cleverly provided documentation that presented the Nemesis Nine as a CIA paramilitary group bound for the Southern Philippines to assist in the threat posed by Abu-Sayyaf rebels indigenous to that region. When they were out of Swiss airspace, they changed course and headed for JFK. Alvarez hacked into the air traffic control system in flight and changed the CDR of their flight so that it appeared they were cleared to land there from the start of their flight upon their approach.

Nemesis Nine followed their pre-planned protocol and left all previously stowed weapons and ammunition on the planes, leaving only with the concealed small arms they could carry on their body. They shuttled to awaiting boats filled with a plethora of arms and munitions that they would take up the north coast of the Atlantic. While Beacon Rock promised to be an oasis of peace in the tempestuous world of Machine Gun Scorzo and the Nemesis Nine, the country the group had come back to was different than the one they had left weeks earlier.

President Courtland was slipping in the polls for his re-election bid only a few months off, and his democratic pundits were slamming him on every side. They made Nemesis Nine their focal point, citing that the president was remiss in his resolve to bring an end to the Nemesis Nine and their wanton lawlessness. The democrats claimed that Machine Gun Scorzo and his Nemesis Nine were the ringleaders inspiring lawlessness and the wanton murder of police by all other groups.

On the other hand, when Courtland attempted to quell the rising tide of violence that was far more prevalent with the activities of AntiCap, BOB, and the Black militants using the acronym CLM, which stood for Colored Lives Matter, the president was accused of being a racist dictator who opposed First Amendment rights of free speech and peaceful assembly. Though the riots fomented by BOB, another multiracial group, AntiCap, and CLM were anything but peaceful groups exercising their right to protest and peacefully assemble, the left-wing media portrayed them as peaceful protestors. The democratic party, the news media, and the social media giants all formed a united front against the embattled President Courtland.

What the media failed to mention, but Scorzo and his group knew only too well, was that each of these groups was led by men and women with a long history with the radical left. While they were the symptom of the problems America was being inundated with by the leftist media, the root of the problem was the enormous amount of funding and logistical support they were receiving to carry out their radical anti-American activities. Scorzo and Nemesis Nine saw this clearer than anyone else.

"Philster, why don't you take Ariana in the other room and brief her on her options at this point. I've got some things I'd need to brief the crew on."

Philster raised his palms at Scorzo and shook his head.

"What? Am I Vegas lounge act now? How many options can I brief her on that would be entertaining? Let's see," he said, taking a long drag off his cigarette and exhaling it, "she deliberately misled her boss as to our whereabouts, so she's gonna be some butch dyke's love doll if she's captured. Christ, Sal! Alvarez told us they already have her boss in the big house and the NSA has a transcript of their conversation using software that proved she was lying during the whole fucking conversation! Her only option is to stay the course with us and have

Alvarez set her up with funds and a new identity."

Scorzo put his face in the palms of his hands and heaved a sigh of defeat.

"There's no going back to the life she once lived," Philster said, turning to Ariana with a look of sullen disappointment. "There's no more DEA for you, no more picnics with the family or meeting up with old friends…no more posts on Yearbook or Chatter. Ariana Carina no longer exists!"

Even though Philster lectured her in his usual bombastic style, there was no emotion in her eyes or her face other than a vacuous look of resignation as she glanced from one person to the next, ending her gaze on Scorzo. Scorzo looked at her intently, almost remorsefully before speaking.

"I'm afraid he's right. I fucked up your life big time when I made the decision to take you with us. Now you see what happens when you think with your heart instead of your head."

"Bullshit," Ariana snapped back. "Your decision in Fox Lake had nothing to do with your heart. I was a bargaining chip that allowed you to put distance between you and your adversaries. It was simple as that."

"If it was as simple as that, I would have tossed you into the water along with your radio."

"That particular radio would have continued to transmit my location, even in the water, and you know it. So, why don't we get on with the business at hand…all present."

"He didn't want you to hear what we have to do," Philster said softly, looking down at the floor.

"Sometimes you have to cut off the arm to save the body," she replied flatly.

All faces trained their eyes on her in dismay. This was no longer the idealistic DEA agent they met in Fox Lake. She was no longer the frightened hostage unaware of her impending fate. She saw the men she was with as providing two options for the direction of her life: She could resign herself to the impotence that would allow evil to prosper, or she could summon the will to power that was required to save her nation. At the very least, she would die trying.

Scorzo got up and walked toward Ariana. Standing behind her, he placed his hands on her shoulders as he began to speak.

"Jake, you did a phenomenal job of taking out a tremendous source of funding for the radical factions in our country. As we are now well aware from our state-run propaganda outlets, the violence from the left is being blamed on President Courtland. Our task then is to put a stranglehold on additional sources of funding, while at the same time disrupting the flow of information from the media. Alvarez has identified four powerful families that are currently providing massive amounts of funding to these radical commies. The first is Mel Bates and his nefarious foundation. They'll be among the easiest to take out since their daughter is having a birthday party. Their whole family, along with many rich donors who align themselves with their causes, will be present."

"Just say the word," Jake said, looking at Nixon, "and we're on-board a 707 westbound."

"You and Nixon will be heading out west along with Gonzo and Sano, but not on that one," Scorzo replied flatly. "The scenario is much different than the op at Sorros' residence. We're not talking about four or five people. We're talking upwards of fifty people minimum and possibly as many as seventy-five to one hundred max.

"What do you have in mind?" Scorzo asked, turning to Alvarez.

"The USS *Chicago* out in San Diego," Alvarez replied.

"Any significance other than the fact that we knocked off the Federal Reserve Bank of Chicago?" Philster piped up.

"Yes, the first and most important thing about the Tomahawks on the USS *Chicago* is they are loaded with both shape charges and cluster bombs."

"Why not just hit them with one big fucking bomb like we did with Lakes and Nervosi?"

"No, he's right," Scorzo interjected. "The thing about cluster bombs is that some of them won't go off, which, in effect, makes them like sitting land mines. So, identification of the casualties and securing the crime scene as well as the neighboring areas make their job a lot more difficult."

"You mentioned the first thing about the Tomahawks on the USS *Chicago*... What are the other things that make it significant?" Philster asked.

"It can control an RQ-1 aerial predator drone that can hover about 20,000 feet above the Bates estate, and the focus can be brought within feet of the blast site, so we have a bird's-eye view of casualties. Another interesting thing about this specific sub is that it was featured in Clancy's novel *Red Storm Rising*, and Don Brown's novel *Black Sea Affair*."

"I can see the necessity of the drone, but who gives a shit about the fact that it was featured in a couple of novels?"

"That's probably the best reason for selecting it," Scorzo added. "What it means is that a hell of a lot of people know about the USS *Chicago* and its capabilities, so that opens the door to a lot more speculation about copy-cat scenarios to the Nervosi and Lakes strikes."

"It's also featured with the USS *Dallas* in a 2009 Call of Duty video game," Alvarez added.

"Well, I knew there had to be at least one retarded reason you chose that ship," Philster said, grinning and shaking his head.

"It's not retarded at all," Ariana said, coming to Alvarez's defense.

"So, when did you become an expert on ship-to-shore marine-based missiles?" Philster asked.

"I'm not, but I did a double major, with one of my majors being in child psychology. I was quite interested in the correlation between violent video games and school shootings..."

"All right, okay, hold up here for a minute," Philster interrupted. "There's a big difference between watching violent video games and shooting up schools than there is in firing sea-based weapons with sophisticated launch codes to hit precisely coordinated targets, don't you think?"

"What I know is that kids today grow up with technology in their hands from the time they're toddlers, and you can find just about anything you want to know about anything online these days."

"I'm sorry, Ariana," Philster began, forming his hands in a time-out sign, "but we're going have to agree to disagree on this one."

"What about him?" Ariana said, pointing over at Alvarez.

"Oh, for Christ's sake, he's a retard with an IQ of about two hundred. He's one in about five billion people with his level of intelligence."

"That leaves a good number of others who might be psychologically predisposed to copy-cat murders."

"She's got a point, douchebag," Max said with a laugh.

"You see, little sister, Philster's accustomed to being the author of ops, not the recipient of advice," Nixon added.

"All right, enough," Scorzo said, holding his hands up and lowering them slowly. "Points well taken on all sides. Alvarez, we go with the USS *Chicago* on the Bates gathering. Jake, you and Nixon will hit Steven Morisey, the CEO of Chatter, at his San Francisco estate. Sano, you and Gonzo will take out Stugenburg and his wife in Palo Alto."

"What about his daughters?" Gonzo asked.

"They have nothing to do with what he and his wife do," Scorzo said emphatically. "In time, they'll know why their parents died, and for their sake I hope they're not stupid enough to follow the path of their parents."

"All right, we don't touch the daughters," Sano and Gonzo said compliantly in unison.

"While these targets may look no different than the ease in which we took out Sorros, Lakes, and Nervosi, there's a crucial difference. They all have to take place at the same time. Max and I will take out Metos. He has to be taken out at close range with a knife to the heart."

"Do you mind my asking why he has to be taken out with a knife to the heart?" Philster asked with an obvious tone of annoyance in his voice.

"No, I don't mind you asking," Scorzo replied. "Remember that physician who went to the FBI with information on all the money that was raised for victims of the Haiti disaster?"

"I remember hearing something about that... He claimed donated money that the Stanton Foundation was raising on behalf of Haiti was missing in action. So what?"

"Well, it just so happens that the physician who provided that information was found dead in Metos' New York apartment, and the death was ruled a suicide. He apparently decided the most effective way to kill himself was by stabbing himself in the heart."

"Metos did it?" Philster asked, perplexed.

"I doubt Metos had anything to do with that, but the Stantons knew Metos. They were a recipient of his donations, and they had access to his New York residence, so I'd like to send them a message in addition to taking out donors promoting leftist chaos. Metos, his wife, and their three children get taken out."

"But, Sal," Jake blurted out, "Metos has four kids, not three. His fourth child was adopted."

"Not possible! I did my homework on that prick's family, and she's going to be at her best friend's house during their assassination."

"Excuse me for playing the devil's advocate here, Sal, but how the fuck would you know that?" Philster grumbled.

"Because I made friends with her best friend online, and I arranged a sleepover, which I'll conveniently back out of once I know that Metos' daughter is with her friend. Aside from that, the Bates strike will go down first. That will have all eyes in America focused away from any other itinerary."

"What's my role in all of this?" Ariana asked.

"You'll remain here at Beacon Rock out of harm's way. Need I remind you, you are not to make any calls, use the Internet, order food, go shopping, or order any on-demand movies. One of the reasons I've made the basement so comfortable is because I don't want any sound or heat signatures emanating from this house while we're away."

"So, there's nothing I can do to assist you guys in any way?"

"Don't give our position away to the militia," Philster said sarcastically. "And help Alvarez with anything he needs."

Chapter 26
War of Words

All communication between Alvarez and the Nemesis Nine was done using a protocol that Alvarez developed which blended features of COMSEC and his own digital encryption system that operated through the dark web. No branch of the military could access it, nor could they decipher it even if they could. When he received transmission that all their teams were in place, he initiated the launch sequence, firing a Tomahawk missile at the Bates' residence during the midst of their celebration. In less than two hours the Bates' residence was obliterated and all guests in attendance were dead or dying.

Alvarez went into immediate action using stationary jammers to block out all media information of the event coming from SNN, KBS, BSN, and other left-leaning sources of information. He then sent out secure communications to alternative media outlets with a narrative that radical left-wing factions of AntiCap, CLM, and BOB were carrying out atrocities on the West Coast. Given the fact that democratic politicians on the West Coast had been allowing radical groups to freely engage in violent activities, the information was believed to be credible by a horrified public.

By the time Nemesis Nine had reconvened at Beacon Rock, there were angry mobs assembled outside the outlets of SNN, KBS, and BSN as well as many other major print media publications who the public felt condoned and thereby promoted radical left-wing violence. With throngs of angry flag-waving protestors outside the major left-wing news outlets, the traditionally left-wing media felt compelled to pick up the narrative of alternative media outlets who had already saturated public sentiment with these atrocities being carried out by the left.

Offices of CLM, AntiCap, and BOB were being fire-bombed by angry patriots who believed them to be the culprits of these heinous murders. Left-wing professors on campuses across the nation were being verbally assaulted for their left-leaning convictions. For the first time since its inception, CLM was being denounced as a radical Marxist organization that cared nothing about the plight of disenfranchised people of color. While most politicians remained neutral or silent on these three organizations, AntiCap and BOB were being openly declared as domestic terrorist organizations while CLM was being decried as an organization that was committed to Marxism and the overthrow of western values which they claimed oppressed people of color.

While the right-wing alternative media as well as the traditionally left-wing media were mourning the loss of these families of such great talent, CLM, AntiCap, and BOB actually hailed their deaths as a great victory for the new world order and the fundamental transformation of America. Adding injury to insult for the FBI, Machine Gun Scorzo interrupted an SNN broadcast through the aid of Alvarez.

"I know I need no formal introduction, having been villainized by the agencies who murdered my daughter and attempted to murder me and my wife as well, but I would like to extend my deepest and most heartfelt condolences to the families who have suffered at the hands of deranged, radical leftists who have taken control of our country and the sensibilities of those who should be pursuing them with a vengeance. Instead of trying to cast aspersion and blame on me and millions of upstanding patriots who are victims of their corruption and tyranny, they should be adhering to the principles of our great constitution that they swore to uphold. These men have not only victimized me, but they have wantonly victimized you, the people of this great nation, by trying time and again to remove your lawfully elected president from office, and not a single one of them has been prosecuted for the crimes they have clearly been proven guilty of. Remember this, my fellow Americans, you have the right to petition your elected officials for the removal of any elected official in the House or Senate who violates his oath of office. If you don't begin to remove those who refuse to uphold our constitution, I can guarantee you that they will begin to remove you, just as they did to my dearly beloved daughter."

Scorzo ended with those words immediately upon a signal from Alvarez, who detected that the NSA would have their location in a few minutes. While the words of Scorzo ended, the words of President Courtland were just beginning.

"I would like to begin by offering my deep condolences to the families that have suffered these tragic losses, but, moreover, I want you to know that we as a nation suffer with you. Today, America has been robbed of some of the greatest minds who offered their talent to our nation and participated in making it the great place it is. I want to make it very clear to the radical cowards who committed these heinous acts of lawlessness that you will be pursued with the entire weight and might of the United States government. We, the people of this great nation, will not continue to suffer under tyranny of a lawless group of individuals that seek change through violence and anarchy. Make no mistake about it, murdering successful entrepreneurs and members of our law enforcement community can by no means be construed as peaceful protests. As such, I will be signing an executive order immediately calling for capital punishment for the murder of police officers and any other murders that result from a person's political affiliation or opinions. We live in a country that allows us to publicly declare our opinions in a responsible manner, and we are a nation predicated on law and order. Tonight, the victims of today's tragedies will see the fruits of my promise to restore law and order to our great country. Our thoughts and prayers go out to the families that are suffering. May God bless each of you as you grieve, and may God bless America!"

President Courtland waved his hand with a slightly clenched jaw and turned his back on a disappointed press that loudly hurled questions at him as he walked away from them. Thanks to the media engineering of Alvarez, and much to the great chagrin of the FBI, the questions concerning Machine Gun Scorzo were conspicuously absent. It looked as though aspersion had been clearly cast upon the radical left elements within the country.

Scorzo and the Nemesis Nine were using the Bureau's own tactics against them. They were no longer waging a war of success based on superior firepower alone. They were using propaganda in a much more powerful way than the Bureau and the media did due to the technical proficiency of Jerry Alvarez. The American public began to see Machine Gun Scorzo as a champion of the people, no matter how unconventional his methods were made to appear by the Bureau. Alvarez inundated newspapers with op-eds he composed that provided documented proof of the Bureau's corruption and complicity in crimes that were tantamount to treason. Moreover, with the cooperation of alternative media outlets who agreed to meet with him at unknown remote locations, he held televised interviews wherein he documented his military service, naming names and disclosing classified operations that he could now speak freely about since his military service was denied.

The saga of Operation Lotus Blossom was substantiated by Pastor Stan Brunsler and scores of others, both professionals and victims who testified to the veracity of Scorzo's claims. Each one of them attested to the fact that Salvino Scorzoletti was a humanitarian hero who was being persecuted because he dared to tarnish the reputation of those who were supposed to be honorable men. In their starched uniforms, polished brass bars, and patent leather shoes, they seemed like nothing less, but Salvino Scorzoletti knew and could reveal the blackness of their hearts, and indeed that's why they tried to silence him and why they continued to villainize him.

Moreover, scores of charitable organizations were requesting open Senate hearings on how they received large charitable donations from the United States Navy in the aftermath of Operation Lotus Blossom. How and why, they wondered, would the US Navy be donating hundreds of thousands of dollars to organizations helping victims of human trafficking? The donations significantly improved the lives of human trafficking victims while at the same time leaving the US Navy in the precarious position of producing a plausible explanation for the humanitarian aid.

With the help of Alvarez, Scorzoletti was saturating digital and print media as well as the television airwaves with incriminating documentation that tied the US Navy to human trafficking. As if that wasn't bad enough for the government, he also levelled charges that the FBI was complicit in covering up the wrongdoings of both ONI and the ATF by arresting and jailing DEA Agent Javier Contreras to keep him silent because they feared that he made the connection between the collaboration of Bickens and Pierpont regarding their mutual interest in pursuing illicit funds from classified operations. Thus, Alvarez had created an adversarial relationship between the FBI, ATF, DEA, and ONI. By setting their private agendas before the public, he placed them at odds with each other.

With ONI under the spotlight of the media, Pierpont could no longer make good on his promise to assist Bickens in his quest for revenge, and with the media inundating the airwaves about chicanery and duplicity abounding amidst the alphabet agencies, the FBI was disinclined to request military support in their pursuit of Machine Gun Scorzo. In their attempt to create an enemy that could salvage the image of the Bureau as a defender of democracy, they instead created the archetypal anti-hero that Americans hailed as a champion for the underdogs.

Far from being considered as public enemy number one, Machine Gun Scorzo developed into a cult status hero. Everything from T-shirts to bumper stickers that were emblazoned with slogans such as "Machine Gun Scorzo for President" were selling faster than they could be produced. Bickens was incensed by the fact that ATF offices were inundated with FFL and ATF 4 forms from people wanting to purchase machine guns, forcing many agents to assume more time on clerical paperwork than criminal investigations. Suddenly, the four most popular destinations in Las Vegas were Battlefield Vegas, Machine Guns Vegas, Machine Gun Experience, and The Range 702, where people could assume the real-world persona of Machine Gun Scorzo. After Courtland lost the bid for his second term in office, people wanted to feel the power of a machine gun coursing through their body, and the face on the paper targets bore a remote resemblance to President Styles Hiding.

The sham victory of President Styles Hiding didn't do anything to dampen the spirit of patriotism that began under President Courtland. In fact, it did just the opposite. News rooms were inundated with mail addressed to Machine Gun Scorzo. At the heart of all their words of praise for his work in giving back to the people what the government had stolen was a heartfelt plea to empower them to do what he could do…rise up and annihilate the corrupt career bureaucrats who no longer represented the American people. The public began to see their politicians as nothing more than the thieves that Scorzo saw them to be. If ever there was a time for a revolution, it was now. But amidst the many things Scorzo wanted to politically correct, there were two thoughts which besieged him constantly. First was his wife. Would he ever see her again, or was there only one ultimate outcome for his destiny? The second thought that tormented him was Ariana Carina. Where would her life ultimately go, or end? She was so young, so full of idealism. So full of life.

"You're like a modern-day Paul Revere," Ariana said, clasping his hands with a broad smile stretching across her face.

"How did you come to that conclusion, princess? I'm just a guy robbing Federal Reserve banks," Scorzo answered flatly.

"People who rob banks do it for profit motive," Ariana retorted. "You're taking money from banks that have nothing to do with the federal government or your own profit motive. Did you ever hear of Eustace Mullins?"

"Yeah, as a matter of fact I have. He wrote a book called *The Secrets of the Federal Reserve*. "I also read another fascinating book called *The Creature from Jekyll Island*. Incidentally, it's what got Alvarez into exploring the dark web to find ways and means of transferring money without leaving a trace from whence it came or whither it went."

Jake and Nixon lay on the couch, listening intently as Alvarez carefully eavesdropped before Philster invited himself into the conversation.

"Bank robber my ass!" Philster opined. "Did you ever know a bank robber who gave all his money away and kept only enough for food, weapons, and supplies? If I could find a costume shop around here, I'd dress this motherfucker up as Mother Teresa instead of one of those raghead Muslims. Shit, at least as Mother Teresa, people would be throwing money at him without him needing a gun."

"I bet people would be throwing money at you if you dressed up as a girl, douchebag," Max added to the levity of all except Scorzo and Alvarez, who exchanged tired glances with each other amidst the laughter.

"What's on your mind, Alvarez?" Scorzo asked seriously.

"Did you ever hear of that Russian sub game I developed called Annigilyatsiya? I sold the rights to a Russian gamer who marketed it in Russia. It's more accurately translated Annihilation!"

"All right...what does that have to do with us?"

"The reality of it is that there's approximately twelve nuclear attack submarines about twelve miles off the coast of a major Navy base on the Atlantic seaboard."

"What's so unusual about that, chowder head?" Philster asked.

"They're not ours, Philster. They're Russian subs."

"Hold up a minute, pothead... You're trying to tell to tell me you invented a game that the Ruskies actually decided to copy in real life? And moreover, they have twelve nuclear subs within twelve miles of our coast?"

"That's exactly what he's telling you," Scorzo shot back flatly.

"What's more is they're armed with the BrahMos missiles, capable of flying at speeds of Mach eight and carrying nuclear warheads as well as conventional weaponry," added Alvarez with authority.

"So, what did you do, Einstein, sell this game to the Ruskies to acquire that house up in Kenilworth you have?"

"Hell no! Games I created were out there on the open market for anybody to buy. I don't have any control over the markets my games sell in. Most of them sell over the net."

"It's a good thing the ragheads are pretty much landlocked, or we'd be French toast by now," Philster added

"The real question is…" Alvarez began, "how can we use those to our advantage in the siege on the New York FED?"

"You can hack into those things, Alvarez?" Jake said with astonishment.

"I speak and read Russian and Chinese," Alvarez replied. "I designed them for wargames against the two communist powers. You see, the Soviets were supposed to breach our Atlantic coast, and the Chinese were supposed to breach our Pacific coast."

Philster smiled and shook his head nonchalantly as he glanced toward Ariana. "Aren't you glad this pothead is on our side?" he asked wryly.

"I guess I'm glad you're all on the side of righteousness," Ariana said softly.

"A great example of the Helsinki syndrome," Philster added

"It's the Stockholm syndrome, you know-nothing douchebag," Max piped in quickly.

"Oh, really, Brillo head, how's that?"

"The Stockholm syndrome originated in Sweden in 1973 when two bank robbers in Sweden took six hostages and held them in a vault for six days, and when they were released, they didn't want to cooperate with the police because they had formed a bond with their captors."

"Helsinki, Stockholm, Sweden, what the fuck does it matter?"

"No particular reason other than to prove you're a douchebag."

"I don't care what the fuck it's called; it can't happen to our princess here," Scorzo said authoritatively as he looked at Ariana.

"*Cos altro ho*, Sal?"

"You've got your whole life ahead of you, that's what you got!" Scorzo shot back somewhat indignantly.

"*Mi hai aperto gli occhi. Sei la mia vita!*"

"I'm your life? I've killed more people in a month of Sundays than you have in your whole career, and that somehow opened your eyes and made you fall in love with me?" Scorzo said with disapproval apparent in his voice.

Ariana looked around the room, seeing no sympathy in any eyes present, for they knew the terrain that Sal walked and the talk he talked, but Ariana fired back.

"Tell me, Philster, weren't you the one who educated me on the crimes of the DEA. Are you gonna change your tune now and tell me that all that embezzling and outright theft was somehow done in the name of the greater good?"

"Hey, kiddo, sometimes I tend to run off with my mouth. I mean… everyone here knows that." The room filled with a brief chuckle.

"And what about you?" Ariana said, pointing accusatively at Philster. "All those children you sold into slavery. Were you just running your mouth off about that?"

"No, he was running his mouth in circles around the congressional oversight committee on intelligence," Max said with a half grin, attempting to lighten the mood. Jake and Nixon rolled their eyes as Sano laughed with a singular focus on Philster. Gonzo shook his head at Sano disapprovingly whereupon his laughing stopped.

"Have you taken any time to read the mail that people are sending you through the news media and on social media platforms?" Ariana asked.

"No," Scorzo replied, cupping his face in his hands. "If it's not heavily censored, it's blatantly canceled…you have heard the term 'cancel culture'?"

"Yeah, it means they eradicate certain speech or points of view." Ariana replied.

"But do you know what it really means?" Scorzo pressed.

"Well, at its root, it's basically human oppression."

"Wrong, wrong, wrong! It's one big fucking dress rehearsal," Scorzo shot back.

"Dress rehearsal?" Ariana said softly, confused. "What do you mean?"

"It's a dress rehearsal for genocide. Think about that for a moment," Scorzo said, stroking his chin. "The first part of genocide is silencing your opponent's thoughts, then his speech, his dialect, his culture, and then finally you silence his being, permanently…you cancel him."

"But people aren't talking about you or the Nemesis Nine like that. To the common people you are heroes!"

"Ariana, let me ask you something." Jake spoke up. "When was the last time you saw the common people in control of anything?"

"They're in control of everything…the farms, the factories, the taxis, the airplanes, the schools…"

"Wrong!" Gonzo interrupted. "They run the farms, the factories, the taxis, the airplanes, and the schools, but they're not in control of them. Our rulers are in control of everything!"

"Okay, our representatives and senators legislate our laws with the checks and balances of the other branches of government."

"Wrong!" the men all said in unison.

"We no longer have representatives and government," Scorzo continued. "What we now have are rulers, and we are the ruled class. They make the rules, and we simply follow them like supplicant slaves."

"If that isn't the truth!" Philster blurted out. "Think about this shit the Department of Education is foisting onto second and third graders about how it's okay to say you're a girl if you're biologically a boy and vice versa, and the only group that it's okay to hate these days is the all-American white male! God forbid you want to defend yourself against a group of Black or Latino gangbangers that want to kill you, especially if you're up against a group of thugs and you're armed with a gun and all they have is machetes! You're shit out of luck in that situation because according to the fucking liberal media, machetes don't count as weapons…so, they're considered unarmed! What a crock of shit! All our fucked-up, enlightened leaders are trying to do to us is turn us all against each other while they live safely with their security guards in their fucking gated communities. That's why they're bringing American-hating foreigners in here by the busloads, boatloads, and planeloads.

"Then…then get this! They have border patrol agents giving them identification, food, clothes, cash, or debit cards to get a hotel for seven days if they test positive for covid. Can you believe this mother-fucked-up cock-sucking shit! Then, if all that's not bad enough, they're put on busses and planes and shipped to sanctuary cities so they commit crimes there with impunity if they somehow can't milk the system!"

"Here, suck on this, Philster," Jake said softly, throwing him a beer.

"Can't you see why I want to stay with you, Scorzo?" Ariana said, using the rationale of the group's assessment of American life.

"Look," Scorzo said, looking at Ariana in a very frank manner. "There's only one way out of this situation if you don't go back to your family."

"And that is?" Ariana queried softly.

"Death," Scorzo answered coldly.

"The world you guys have been describing doesn't seem like a world much worth living in," Ariana replied.

"Tell me about these letters and social media platforms," Scorzo said, changing the subject. "What are the people saying about me?"

"In a nutshell, Sal, you're a hero. The fact that you aren't willing to be subjugated to a ruling elite class makes you a legend. Think about it—the people who stormed the governor's office in Michigan over the lockdowns weren't trained SEALs or sharp-shooting assassins. They were just plain old ordinary folks…the ruled class, rising up against their tyrannical rulers. And what about the Italians that banded together to guard the statue of Columbus from being knocked down, or the Proud Boys protecting monuments in the South. None of this stuff was happening before you started hitting Federal Reserve banks and disbursing money to people and groups that needed it. You opened a door for me, and showed me another side where this shit doesn't have to exist, and now you want me to just walk back through that door and live in that world of shit? Look at my boss. All Contreras did was good, and look where he is now. He's in jail being blamed for aiding and abetting all of you when the only thing he was trying to do was put all of your asses in jail. Does he deserve that? If anyone deserves to be in jail, it's me!"

"Look, Ariana, maybe there's a way to salvage Contreras's life if not his career," Scorzo said resolutely. "Me, Alvarez, and the Philster are gonna do a little brainstorming. You kick back with the guys and have a few cold ones."

When Scorzo, Alvarez, and the Philster were sequestered in Jerry's little alcove, Scorzo came to the first order of business.

"Are you able to obtain the routing number for the Federal Reserve Bank of New York?"

"Obtain it," Alvarez said with dismay. "It's 021001208."

"But the routing number in and of itself is of very little use," Philster balked.

"To a degree true, but when we took the Fed Reserves in Chicago and San Francisco, I breached their systems. That, in turn, allowed me to steal payment transfer systems. I downloaded thousands of them. We can totally wipe out the Federal Reserve of New York."

"How much are we talking about?" Scorzo asked bluntly.

"We're talking about 3.7 trillion in transferable funds, not counting the gold in the vault," said Alvarez.

"And the gold?" Philster piped in curiously.

"About 6,310 metric tons."

"Fuck the gold," Scorzo said, shaking his head coolly. "That's a logistical nightmare."

"But it definitely has a purpose," Philster said.

"And what purpose would that be?" Scorzo and Alvarez said in unison.

"First, we clean out all the cash electronically; then we get word to those jackasses in CLM, AntiCap, and BOB that we're hitting the gold in the New York Federal Reserve. Now you know those rioting motherfuckers are gonna want a piece of that ass, so they're the ones that are gonna get their asses shot up and their reputations disparaged."

"Every now and again, you come up with a common-sense idea." Scorzo grinned and nodded at Alvarez.

"Common sense, common sense!" barked Philster. "Those

motherfucking assholes will replace you as public enemy number one. The thing I can't wrap my head around is how AntiCap is going to be able to rationalize their participation in a gold heist being the cock-sucking commie motherfuckers they are!"

"They'll claim it's for the less fortunate or some shit like that," Alvarez suggested.

"You can bet that will happen," Scorzo added.

"And what about these subs?" asked Philster. "How do they figure into our plan?"

"We use the subs on our Eastern Seaboard to take the network that made Sal public enemy number one," Alvarez said casually.

"The J. Edgar Hoover Building…" Scorzo said, shaking his head in agreement. "They not only publicized me as public enemy number one, but they also treated President Courtland like he was public enemy number one, supplanted by me only when they couldn't make anything stick on him."

"Indeed," Alvarez concurred. "But it doesn't stop there… We fire a few salvos at the Federal Reserve Bank of New York and melt a bunch of CLM, AntiCap, and BOB ringleaders in 6,300 tons of gold we leave for them."

"What about the Chinese subs off our western coast?" Philster inquired with excitement. "Do they play any part in our plans?"

"I'm glad you asked," Alvarez said, looking first at Philster and then smiling as he looked at Scorzo. Alvarez took a long swig off his beer and placed it down on the table with emphasis. "Sal, after political graft and outright corruption, especially where concerns the theft of this last election from President Courtland, the left is using illegals to incite more chaos as well as retain their power via more votes from people they are pandering to."

"That's a no-brainer!"

"Damn fucking straight!" thundered Philster. "So, what are we talking about?"

"We're talking about four SSN nuclear attack subs of the Shang class, and three SSBMs in the Jin class. The SSBMs are each armed with two nuclear armed ballistic missiles. The nice thing about it is that with the exception of one Jin class sub off the coast of San Diego, all the others are offshore in different regions of Mexico and Central America."

"Leave this to me if you want to get the most mileage out of this op," Philster blurted out. "Einstein here has the highest combined IQ in this room, but nobody beats the Philster when it comes to planning ops!"

"All right, let's hear what you got," Scorzo said, with Alvarez nodding in agreement.

"Okay, our first two primary targets are the J. Edgar Hoover building and the NSA in Maryland. It's essential that we take out the NSA's capacity to track us via voice prints, retinal scans, facial recognition, satellites, and God only knows what other shit they use. Once they're out of the picture, their other posts throughout the States are rendered useless. Next, we take out the Bureau's field office on the west side of Chicago, and target another missile within close proximity of the Chicago Metropolitan Correctional Center. They will do an immediate evacuation of that facility, with the least dangerous, such as our friend Contreras, given very minimum security. I'm sure he'll find some way to put distance between himself and his lovely cohorts. It will also cause enough havoc for that stumble-bum president Hiding, that nobody will be looking for Machine Gun Scorzo and yours truly, accompanied by the lovely Ms. Ariana Carina, who we will unite with her parents."

"I'm curious why you didn't mention taking out the BATF field office in Washington?" Scorzo asked wryly.

"Maybe I like your plan better…thinking of Bickens growing old in a wheelchair crapping his pants whenever his bed nurse is occupied texting her boyfriends," Philster ended with a rancorous laugh. What he didn't tell Scorzo, though, was that he knew Bickens would be in the J. Edgar Hoover building trying to gather information that would lead to nowhere.

"So far it's sounding good," Scorzo assented, "but what about the

Chinese fleet of subs over in the Pacific? How do they fit into our plans?"

"They deal with our crisis on the border?"

"I don't know about that, Philster. Why in Sam Hill would they want to solve our border problems. If anything, I would think they would benefit by seeing them get worse."

"No, he's absolutely right," Alvarez interjected. "It's a concept we call softening up the enemy."

"I'm familiar with the concept," Scorzo said sarcastically, "but I can't go along with hitting targets in our own country..."

"Just hear him out, Sal," Alvarez interrupted.

"Remind me to thank you later, Einstein," Philster said, grinning at Alvarez before turning quickly to Scorzo with a focused look of seriousness. "The beauty of this op is that it only hits one domestic target...Fort Bliss."

"Why in the hell would we want to hit our own people?" Scorzo fired back.

"Because Fort Bliss has been turned into a huge migrant camp where they're housing a bunch of illegal immigrants instead of home-less vets...which is what they should be doing!"

"Well, fuck me!" Scorzo retorted angrily.

"Next, we target foreign nationals near the Mexico-USA border that are close to large military installations. Does Ciudad Juarez ring a bell?"

"Yeah, it does," Scorzo agreed.

"Well, it should! It's right next door to the Sixteenth Brigade Engineer Battalion, the Fort Bliss Army Reserve, the US Naval and Marine Corps Reserve, the Department of Homeland Security, and a bunch of other Army bases. We waste Juarez, and Fort Bliss turns into Fort Blitz! At the same time, we take out Reynosa Airport, which again is close to the Texas National Guard, the Army Reserve, two field offices of the TSA, and not too far from Moore Airfield. Any logical commanding officer is going to look at it as an absolute siege. They're going to give orders to shoot any man, woman, or child that moves toward our borders!"

"They always did say at ONI you were the man with the plans," Scorzo said.

"But wait, wait!" Philster said, putting his palms up in front of Scorzo.

"There's more." Scorzo raised his eyebrows.

"Hell yeah, Sal, I'm just getting fucking warmed up! Before the Chinese know what's happening, we hit the port of entry where all these fucking caravans start...Chiapas Mexico! After that we go right down the line and hit Guatemala, El Salvador, the home of the wonderful MSD-15 gangbangers, or whatever their name is, and then Honduras and Nicaragua."

"That's it?" Scorzo asked

"That's it he asks incredulously?" Philster grinned at Alvarez. "Well, when the Russians are retreating back into international waters, we could have Alvarez launch some of their nukes on South Africa, Syria, and Pakistan and clean up the European refugee crisis, but I think we should call it a day and let that German broad clean up the refugee mess she made over in her own country. As far as my op is concerned, I think our good is done here...problem solved!"

"What about Ariana," Scorzo asked.

"Good question," Philster said sarcastically as he glanced at Alvarez. "Do you really think with half the world in a torrent of fire, the feds are going to be looking for a woman who is already presumed to be dead?"

"No, I guess not," Scorzo said stoically, pushing his chair away from the table with the others joining him.

The banter in the other room was jocular and upbeat until Scorzo, Alvarez, and Philster ended with looks of solemnity.

"Why the serious faces?" Ariana asked.

"Yeah, even the douchebag looks a whiter shade of pale," Max added.

"You're going home." Scorzo pointed at Ariana with a lack of emotion she had never seen before.

"How's that going to happen with every law enforcement officer in the country looking for you two?" Max asked.

"Philster came up with the idea that we'd go low profile and take a Mover from here to Chicago. Nobody's gonna stop a Mover driver that doesn't speed, follows all the rules, and has a GPS to keep him on track. We give him 10K there, put him up in hotels, cover his meals, and he gets 20K to head back empty with food and lodging allowances."

"Plus, we'll give him a five bones rating," Philster said with a laugh. "Now what fool is going to say no to that when those guys have to practically sleep in their cars to make 2K a month?"

"Have you guys forgotten that everyone in this country knows what we look like?" Ariana asked.

"They know what we look like, but they don't know what you look like because you've been undercover throughout the duration of the op against us. And we won't be looking the same," Scorzo said, looking at Philster with a grin.

"Oh no, don't tell me I have to wear a turban and a dress again," Philster said, with his face twisting in chagrin.

"We'll add a masculine touch this time."

"How do you make a dress-wearing motherfucker with a turban look masculine? How? Will you tell me that one?"

"We'll both grow bushy beards that cover our face. We'll play the part of tourists?"

"Why not just play the part of undocumented refugees from Pakistan?"

"Because the Mover driver would probably be asking us questions about our lives. The object here is to keep him busy answering our questions about himself and his life in America."

"What if he starts hitting on Ariana?"

"She'll just answer everything in Italian, and he'll give up on her."

"What if he asks us questions about her," Philster asked with growing annoyance.

"Look, we're rich sheiks. We say we bought her in France for entertainment," Scorzo shot back.

"So, I don't have anything to say about this," Ariana said with a look of discontent.

"No," all the men present said in unison.

"I think it's pretty clear you've grown on all of us," Max said with a grin, "especially douchebag over there." He thumbed his hand at Philster. "He probably has to pull his pud a few times a day before he can get to sleep thinking about you."

"Oh, and you're some kind of fucking monk when you're around hot ladies, huh Brillo head?"

"Not when he pummeled this chick in Mindanao. He went at it with her for about thirty minutes straight," Sano piped in.

Scorzo put his hands together in a staccato motion calling for a break in the present conversation and the room went silent.

"Here's our present directives… We three," Scorzo said, circling around Philster, Ariana, and himself, "are heading to Chicago via a Mover rideshare. The rest of you will remain here and keep our residence secure."

Jake shook his head slowly with an inward look of discontent.

"What's on your mind, Jake?"

"President Hiding will be making his first visit to a military base since he's taken office, and he's coming right up to the naval station here in Newport, Rhode Island."

"Jake, does the phrase 'you don't shit in your own backyard' mean anything to you?"

"Yeah," Jake sighed.

"That old fucker will be lucky if he doesn't have a heart attack or a seizure when we initiate our firing sequences. He'll probably crap his pants at the very least."

"Can you just imagine what kind of answers his press officers are going to be writing on his notecards. That old fuck will probably look like a drunk shuffling through a disheveled deck of cards looking for the joker," Philster added with laughter that brought levity back to the room for a moment before Scorzo motioned for another time-out.

"Okay, we lie low here for two weeks to put on a little weight and change our appearance with some bushy beards while Alvarez hacks the launch codes for our East and West Coast strikes."

"Sal, how can I go back to the kind of life I was living, knowing what I now know?" Ariana asked softly, peering deep into his eyes.

"You won't have to," Alvarez answered before Scorzo could speak. "I set both you and Contreras up with four billion dollars each in numeric accounts registered as charitable foundations."

"Which means two things," Scorzo added. "First, it's tax-free money, and second, it has nothing to do with either of your names."

"But at the end of the day, it's stolen money."

"No, at the end of the day, it was money stolen from all of us," Jake added emphatically. "We only took what belonged to the American people to begin with before a bunch of robber barons created legislation to make theft legal. And most of that money we've given back to people who really need it, like sick coal miners in Pennsylvania, starving families in rural Appalachia, and people like Reverend Stan Brunsler who help women that are victims of human trafficking. We also started a company that builds houses for homeless vets."

"Think about the fees banks charge on the credit cards they offer," added Sano. "Fifteen, 21.9, and up to thirty-five percent on cash withdrawals. There's a word for that which puts people like you and me behind bars. It's called usury!"

"He's right," added Alvarez. "The maximum amount of interest allowed by law is eight percent, but they get around this by specifying that there are exceptions for home loans less than 300K, or equity lines of credit, and all sorts of other stuff."

"Tell her about the First Marquette National Bank versus First of Omaha Service Corporation in 1978, Einstein! That's motherfucking thievery in motion!" Philster thundered.

"Well, in a nutshell, Marquette Bank was based in Minnesota, where their interest was capped at twelve percent, but under Nebraska laws, where First Omaha was based, they could charge up to eighteen percent interest."

"So, what do you think those fuckers in First Marquette National bank did?" Philster erupted.

"You got me," Ariana said, shaking her head in dismay.

"Those motherfucking shysters changed the terms of the contract to add annual charges that would make up the difference, bringing them up to eighteen percent interest too. How's that for sleight of hand?"

"So, you do some serious thinking, baby girl," Nixon chimed in. "When you talk about stolen money, you need to ask yourself who the money was stolen from and where did it end up."

"Damn straight!" Philster barked. "The money was stolen from people like you and your parents, as well as people like me, Scorzo, and the rest of us here who put our asses on the line every day of our life so a bunch of smooth-talking shysters could line their pockets with it and live in Martha's Vineyard and other places for the well-to-do crooks. I get so fucking mad thinking about it that I don't even want to talk about it anymore! That's why you and Contreras are going to take that money and use it for some good! That guy's got a good head on his shoulders, and you've got a good heart, kid. Like old Gandhi said, 'Be the change you want to see in the world.'"

"So, what's next?" Ariana asked.

"We relax and enjoy our anonymity in this beautiful estate with a proud naval history, and the rest you don't need to know."

"Why, are you guys planning a coup d'état to bring back President Courtland?"

"You ever heard the term plausible deniability?" Philster asked.

"Yes, it's the ability to deny knowledge or actions based on a lack of information or participation in the planning of those actions."

"So, what the douchebag is trying to tell you is that the less you know about our future plans, the better off you'll be when you're debriefed."

"And they will debrief you," Philster added.

"And wouldn't you like to be a part of that debriefing session, douchebag," Max added with a mischievous grin. "You'd probably include a full cavity search as a part of the debrief."

The room erupted with laughter, and even Ariana joined in when she looked at Philster's anguished red face, searching for a comeback.

"Look who's talking, Brillo head," Philster fired back. "You're the one who's a proctologist. I guess looking up people's asses does it for you! You probably don't even wear gloves when you go probing. In fact, I bet you even sneak a sniff now and then, ass man!"

Ariana doubled over with laughter as did the others. The Philster was never one to be outdone when it came to insults. After the laughter slowed to sporadic bursts, Ariana asked, "What do you need me to do in the next couple of weeks."

"We need you to be as dumb as a stump," Philster quipped.

"He's absolutely right," Scorzo said, raising his eyebrows and nodding his head affirmatively.

"Can you cook, Ariana," Nixon asked.

"Yes, I'm a wiz in the kitchen," she replied with a coy smile.

"All right, you put some lists together of foods and ingredients you need, and me and Gonzo will go shopping since we're the most low-profile individuals in this crew."

"Oh Jesus, Nixon," complained Philster, "you silly ass Snoop Dogg-looking motherfucker, you're bound to draw attention everywhere you go. And, by the way, who knows how many outstanding warrants the real Snoop Dogg has out on him. You could get busted for something stupid like jaywalking up in this area, and then we're all fucked."

"Well, maybe I should just buy a pair of scrubs and say I'm a caretaker. You know all us niggers up in these highfalutin areas either work in nursing homes or at McDonald's."

"All right, all right, you two cease fire," Scorzo interrupted. "Nixon, you'll stand down. Jake and Gonzo will do the shopping."

As the days passed, Alvarez worked assiduously breaching the launch codes of the various submarines that would carry out his mission. Ironically, it was the NSA's decrypting software that was enabling him to achieve his work with efficiency and lightning speed, but when the agency served its purpose for Alvarez, it would be obliterated.

There would be no telltale signs that missiles were launched from

Chinese and Russian subs. Only the onboard crews of the fated vessels would know what happened, but they wouldn't know until after the launches were made, and they would be powerless to change the course of destiny their destruction would reap. Nor would they claim responsibility. Instead, they would claim that America was in the midst of an insurrection due to the conservative narrative that President Courtland's second term had been stolen by President Hiding through a wanton act of voter fraud.

As the day drew closer to what the group now called Operation Border Control, Scorzo grew uneasy about using a civilian Mover rideshare. He called Philster and Jake into Alvarez's labyrinth of monitors ad electronic equipment.

"Philster, how do you and Jake connect with Mohammed Hussain?"

"Through books in public libraries," Jake answered.

"He's serious," Scorzo said, looking at Philster skeptically.

"Yeah, why? What's up?"

"I'm not comfortable with the idea of a civilian Mover driver, so how long will it take to connect with Mohammed?"

"He hangs out at the New York Public Library in midtown Manhattan… It's the Stephen A. Schwarzman branch…great place for a Jew-hating Muslim to hang out, huh," Philster wise-cracked.

"Sal, that's about a three-and-a-half-hour drive south on 95 from where we are now."

"That means you should have been gone about three hours ago," Scorzo said with authority. "Take Sano with you."

"Roger that, boss. We're gone."

Within moments a Mover driver pulled up to the estate and was surprised by the demeanor of his riders.

"Wow, you two look like you just came from a rodeo. Man, I didn't think nobody even lived at the Beacon Rock estate. I guess you don't really need to dress fancy when you have enough money to live at a spread like this."

"Look, we're here on business, just renting the place for a few days. We're really tired so we're gonna sack out back here. Get us to

348

the Stephen A. Schwarzman library as fast as you can, but don't speed, okay? We'll take good care of you."

As instructed the driver complied and said nothing to Jake and Sano until they reached the library. Upon entering, they saw Mohammed sitting at a table. Sano sat down across from him and Jake selected *Red Scarf Girl*, which signaled that their need was urgent, but had nothing to do with weapons or money laundering. Jake placed a note inside that instructed Mohammed he needed him as a driver to and from Chicago. He offered 200k when they reached Chicago, and 200k upon return to New York. Mohammed nodded his head in agreement, but Jake wasn't finished. He walked away from the table and retrieved another book called *First They Killed My Father*. Mohammed's head rose with his eyes slowly meeting Jake's. Before he even opened the book, he knew he would be engaging in a wet job. Jake and Mohammed walked to a secluded area of the library where Jake handed Mohammed a pair of gloves and silenced twenty-two along with a fake Mover account. He was instructed to take the driver to Fordham in the Bronx, put two in the back of his head, and take the driver's wallet to make it appear like a robbery...a very plausible scenario in that area of the Bronx. Thereafter, he made his way to Queens Audi and purchased an Audi a6 four-door sedan with tinted windows. By nightfall he was at Beacon Rock estate.

Chapter 27
Revelation

—∿∿—

Alvarez took advantage of the Memorial Day holiday to clean out the entire cash holdings of the New York Federal Reserve Bank and equally divide one trillion dollars as donations to the Wounded Warriors Foundation, the Paralyzed Veterans Association, and a newly founded association they created that built homes for homeless vets. Prior to this he carefully seeded information in CLM, AntiCap, and BOB publications that Machine Scorzo would be pillaging the gold with a fleet of armored cars which were anonymously ordered to line the streets surrounding the Fed.

As Alvarez predicted, all three groups not only convened with their New York chapters, but had members bused in from around the US. Their heavily socialist orientation not only made them feel that they had the right to one of the world's biggest gold reserves, but that they in fact had an obligation to take the wealth of the privileged white capitalists away from them. However, in their insipid greed, they failed to carefully plan the necessary logistical support to transport the gold from the vaults to the trucks and load them. The result was ensuing pandemonium.

"Now we need a little mood music as the fireworks begin," Alvarez said.

The others looked on in amazement as Alvarez allowed the scene to play out for them on live satellite feed.

"Mood music," Jake said questionably as Sano began to laugh.

"Yeah, nothing like a good soundtrack in an action movie," Nixon added.

"How about 'London Calling' by the Clash," Alvarez said with a wide grin stretching across his face. He queued up the music and within seconds he had armed and fired his first missile from Russia's Borei A class sub, the Knyaz Vladimir, Russia's most advance ballistic missile submarine as the music blared.

"How many you need to fire," Jake questioned Alvarez.

"That sub is equipped with about sixteen RSM-56 Bulava ballistic missiles. The one I launched has six MIRVS on it."

"MIRVS?" Ariana asked.

"Yeah, multiple independent re-entry vehicles, meaning it can target six independent targets from one missile," Max explained.

"I thought we were only hitting the Fed and the J. Edgar Hoover building?" Nixon queried.

Alvarez put his finger up to his mouth to signal silence. He listened in mesmerized silence as he heard a frenzy of frantic chatter on the Knyaz Vladimir. The lieutenant commander was frantically shouting to the captain that "a missile is aloft bearing toward the US Eastern Seaboard."

The rear admiral shouted, "Override the firing sequence; it will self-destruct."

"Something is jamming the override, Admiral!" the captain shouted frantically.

"Descend to a depth of five hundred feet and bear north starboard, full speed ahead!" the rear admiral ordered decisively. This stealth class sub would have no problem fleeing undetected into the Arctic sea.

Alvarez slowly turned the music back up, and the men watched as the Fed, the J. Edgar Hoover Building, and the BATF Washington field office were decimated. Next, they saw the massive NSA structure in Maryland demolished seconds before the Washington DEA office was devastated. Twenty minutes later the Chicago FBI field office was obliterated, and while the Metropolitan Correctional Center itself was not targeted, it was within range to feel the blast shock waves and sustain limited structural damage that was nonlethal to the inmates. Nevertheless, as Alvarez predicted, the building was evacuated, and in the melee, Contreras managed to evade and escape his captors.

Simultaneously, four Jin class Chinese submarines had their firing systems breached by Alvarez. Each sub carried twelve JL-2 SLBMs carrying a single nuclear payload. His first targets were Juarez, Mexico, and Fort Bliss as well as the surrounding military installations. Next, he hit Mexico's Reynosa Airport. In frenetically quick succession he fired SLBMs from two other subs targeting Chiapas, Mexico, Guatemala, El Salvador, Honduras, and Nicaragua. The devastation was unprecedented in human history, and while the Chinese knew the weapons were launched from their vessels, they were powerless to do anything other than submerge and flee back toward the South China sea.

The Chinese quickly pointed the finger of devastation at the USS *Pasadena*, the USS *Scranton*, and the USS *Alexandria*, which were closest to the Mexican and Central American targets, but their propaganda was quickly debunked because the Ohio class nuclear armed subs were in the Atlantic fleet. The three aforementioned vessels were armed only with Tomahawk and non-nuclear cruise missiles.

President Hiding was at a loss for words in responding to reporters at an immediate press briefing. He would have loved to lay the blame at the feet of Machine Gun Scorzo, but it seemed unfathomable that a group of nine men could carry out such large-scale attacks both on the US and other nations. By the same token, foreign and domestic attacks would likely be limited to attacking the USA alone instead of other third-world nations that they perceived to be victims of the USA. His only statement was a weak and barely discernable attack on his predecessor.

"Unfortunately, at this point, the only thing that seems clear is that this is part of the legacy of President Courtland, who embraced the policies of dictators and despots around the world. Rest assured the culprits of these heinous acts will be brought to justice."

"Mr. President, Zara Abdulla, Socialist News Network. What plans do you have to find and deal with the perpetrators of these terrorist attacks?"

"We have a variety of options open to us at this time which I am not at liberty to discuss. That's all for now, folks...no more questions."

President Hiding turned quickly and stumbled as he left the platform, but his fall was caught by a secret service agent who kept him from hitting the ground. Thereafter he was quickly shuffled back into the White House by several secret service agents. The president was neither forthcoming or transparent in who the culprits were or how he planned to deal with the destruction that ensued in the attacks. He was truly clueless, but with a largely socialist news media that supported his socialist agendas, there was a virtual media blackout on the attacks.

One thing was clear, the southern border crisis was halted in its tracks. Money previously spent on busing immigrants to the Mexican-American border and supplying them with food and logistical supplies for their journey had to be diverted to visiting doctors, medical supplies, and tent communities. Those not immediately killed by the blasts were quickly succumbing to radiation sickness.

While Scorzo, Philster, and Ariana were deliberately kept in the dark, they knew that Alvarez would accomplish the necessary carnage that would end the socialist dissolution of the United States. Upon entering South Bend, Indiana, Ariana began to slump into a comfortable sleep, leaning against Scorzo in the back seat of the car. He slid his arm around her shoulder and began to softly pet her fine hair. Though she was tired from the fourteen-hour journey, deeply amorous feelings of safety and comfort summoned her to an aroused state of wakefulness.

She peered up at him and placed both of her warm and softly delicate hands on both sides of his cheeks.

"Salvino, why can't I work with you and join forces for the good of people?"

"You want to end up as another Patty Hearst doing jail time for joining forces with a criminal gang? As it stands now, you were an unwilling hostage who can also help clear your boss, claiming you were intimidated and coerced by us."

"I just want to be with you, Salvino."

"Really, you want to be with a man who gave the orders to destroy millions of innocent lives?"

"What are you talking about?"

"Before we left Beacon Rock, Alvarez breached the launch codes of a Soviet sub off the Atlantic coast to destroy six targets with a MIRV cruise missile. All of them were corrupt federal agencies, but the sad truth is that it also involved collateral damage to people inside and around those buildings who were totally innocent. Among the East Coast targets were the Chicago Bureau office that arrested and interrogated your boss as well as a building in close proximity to where he was being held in the Metropolitan Correctional Center in downtown Chicago."

"But the Chicago Bureau SAC, Bickens, the Bureau headquarters at the J. Edgar Hoover building as well as the DEA and BATF offices in Washington were cesspools of corruption, and we both know that."

"But there's more… much more."

Ariana took her hands off Scorzo's cheeks and placed them over his heart. "What? Tell me whatever it is. It's not going to change the way I feel about you." Ariana slid her hands around Scorzo's back and laid her head against his heart. "Tell me."

"I also ordered Alvarez to breach the launch codes of several Jin class Chinese subs off the Pacific coast armed with cruise missiles carrying nuclear payloads to strike seven targets within Mexico and central America, killing millions of innocent civilians within seconds."

"Sal, you know damn well that those weren't innocent civilians. They were an invasion force carrying their own countries' flags, and they were well financed from the start to the end of their journey."

"And what about the pregnant women and the small children travelling alone."

"Sal, you know as well as I do that they were being used as pawns in a partisan political scheme to undermine Republican support. How many of them were likely infected with Covid and not even being tested? Moreover, a good majority of those people have no viable skills applicable in the USA, and few if any speak English. You were the one who told me that the quickest way to divide a country into warring factions was to substitute a common language with multiple foreign languages. Remember that?"

"Yes, I remember it, and I have seen it in action in other places in the world."

"And what about the differences in cultures? Immigrants these days aren't being encouraged to assimilate into American culture. American culture is accommodating every group of foreign nationals that comes here."

"You're starting to sound more like me than me." Scorzo chuckled.

"These are always the beginning stages of the dissolution of a nation state," added Philster.

"And the battle cry of the day from the halls of Congress to every news media on the air is that America is a systemically racist country, with white people being the focal point of the problem," Ariana countered.

"And what I can't understand," the Philster chimed in, "is why all these fucking bastards of different races would want to come to a country that's constantly being accused of being the most racist country on the face of the earth! For Christ's fucking sake, have you ever received a government document? There're instructions in about twenty different fucking languages on it. You actually have to search for the instructions that are in English, and you tell me that's a motherfucking racist country! If you ask me, the only victims of racism are white, heterosexual males. We don't even have our own fucking bathrooms in public anymore. We have to share them with women, or women who identify as men, or peter-pumping men that identify as women. What the fuck is that all about? Oh, I forgot, it's about embracing unity in diversity, yet we're considered the most divisive country on the planet these days! Fuck I need a bar...maybe two Xanies!"

"That's the last thing you need," Scorzo ordered.

"Besides, I like your impassioned dialectics; they make sense," Ariana added.

"Oh, come on, admit it, kiddo, you just like to see me get all worked up like the rest of the crew does."

"No, I just like the way you talk about the insanity of this country in a way that makes me laugh."

"Be that as it may, civil war is nothing to laugh about. Women and young girls that look like you are usually victims of gang rape before they get their throats slit or their brains blown out after they've served their purpose. Anyone who's a doctor, lawyer, or person who is wealthy or educated gets executed because an educated mind is considered the most dangerous enemy of a socialist coup. It's fucking hell on earth."

Ariana looked up into Scorzo's eyes with a deep sense of empathy.

"Who knows how many more would have died in much more brutal ways if you hadn't given Alvarez those orders?"

"I can't really say, but then I've got to live with that."

"Don't start thinking with your heart, Sal; keep thinking with your head. Your actions today probably saved this country from unimaginable bloodletting."

"Yeah, Sal, think about all those cock-sucking commies from CLM, BOB, and AntiCap from all over the country that you took out in one fell swoop."

"Well, that was Alvarez's and your brainchild."

"My brainchild," Philster groused. "I was the one that wanted to annihilate as many of those cock-sucking commie bastards posing as social justice warriors as possible! Alvarez just wanted to bleed the Fed dry."

"Will you guys keep any of that money?" Ariana asked.

"Enough to disappear with and retire," Philster replied.

"You and Contreras are getting a tidy sum of that money as well, because you both know your days with the DEA are over."

"Sal, we can't take that money."

"Well, then use it to help coca farmers set up coffee plantations in Hawaii. Kona coffee is the most delicious coffee on the market, and it also demands a premium price. Put the cartels out of business by dealing with the disease instead of the symptoms. Then set up a bunch of non-profit organizations you and Contreras can run and draw a legitimate salary from that. You each have fifty billion dollars in numeric accounts set up as foundations that have nothing to do with your names."

"Whose names are they associated with, and I thought it was only four billion?"

"Dead people." Scorzo replied and added, "I'm feeling generous when it comes to you and Contreras."

"But how can a foundation have a dead person as its founder."

"The same way that dead people voted for President Hiding." Philster laughed.

"Now, to change the subject we need to connect with your former boss."

"But his phones are tapped."

"Not anymore. We took out the NSA and the Bureau's Chicago field office, so you can call him."

With her hands shaking slightly, she dialed Contreras, and he picked up.

"Contreras here."

"Boss, it's me, Ariana; where are you."

"I can't talk. This isn't a secure line."

"Trust me, I know some people who are very knowledgeable about certain things and your line is secure. The NSA and the Bureau's Chicago field office are no longer operational. Now, where are you?"

"I'm on the elevated purple line heading north into Wilmette."

"Get off at Evanston on the Noyes Street stop and go to my parents' home."

"Ariana, where are you? What happened to you? What's going on?"

"I'll meet you at my parents' home in thirty minutes. Tell them that you secured my release, and I'll brief you on everything."

"Gotcha, see you in thirty."

Contreras did as he was instructed, much to the delight of Mr. and Mrs. Carina, who had already presumed their daughter dead. To the both of them Contreras was like Jesus, who called Lazarus out of the tomb. They both embraced him for several minutes and Mrs. Carina kissed him several times on the cheek before fixing him a sandwich and bringing him some coffee. They were full of questions, but Contreras insisted that their daughter was the hero and he wanted them to have their questions answered by Ariana herself.

As Ariana's keys began to sound in the lock of the Carina home, there was an immediate sense of joy. The Carinas bounded off the couch and toward the door with Contreras in tow. But Contreras was reserved and feeling ill at ease because he knew exactly who Machine Gun Scorzo and Philster were.

"So, this isn't over," Contreras said cautiously.

"Indeed, it is over, compadre," Scorzo said with an amicable smile. "You're here because of the blast we targeted near the facility you were being unlawfully held at. We know what happened to you courtesy of Bickens, Pierpont, and the Bureau's Chicago field office."

"I also happen to know how you were personally fu... Excuse me, Mr. and Mrs. Carina," Philster said with a congenial smile. "You were buggered to put it a little more pleasantly because billions of dollars were going to be transferred to ONI Deputy Commander Richard Pierpont and Gary Bickens, but you and my friend here who's now known as public enemy number one, Machine Gun Scorzo, got in the way. You were taken out of the way by the Bureau, and Scorzo settled the score by permanently terminating the principles in Operation Lotus Blossom, but since there was only vaguely circumstantial evidence against him, he was dishonorably discharged and relegated to a civilian job thereafter.

"However, the twenty-billion-dollar question on Bickens' and Pierpont's mind before their untimely demise was where did all that vast fortune disappear to. Their logical conclusion was that Scorzo set it up in several shell companies, and they were determined to get it. So, Bickens traveled out of his jurisdiction on a weapons charge to torture Scorzo into giving up the money. Unfortunately for Bickens, Pierpont didn't share Scorzo's highly classified service history so he wasn't prepared for what he was up against. He also knew nothing about Scorzo's wife and daughter. Tragically, Scorzo's daughter was killed in the siege, and I'm sure you know the rest of the story from there on with a few twists and turns."

"So where did the money go?" Contreras asked.

"It was set up in an account for a man named Reverend Stan Brunsler, who helped the victims of human trafficking that the Navy was an active participant in. The Navy used the ill-gotten gains to finance black bag jobs without having to go to Congress to grovel for the money. Scorzo took nothing, but having failed in their siege, Bickens and Pierpont were even more determined to villainize Scorzo and pursue the money they thought he had. After all, they reasoned, how could he be happy with a dishonorable discharge after years of valiant service and a civilian job as a military mechanic with no pension.

"My sentence was commuted for information I provided on Scorzo, most of which was BS, and then I tipped him off that he was likely to take a hit, which actually happened moments after I called him. With his daughter dead, and his wife's status being that of a foreign national, it was safest to leave her behind."

"That's where you enter the picture," Contreras added.

"Exactly, Scorzo needed to find out what I knew, what I told them, and then make it look like he came up north to terminate me. It was a good plan, but I knew we would need battle supplies, so we hit Sonny's Drugs up in Winnetka. That's where you came into the picture with your team. Naturally, that was a problem for Bickens, so he took jurisdiction over your team because he suffered casualties during the siege."

"And our daughter brought these men to you, Agent Contreras?" Mr. Carina asked with pride.

"That she did," Scorzo replied humbly. "But she did a lot more than that, which you can be very proud of. She actually led several agencies in pursuit of us, and she actually got the drop on us in the siege at Fox Lake, even though she was wounded in the process. That was the only thing that stood between her becoming a hostage and our capture."

The Carinas beamed in pride with their arms around their daughter the whole time. They wanted to know so much more about

Ariana's long absence, but Scorzo intervened and informed them that they would have to let the agent bring them in with their daughter for booking and to debrief both the agents.

As soon as they left the premises and were outside, Contreras put his hand on Scorzo's back ever so lightly and turned to him pointedly.

"You aren't really turning yourselves in, are you?"

"That wouldn't be a wise idea for any of us. First of all, you're no longer with the DEA, and second, you're currently a fugitive. Ariana's not in a much better situation than you."

"So where do we go from here?"

"We disappear."

"With what? No money? No job? An identity as a federal fugitive…"

"You've got a hundred billion dollars in numeric offshore foundations between the two of you. Alvarez set you up with new identities, and your status as a fugitive was removed from the national databases by Alvarez. Both of you are free and clear to use that money to do some real good in the world. I already made one such suggestion to Ariana that involves helping coca farmers get into a more lucrative crop, but there are hundreds of good causes you could use that money for, and you don't have to touch a cent of it if you think it's dirty or stolen money. You can draw your salaries as non-profit principals. You're a good man, Contreras…we stole money from thieves who pillaged the American public through legislated graft. You have an opportunity to give that money back to people who deserve it. You also have a damn good woman here who needs a good man to love her and take care of her. Alvarez already purchased a spacious home for you two as a wedding gift, so if I were you, I wouldn't wait too long to pop the question."

"And what happens to you guys?"

"Well, I like to think about that song 'Imagine' by John Lennon, but who knows," Scorzo said with a wry smile as he shook his head. "There's about fifty countries with non-extradition policies with the US, so our options are open. Say, how about we drop you off at your new home. I think you'll love it. Alvarez has very good taste in furniture and art."

As Scorzo predicted, Contreras and Ariana loved their home. Contreras even carried her over the threshold. After minimal conversation, Contreras and Ariana walked Scorzo and Philster to Mohammed, who was waiting in the car.

"I really misjudged you, my friend," Contreras said to Scorzo.

"I didn't misjudge you," Scorzo replied. "Well, maybe one time."

"Oh yeah, when was that?"

"Up in Fox Lake when you played that corny U-2 song from the gunships."

The two men laughed, and Contreras opened his arms, and Scorzo hugged him and then Ariana. Then they turned to Philster, who warmly embraced Ariana. Then he extended his hand to Contreras.

"I don't go in for this hugging shit with men," Philster said with a somewhat smug smile. "A handshake will suffice. Have a nice life. You two deserve it more than most of the people I've met in my life."

With that, Scorzo and Philster got back into the car, and Mohammed gave a brief wave as he slowly backed out of their driveway. The trip back to Beacon Rock was a bit more eventful that the trip to Chicago. For one thing, all traffic was routed away from Route 94 heading into the city as it was still considered a potential target for further attacks. Similarly, they were routed from Route 80/95 into New York up to 287 after Denville, where they had to travel an extra couple of hours until they were able to pick up 95 at Port Chester and head straight north to 138 into Beacon Rock. New York and Washington were still considered potential targets.

Just when it seemed that the men were home free, they saw a squad car stopped ahead with an officer waving for them to stop. About another fifty yards beyond them were two more squad cars blocking passage, and there were no cars in sight other than the police vehicles.

"Oh, what the fuck is this?" Philster fretted.

"Reach under your seat," Mohammed said calmly. "You'll find two Glock nine-millimeters with hundred-round clips." Mohammed did the same thing, as Philster passed one to Scorzo.

"Exit the vehicle with your backs facing me," the officer ordered over his loudspeaker. As the officers approached, Mohammed and the others initially complied, but none of them closed their doors or turned around. Instead, they crouched behind their doors and opened fire with a torrent of bullets ripping the two officers to shreds. The other cars blocking the road in the distance began to open fire.

"Behind the car!" Mohammed shouted with command. Scorzo and Philster took cover behind the car as Mohammed opened the trunk to expose four Stinger missiles. Within seconds they flanked the car and quickly aimed and fired the Stingers, blowing the two cars completely off the road. A third car behind it was hit and was blown at least ten feet into the air before hitting the pavement and tipping over into the water.

"Fuck, we've been made. How the fuck did that happen?"

"Most likely the Mover we used to go into NYC?" Philster fretted. "The dick who found our driver probably got curious because the first lead went cold, so he started checking all the pickups, with ours being the most suspicious. I mean, think about it, Sal, who the fuck that lives at a place like Beacon Rock is going to have a Mover rideshare take them into a New York City library. They would have a personal driver! Fuck! Fuck!"

"Calm down, Philster!" Scorzo ordered.

"Sal, they probably have our northern perimeter teaming with heat!" Philster fumed.

"It's not likely," Scorzo countered. "Otherwise, they would have moved in on us and stormed the estate, and that didn't happen."

"He's right," Mohammed added, "but it's likely that the Coast Guard just a few miles north of the estate heard, and we won't be able to escape the eyes in the sky. We're wasting time! Let's get back to the estate, where we have enough firepower to repel an attack."

"He's right," Scorzo said, nodding at Philster.

The three jumped back into the car and sped toward the estate.

As Mohammed correctly assumed, there were no teaming forces surrounding the estate, but there was a Coast Guard helicopter hovering over the carnage on Bridge 138, and they were no doubt calling in for backup. Given the fact that there were explosive munitions used, they were probably briefing incoming personnel that they may be facing the terrorists responsible for the devastating US and international attacks.

"What the fuck happened up here?" Scorzo demanded of the men.

"A detective came up here asking about a pickup from this location," Gonzo answered, "and I told him I didn't know of any pickup because I was out of the loop on this one, but Nixon salvaged it by saying I was just temporary help, and he ordered the Mover because our driver was sick."

"Then what happened?" Philster asked.

"Then he asked how our partners got back from the city," Nixon replied.

"And…what did you tell him," Philster plied.

"I told them they were catching a flight to the West Coast from the city."

"And I bet you gave them fake names?"

"You know I did!" Nixon barked back. "I wasn't gonna give you guys up."

"Well," Scorzo replied, "you basically did. Do you know how easy it is to check names on a passenger manifest for West Coast flights? As soon as he caught you in that lie, he probably had this place under surveillance."

"All right," Nixon conceded humbly. "I fucked up. I thought our whole place was going to be under siege, so I got nervous."

"Forget it. Now we've got to think of our way out because they're gonna come at us in military force from this point on. Downstairs… the situation room!"

Scorzo announced the plans with unquestioned authority.

"Okay, fortunately for us, the Newport, Rhode Island, naval base has been decommissioned. That's probably why President Hiding decided to visit it. The only thing they have operating out of there is the Coast Guard, so we don't have to worry about any firepower coming from the north. But they could send in reinforcements from 138, and the bridges coming from routes 114 and 24. We have to blow all of those bridges immediately. Have you breached any of the subs at New London, Alvarez?"

"No sir, I chose the C-class subs in Kings Bay, Georgia."

"Are you out of your fucking mind, Alvarez?" Philster blurted out.

"Why Kings Bay?" Scorzo asked calmly.

"Because the C-class subs are much more powerful. They're armed with Trident II D5 missiles with five MIRVs each that travel at a speed of 18,030 miles per hour. That means they would blow out all three bridges and obliterate Jamestown, where an offensive could be mounted in exactly three minutes."

"Make it happen three minutes ago," Scorzo ordered decisively.

Alvarez quickly moved away from the table, saluted Scorzo, and headed to his battle station. Within seconds Alvarez breached the launch codes of a single sub and launched three missiles containing five MIRVs each. Within minutes, not only were the three bridges taken out but Jamestown, Prudence Island, and Rhode Island to the west from Little Compton up to Tiverton were left in total ruins. Alvarez reported back with a salute at Scorzo. "Mission accomplished, sir. Not only are all the bridges taken out, but all surrounding land masses where offensives could be mounted were destroyed."

"Good work, soldier! Max, I need you, Sano, Gonzo, and Nixon to go topside with Stingers and force those Coast Guard helicopters to land on our north side. Alvarez, you jam their communication systems so they can't relay any information. There's three of them, but we'll only need two, so shoot one down over the water to make it appear like they were all shot." down."

Gonzo and Nixon were the first ones out on the north perimeter, but before they could get a shot off, they were fired upon and both Nixon and Gonzo were hit. Nixon was mortally wounded but Gonzo managed to make it back inside and warn the others before he died.

"Scorzo, those aren't ordinary Coast Guard choppers. Those fuckers are HITRON choppers. They're armed with stun grenades, M16A2 rifles, FN M240 machine guns, and a Robar 50 long-range rifle."

"All right, change of plans... We shoot one down from inside so they think we have the advantage. Max, you look after Gonzo and do the best you can for him. Sano, you and I are going to draw them to the north perimeter and get them to come down as low as they can, making it look like we want to surrender. Then, we'll take cover behind the trees. Jake, I'm counting on all the skill you possess to take out the pilots. Hopefully, the crafts will be low enough that they'll still be functional after a not so easy landing. The gunners should be disoriented enough that either you or all three of us can take them out. Alvarez, even though NSA is out of the picture, the DOD can still track us on live feed with their satellites. I need you to put those out of commission."

"Consider it done, sir."

Without their ability to communicate, the HITRONs couldn't call in any backup, so they played into the hands of Scorzo and Sano, who acted as though they were ready to surrender. Rather than wait until the crafts were hovering above Scorzo and Sano, Jake waited until they both landed. His first shot was a direct head shot into the first pilot that went unnoticed. He drew his breath in slowly and fired on the second pilot, hitting his left arm with the bullet entering his heart. As men dispatched to take Scorzo and Sano into captivity, Jake began picking them off one at a time until they realized they had been set up. Sano mounted one craft and killed the remaining gunner, and as the gunner from the second ship took aim at him, Scorzo took him out from behind.

With the ship's crews dead, Scorzo bolted back into the estate to get Mohammed and Alvarez.

"Mohammed, wire this C-4 to all of Alvarez's equipment and blow it in place. You've got two minutes to be onboard that chopper or we're out of here without you."

"I'll have it done in sixty seconds, my friend."

"Alvarez, we've got a chopper to board."

Scorzo and Alvarez quickly made their way to the humming chopper, but as they passed one of the gunners lying face down, he pulled a side arm and shot Alvarez twice in the back before Scorzo spun around and returned fire, killing the gunner.

Scorzo leaned over Alvarez, who was coughing up blood.

"Come on, kid, hang in there, were out of here…we made it!" Scorzo said in a pleading tone, but as he saw blood pulsing out of Alvarez's chest, he knew he wasn't going to make it.

"I'm cold, Scorzo. I won't make it."

"I'm not leaving you here…not like this."

"No, Scorzo, leave me. I want to die on American soil. This is what I fought for. You gave my life meaning…" His words trailed off, and Mohammed was running toward the chopper as the C-4 rocked the basement and set the estate on fire.

The men headed to the C-110s. They left JFK Airport free and clear of any pursuers and boarded the plane. The last remnants they had of Alvarez were the documentation to take off heading to Taiwan and the new identities he had made for them along with the numbered accounts he created for them. Mohammed, their silent ninth partner, bid them farewell at the airport and returned to the New York City Library.

Just as the America the men had returned to after their military service ended was no longer the same place they left, now the place they were leaving was no longer the same. America was descending into civil war, with Blacks rising up against whites, Muslims against Christians, and Jews and patriots against liberals. The members of BOB, CLM, and AntiCap who survived the NYC Fed bombing found themselves despised by all as the few film clips of them that survived portrayed them as wolves in sheep's clothing, a far cry from the social justice warriors they claimed to be.

In the midst of all this turmoil and upheaval, President Hiding falsely claimed that the authors of all this anarchy, Machine Gun Scorzo and his gang of murderers, were killed in a courageous raid on the Beacon Rock Estate, where they had been living in anonymity with the well-to-do. "Now," he pronounced with a sense of victorious vanity, "is a time for Americans to come together and rejoice in the fact that a hugely divisive force in our society has been forever vanquished…" Just as he was speaking his last word, an egg splattered against the side of his head, causing him to fall into the arms of an attending secret service agent. The president was swiftly whisked back into the White House.

With the exception of Mohammed Hussain, the five remaining members of the Nemesis Nine would settle in countries that had non-extradition treaties with the US, and were off limits to Interpol as well since none of the crimes that Interpol is chartered to investigate were committed by the Nemesis Nine, nor could those that were alleged against them be conclusively proven. Sano and Max settled in Taiwan, Jake took to Brunei, and Philster settled in a beautiful seaside estate on the shores of Cambodia, where he came to be known as generous uncle Phil.

In Taiwan, Salvino would board a flight for Xian, China. As his plane rose above the clouds, music from the headphones crept sonorously into his ears. Chopin's Prelude in E Minor was a fitting piece as the man who came to be known as Machine Gun Scorzo ascended into the sky and evaded capture. His plane would take him to the land where the sun also rises, and into the welcoming arms of his beloved wife. America would have to fight the rest of their war without Machine Gun Scorzo, but he had galvanized the forces that would politically correct America. The soul of America was still intact.

www.ingramcontent.com/pod-product-compliance
Lightning Source LLC
Chambersburg PA
CBHW022002050726
47499CB00002BA/266